NO MORE LIES, Alec Brock

ALEC BROCK SERIES BOOK 2

Larissa Lopes

To my dear Brockies.
Because Alec Brock really does have
the best fans in the entire world!

SATURDAY, OCTOBER 25

LOS ANGELES, CA

Linda's old cell phone vibrates
3:47 A.M.
1 NEW MESSAGE RECEIVED

**I tried to hold myself back, but I can't. I won't be able to…
Not knowing you're there with him right now.**

You said you would forget everything about him, Linda. And I can't keep my promise if you don't keep yours.

**Please stay away. Please!
I don't want to end up hurting you more than I already have.**

"Baby, come on—it's past midnight! I'm not gonna let you spend another night writing…"

"I'm coming soon, okay? I just want to finish this—" The

serious look on his face shut me up. He was focused on the screen now, reading the words I'd just typed.

I hated to see him like that—so *worried.*

"I'm halfway through the story," I explained quietly.

"I know, I just..." He searched for the right words, his eyes full of regret. "I'm sorry about that. I shouldn't have—"

"Hey! I've already forgiven you, remember?" I closed my laptop and got up from my chair, wrapping my arms around his waist. "Thirteen years ago! This is all in the past, baby. Everything is okay now."

Then why do you have to do this? I read it on his face for the thousandth time, though he never had the courage to say the words out loud.

It had all started as an experiment for my PhD in Psychology: something to help me understand myself better. And he was doing his best to be a supportive husband, I knew he was. But when I told him I wanted to finish the book before we started trying to get pregnant, things got a little more...uneasy.

It was just too hard for him to hide how much this affected him. I wasn't writing only my story, this was *his* story too. It was *our* story, actually—the story of the three of us. We'd all made mistakes back then, we'd all made *choices.* And I guess he was afraid that, at some point during this trip down memory lane, I would end up regretting those choices I'd made. One choice in particular.

"Sometimes I still can't believe you came back to *me.* After everything..." He cupped my face in his hands, staring deep into my eyes. "I really thought I'd lost you during those few months..."

I tightened my arms around him, remembering the scene I'd just written—the first time Alec kissed me in Vegas. I genuinely thought I'd gotten my happy ending that night.

I had no idea that my darkest battle was just beginning.

Chapter 1

D*reams do come true.*

    I mean, they might not happen exactly the way you expect, but I guess that's for the best. We don't always know what's good for us, but life does. And that's why it gets in our way sometimes, forcing us to take a detour. But the dream you wished with all your heart—the core of it, the essence of it—is always there at the end, waiting for you.

"What are you smiling at?" Alec asked in his morning voice, turning off the alarm I didn't even realize was ringing.

I grinned at him. And, God, he'd never looked more beautiful. His green eyes were just half open, but his hair was all wild and his dimples were showing.

I felt like my heart didn't fit in my chest anymore. It was overwhelmed with love and happiness. I wanted to show it—to tell Alec how much I loved him. How much I'd waited for that moment, how much I'd dreamed of waking up next to him. But I knew he wouldn't take it well. Even if it was the truth—I really loved *him*—he wasn't ready to hear it yet.

"I just love…Vegas." I smirked, combing his curls with my fingers.

Alec chuckled, then leaned in for a kiss. "We're gonna have to come back, then. I want to show you the city next time."

I snuggled into his chest, hiding my excitement. *This can't be happening. This can't be real life.* My *life!*

Alec put his arms around me, adjusting the comforter so it covered my shoulders. And I closed my eyes, holding him tight.

If I'm dreaming about all this, I don't want to wake up. The warmth of his body. The faded smell of his cologne. The steady pace of his heartbeat. *I don't want to wake up. I don't want to wake up. I don't want to wake up.*

"Alec, are you there?" A hard knock on the door made my heart jump.

"Yeah…" Alec answered groggily. I wasn't the only one who had fallen back asleep.

"Oh man, you said I didn't need to wake you up today!"

"Sorry, Jimmy," Alec shouted, startled. "What time is it?"

"Late! We have to leave in fifteen minutes! And there's a group of fans downstairs. If you want to give them some attention, you have to come down now!"

Alec sat up on the bed, stretching his arms. "I'll be ready in five."

"I'll order breakfast to go…"

"Thank you," he said to the door, then turned to me apologetically. "I'm sor—"

"Oh, and your father called," Jimmy continued. "He said he talked to Dan… You forgot to tell him about the paparazzi yesterday, didn't you?"

Alec's eyes widened, and he reached for his cell on the night table. "I'll call him. Thanks, Jimmy."

I got up, alert, watching him find some clothes in his suitcase with the phone to his ear. His mood had shifted so fast that now *I* was the one worried.

"Hi Dad," he said, his tone uneasy.

I pretended to be busy with the hairbrush but kept paying close attention to the conversation.

"Sorry. Yeah, but… I was going to… Already?" He rubbed his eyes, exhaling. "I know… I know, okay? I'm going down now to talk to the fans, and we're leaving as soon as she… No, what message? All right, let's talk when I get there. We'll be home for lunch… Bye."

"What's wrong?" I asked. I didn't need to hear that he'd gotten bad news; it was written all over his face.

"Nothing. Everything is okay, don't worry."

"Please don't lie to me. Not *you*."

"Sorry." He bit his lip, catching me in a hug. "But everything *will be* okay, I promise. They just need some time to get used to it."

"Who? Your parents?" I looked up at him, fretting. Until that moment, I'd never really thought of what Amanda and Oliver would say about us.

Alec's eyes lingered on mine, but he didn't answer me. He kissed the top of my head instead, then walked to the bathroom. "I hate to leave you like this, but I don't want to rush you and I do need to go say hi to the fans before we—"

"It's okay, I don't mind." I stared at the empty room, still thinking about his father's call.

"Thank you!" Alec shouted from the other side of the door. "I'll make it up to you this weekend… And don't worry about my stuff; I'll ask Arthur to come pick it up."

Arthur. A shiver ran down my spine.

He was Alec's bodyguard; I knew he couldn't be the impostor. My paranoia about him was totally unfounded. But the mention of his name made me remember *why* Alec had yelled at the paparazzi yesterday. The *real* reason behind his panic attack and our fight on the rooftop.

Last night I had decided to shut down all my worries, all my problems—forget the unfinished business I had with my past. But now it was morning again, and I would have to start thinking about *him* eventually.

Has he seen the photos yet? Is he mad that Alec and I are together? Will he try to contact me? To get revenge? I was already feeling exposed, defenseless.

Now he would know I was living in LA; he would know where to find me! And the fact that he could be literally anyone outside that room and I wouldn't be able to tell made it all even more terrifying.

"You look great in red," Alec said, fully dressed, hiding his messy mop of hair with a beanie.

I smiled at him, shaking the anxiety out of my head. "I guess your stylist thinks it's my favorite color. The dress, the sleepwear…"

"No." He smirked. "She knows it's *mine*."

I raised my eyebrows, amused. "Well, that's not fair, is it?"

He shrugged shamelessly, his dimples peeking out. And just like that, I was lost in my dreams again. He looked so perfect standing there—staring at me. I wished we could spend the whole day in that room, just the two of us.

"Ready?" Jimmy knocked on the door.

"I'm coming!" Alec found his phone, then shoved it into his pocket while walking toward me. "I'm really sorry. I hate to leave you like this… Maybe I shouldn't—"

"Don't worry, go." I touched his cheek in reassurance. "It's only for ten minutes anyway, right?"

He smiled with a nod. Then he put his hand over mine and brought it to his lips, kissing my palm. "I'll be in the lobby, okay? Anytime you're ready, I'm waiting," was the last thing he said.

I didn't want to make us even more late, so I got dressed as fast as I could while gathering all of our things. I had just finished brushing my teeth when my cell buzzed. I knew who it was; Nina had sent me a dozen messages that morning. But before I had the chance to read any of them, I heard Arthur's voice outside.

"The car is here. I've already talked to the driver. Yes, he is distracted with the fans…"

Everything in me went quiet. It took me a few seconds to realize *why*—what I was doing. I was trying to recognize *his* voice.

You can't keep secrets from your bodyguard, I remembered the impostor saying.

It would be so easy for Arthur to pretend he was Alec. They were together all the time; he knew every single detail of Alec's life!

"No, she won't leave before me. I'm waiting right in front of her room…"

I couldn't tell if I knew his voice or not. Voices change over the phone, and the impostor had probably disguised his anyway. To me, it had always sounded like Alec's.

I can't believe you fell for this, Linda. You're so stupid! I reminded myself. And the realization made me open the door a crack. My suspicions were just ridiculous; the impostor couldn't be one of his bodyguards! I was being paranoid—like I'd been with his guitarist, James.

Arthur said goodbye to the person on the line, then politely asked me if he could enter the room to pack Alec's belongings. He seemed happily surprised when he realized I had already done it but scanned the room one more time anyway.

I didn't wait for him. I rushed to the elevator, pulling my new suitcase behind me. It was awkward to be alone with him. He wasn't funny and talkative like Jimmy. He was too serious, too formal. And what bothered me the most, too *familiar*.

I wanted to ask him about the pictures for Alec's stylist—to confirm that it was really him who had stalked me in order to take them. I felt like I'd seen his face before, and I was sure someone had followed me to the bus stop on Tuesday... It *had* to be him, there was no other logical explanation!

But I couldn't bring myself to say anything. The energy in the elevator was too heavy; I needed Alec to mediate the conversation.

Thirty-eight... Thirty-seven...

I watched Arthur pay attention to the floor numbers on the display. I'd never noticed how tall he was. And muscled... Not the scary type, like Jimmy, but still kind of intimidating.

He didn't seem very old, either. Early thirties at best. His pale face was always straight, and his short, dark hair had that wet, shiny look.

Sixteen... Fifteen...

He glanced at me, and I let my hair fall over my shoulder, forming a curtain between us. There was something about him...a tension. I didn't dare to look up again, keeping my head down until the doors opened.

On the wrong floor, I realized.

We weren't at the lobby—we were two floors below the street level. But Arthur grabbed both suitcases, already stepping outside.

My whole body went into alert mode.

The corridor ahead of us was dark and empty. There were many housekeeping carts in front of gray metallic doors, but no one in sight. I was sure we weren't supposed to be here; it was clearly some kind of staff-restricted area.

"Where are we going?" I blurted.

"To the car," Arthur said without stopping.

You've got to relax, Linda. This is probably just a strategy to escape the paparazzi. After what happened yesterday, they must be waiting in front of the hotel, ready to attack us again. I followed him to the service entrance, trying to calm my racing heart.

When we left the building, there was a car waiting for us, but Alec was nowhere to be seen. The driver placed the bags in the trunk as Arthur opened the door for me, pointing at a paper bag already lying on the back seat. "Your breakfast, miss."

I didn't answer him. I kept looking over the roof of the car, searching for a familiar face among the people passing by. "Where's Alec? And Jimmy?"

"They—aren't coming with us." Arthur dropped his gaze, walking to the passenger seat.

"Alec said he would be waiting for me." I took a step back, then another.

Arthur rushed in my direction, his eyes never leaving mine. And something in the way he moved made my chest tighten, releasing a cold wave of fear into my bloodstream.

"Please, miss, get in the car," he said quietly.

But his tone only made my suspicions grow.

"I'm not going anywhere with you!" I turned around, ready to run.

Arthur caught me by the arm. "Please, Linda. You have to come with me."

Oh my God, it's him, isn't it? My name. The way he said my name!

I held his gaze. It was too intense, too purposeful.

He planned all this—to separate me from Alec! I bet this driver is a friend of his. I bet he paid some staff at the hotel to let us use this entrance. He doesn't want anyone to see us leaving the lobby. He is...kidnapping me!

My pulse raced out of control.

"Help!" I shouted in despair. And luckily, my reaction distracted Arthur long enough for me to wrench my arm from his grip.

I used too much strength, though. So I lost my balance and

stumbled backward, falling hard onto the ground of the parking garage.

"Help!" I screamed louder, shaking from adrenaline. He was too big, too strong! I wouldn't be able to escape if he put his hands on me again.

But to my surprise, Arthur didn't even try. "I'm sorry! I didn't mean to scare you!"

"Are you okay, honey?" A middle-aged woman took me by the elbow, helping me up from the cement.

"I'm sorry." Arthur sounded regretful. "I'm just following Mr. Brock's orders, miss. I didn't mean to—"

"You're lying! Alec told me to meet him in the lobby!" I hid myself behind the woman.

"Not Alec, miss…Oliver."

My heart skipped a beat.

"I'm sorry but I received orders not to let the paparazzi spot you today."

I dropped my eyes in realization. *They just need some time to get used to it,* Alec had said.

Oliver was the one talking to Arthur on the phone. He didn't want Alec to be seen with me. He didn't like the idea of us dating. He didn't think I was good enough for his son.

"Look at your hand, honey! You're bleeding," the woman said, glaring at Arthur. Then she pulled out a kitchen towel from her apron and wrapped it around my palm. "Let's come inside, and you can call—"

"We're already—late," Arthur's voice broke as I raised my head to look at him. There were more people staring now, judging him with their eyes. And for the first time, he looked more afraid of me than I was of him.

That's when I realized how far I'd taken my paranoia. The fear, the anxiety, the danger—it was all in my head! Arthur hadn't tried to kidnap me, he had no reason to. He was just following orders, doing his job. And I was not only making it harder for him to do that, but also making a complete fool of myself in front of all those people.

"Let's go." I shot Arthur a glance. Then I turned to the woman, giving her the kitchen towel back. "Thank you, but I'm okay. It was just a misunderstanding," I said loud enough so everybody could hear it.

The woman knit her eyebrows in disbelief, gesturing for me to keep the towel. "Sweetie—"

"I'm okay, really." I rushed to the car. I was so embarrassed by the scene I'd just made that I wanted to disappear from that place.

But Arthur didn't move. He was still studying my reactions, paralyzed with shock.

"Let's go!" I shouted.

And he finally went to his seat, only speaking to make sure the driver knew where he was taking us.

♪♩♡

Shame. Shame. Shame. I couldn't stop my face from burning.

What have you done, Linda? That was so stupid!

Now everybody will know you're paranoid. What will Alec say? What will his father say? Arthur is going to tell them you're crazy. And the worst part is that he might be right!

Ignoring my breakfast, I took the bottle of water from the takeaway bag and did my best to clean up the scratches on my right palm. They weren't so bad, actually—apart from this deeper one.

I tried to hide them with the sleeve of my jacket, but I was still bleeding. I would have to keep the towel. I would have to tell Alec.

You're so dumb, Linda! How the heck are you going to explain this? I put pressure on the wound, anticipating what I would say when my phone buzzed.

But to my total shock, it simply didn't ring. Alec didn't call.

I knew he had his phone with him; I'd seen him putting it in his pocket. *Did he know we were leaving in separate cars?*

No, he would have told me.

Maybe he's used to it. Maybe he does this every time he's with a secret date.

Suddenly there were all these little movies playing in my head. Alec with Tera. Alec with Hailey. Alec with every single one of the girls from his dating rumors.

Urgh! I groaned in my head.

Everything in me was restless—I *was* going crazy. If I didn't find a distraction from my anxiety, by the time we got to the heliport, I would officially be insane!

Hey… Are you there? I wrote Nina a text.

But she didn't bother replying.

"Tell me *everything*!" she said the second I answered her call.

"Hello to you too!" I laughed. I could always count on her to make me feel better.

"No chit-chat, Linda. Come on, give me the juicy!"

"I can't…talk details right now." I glanced at the driver, careful not to look at the passenger seat where Arthur sat.

"Is someone with you?"

"Yes."

"Him?"

"No."

"Oh." Nina sounded disappointed. "Can you keep talking like this, at least?"

"Yes."

"Great! So did you kiss?"

"Yes." I bit my lip, remembering.

And Nina squealed in celebration. "You have to tell me every-thing later! How was it? Was it awesome?"

"Yeah…" I smiled. Just the memory of him was enough to make my stress go away.

"Everything you expected?"

I thought about how good it felt to fall asleep in his arms. "Somehow, even better."

"Really? Oh my gosh, L. I'm *so* happy for you two! You have no idea!"

"Don't get too excited, okay?" I recalled what had just happened with Arthur and the fact that Alec's father clearly hadn't taken the news very well. "Things are…*complicated* right now."

"What do you mean?" she asked.

But I didn't have time to answer. The car had stopped near the helicopter, and before I could even search for him, Alec was already there—standing by my door.

"I'm so sorry." He hugged me as soon as I stepped outside. "I promise you, this will *never* happen again."

"It's okay…" I rubbed his back, wondering what exactly he was talking about. How much did he know?

"No, it's *not* okay!" He leaned back to look at me. "This is unacceptable! I've already warned my father on the phone, he should have—" Alec frowned, then caught my hand in his, moving the towel to examine my palm. "What happened?"

So, he doesn't *know.* I glanced at Arthur. *Will he tell them the truth if I decide not to?*

"It was nothing. I just fell down on the sidewalk when I was getting into the car."

Arthur pressed his lips together in agreement, and I knew right then that it would be our little secret. I was happy, actually. Grateful. The last thing I needed today was to have to explain to Alec how much his impostor still messed with my head.

"We should take care of this before flying home," Alec said, still staring at the wounds. Then he turned to Jimmy. "Sorry, but can we—"

"I got this." Jimmy nodded, rushing back to the heliport building.

"Hello? Hello?" I heard a muffled scream coming from the back seat. I had completely forgotten Nina was waiting on the line.

I pulled my hand from Alec's and jumped back inside the car, putting the cell to my ear. "I'm so sorry, Nina. I'll call you later, okay? I can't—"

"Oh, is it Nina?" Alec climbed in, closing the door behind him. "Let me talk to her. I wanna say hello."

I froze for a second, having problems processing his request. So Alec took the phone from me.

"Hey, pal! How are you?" he said, excited. "Yeah, now we can have that double date. When can you come to LA?"

My jaw dropped.

"I think it might work for us. I'm gonna check with James."
What?

"But now I have to hang up, okay? I think your BFF might be in shock… All right." Alec smirked, passing me the phone. "She wants to say goodbye."

I had absolutely no reaction.

"Linda?" Nina said on the line, reminding me to actually put the cell to my ear.

"Y-yeah."

"Are you okay?" She giggled.

"I'm not sure. Can I call you later?"

I didn't wait for her answer before hanging up. "How often *exactly* do you two talk?"

"A little…" Alec took my hand in his, avoiding my gaze, and examined the scratches again.

I blinked twice in disbelief. "And what was that about LA?"

"I kind of owe her a date with James." He chuckled to himself.

"What? *Why?*"

"She told me she has a crush on him, and we made a deal. I've been wanting to talk to you about them... I really think they match; we should set them up!"

"I..." I couldn't articulate my words. Thoughts were running too fast through my head. All kinds of thoughts. All kinds of feelings.

"But first, I have to ask you something—about all this mess." He nodded at the other car parked next to us. "When we get home, I know my father is going to say a million things about yesterday. And I want you to, *please*, just ignore everything, okay?" Alec held my chin to make sure I was paying attention. "This is very important: don't listen to him! I know we can do this —I *want* to do this." He rested his forehead against mine.

"Okay." I closed my eyes, anticipating the kiss. But Alec didn't move.

I felt him smile, his lips barely touching mine. "And I was thinking about what you said yesterday..."

"Yeah?" I kept my eyes closed. I wanted that kiss so bad.

"You said you never wanted to start this investigation anyway, right?" He kissed me once, then twice.

"Right." I held my breath, waiting for more.

"So..." Alec cupped my face with his hands, then tilted my head, whispering in my ear, "If you don't want to find this guy, and I definitely don't want him to find *you*..."

He lowered his kisses to my neck, and I shivered, not even thinking straight anymore.

"Why are we *searching* for him? I mean, how do you feel about calling off the investigation?"

I leaned back in surprise, and the green in his eyes grew

darker. I had to smile a little, enjoying the cute trace of jealousy on his face.

"I would really love that," I said genuinely. I hadn't realized it until that moment, but as long as we didn't try to find him, I was safe!

I confess I'd always been afraid he would come after me one day. In the beginning, I *hoped* he would—I wanted him to tell me the truth, to explain everything. Then, after the investigation started, I was scared he would find out about the trap Jack and Oliver were setting for him and want revenge somehow. But if there was one thing I knew for sure about Impostor Alec, it was that he didn't want to be found. So why would he risk exposing himself by coming anywhere near me, right?

He didn't love me enough to show me his face; he had made that clear. So as long as we kept our distance from him, he would never risk coming after me! There was no need to be paranoid. I was safe! I was really safe!

"I'm gonna talk to Jack about this when we get home, then." Alec's lips curved up at the corners. Then he glanced at his watch. "If we manage to get there in time…"

"You mean *today*?" I knit my brows.

"Yeah, that's the meeting we have at lunch. Didn't I tell you yesterday?"

"No," I murmured.

Alec studied my reaction. "Are you sure about this? Calling off the investigation?"

"Yeah."

"Really?"

"Yes!" I rolled my eyes, grinning at him. He looked adorable when he was jealous. I couldn't get over it.

"You're not saying this just—"

"No! Stop questioning me!" I giggled, pulling his beanie down until it covered his eyes.

He laughed out loud, and I couldn't resist—I kissed his dimple, helping him fix the beanie again. "I think I'll feel safer like this, to be honest. Because he won't feel threatened by us... He obviously doesn't want to expose himself, so no investigation means no reason for him to be scared and try to disturb our peace!"

Alec's face lit up with my favorite smile. And, God, all I wanted in life was to live for that smile...

I was so ready to forget my past and all the untold truths that would only hurt me. I wanted to start over, from scratch—with *him*—today!

Before I realized what I was doing, I pulled him by the shirt and brought his lips to mine. Alec chuckled against my mouth, moving his hand to the back of my head. Then he deepened the kiss, sending chills all over my body.

"Found a first aid kit, Alec! Let's go!" Jimmy knocked on the roof of the car.

"Don't forget where we stopped." He breathed in my ear. "We'll continue this later."

Chapter 2

"You're an hour late!" I heard Oliver's voice as soon as we walked into the Brocks' house.

"Well, we had an unexpected *change of plans* while leaving the hotel, so don't blame it on us!" Alec snorted.

"Please don't start this now, Oliver. Let them have lunch first." Amanda hugged me, then Alec. "I haven't seen my son in two weeks! How was the trip, baby?"

"Great!" He smiled at her. "You would have loved—"

"We're not pretending nothing happened, Amanda. This is too serious! He crossed the line!"

"Calm down, Oliver, you're too stressed. Let me talk to him, okay?" another voice surprised me. I glanced at the living room, and Alec's manager was there, rolling a magazine together in his hands.

My stomach froze when I noticed the newspapers and printed pages from websites scattered all over the coffee table. And to make things worse, Dan wasn't alone.

I didn't recognize any of the other people, except Jack—the detective—looking quite alarmed on the other end of the couch. I wasn't sure what exactly we'd done wrong, but it was pretty obvious that we—Alec and I—were in *big* trouble.

"Okay, let's get this over with." Alec exhaled, relaxing his shoulders. "Dan, I'm sorry. I messed up; I should have been more careful. But this is worth it." He reached for my hand, making sure everybody was watching him. "I know there will be consequences, but I'm ready to face them."

"Alec, it's not that simple…" Dan frowned.

"Yes, it is! They will get used to it." He squeezed my hand.

And Oliver snapped. "How could you expose… Do you have any idea…? Haven't you learned anything by now, Alec? What were you thinking?"

"I just wanted to live in the moment, Dad! For once, okay? Just *live*! Who knows how much time I have left anyway?"

Everybody went quiet for a second. The weight of his words filled the room with meaning.

His cancer. My heart raced. *No. No!*

"Come here, baby." Amanda wrapped her arms around him.

"Alec?" I widened my eyes, begging for more information. I was clearly the only person in the room who didn't know what he was talking about, and I was already freaking out.

But Alec didn't say anything. He looked down instead.

"He's fine, honey." Amanda rubbed his back, smiling at me. "But his follow-up scans are coming soon, and he always gets a little—"

"—irresponsible! You went too far this time, son."

"Come on, Oliver, you know he didn't mean to—"

"I think I should come back another time." The detective got up from the couch.

"Actually, Jack," Alec raised his voice, "Linda and I were discussing this morning… Now that we know it's not anyone from the crew, we're considering calling off the investigation. What do you think?"

Oliver laughed out loud. "You have got to be kidding me."

"No, Dad. He hasn't tried to contact her since…you know. And she has already forgiven him, she doesn't want any revenge."

"You—*forgave*—him?" Oliver's gaze was a mix of skepticism and mockery. I had to look away.

"Yes!" Alec answered for me.

"This is very mature of you, sweetie," Amanda spoke.

"*Too* mature." Oliver raised an eyebrow. "And right after the paparazzi—"

"What are you insinuating, Dad? She's nothing like Hailey!"

"Well, something doesn't make sense here…"

"It was *my* idea, okay?"

"You obviously don't know all the facts, son." Oliver's attention turned to me again.

"Talk to *me*! Leave her alone!" Alec put himself between his father and me.

"Enough!" Amanda yelled. "Alec, to the office!" She pointed at the library. Then her eyes traveled across the room, stopping on Dan. "Do you wanna go first?"

He nodded, gathering up the newspapers from the coffee table.

Alec looked back at me, then said in the direction of the stairs, "Ben, can you take her with you?"

"Yeah." Only then did I notice his twin standing behind us.

"Are you sure you don't want me to come with you?" I asked Alec.

"Yes." He kissed my cheek. "I'll come meet you guys soon, okay?"

I watched him walk to the office with his manager. I didn't want to let Alec face all of that alone. But at the same time, I had a feeling anything I said would be turned against me. And to watch the discussion without being able to defend him would be even worse than not being there at all.

"Go get her something to eat, Ben." Amanda's voice was softer this time. "This might take a while."

Benjamin started walking, and I followed him in silence. I was still trying to understand what was happening, putting all the pieces together in my head.

"What do you want to eat?" He opened the fridge.

I couldn't help myself. I had to ask. "Alec is not sick again, is he?" I held my breath, waiting for the answer.

"No, he's just dramatic. And attention-seeking." Ben rolled his eyes, turning to the fridge again. "Bean salad? Or do you prefer a sandwich?"

"I'm good, thanks." I shook my head, a little surprised at his indifference.

"Come on, you gotta eat something…"

"I'm really not—"

"Liar." He studied my face. "You're pale—I can tell you're *starving*. Did you even have breakfast today?"

I dodged his gaze.

"Seriously? I was bluffing!" He raised his voice, looking me up and down. "What the hell are you trying to do to yourself?"

I crossed my arms over my chest, terribly self-conscious. "I was too anxious to eat, okay? I still am!" My stomach tightened, remembering Arthur at the hotel.

"You guys are making a storm in a teacup," Ben mumbled to himself.

And I lost my breath in shock. *Does he know about Arthur?*

"Come on, do you really think you're in danger?" He scoffed. "That was a poor choice of words, not a threat! There's no reason for all this drama."

Wait, words? Threat? "What are you talking about?"

"The text!"

"What text?" I knit my brows.

Benjamin frowned too, then stared at me, visibly confused. "What are *you* talking about?"

So, he doesn't know…

"Nothing," I said too fast, composing myself. I couldn't believe paranoia was taking over my mind again. Arthur had no reason to tell them what had happened—it would be as embarrassing for him as it was for me!

He will keep this between us. I know he will…

Ben watched my reactions, as if trying to decide whether I was crazy or not. "Are you okay?" he said in a low voice.

My cheeks burned with shame. "Yeah, I'm fine."

"All right… I think I better…" He walked to the pantry without finishing his sentence.

I let out a breath in relief. I really hoped he would just leave me alone.

But my peace didn't last long. I turned to the other side of the kitchen, listening to the voices in the living room, and suddenly, all I could think about was Alec. I wanted to see those newspapers. And listen to what Dan was saying. And find out why Mr. Brock had been so rude to me…

I tried not to take it personally—the whole leaving-in-separate-cars thing—but now I was convinced that it *was* personal. Very personal, actually. I didn't think Oliver liked me at all!

"I'm sorry I was rude before," Ben said softly, bringing me back to the present.

"It's okay." I leaned against the counter. "I think I better get used to it…"

"Why? Why are you saying that?"

"Your dad doesn't like me very much, does he?"

"No! I mean…" Ben stopped stirring to look at me. For some reason, he'd ignored what I said about not being hungry and was now cooking something on the stove. "Alec was just stupid for not telling him about the paparazzi before he saw it on the news. He's mad at *him*, not you."

"But he said… I don't know. I think he believes I *wanted* the paparazzi to see us together—as if I was planning something or hiding something. Who is this Hailey, by the way? Hailey Dawson?"

"Yeah." Ben kept his eyes on the pan this time.

"What happened? I know she was Alec's girlfriend, but—"

"*My* girlfriend," he interrupted me. "The paparazzi photographed her with *me*, not Alec."

"What?" I immediately recalled the pictures of them at the beach. The twins were pretty much alike from that distance—apart from their hair. And Alec was wearing a beanie that day.

Benjamin was wearing a beanie that day!

I can't believe this. Impostor Alec and I had had so many fights over those pictures. We even broke up for a week because of Hailey! If I'd known she was with Benjamin all along…

"But why didn't she tell everybody it was you? I mean, if she was *your* girlfriend…"

"She preferred to let them think the rumors were true."

"Why would she do that?"

"Let's just say it was…beneficial for her modeling career."

"No…" I tilted my head in sympathy. "How could she do that to you?"

Ben pretended not to hear me, adding some cheese to his mixture.

"So that's what your father thinks of me, then? That I'm a profiteering bit—"

"Don't call her that." His voice was small, hurt.

"Sorry," I said out loud, cursing her in my mind.

I *knew* there were valid reasons for me to hate Hailey! How could Benjamin even defend her? Oliver was right to be suspicious of me—or of anyone who befriended the twins, actually.

"Do you want to eat here or at the studio? The dessert is there anyway," Ben said, handing me a bowl full of macaroni and cheese.

My mouth watered. I really wasn't in the mood to eat right now, but mac and cheese was that one dish I could never say no to. My favorite comfort food in the world.

"How did you know this was my weakness?" I took it from his hands. Just the smell was enough to empty my mind, to calm me down.

"Who *doesn't* like mac and cheese?" He gave me a crooked smile.

I laughed, taking the first bite. And, yes, it was as delicious as it looked.

♪♩♡

After I finished eating, Ben said he had something else I would like in his music studio. So we crossed the back yard to a guest house at the highest part of the property.

It was almost the size of my mom's home in West Virginia. I had watched him coming in and out of that place all weekend the last time I was here, but I'd never seen how it looked inside.

Ben stopped in front of the studio, pulling the keys from his pocket. But then he hesitated, glancing shyly at my bandage. "Can I ask you a question?"

"Sure." I started rehearsing the lie in my head.

"What happened to your hand?" he said, opening the door. And his tone was so thoughtful that I thought I wouldn't be able to lie.

"I-I lost my balance and tripped. When I was getting in the car."

He pressed his lips together, then turned around, entering the room. "Chocolate might help." He showed me a secret cabinet over the minibar. "Mom doesn't like when we eat these things, so we keep them here. But if you ever—"

"Oh, so *you're* the keeper of the good stuff!" I chuckled, recognizing all the snack brands I liked the most. "Good to know."

"Alec also has a key—in case the studio is locked. But don't hesitate to take whatever you want."

"I'll definitely remember that. Thanks!" I grinned at him, finding myself a Reese's Cup.

"You're welcome." He watched me devour it, a self-satisfied smile on his face.

"So this is where you hide, huh?" I threw the wrapping in the trash can, exploring the studio. I had barely seen Benjamin the last time I was at their house, and now I understood *why*.

"This place is sick, Ben! I can't believe Alec never brought me here!" I walked around, touching everything.

I felt like I was in a cozy little cabin. The walls were cherry-red with details in wood, and there was this big sofa in the middle of the room, surrounded by instruments scattered all over. Mostly guitars, but there were also a few violins...a grand piano—and a drum set—and a cello!

"He was probably keeping you away from *that*."

I followed his gaze to a closed door next to the recording booth.

Curiosity sparked inside of me. "Will you get into trouble if I go check it out?"

"Probably..." He frowned. "But go ahead, I don't mind."

I had to laugh at the indifference on his face. Ben had this way of saying things—I couldn't tell if he was being sarcastic or trying to be funny. I just knew that his answer made me even more curious about that mysterious door.

I turned the knob, excited, then held my breath, covering my mouth with my hands. The room was filled from floor to ceiling with big glass cabinets. It was like those displays you see in museums. It was Alec's museum! The awards, his platinum album, the official photos—it was all there!

"Are you seriously gonna cry?" Ben laughed next to me.

"Of course not." I laughed with him, trying hard to hold back the tears. "I'm just…so proud of him."

I recognized every prize Alec had gotten; I'd really been with him every step of the way. And seeing everything all at once like that—it was like déjà vu.

Stop fangirling, Linda. You're his girlfriend now. Act normal! I composed myself, glad that Alec wasn't there to see my reaction.

"You really are his biggest fan, aren't you?"

"I think I probably am." I giggled, wiping my eyes. Then something crossed my mind. "Has he ever dated a fan before?"

Ben looked away, but I insisted, meeting his gaze again.

"Made out with, yeah. Fallen in love, no."

His words lit up my whole spirit. "Do you really think he's—"

"Yes," Ben said in a low voice.

I turned to the other side of the room, trying not to look so happy. And that's when I noticed a whole shelf with photos of Alec as a kid—playing the piano, the drums, the guitar.

"Aw, look at you two!" I smiled at a picture of the twins performing together in primary school, Alec on the piano and Benjamin on the violin. It was the cutest thing ever! They looked so alike that I could only tell them apart because of their instruments.

"Was this before or after…you know?"

"Before. This one is from after he got sick." Ben showed me a different shelf. But this time I couldn't pay attention to Alec.

"Is that *James*?" I stared at the little blond boy holding a guitar.

"Yeah."

So they've been playing together for that long? "How old were they here?"

"Hmm…eleven, twelve? I don't know. It was right after AJ joined the band."

I frowned, puzzled, so he continued, "They were a band before—Alec, James, Zach, and AJ."

"I thought Alec had always played solo…" *How haven't I heard of this band before?*

"My dad thought it would be better not to mention that to the press."

"Oh." I understood that right away. Alec had told me about his father's obsession with "keeping private things private." Oliver was a publicist, so he'd always done everything he could to keep his family as safe from the media as possible. *He only tells them what they truly need to know,* I remembered Alec saying.

No wonder Oliver is so mad at us today! This is probably the first time Alec exposed himself without discussing it with him first.

I glanced at the photo again. "And what happened to the band? These aren't Alec's bassist and drummer, right? I don't remember—"

"They had a…disagreement." Ben shifted his weight from one foot to the other, suddenly uneasy.

I was about to ask him what had happened when he continued, "Things simply didn't end up well, so don't talk to Alec about this, okay?"

"Okay," I said automatically. Ben's tone was too serious for me not to agree with him, but there was no way I wouldn't ask Alec what happened to the band later.

"I mean it, Linda. It triggers his anxiety!" Ben exhaled, glancing down. "I shouldn't have let you come here…"

"Hey, relax! I won't say anything." I was honest this time. But now I couldn't tell if I was more curious or worried about the whole thing.

We both went silent for a second. And at that moment, I realized how little I knew Alec. Even if I recognized every single one of these awards, even though I'd been following him since his career started, there was a whole lot of history I knew nothing about. Things that upset him, that hurt him, that challenged him… Everything Oliver had made sure to keep secret from the public eye.

"We should go back to the house." Ben sounded regretful.

No, I still have so many questions! "Please tell me one more thing? Just one?" I begged.

"What?" He rolled his eyes, his mood lighter.

"Is it because of this band that Alec thinks so highly of James? Because he was the only one who stayed?"

"No." Ben chuckled. "He thinks highly of James because James is a very genuine guy! And he's not the only one who stayed, you know? Don't you recognize AJ?" He pointed at the tallest boy, who was playing the bass guitar.

I focused on the picture, trying to remember. Brown skin, thin eyes. "Is he one of the bodyguards?" *I think I saw him with Alec a few times…*

"Yes. After the *disagreement*, AJ didn't want to play anymore. But he was close to the family, so Dad found a place for him in the crew."

"And what happened to the drummer?" Gray eyes, blond bangs—I was sure *that* face I'd never seen before.

"No, Linda. You said *one* more question." Ben held my arm, gently pulling me out of the awards room. "He's already gonna kill me for—"

"For *what*, brother?" Alec asked from the front door.

"For showing me how cute you guys were!" I said quickly, grinning at them both. I wished I could have seen them together when they were little—they looked very different now. And not only because Alec's hair was longer, and Benjamin didn't have any tattoos. Their energy, their personality, their style—everything was so contrasting that, standing side by side, they didn't even look like identical twins anymore.

"We *were* cute? Past tense?" Alec faked a frown, locking his arms around my waist.

"I think I'm gonna go." Ben picked up one of the violin cases from the floor.

"Thanks for keeping her company, bro."

"No problem." Ben nodded.

"Did you guys have lunch?" Alec asked me.

"Yeah. Mac and—"

"You should pay more attention, by the way," Ben blurted from the door, exchanging a serious look with his brother. "She didn't eat breakfast this morning."

"What?" Alec gave me a disapproving frown. And I wanted to kill Benjamin for that, but he wasn't even in the room anymore.

"I was too anxious. I'm sorry… But tell me what happened in there? Are you okay?" I asked, anxiety circulating through my veins once again.

Alec went quiet, then squeezed me in his arms, snuggling his head on my neck.

"What did they say?" I tried a different question. It was pretty clear that he *wasn't* okay. "Are you in trouble because of me? How bad are the pictures?"

"I don't want you to worry about this," Alec said in my ear.

"But—"

"No." He leaned back, catching my face in his hands. "Everything will be okay, *I promise you.*"

I looked into his eyes, searching for the truth he wasn't telling me.

Alec dodged my gaze, letting me go. "The only thing you need to know is that we have to be careful from now on. They didn't catch us kissing, so Dan is telling the press that we're just friends. But we can't be seen dating in public anymore, okay?"

"Okay… What about your dad?"

"We're fine. I should have called him yesterday; it was my fault."

"And Jack? What did he say about the investigation?"

Alec's eyes flickered down for a second. "You didn't bring your old phone to Vegas, did you?"

"No, I don't carry it around anymore."

"Can I have it?" he said with a grin.

I hesitated, confused. His mood swing had surprised me.

"Please?" Alec insisted.

"Y-yeah, sure. But…why?"

"So you won't have anything to remind you of him." He grinned again. "I want you to forget your past, Linda—and be happy with *me*."

He was making that cute jealous face again. I couldn't help but smile.

"Give it to Mario as soon as you get home tomorrow, okay? *Please*. Don't even turn it on; I don't want you looking back at your past ever again!"

I nodded, feeling this warm blast in my chest. There was nothing I wanted more than to get rid of those memories—to start a new story with him.

"That's my girl." Alec tucked a lock of hair behind my ear.

His green eyes were soft now, relieved. I opened my mouth to ask what else had happened in the meeting, but he pulled me by the waist, leaning down slowly.

"Now, about the future…" He pressed his lips to mine, and every other thought faded from my mind.

Chapter 3

"She's here!" Claire came running the second I opened the door to my dad's house the next day.

"Hey, sweetie. You're still up?" I stumbled on the doorstep, trying to hug her and pull my suitcase inside at the same time.

"I was waiting for you." She grinned up at me.

I took off my backpack, kissing the top of her head. Claire and I had a too big of an age gap to build a strong sibling bond, like Alec and his brothers. I confess I saw her more like my own child than a sister. But I did love her. And watching her so excited just to see me kind of melted my heart.

"So how was it?" Caroline smirked at me.

"Awesome!" I smiled from ear to ear. I was too happy to hide —from anyone.

"Tell us…" she started saying.

But then I remembered Mario, waiting in the car. "Sorry, I'll come back in a minute."

I ran upstairs and found my old phone right away. The battery was completely dead—which reminded me it would need its charger too. And when I went back to the car, I handed everything to Mario without hesitation.

"Have a good night, miss."

"You too." I waved, watching him leave.

I couldn't believe how relieved I felt. Alec was right; there was too much history attached to that phone. Getting rid of it was like washing away the last bad memories from my past.

I turned around and smiled at my house. Now I was clean. Now I was ready to really start my new life in LA.

"You're grounded," Dad announced when I came through the door.

My face fell. "For this?" I pointed at the street. "I'm sorry, Dad. I had to send this thing to Alec, and Mario was waiting…"

"You're grounded because you missed dinner." He crossed his arms over his chest.

"*What?* I thought you told Alec to bring me back before curfew, not dinner." I checked my watch. "And I'm an hour early!"

"You're grounded, Linda," Dad repeated, his tone harsher. "End of discussion!"

I glanced around, searching for backup. Caroline wasn't there anymore. She must have felt the storm coming and decided to take Claire to her room. But that's when I noticed the magazines on the dining table.

Alec Confronts Paparazzi… To Defend His New Girlfriend!

Everything About Alec's Sleepover Date in Vegas

Alec Brock Spotted Making Out With A Mystery Latina

"At least have the courage to tell me the real reason you're doing this!" I grabbed my bags, walking to my room.

"All right, you wanna talk about this? Let's talk about this!" He raised his voice, speaking in Spanish.

"Not now, Dad," I also changed languages, marching up the stairs. He had just ruined my mood, and I was too angry to look at his face.

"Do you think this is normal, Linda? Do you think this is

right?" He followed me, still speaking Spanish. "You just spent the *weekend* away—with a boy you barely know! And now the whole country is talking about it. Did you read what they're saying about you? He's just ruined your name!"

I dropped everything on the floor, then fell onto my bed, covering my ears with my hands. I couldn't believe my perfect weekend with Alec was going to end like this.

"No more sleepovers or trips from now on! I want you home every day by 8 P.M.," he said from the door.

"But Dad…" I had just told Amanda I would come to her Halloween party on Friday night. "We live on opposite sides of the city! And Alec doesn't stay in LA much—we have to make the most out of the time he's here!"

"That's *exactly* the problem. This boy is—"

"He's the nicest guy in the world, Dad," I said reassuringly.

"I'm sure he is." He snorted, glaring at my new suitcase. "You can tell him to stop with the expensive gifts, by the way. I mean it! This isn't right, Linda!"

"He surprised me at school. What did you want him to do? Let me borrow his clothes the whole weekend?"

"I told him your suitcase was ready at home. Couldn't he have just passed here before—"

"We were already late for the concert!" I said, my patience wearing thin.

"I don't like this, Linda. I don't like this at all!"

"Well, you're gonna have to get used to it," I snapped.

"*I'm* gonna have to get used to it?" He pulled the door closed behind him, suddenly furious. "How dare you talk to me like this?"

"I'm tired, Dad, can we please talk another time?"

"No, Linda, look at you! This boy is bad news, and you're completely out of control! You're seventeen—you're gonna have to respect me! You can tell this friend of yours that—"

"He's my *boyfriend* now," I announced, savoring the word. I had seen my father mistreating Alec since that first night they'd met in LA. It was time for him to understand that Alec was important to me; he wasn't going anywhere.

"You're so naive, Linda. *Boyfriend...*" He rolled his eyes. "You're his groupie! He's going to take advantage of you and then leave! How long do you think this is gonna last? Do you actually believe you're gonna fall in love and live happily ever after?"

I felt the tears coming, so I turned to the other side of the bed, using my pillow to cover my face. "Get out of my room!"

"We're not done talking… You are both kids! And you, young lady, have no idea what you're doing! I hope you're at least being responsible, because—"

"Ahh!" I groaned, throwing the pillow at him. "Shut up, Dad! Shut up! *You're* the one who has no idea what you're saying! And just for the record, you don't *ever* have to worry about that—I'm not getting pregnant in high school! I'm not as stupid as you and Mom!"

Dad's face went red. Then he walked to the door, looking at me with deep, angry eyes. "From now on, I want you home straight after school, do you hear me? No leaving the house on the weekends either! You're grounded indefinitely—until you learn how to be more respectful!"

♪♩♡

"What do you think your parents will do when they find out you have a secret boyfriend?" Alec said on the phone.

"Well, Mom likes your songs, so she will probably fangirl a little." I laughed.

"What about your dad? I can see he's way stricter than she

is… I don't like it when you're at his house. You're always anxious around him."

"Yeah, I prefer to stay with Mom too. Nothing seems to be good enough for him, you know? I don't think I could live in San Francisco, honestly. Spending the summer here is already driving me crazy!"

"I can see that… He's probably gonna hate me, isn't he?"

"Probably, yeah." I snickered. "But don't take it personally, babe. It's not because it's you—he's always made it very clear that he didn't want me to date in high school. His worst fear is that I'll end up making the same mistake that he and Mom made."

"Oh. Well, I can't even *touch* you, so I guess he doesn't have to worry about that."

"*Yet*," I said with a smirk, making Alec laugh.

"Do you realize we've never been so close before? I mean, physically?"

"It's true! This is the first time we're in the same state." I grinned. "It's a shame you're only in LA for the festival tomorrow."

"You know what? I'm pretty tempted to take the car right now and go after you."

"You're crazy." I chuckled. "You would spend the whole night driving and then have to leave immediately just to make it back in time for your show. Even if you took a plane, just a few hours wouldn't be worth the trouble."

"I disagree. Just looking at you for a *minute* would be worth it," he said, sounding like he really meant it.

"No." I shook my head. "We're gonna have *plenty* of time to be together when the tour is over. I can wait; it's okay."

"I don't think *I* can. I want to see you so bad, love—I could drive all night just to have a glimpse of you. I have to see you, at least once…"

I have to see you, at least once... His voice kept echoing in my head.

I woke up panting, my heart pounding loudly in my chest. I remembered that night as if it'd been yesterday. I had been visiting my dad last summer, when he still lived in San Francisco. Caroline had just given birth to Jesse, and they needed someone to help with Claire, so I spent a whole month with them.

Alec was on tour, so we didn't even consider meeting in person. Except for that night. That one conversation.

I have to see you, at least once... Now I understood the urgency in his tone. *At least once...*before the truth came out and he was exposed.

I couldn't believe I had forgotten about this—I hadn't mentioned it to Jack! We'd stayed on the phone for an hour that night, talking about the possibility of him coming to see me at my dad's. He'd never been so serious about meeting me before. And his phone number was also from LA! That whole conversation was probably a confirmation that the impostor really lived in California!

Alec had explained that the detective hadn't found any evidence against anyone from his circle. That's why his dad had agreed to call off the investigation—they knew the impostor wasn't a risk for Alec. But even if he wasn't *that* close, he could still be close enough! He could still live in LA! And now that the photos had gone public and everybody knew I was here... Would he try to contact me? Would he try to *see* me?

I would never know.

He surely wouldn't give himself up by revealing his true identity, especially now that I was with the Real Alec. But if he wanted to pass by me on the street or talk to me at a public place or simply watch me from a distance—I would never be able to tell! He could *see* me anytime he wanted, and I wouldn't even know!

I forced myself to take a deep breath, watching the sunrise colors through my window. I'd never believed Impostor Alec was someone bad. I thought he was sad and probably lost, but he wasn't *bad*—he couldn't be. But if the relationship we'd had was somehow real for him… If any part of this lie was true…

He's gonna find me. My chest tightened. If he lived anywhere near LA, I knew he would at least *try*.

And there was absolutely nothing I could do to stop him, to protect myself from him. This was my life now. There would always be someone out there who knew who I was—who knew everything about me. And with the investigation off, the only thing I would ever know for sure about him was that his name wasn't Alec Brock.

"Are you leaving already? I thought I was dropping you off," Dad said in the kitchen, giving Jesse his bottle.

"I'm gonna walk." I avoided his gaze.

"Come back here right now! Do you think I'm going to let you leave without eating?"

I huffed, then marched back to the kitchen.

"It's too early, Linda, sit down to eat your breakfast… And the school is too far. You should—"

I grabbed a snack and left the room before he could finish his sentence. I was still mad at him over last night. I didn't know what I would do about it yet, but there was no way he would keep me from seeing Alec this weekend!

I tried to eat while walking down the street, but my levels of anxiety were too high. I couldn't stop thinking about my dream. I couldn't stop thinking about *him*.

I have to see you, at least once… I wondered if he'd seen the photos yet. If he had figured out I was living in LA.

He could be anyone. He could be anywhere. How was I supposed to live my life like that? Every random guy's stare now sent my whole body into panic mode! It was so scary to simply walk on the street that I wound up hurrying and arrived at school in no time.

Breathe, Linda. Breathe. I tried to calm myself down using Dr. Brown's relaxation techniques. I didn't want to take my anxiety pill this early in the morning.

He said that over a year ago, remember? It's not like he's planning to come see you now. And just because his number was from LA, it doesn't mean he lives anywhere near here. He could be miles and miles away. He might not even live in the state! Maybe he just bought the phone here...to make his story more convincing.

Plus, he lied to you—he never asked you to forgive him. He probably doesn't care about you at all. He might have even forgotten you exist already.

I took one last deep breath at the sound of the bell, then left the bathroom stall I had locked myself into. I'd been the first to arrive at school, after all; it would be too ironic if I was late for class.

But the moment I walked down the corridor, I felt like something was off.

I double-checked my clothes to see if I had toothpaste on my shirt or something. Then I looked around, wondering what everybody was staring at. But there was no one behind me, and each step I took was followed by more and more eyes.

My stomach froze. It was like I was living a nightmare. Like they could all tell how paranoid and terrified I felt having their attention focused on me.

I ran to my first classroom and sat down at my desk, avoiding any eye contact. My anxiety was so out of control now that my hands were shaking.

I reached for my backpack and found Dr. Brown's pill. There was no way I could just breathe deeply this time.

"Hey, you okay?" my lab partner said.

"Yeah, thanks." I nodded, taking the medicine right before Ms. Jones started her biology class. That's when I saw two girls laughing over a gossip magazine in the front row.

Of course! I exhaled. There were so many things in my head today that I'd completely forgotten about the paparazzi and the news.

"Put that away, girls." Ms. Jones pointed at the magazine in their hands. But then she narrowed her eyes, taking a second glance at the picture.

"Is that…" She met my gaze.

And that's when everybody turned around to look at me.

Chapter 4

I'd been warned about this. Alec had explained to me what people would do and ask and think. We had anticipated everything.

"We're just friends," I would say. No comments about Vegas, no details about his life. What we did together was no one else's business, and Alec wanted to keep it that way.

I was ready for it. To lie to everyone, to defend our privacy—our right to just live our lives. But I was not ready for *this*.

Not the attacks, not the insults…

What do you do when people decide to hate you for no reason at all?

First it was Dad, making all kinds of wrong assumptions about Alec. And now, everybody at school seemed to hate *me*.

When I stopped at my locker before lunch, it was covered with hateful notes—even a couple of death threats! I ignored them, of course. Especially because I knew there were a lot of eyes watching my every move. But when I opened the door, more notes fell out at my feet.

It didn't take long for the audience of teens in the hallway to grow. And then I wasn't sure what to do anymore. *Should I clean this up? Should I pretend nothing happened?*

"Hey…*Linda*! How was your weekend?" said this girl I'd never seen in my life.

I pretended not to hear her.

"Well, we know what *you* did. Romantic getaway in Vegas… how classy!"

"We're just friends," I said sharply, trying to end the conversation.

"Oh, I *bet* you are." She laughed out loud. "So, tell us… Is he as delicious as he looks? I bet he has a big—"

I slammed the locker door and started to walk away.

"So moody… I bet he dumped her already," she said to the crowd, making everybody laugh with her.

I glanced at all those eyes—staring at me—and my heart raced again. So I went back to the bathroom, back to my stall.

My new school had only been tolerable so far because I felt invisible. *Will it be like this from now on? Will they ever leave me alone?*

It didn't matter if what they were saying about me was good or bad, I didn't think I could deal with all that *attention*. Not when the impostor had just found out I was living in LA. Not knowing that every guy who looked me in the eye could actually be *him*.

My hands were shaking again, my breathing rapid and shallow. I had another pill in my locker, but I couldn't go back there now.

I let my head fall back against the door, gasping for air. I needed to go back to Alec's world. When I was with him, I was never anxious, never sad. His light was strong enough to illuminate us both, and without him by my side, I was only darkness.

"Linda?" Someone knocked on the stall.

"Leave me alone!" I yelled, choking on my tears.

"It's Liz—Elizabeth. From biology… I saw what those idiots

did. I locked the bathroom; you can come out if you want. It's just you and me."

I wiped my eyes, composing myself. "Thank you, but I'm fine."

"No, you're not. I saw you taking your meds before classes even started." Her voice was low. "But it's okay, you know—not to be okay."

Who is this girl again? Biology?

No, it can't be. This soft-spoken person trying to calm me down is the punk chick that sits next to me in the lab?

I opened the door slowly, more out of curiosity than anything. And yep, it was her. Pale skin, thin eyes, dark makeup, purple hair.

We'd never spoken before, besides the minimum communication required for class. She was one of those girls my abuela would have warned me to stay away from. But in LA, there were more of them than Abuela could have thought. And being the only new student in biology, I hadn't had much of a choice. The only seat left was the one next to her.

"You will survive, don't worry. I've seen worse…" She gave me a sympathetic smile. "Do you want to go have lunch?"

I shook my head. "I don't think I'll leave this bathroom anytime soon."

"Come on, don't give them what they want!" She reached for my backpack on the floor. "You have the right to sleep with anyone you wish. If they have a problem with that, it's their problem, not yours."

I cracked a little smile. "I didn't… We didn't…"

"Whatever, girl. Not my business." She handed me my backpack. "So, lunch?"

I knew I would regret it, but I followed her anyway. Something about Liz's attitude reminded me of Nina, and I was so desperate for any kind of comfort that I couldn't help but hold onto it.

"Guys, this is Linda." Liz sat down at a table in the cafeteria, making room for me next to her. "She's our friend now."

Only half of the girls turned their heads to say hi. I recognized some of them; I'd watched this table of people before. They were the girls' soccer team.

"Thank you for letting us know, Liz." A smiling brunette offered me a handshake. "I'm Aisha, nice to meet you."

"Is she the chick who—?"

"Mind your own business, Brianna!" Liz raised her voice to the girl at the end of the table.

"Jeez." She turned her back on us, looking offended.

The smiley one spoke again, "You're in my chemistry class—and math! You're new in LA, right?"

"Yeah." I bit the inside of my lip, trying to remember her from class.

"Sam has just moved here too." Aisha nodded at the curvy redhead sitting across from her.

"Hi." The redhead grinned.

This one I remembered. And I confess it wasn't even because we had most of our classes together. It was because she was…*pretty*. Like, photographic model pretty. The red hair, the little freckles, the blue eyes… She had that raw beauty you can't help but notice—and be a little jealous of.

"Where are you from?" I asked, curious. I had no idea she was also new to LA.

"New Jersey. I moved this summer."

"Me too! I mean, I also moved in the summer. I'm not from Jersey—I'm from West Virginia."

"Cool." She nodded, opening her salad. "And how did you end up here?"

"I came to…live with my dad." The words tasted bitter in my mouth. "What about you?"

"My mom remarried." She shrugged.

"Oh." I frowned in sympathy. I could see the words hadn't tasted so good to her either.

"Great, you're already feeling sorry for someone other than yourself." Liz smirked. "That's a good start."

I couldn't help but smile.

But then my heart stopped. They had just turned a stereo on, playing Alec's first single.

I glanced around the room and found where it was coming from: a table full of boys dancing and singing along. But before I had time to react, other people were rushing to join them—to make fun of Alec.

One of the guys pulled his girlfriend into the middle of the circle, then kissed her mouth theatrically, moving his hands all over her. The whole cafeteria laughed out loud, but I didn't hear any sound. I could only pay attention to their eyes. I could only imagine *his eyes* hidden somewhere in the crowd.

That's when I couldn't take it any longer. I grabbed my backpack and ran to the bathroom as fast as I could. I promised myself I wouldn't leave this time. Not until everybody was gone.

♪♩♡

I don't feel all right when I'm not with you, I texted Alec when I got home.

He didn't answer.

I decided to take a shower, then find something I could eat in my room. Caroline had said a few words to me, but I'd avoided Dad. I wasn't ready to talk to him yet.

I finished my homework, texted with Mom for a while, then

Claire came to kiss me goodnight before going to bed. Still, no news from Alec.

Did something happen? Is he avoiding me? I fell asleep with the phone in my hands. So I wasn't sure if I was dreaming or awake when I finally felt it buzz.

"Hello?" I said groggily.

"Did I wake you? I'm so sorry. I wasn't allowed to have my phone with me all day, and I didn't want you to go to sleep thinking I was ignoring you…"

"It's okay." I grinned. "I'm happy you called."

"I missed you today." He had a smile in his voice.

"Me too. I had a *terrible* day."

"Me too." He sighed.

"Do you want to talk about it?" I rolled to the side of the bed, worried. I knew that whatever consequences those paparazzi photos had had in my life, it had been a thousand times worse for him.

Alec took a deep breath, as if preparing to say something important. But then he murmured, "Not today… Wanna talk about yours?"

"No." *Absolutely not.* It would only make him more stressed.

We both went silent. But I swear that just being with him— with his presence—already made me feel a lot better.

"You sound sleepy," he said. "I should let you rest."

"No, don't go!"

I heard him chuckle.

"Stay with me on the line like this? Just for a minute?"

"Sure." His voice was soft, gentle.

I closed my eyes, feeling his arms around me. All I needed today was that—a little bit of his warmth. A little bit of his light.

"And, babe?" he said drowsily.

"Yeah?"

"It's just a wave, okay? Whatever it is…"

I squeezed the phone in my hand, my eyes filling up with tears.

♪♩♡

Things didn't get any easier in the next couple of days. It was hard to decide which was worse—to face the bullies at school or my dad at home.

The dating rumors had completely taken over the news, and Dad was not only *displeased*, but also made a point of showing *how* displeased he was every opportunity he got. So, yeah, I guess school was probably better.

Liz, Aisha, and Sam were helping me cope with my anxiety, and since I had at least one of them in each of my classes, their company also discouraged the bullying a little. But just when I thought things were starting to get better at school, the paparazzi found me.

I'd never been so afraid in my life. I was so anxious that I couldn't eat the whole day! Now I knew for sure that Impostor Alec would know where to find me if he wanted to! I'd been photographed in front of my school, in front of my house… I didn't even have the guts to go to my appointment with Dr. Brown, afraid Dad would see the pictures of me on the other side of the city when I was supposed to be grounded.

I told the paparazzi that Alec and I were just friends and assured them they could go away—they wouldn't spot Alec anywhere in my neighborhood. But there was this one persistent car that never went away.

It was like being in a reality show, knowing people were judging me and talking about me 24/7. And I felt really bad for Alec. I didn't know how he coped with all that attention every single day.

My only moments of peace that week had been his goodnight calls. And I had the feeling I was *his* only escape too.

He was quieter than usual—much more serious. I asked him a few times if something was going on, but he always changed the subject. And I couldn't bring myself to pressure him. Not when I was keeping things from him too.

We talked about the paparazzi and the media, but I chose not to say anything about school. It would only hurt him. Alec cared too much about his fans' opinions, and judging by the hate notes I was getting, it was obvious that the fandom wasn't taking the dating rumors very well. Even if for them it was just that: only rumors.

It was already bad enough that I had to tell Alec I was *grounded*.

I didn't talk details, of course, but I let him know that, although Dad had never said anything about *receiving* visitors, I wasn't allowed to go out of the house for a while, aside from school. Which meant I wouldn't be able to go to his mother's Halloween dinner on Friday.

It crushed me to hear how disappointed he was. He told me his mom had even gotten me a special costume already! But it was okay, he said—my dad could make it as hard for us as he wished; we were not backing down. We were going to make this work.

And his words reassured me.

Every time someone mocked me at school, every time I had to see my dad at home, Alec's promises were the thing I came back to. My safe haven.

But I couldn't exactly say things were going *well*.

On Thursday, the bullying got so bad at lunch that I was called to the principal's office! I couldn't even believe it; I didn't do anything wrong! *They* were the ones who kept provoking *me*.

I was on the verge of a panic attack when I walked into that room—I'd never been called to the principal's office in my entire life. And when I saw my dad sitting there too, I honestly thought that was the day I would die.

But things turned out better than I expected. The principal suspended the boys and made them apologize to me, spreading fear all over the school. So no one dared to sing Alec's song in the hallways anymore, and the bullying had been drastically reduced to the anonymous hate notes in my locker. Which was still kind of bad, I guess—but it was at least some sort of relief.

But the best thing of all was my dad's reaction. We'd barely been speaking at home, so he had no clue what was happening at school. And when the principal started telling him about the bullying, he seemed even more regretful than concerned. I guess the message sank in. It made him realize he was one of them—one of my bullies.

I could not believe it when I heard him talking to my mom that night. The two of them hadn't spent so much time on the phone since…ever! And then this morning, he woke up early to cook and asked if I could have breakfast with him before heading to school.

It was so unexpected that I didn't know how to react.

He didn't say he was sorry, but he announced I wasn't grounded anymore. If I wanted to see Alec, I could—as long as we split our time together between our houses. He even said I could stay the night occasionally, since we lived on opposite sides of the city. But he didn't want me to spend the whole weekend there anymore. If Alec wanted to be with me, he would have to spend some time here too, under *Dad's* watch.

"Thank you," was all I could say. I also tried, "I'm sorry for what I said about you and Mom," but the words got stuck in my throat.

I knew he'd understood it, though. Because he had a little smile on his face when he served me more pancakes.

Chapter 5

I called Alec the minute Dad dropped me off at school. "I have good news!"

"Me too," he said with a smile I could hear. "You first."

"I'm not grounded anymore! I can come to the party tonight!"

"Are you serious? That's great! I'll tell Mom you're coming; she's gonna be thrilled."

"Oh yeah, the costume! I can't wait to see it," I squealed. "Go ahead—your turn."

"Well, now I don't have to do this over the phone. I can tell you when you get here."

"Come on, I'm curious… Tell me!"

He laughed out loud. "No. Tonight."

"Alec, that's mean! How can you—"

I stopped talking when I noticed this girl turning her head to look at me. But it wasn't her stare that had caught my attention. It was a paparazzi watching me from a parked car.

"I've gotta go. Talk to you after school, okay?"

"Okay."

I hung up the phone, focusing on the driver. The windows were too dark for me to see his face, but I recognized the car—he had followed me all week! It was getting ridiculous. I would have to talk to Alec about this.

Tonight. I grinned again, glancing at the sky.

♪♩♡

"Someone seems happy today," Liz teased at lunch, passing me the Halloween candy bucket.

I bit my lip to keep from smiling, then found the last mini Reese's Cup. I had eaten, like, five already—it was by far my favorite treat.

"Does this have anything to do with your boyfriend?" Aisha smirked.

I rolled my eyes at her.

"All right, all right—your *friend*."

"Kind of…" My cheeks burned.

It was getting harder to lie about Alec. To strangers, I didn't mind. I was actually good at it—the words came to me automatically. But Aisha was becoming a friend, and it's hard to lie to people you care about.

"Are you sure you can't come to my Halloween party, Linda?" Brianna said from the other end of the table. "You can bring Alec. It would be a pleasure—"

"I've already made other plans, thank you," I said politely.

"Maybe next time, then?" She twirled her hair around her finger.

"Sure." I gave her a fake smile.

Another thing I was getting good at was identifying people who were only being kind to me to get closer to Alec. It was easy, actually, since no one at school seemed to treat me normally anymore. They were either too awful or too nice.

"Sorry, I'm late." Sam exhaled, laying her oboe case on the

table. "I hope you haven't eaten all the good ones, I really need a treat today."

"What happened?" Aisha asked.

"I hate this band! It was so much better at my old school."

"So, quit." Liz shrugged.

"I can't! I need this in my curriculum if I wanna get into UCLA."

"Oh, cool, that's where I'm going too!" I said. "You're all staying in LA next year?"

"Not me." Liz shook her head. "I'm backpacking in Europe."

"Sounds like a better plan." I chuckled. "What about you, Aisha?"

"I'm still trying to convince my parents to let me go with Liz… So yeah, I'm probably staying."

"You should come with us to UCLA!" Sam said, grabbing the bucket. "Maybe we could all… Where did you guys find the Reese's?"

"It's over. Linda went wild on them." Liz nodded at the empty wrappers in front of me.

"Oops." I frowned, making everybody laugh.

"Well, I was about to suggest we could be roommates, but now…" Sam teased.

But just then my phone started buzzing. And to my total surprise, it was a call from Alec's mom!

Amanda asked if I could curl my hair for tonight, and when I said yes, she told me to leave the curlers in until I got to her house. It would be some kind of surprise for Alec.

I know most people would be *very suspicious* about this, but I was accustomed to the Brocks by then. It turned out that the concert in Vegas and the Early Christmas Alec had set up for Claire weren't out-of-the-blue things. Apparently, his whole family had this compulsion to make other people happy. Sometimes for no reason other than they felt like it.

It was a family thing. A competition, even—they kept trying to outdo each other's surprises. And it wasn't only for their family members. Whenever they had the opportunity to do something extraordinary for someone else, they just did it.

I wondered what Amanda was planning. I couldn't decide what I was more excited about, Alec's costume or mine.

That was…until I saw him.

It took me a solid minute to stop staring at his Navy officer uniform and process what was happening around me. He looked so hot in that white suit—I couldn't believe this was my boyfriend. I couldn't believe he was mine.

"You look *great*," I finally said.

He showed me his dimples, then planted a kiss on my lips. "You too."

"No, I don't." I raised my hands to my head, trying to hide the hair curlers. "I'm not ready yet; stop looking at me!"

He laughed, taking my bags out of the car. "Go change, Mom is upstairs."

We entered the living room, and I saw Ben and Oliver on the sofa, watching the news. But I didn't want to say hello. Not dressed like this.

Still, seeing them gave me a hint of what would be my costume. Ben was in a green Army dress uniform costume, and Oliver in blue, honoring the Air Force. So I was pretty sure I would be a nurse—or someone else in the military.

I turned to Alec on the stairs, remembering the other thing I was curious about. "Tell me your good news!"

"I thought you would have guessed by now." He smirked. "Didn't my mom tell you what we celebrate on Halloween?"

"Not really. She said it's a benefit dinner with her Hollywood friends. She does it every year, right?"

I was *so* excited for it. I couldn't believe I was about to have dinner with real Hollywood stars!

"She didn't tell you what she's raising money for?"

"No."

"I'm gonna let her tell you, then." He knocked on her door. "She loves telling this story."

"But you said you would—"

"Sweetie, I'm so glad you made it!" Amanda hugged me. "I was devastated when Alec told me you weren't coming anymore."

"Yeah, my dad finally agreed." I smiled, noticing she wasn't ready either. Her makeup was impeccable, but she was wearing a robe, and her hair—just like mine—was still full of curlers.

"Come." She gestured for me to come into the bedroom. Then she turned to Alec. "Are you guys ready?"

"Yeah…and bored!"

"Don't worry, people will start arriving in a minute." She stepped out of the room and adjusted a golden medal attached to his suit. "Make sure everyone feels at home until I come down, okay?"

"Fine." He sighed, walking away. "And Mom, you forgot to tell Linda what we celebrate on Halloween."

"He didn't tell you?" Amanda widened her eyes, closing the door behind her.

"No! Can someone please just tell me already? I've been curious all day!"

She giggled. "He just got his follow-up exams back, sweetie. Cancer-free for nine years now—thank God!"

My jaw dropped. *Is that why he was so serious this week? He was waiting for the results? Why didn't he tell me? I could have—*

"So, since Alec went into remission on Halloween, I decided to organize this benefit every year and raise funds for the Children's Cancer Research Institute that developed the experimental treatment that saved his life. I'm surprised he didn't mention it to you."

"Yeah, me too." I frowned. I couldn't believe I'd spent the whole week lost in my silly problems while Alec was dealing with something so serious all on his own.

"Well, now you know… My boys are fine, you're here with us, and we're going to raise a lot of money and save a lot of lives tonight!" She smiled, carefully removing the first curler from my hair. "I'm so proud of this institution and of what they've been doing in the past years. They showed me the plans for this new hospital they want to build…"

She kept working on my hair, but I got distracted by her enthusiasm, her ambition, her faith. I felt inspired just witnessing it, as if it was something contagious. Now I knew where Alec had learned it—that blindly optimistic way of seeing life. They both dreamed so high that I wondered if they actually believed in fairy tales.

I think *that* was the major difference between Alec's world and mine. My family didn't know how to *dream* like that. We had hopes and dreams, yes, but we were all…reasonable. We didn't believe in the impossible like they did. Our world was cynical and realistic.

That's why Dad didn't believe Alec and I could truly be in love—a love that could last. He didn't believe in fairy tales.

"Are you ready to see your costume? Or should we do makeup first?" Amanda's voice brought me back to the present.

"Costume!" I said without hesitation. "Am I also in the military?"

She laughed out loud, walking to the closet. "No, that's just for the boys. Alec told me you guys watched *Pearl Harbor* together, so it gave me the idea…"

"We still haven't finished it," I told her.

"You should—it's a great movie." She grinned, holding a hanger under my chin. "I'm so happy I get to dress up a girl for once!"

I glanced down at the white dress she had picked for me. There were wings attached to it! "I'm an angel?"

"Yes, you are," she said with a smirk.

"It's *so beautiful!*" I touched the wings. They looked like real feathers—soft and fluffy.

"Go ahead, try it on! Use the closet so you can see the back in the mirrors." She guided me to the other room.

I couldn't call it a closet, though. It was bigger than my bedroom! And don't even get me started on the clothes…and the shoes…and the accessories.

"Oh, I forgot the boots," Amanda said, handing me the dress. "Make yourself at home. I'll be back in a minute."

I nodded at her, enchanted by the lights and the mirrors. Everything looked so glamorous that it was like I was walking into my dreams.

I put the dress on the antique sofa in the center of the closet, thinking about the Navy officer waiting for me downstairs.

Seriously, this can't be real life! I beamed, taking off my pants, then my shirt. And that's when I saw the bathroom scale.

I had a sudden urge to step on it, but as I moved forward, I wasn't sure I'd have the courage. I knew I had lost weight again. My body felt weaker, more tired. I could *feel* the effect Impostor Alec still had on me.

Trying to think of something else, I put on the costume, then got a full glimpse of myself in the mirrors. But the scale was still there—calling me.

So I stepped on. And what I saw made me feel sick to my stomach.

"There you go." Amanda entered the door with a pair of tights and white, knee-high boots.

I stepped off the scale quickly. "Thank you."

"Look at you…" She clasped her hands over her mouth,

watching me sit down to put on the shoes. "You're absolutely stunning!"

I tried to smile back at her, but I couldn't. I was *disgusted* with myself. It had been so hard to put on a few pounds... I couldn't believe all that stressing about *him* was taking me back to square one!

"Is everything all right?" She sat down next to me.

"Yeah, I'm fine." I dropped my eyes, not knowing what else to say.

Amanda examined my face. "It's okay if you lost a little weight, honey—don't beat yourself up. You're still following the nutritionist's instructions, right?"

"Most days, yeah. I just...I had a bad anxiety week."

"Oh. Do you want to talk about it?"

"It's nothing, really."

She reached for my hand. "It's all right, you can talk to me."

I wouldn't be able to lie. Not with her looking at me like that.

"Please don't tell Alec, okay? I don't want him to worry about this."

"Sure." She nodded.

"It's just that... Now that the photos are out, *he* knows I'm living in LA. And it's hard to turn off the alert mode—"

"Did he contact you again? Did he go after you?" she said too fast, too serious.

"No!" I raised my voice to break through her questions and try to calm her down. "I know this is all in my head! He probably doesn't even remember I exist. But since his number was from LA, and I don't know what he looks like... I can't stop stressing that anyone could be him—everywhere I go!"

"Oh, honey, I'm sorry to hear this. I know exactly what you mean."

"Do you?"

"I do, actually." She pressed her lips together. "Years ago, when the twins were still toddlers, I got this death threat and—"

I widened my eyes in shock.

"No, you don't have to worry—it was probably just a mean joke. But I know how this kind of thing can mess with our heads; I remember I went *crazy* at the time. I hired more bodyguards; I didn't want to go out of the house or leave the kids with anyone. It's terrible to know you're in danger without knowing what that danger looks like."

"Yeah." I sighed. Impostor Alec hadn't sent me any threats like that, and I was already losing my mind! I couldn't even imagine how she had handled that level of stress for so long.

"And what did you do? Or have you been just living in fear since then?"

"No, honey. He would have actually killed me, if I'd chosen to *live in fear* like you said." She giggled. "Of course, we all became a little more careful after that. Especially about security and privacy and what kind of information we shared with the media.

"By the way…" She raised her hand, moving slightly on the sofa. "I wanted to apologize to you for what Oliver said on Saturday. Since that threat, he's never stopped being a little overprotective, you know? He just wants to keep everybody safe, and now that Alec is so exposed…"

"It's okay." I gave her a reassuring smile. It was good to finally understand why Oliver was so obsessed with his family's privacy.

"But what I want you to take from all this, honey, is that the antidote to fear and anxiety is *faith*. There was literally nothing I could do to protect myself and my family outside the house. So in order to have the courage to keep going to work and living a normal life, I decided to live in faith, not in fear."

"What do you mean?" I narrowed my eyes.

"Take Alec, for example. My boy's biggest fear is that his cancer comes back, right? You saw how his behavior changed this week—he's terribly afraid of doing these scans. But you don't see him like that during the rest of the year, do you?"

I shook my head. I'd never seen Alec so *quiet* before.

"That's because day after day, he chooses to live in *faith*. That doesn't mean he's not afraid, just that he chooses not to listen to his fear. And when he gets up choosing to believe he's healthy, he has the energy to eat well and to exercise and to do whatever is in his power to actually *stay healthy*. If he woke up and listened to his worries, do you think he would have the same motivation throughout the day?"

"No." I shook my head again.

"See? Our faith and what we choose to believe have a direct impact on our behavior. You can't change the situation you're in —the same way Alec can't change his predisposition to cancer. But you can follow his example and choose to live in faith. Because the more you feed your fear of this guy, the more negative effects he will have on your life."

I dropped my eyes. I knew she was right.

"The truth is that you have no idea of what's in this guy's mind. But you're not doing yourself any favors by being pessimistic! You have to tell yourself every day that you're safe, that he won't ever touch you. Because if you don't… If you let your fear take over your mind like this, you'll be giving your life to him. And he has already taken so much from you, honey. Don't let him take anything else—not even one more day."

I looked into her green eyes. Alec's eyes. She was absolutely right. They were both right.

It'd been a year and a half since that guy entered my life. A year and a half that he stole from me—that I would never get back. I couldn't let him take anything else. Amanda was right, not even one more day!

"Promise me you're going to take care of yourself?" She hugged me sideways.

"I promise," I said, and I meant it.

"Good." She got up from the couch, pulling me to her dressing table. "Because my son needs someone strong by his side. And I know you're just as brave as he is."

"He's really amazing, isn't he? I mean, I already thought he was amazing before we met, but now… His fans don't even have a clue how brave he really is."

"Yeah." She grinned, applying something creamy on my cheeks. "And you know what? That's actually the end result of choosing to *live in faith*. I'm very proud of each one of my sons. Matt is a truly brilliant boy, Ben is the sweetest kid on earth, but I have no doubts that Alec is by far the bravest one. He's not afraid to dream; he's not afraid to take risks; he's not afraid to fail. And I can assure you that isn't something he inherited from his mom and dad either." She laughed. "He is like that simply because he's used to the fight, you know? His daily victories against his own fears is what makes him so strong and so brave."

I thought about my Navy officer again. "I honestly don't know what he saw in someone like me…"

"Oh, I do." Amanda smirked, holding the jar of blush. "I can't wait to see his face when he sees you tonight."

♪♩♡

I really didn't get her enthusiasm. She kept babbling over my dress, my hair, my makeup… I only understood why she was so excited when I saw Alec staring at me from the bottom of the stairs.

He seemed genuinely stunned—even a little emotional.

"Did you like it?" Amanda said, ecstatic.

"I love it!" Alec raised his hand in the air to take mine, then shook his head, smiling. "Thank you, Mom."

"What's happening here?" I glanced from Alec to Amanda and back to Alec. I was clearly missing something.

"He's been calling you an angel since you came here for the first time," Amanda explained, adjusting my wings. "So I thought about making my boy a little Halloween surprise."

"You're the best, Mom." Alec kissed her cheek, then gave her a long hug.

I bit my lip in delight. I loved everything about that scene—Alec's reaction, the fact that he'd been calling me an angel, the beautiful relationship he had with his mother.

"Oh good, you're ready." Oliver stopped walking when he saw us in the living room. "Come, love! They are calling you."

"Right." Amanda grinned at Alec and me, then went to greet her guests, who were already gathering on the outdoor patio.

The room was quiet for a minute, despite the music playing outside. Alec's eyes lingered on mine, soft and meaningful. And I stared back, thinking about what his mother had said... Everything he'd gone through that week, what Halloween really meant to him, how brave he was for fighting his fears every single day.

I wanted to say something—to let him know that I was there for him. That I was proud of him. That I loved him! And though I didn't use any words, I knew he had understood. Because his arms were suddenly around me, his mouth soft against mine.

"Alec, you can't do that in public, remember?" Oliver shouted from the kitchen.

And his son huffed, letting me go. "I can't wait for these parties to be over so I can be alone with you."

"Parties? Plural?" I said, surprised.

"Yeah." He half-smiled. "You're meeting my friends tonight."

Chapter 6

By ten o'clock, I had decided I never wanted to leave Alec's world again. And not because his world was, you know —*his* world, full of glitz and glamor. But because here I could be with him and touch him and kiss him anytime I wanted.

Well, as long as no one was watching.

But even this dating-in-secret thing was so much better when we were together. In my world, it was just lie after lie, but in his world…

Amanda presented me to her guests as Alec's *friend*, and every time she said the word, Alec's dimples sank deeper. He started doing all these little things—like holding my gaze and smirking for no reason. I guess he wanted me to know what he was thinking. He wanted to show how much he longed for me.

Every time I got up, he came along. Hand-holding, stolen kisses—he always tried something when no one was watching. But my favorite part of the night was when I had to go to the restroom. I didn't see him follow me, but when I opened the door a minute later, he was there—waiting.

It was the hottest make-out session I'd had in my life. He left me breathless with crooked wings.

I hoped none of the guests had seen us. Although I had a feeling they wouldn't tell anyone if they had. Most of them were celebrities—they knew too well how it felt to have a secret exposed. I didn't think they would purposefully do that to someone else.

And they were very nice, actually—more than I expected. I know in theory we all know that, but they were really real people. I mean normal human beings, like *me*. If I disregarded the expensive costumes and the way-too-much makeup, I could even picture them in *my world*, doing something ordinary like cleaning the house or watching TV on Sunday afternoon.

I had come with no expectations besides spending time with Alec, but it turned out to be one of the best parties I'd ever attended. I enjoyed everything—the music, the food, the people. They were all older, and I liked that.

My mom always said I was born with an old soul. I had zero patience for drinking games and "woos" on the dance floor. But give me a dinner party or a bingo night, and I was at home. So when Alec asked if I was ready to go to his friend's house, I had to lie.

"Sure." I nodded, getting up from the table. "I hope to see you again, Mr. Richardson. It was very nice meeting you."

"The pleasure was all mine, darling." He smiled his kind, wrinkled smile. "You got yourself a real angel, boy. Don't let her fly away."

"We're not—we're just friends," I blurted.

But Mr. Richardson laughed. "Ah, Hollywood love. I remember when I couldn't take my eyes off my Rachael on set, but we had to keep hiding…"

"Were we that obvious?" I lowered my voice, fretting.

"You were okay, sweetie. Him, not so much… But you're right, boy. Don't waste a minute. Don't let her fly away," he said again, even more meaningfully this time.

"I won't, sir." Alec grinned, putting his hand on the small of my back. "Let's go?"

"Yeah, let me just grab my purse." I said goodbye to Mr. Richardson, then felt my cheeks go red on our walk back to the house. Now that I knew we were being so obvious, I couldn't look anyone in the eyes anymore.

"Did you have fun?" Alec followed me on the stairs.

"Yes!" I turned back to look at him. "I met someone who actually won an Oscar, can you believe it?"

"Who? Melvin or Forman?"

"There were *two*?" My jaw dropped.

Alec smiled, his eyes blazing. And as soon as we reached the top of the stairs, he grabbed my waist, pushing me hard against the wall. It happened so fast that my only reaction was to hold my breath as he slammed his mouth over mine.

"Mr. Richardson was right, you know? You're incredibly cute tonight." He kissed my bottom lip, savoring it. "It's hard to control myself."

"Then *don't*." I pulled him closer with my leg, and Alec inhaled, tightening his grip on my waist.

"Girl, what are you doing to me?"

I laughed. "Are you sure we have to go to this other party?"

He held my gaze for a second, then sighed at the ceiling. "I haven't hung out with them in a long time; I have to show up. But the sooner we go, the sooner we can come back..." He lowered his lips to mine again.

"Oh, there you are!" Ben came up the stairs and rolled his eyes when he saw us. "Are you coming or not?"

"No bodyguards?" I asked when we got into the car. Ben was the one driving, and it felt a little odd to go out with Alec without any kind of adult supervision.

"Their house is in the neighborhood." Alec smiled back at me from the passenger seat.

And just like that, I liked that party already. I normally hated the crazy chaos of teenage parties. But if it meant I would finally have an unsupervised, undisturbed, lighthearted moment with Alec, I was one hundred percent up for it.

But, boy, was I wrong.

As soon as we entered the house, Alec was taken by his friends. And when I say *taken*, I really mean in that predatory way —almost as if they were his fans! *Everybody* wanted to talk to him. Ask how things were going, ask about what he'd been doing lately.

I took it badly at first, mad that he had practically abandoned me with a bunch of strangers. But then I realized how happy he was. He had clearly missed them too; they all just wanted to spend some time together. And it was unfair of me to be jealous— they got even less time with him than I did.

So I decided to go find myself a treat and let him be. His friends could have him for the rest of the night; tomorrow, he was mine.

The only problem was…I really hated high school parties. In West Virginia, I'd only been to a handful of them. And never by my own will. I'd always been more the reading-under-the-blanket type than a party girl.

I searched for Ben, to see if he was less busy than Alec, but I couldn't find him anywhere. So I did my best to talk to people and engage in conversations, like I'd done at Amanda's party. But this time, I failed miserably. That's when I gave up on small talk and decided to isolate myself on the balcony.

I was really not a *cool person*, I realized. Being around people my age always made me feel like that. I never—

"Can I hide here with you?" A deep voice interrupted my thoughts.

"Sure." I gave the boy a little smile, and he leaned on the parapet next to me.

He was tall and dressed all in red. It took me a second to realize it was a devil costume. His hair was black—a dull, dyed black that made his face paler and his gray eyes even more intense.

"We match." He stared at my dress, amused.

"I guess we do." I giggled, turning back to the view.

But the guy, he never stopped staring.

I felt his eyes on me and ignored the knot in the pit of my stomach. *I refuse to be paranoid again.* I remembered my conversation with Amanda. *This is just a random guy at a party—I won't let Impostor Alec take my sanity away from me anymore. Especially not tonight!*

"Sorry." The boy shook his head, turning to the ocean. "I didn't mean to make this awkward. I know you're here with Alec…"

"We're just friends," I said automatically. But then I regretted it. This was definitely not a good time to lie about having a boyfriend.

"Oh really?" The guy smirked, then turned to me again. "Does this mean I might have a chance?"

I frowned at him. I didn't know what to say. *Should I lie again? Should I tell him the truth?*

"I get it, don't worry." He snickered. "I bet his dad is forcing you to keep it a secret."

My breath caught in my throat. *How much does this guy know about the Brocks?*

"May I just say something?"

I opened my mouth to answer, but he didn't let me speak.

"You deserve better than this." His tone was low, honest. "If you had come to this party with *me*, I wouldn't leave your side for a second."

I dropped my eyes, suddenly embarrassed by Alec's neglect.

The boy caught my chin with one hand, making me meet his gaze. "I'd be bragging to the entire world that you had chosen *me* —that you were *my girl*."

A shiver ran down my spine. There was something familiar about his eyes. And his words, they were…heartfelt. Almost as if he was trying to warn me somehow. To *protect* me from—

"Back off, Zach!" Alec shouted, rushing toward us.

My heart jumped at his voice.

"Why so mad, Alec? I heard she's just your *friend*."

Alec clenched his fists in silence but stared at him with angry eyes.

"Don't know what to say, do you? Or you *do*…but Daddy doesn't let you say it?"

"Just shut up!" Alec grabbed my hand, yanking me away.

I followed him, startled, but glanced back at the balcony, trying to understand what was happening. Trying to understand who *he* was.

"Oh, I see…" The boy looked me in the eye. "He didn't tell you his secrets, did he?"

Alec stopped, letting go of me. "Linda, can you please give us a minute? I'll meet you inside."

I didn't even have time to react.

"You don't want her to know?" Devil Boy laughed out loud. "I'm just trying to warn you, love. *Stay away*—for your own good! He's gonna use you for a while, then toss you aside, like he does with everyone else."

"Linda, *please*." Alec clenched his fists again, not meeting my eyes.

I walked back into the house, my whole body overtaken by adrenaline. *What the heck is happening? Who* is *this guy?*

"But don't worry, love," the boy shouted at me, catching everybody's attention. "You can join our club when he's done with you. It's called All The Losers Alec Brock Has—"

He didn't finish his sentence.

I held my breath in shock. I was sure Alec had punched the guy in the face. But when I looked back to see what happened, no one was hurt. Someone else had stepped onto the scene: *James.*

My heart immediately reacted to him, pounding faster in my chest. I watched James stand between Alec and the other boy, but all I could think about now was *James.* I hadn't seen him since that day at the studio.

"I really thought Alec would hit Zach this time."

I glanced at the voice behind me.

"Me too," someone else said, disappointed, before turning back to the party.

That's when I realized the tension in the room had nothing to do with shock. It was *expectation.* I was the only one surprised; they had all seen this before. They were all used to it.

But why...? I turned to the balcony.

James was furious now, scolding them. Alec focused on the view, taking deep breaths to calm himself down, while Devil Boy seemed resentful, staring at the wall.

I felt like I was there with them—I was so stressed my hands were tingling. But apparently, I was the only one worried. People had quickly lost interest in the scene after James arrived. And I asked myself again, how many times had they witnessed something like that? I still couldn't believe Alec had almost gotten into a fight with...

Zach. I finally connected the name to the person. He was the drummer in Alec's former band! He wasn't blond anymore, but I knew I'd seen those gray eyes before.

Benjamin had used the word *disagreement* when he explained to me why the band ended on bad terms. But now I was guessing there was a lot more to that story.

I focused on the balcony again. Alec wasn't there anymore, but James was still talking to Zach. They seemed very close, actually—which surprised me. I thought James had taken Alec's side after the *disagreement*. I didn't see how he could have kept his friendship with both of them. Especially now that I'd witnessed the effect Zach had on Alec.

"Let's find Ben and get out of here." Alec grasped my hand.

I jumped in reflex. I hadn't seen him coming.

He interlocked our fingers, pulling me across the room. And I squeezed his hand, reminding him that we couldn't be seen doing this in public.

"I don't care," he said icily, marching to the stairs.

I didn't dare say anything else. He was too nervous, too anxious.

We checked every room, searching for Ben, but with no success. "Do you think he left without us?" I finally asked, when we finished our little tour of the house.

"Maybe…" Alec scratched his head. Then he turned to a girl passing by us. "Lucy, have you seen Hailey?"

Hailey Dawson? I froze. *Ben's ex! The one who used Alec's name to promote herself.*

"I think she left."

"Was my brother with her?" His voice was urgent.

"I don't know. I saw them together earlier, but—"

"You've got to be kidding me," Alec growled, letting go of my hand and grabbing his phone out of his pocket.

Chapter 7

Forty minutes later, we still had no news from Ben. Some people had seen him leaving with Hailey hours ago, but no one seemed to know where they'd gone. Alec was sitting on the couch with me, calling his brother's number every two minutes, while James paced the balcony, trying to reach the girl.

I'd never seen Alec so stressed before. He hated Hailey, I could tell. And I was relieved, to be honest, because I hated her too. I didn't know what I would have done if he had introduced her to me as a dear friend or something like that. After what she had done to Alec—*and* Ben—I didn't think I could ever pretend to like her.

"They're almost here," James announced, collapsing on the other end of the couch.

I couldn't help but notice his eyes, focused only on Alec. It was the sixth time he'd done that tonight—talked to people around me as if I wasn't even there.

"Did you talk to her? Where are they?" Alec said too fast.

"At the beach." James shook his head, distressed. "And she sounds happy, so get ready. You know that's never good."

Alec sighed, listening to the details.

Apparently, Hailey had had a grip on Ben since they were thirteen. She was his first girlfriend—the only one he'd had, if I understood correctly. Alec said she used to be a nice girl until two years ago, when she started hanging out with a drug-using crowd. After that, every time Benjamin disappeared with her, he got into some sort of trouble.

"I don't know why he's doing this again," Alec said, anxious. "He promised me he wouldn't—not after the circus she made out of those pictures! I can't believe they're back—"

"Hey." I stopped him. Ben seemed to be a very well-balanced person; he wouldn't let Hailey take advantage of him *again*. "Maybe they're just talking, in order to close the chapter. We have to stay optimistic, right?" I stroked his knee, remembering my talk with his mom.

Alec smiled slowly, staring at me. Then he slid his hand under mine and brought it to his lips, kissing my fingers.

"So this is the famous Linda González, huh?" Hailey broke through the crowd, coming in our direction. She was wearing a tight leather dress, showing off her tanned legs, and a pair of cat ears over long, blonde hair.

"Where's Ben?" Alec got up, angry.

"He's peeing, relax!" She stroked his chest for a second, then in one quick movement, pushed him down onto the couch.

I glared at her.

"I guess we haven't had the pleasure of meeting yet." She leaned down, offering me a handshake. "I'm Hailey."

I couldn't help but look at her boobs—they were right there in my face! But then I realized: she was doing it on purpose. So people could see them. So *my boyfriend* could see them!

"I'm Linda." I squeezed her hand, scowling.

Hailey laughed out loud. "Possessive—I like her, Alec! But you don't have to worry, hon. I don't want your boyfriend. You got the wrong twin; Benji is way more fun to be around." She glanced back at Ben.

My mouth fell open when I saw him come in. He was stumbling on his own feet!

"What the hell did you give him?" Alec jumped off the couch.

"Just a few drinks to chill out, right, babe?" She touched Ben's forehead and pushed his hair back, visibly proud of herself.

But he didn't even acknowledge her. He didn't seem to be there at all.

I stood up, worried about Ben, but Hailey was suddenly in front of me.

"So tell me about yourself—*Linda*. You seem to be a *very interesting* girl. Feels like I've been waiting for *forever* to meet you…"

I raised my eyebrows, speechless. From the way she was staring at me, I couldn't tell if the girl was crazy or seriously intoxicated.

I stepped aside when I saw Alec supporting Ben, his arm under his twin's shoulders. But Hailey got in my way again, so it was James who stepped up and helped Alec steady his brother.

"How is the teddy bear?" Hailey tilted her head. "Which one do you like better, the first or the second one?"

Her gaze made me shiver. It was like she knew how much I hated her, and for some reason, she hated me just as much. "Wh-what do you mean?"

"Hailey's mom is the owner of the toy store, baby. Where I got your bear—to replace the one you used to have, remember?" Alec explained.

And just like that, I liked Mr. Bear a little less.

"Let's get out of here," Alec continued, searching for the car keys in Ben's pockets.

"We took a cab." Hailey shrugged. "He left the car at my house."

Alec held his breath, glaring at her.

"At least she didn't drive like this, Alec. Come, I'll take you guys home." James put Ben's arm over his shoulder, already pulling him outside.

"The *loyal* sidekick." Hailey snickered, following us. "I have to confess, you almost fooled me. I've always thought you were a *good boy*." She glanced from James to me and back to James. "Seems you're a real McLaren, after all."

"What is she talking about?" Alec asked James.

"No idea." He shook his head, then looked me straight in the eyes for the first time tonight. "She's drunk, just ignore her."

Hailey laughed again, but I couldn't focus on her. My heart was pounding now. It had caught me completely off guard, the way James stared at me.

"Where is Zach, by the way?" Hailey glanced around the party. "I can't believe he's missing this."

"He left," James said sharply.

Hailey brought her hands to her chest. "Zachary McLaren left a party earlier? What did I miss here? Did they finally…? Oh, no." She touched Alec's arm. "Please, don't tell me you ruined that pretty face."

"Why can't you just shut up?" Alec snapped, pushing her hand away.

"Don't wanna tell me? Fine! He will." She grabbed her phone, smirking. "It was because of *her*, wasn't it? This is going to be so entertaining…"

"Hailey, I swear that—"

"Let's go, Alec!" James walked faster with Benjamin, unlocking the car from a distance.

♪♩♡

"Where is Hails? HAILS? Where are yooou?" I heard Ben saying from the other side of his bedroom door.

"She went home, Ben." Alec sounded tired, as if he was repeating himself for the tenth time. "Here, have another sip."

I hesitated over whether or not to enter the room.

I had gone downstairs for some snacks while Alec and James changed Ben's clothes and made him drink water. We were trying to sober him up. Ben had spent the whole drive home sleepy, not saying a word, so Alec thought it was dangerous to just let him sleep like that. He was too wasted to be left alone.

"Let's make sure he eats something, and then we can let him sleep," James said.

"The food is already here. Just so you know," I whispered from the corridor, holding two plates with leftovers from Amanda's party.

"Baby?" Benjamin said, hopeful.

"No, Ben, it's Linda. See?" Alec held the door open for me. "I told you, Hailey went home!"

Ben stared at me from his bed, as if seeing my face for the first time in his life. Then as if he was seeing a ghost. Then as if I was his favorite person in the whole world.

I had to laugh. Drunk Ben was a lot funnier than Regular Ben.

"How is it going?" I asked Alec, setting the plates on the computer desk.

"He seems better." He hugged me sideways and planted a kiss on top of my head.

"I need to find Hails! HAILS?" Ben started asking for Hailey again. "Where is she? Help me find her, James?" he said, anguished.

But James didn't even look at Ben. "You guys can go to sleep, if you want." He stood up, focused only on Alec. "I'll make sure he eats before going to bed."

I couldn't help but notice James's tone—urgent, distressed.

The same tone he'd used to dismiss me every time I'd tried to help so far…except when it would get me out of the room. Twice! First to go find a bucket, then to bring Ben something to eat.

I took a second look at James, suddenly annoyed.

"It's all right. Linda and I can take care of him." Alec argued, thanking James for his help and telling him that things were under control now. He could finally go home.

And I think Alec was close to convincing James when Ben took advantage of our distraction to get out of bed and call Hailey.

"No, you're *not* calling her!" Alec reacted fast, yanking the phone from his brother's hand and turning it off.

Ben glared at him. "Give that back!"

"Shhhh, you're gonna wake up Mom and Dad!"

"Give it back!" Ben almost fell on the floor trying to reclaim his phone.

"Stop it!" James put himself between the twins, then helped Benjamin back to bed.

"I need Hails." Ben looked at James with watery eyes. "I don't wanna be alone tonight."

"I'm here, buddy. You're not alone." James sat next to Ben, one hand on his shoulder. "You know what, Alec? Just go… I can handle this on my own." He exhaled, biting his lip ring.

"But you—"

"It's okay, I don't mind. You have…*company*." James nodded at me.

And until that moment I thought I was imagining all this. I was telling myself James was trying to keep me away because I had no experience taking care of drunk people or because I was a girl and couldn't help as much as a boy could in this situation. Until he glanced at me again. Until our eyes locked for the second time that night.

It lasted for just a fraction of a second, but it was enough for me to feel it—his *discomfort*. He was trying to get Alec out of the room because of me! Because as long as *he* stayed, *I* would stay too!

"Are you sure?" Alec hesitated.

"Yeah. Go…be with your girlfriend." James waved without looking at us, turning his full attention back to Ben.

Two hours later, I still couldn't relax.

Alec was sleeping on his stomach, one arm around my waist. But I kept thinking about James there, in the next room. I couldn't forget the way he'd looked at me.

Both times we'd met, he seemed *tense* somehow. And he'd always kept this distance between us—dodging my eyes, never letting me in. As if he feared I would figure something out if I got too close.

I hated my suspicions. Alec had already explained to me what the detective had said—that the impostor couldn't be anyone from his immediate circle. And I wanted to rationalize, to stop being paranoid. But James…I had this gut feeling about him.

And the worst part was that, at the same time I wanted to get closer and figure James out, I felt like I shouldn't do it. Like he was keeping me out for a reason, and deep down, I knew he was right. I wouldn't want to know.

I turned to the other side of the bed and tried to calm my thoughts, watching Alec sleep. I was happy to see him so peaceful. After what had happened with Zach, then Hailey, then Ben, I wasn't sure he would be able to relax. But apparently, he wasn't worried about Ben at all—which proved how much he trusted *James*. And the guy had indeed managed to put out the fire three times in a row, like a superhero. He'd stopped the fight, he'd located Hailey and Ben, he'd driven us home…

I exhaled. *Just drop it, Linda. James has been nothing but a great friend tonight—you're crazy for thinking he could be an unscrupulous liar. The liar you fell in love with.*

Impostor Alec was probably someone lonely and sad. Not a nice, attractive, and successful guy like James. I really should stop with the paranoia and go to sleep.

I closed my eyes, snuggling closer to Alec. And I was starting to lose consciousness when a sudden noise woke me up. The sound of a door being opened and then carefully closed.

I slid out from under Alec's arm, worried about Ben. I was sure James had fallen asleep on duty, and letting Drunk Ben walk alone downstairs was definitely not a good idea.

"Ben?" I searched for him in the living room, then the kitchen, walking on tiptoes.

But then I froze where I stood. The light was coming from the library—also known as Oliver's office. *He* was the one who had come down, not Ben!

Did he see me? What do I do now? Should I hide or pretend I came to the kitchen for a late-night snack?

To my total despair, the lights went out, as if someone had just flipped a switch.

Urgh! Why did I have to get up? I ducked down to hide behind the counter. Things had been better between Alec's father and me this weekend, but I still had this feeling he didn't like me very much, and I didn't want to give him a reason to dislike me even more.

"Hi." James's voice made my head go blank.

He turned on the kitchen lights, walking in my direction.

Say something, Linda! Anything!

"H-hi." I stood up, my face burning. *What was he doing there —in Oliver's office—in the middle of the night?*

"I was going to leave a note, but..." He folded a piece of

paper and put it into his back pocket. "I'm going home. Can you tell everybody in the morning?"

I nodded, breathless. My whole body was stiff with tension.

"Thank you," James said, serious. A little cold, even.

I knit my brows, holding his gaze—trying to see inside his mind. And for a second, he stared back—resentfully.

"Have a good night." He turned around.

"Wait!" I touched his arm in reflex. I needed more time to understand all this tension between us. I couldn't be imagining it. I couldn't be *that* paranoid.

"Why are you leaving?" I regretted the words as soon as they left my mouth. "You said you would stay." *Not any better, Linda...* "Ben! What about Ben? How is he?"

James laughed a little. "He's perfectly fine."

I'd never seen him laugh before. It made me notice the blue of his eyes.

"Is he in bed? I mean, sleeping?" *Jeez, Linda. Relax! He's going to notice your suspicions.*

"Yeah. I don't think he will wake up anytime soon, and I have something to do in the morning, so..." James angled his body toward the door.

"Sorry they made you stay!" I said before he moved any further. "If Hailey hadn't left the car—"

"It's okay." He shrugged.

"You're really close, aren't you? To the twins?" I improvised, trying to stall him long enough to get into his mind again.

And seriously, his eyes were the darkest shade of blue I'd ever seen in anyone! How hadn't I noticed that before?

"We grew up together. They're like brothers to me," James said timidly.

"They like you a lot too... Maybe even a little too much." I snickered, remembering the way Ben seemed to feel safe next to him and how strongly Alec had defended James when I thought he could be the impostor. "It's like none of them can survive without you."

"I don't think I'd survive without any of them either." James smiled down at his feet. And the honest embarrassment of his smile washed away all my suspicions.

He was shy, that was it. He was one of those people who was genuinely afraid to look at a stranger's face. That's why he'd kept his distance from me. That's why I hadn't noticed his eyes until now. It was never personal or about me, it was just who he was.

There you go, Linda. You got your answer.

Now go get yourself a treat and stop with the paranoia. Alec is waiting for you upstairs.

"Drive home safely, James." I grinned at him, peace warming my heart. "It was nice to talk to you. I hope we can do it more often."

"Me too." He flushed, looking down again.

And the more I noticed his shyness, the more I realized there was nothing to worry about.

I blamed my anxiety for making me so crazy before. It plays tricks with our heads sometimes, making us believe bad things are real. It was like with Arthur—at the moment he asked me to get in the car, I was absolutely sure I was in danger. And then a minute later, I felt like an idiot, realizing it had all just been in my head.

I had to do what Amanda said and stop listening to my anxiety. I didn't want to waste one more day…one more minute…one more second! From that moment on, I would *choose* to be optimistic.

"I think I'm gonna go, then," James murmured.

"Okay." I nodded, then turned around and reached for the candy basket on the kitchen island. *That's* what I needed after this long, stressful night: a treat!

But James didn't move. For some reason, he didn't seem to be in such a hurry anymore.

"I'll let them know you left," I said reassuringly.

"Thanks." His eyes lingered on mine.

And I wondered if he was considering continuing the conversation—like there was something he wanted to say.

"Can I have one?" He let out a breath, nodding at the candy.

"Of course!" I proudly stretched my arms out to hold the bucket near him. I was starting to figure him out! I knew he was gathering his courage to say something else.

James put one hand inside and grabbed a random treat.

A Reese's Cup, I saw when he pulled it out. *My favorite!*

"Sorry." He dropped the chocolate back into the bucket, trading it for a Kit Kat.

I immediately lowered the basket to find the Reese's he'd rejected. But then I noticed… It was the last one.

He had left it for me. He'd said *sorry* for taking it!

I raised my head startled, searching for James's eyes. But he had walked away without saying goodbye.

Chapter 8

"Good morning." Alec kissed my shoulder.

My eyes burned as I opened them. It felt like I had just fallen asleep ten minutes ago.

"Morning." I rolled over on my back to look at him. He knelt on the bed, smiling. And there was a tray next to him. A beautiful breakfast tray. "Am I dreaming?"

Alec grabbed a piece of watermelon and brought it to my lips.

I took a bite. "I guess I'm not."

He grinned, tossing the rest into his mouth.

"And why all this?" I sat cross-legged on the bed, picking up another piece.

"I just wanted to say I'm sorry for ruining Halloween." He paused, regret darkening his face. "I shouldn't have taken you to that party. We should have stayed home, here in my room."

"That would have probably been better…" I agreed.

"But I'll make it up to you. I'm all yours today." His dimples showed.

And I sighed heavily. I wanted to spend the whole day in that room, staring at those dimples. But my world was waiting for me today. I had to go back to real life.

"My dad doesn't want me to stay here. Do you think maybe… you can come to *my* place?" I bit my lip. I knew how much I was asking of him, and I didn't—

"Of course!" He moved closer and gave me a kiss. "We can finally watch the rest of the movie!"

I smiled, embarrassed, almost wishing he had said no. I knew exactly what would happen; I could anticipate everything.

Claire would never let us control the TV—and she probably wouldn't leave us alone, either. Dad would come spy on us every ten minutes, and Alec would realize that in my house I wasn't allowed to even be in the same room as him with the doors closed. If Dad knew that we slept in the same bed while I was here, I would be grounded for life!

"What's wrong?" Alec stroked my leg.

"I wish I could stay in your world. I don't like mine anymore." I reached for his hair to play with his curls.

"You should move here, then." He tilted his head, enjoying my touch. "I wouldn't mind at all…"

I giggled. "Isn't it too soon to say things like that?"

For him, I meant. I'd been ready to say *yes* to a lifetime with him since about a year ago.

"I guess, yeah. But you're messing with my mind." The green in his eyes blazed. "I've never felt like this before."

My heart melted in my chest. I wanted to say it. I *loved* him. So much.

But our history was so complex… I didn't want to do anything wrong. I couldn't risk scaring him away.

So I grabbed his hand instead, interlocking our fingers. "It *feels right*, doesn't it? I like this—when it's just the two of us."

"Me too." He pulled me into his lap, then kissed me gently. Right before my phone started ringing.

♪♫♡

"Leave the door open!" Dad yelled from downstairs.

"I know!" I yelled back, rolling my eyes. First, he'd forced us to hang out in the living room, where he could keep an eye on us. Then, he'd turned lunch into an interrogation. Poor Alec couldn't even eat dessert because Dad kept asking question after question. And now this... *I hope he doesn't send Claire to spy on us.*

Alec laughed quietly, pretending to be distracted with the documents on my desk.

"Now you know how lucky you are, growing up with trusting parents." I fought the urge to close the door and walked toward him. "My leash here is pretty tight."

"At least you don't have to bring a babysitter every time you go out," he said to himself.

"Touché." I thought about Jimmy downstairs with Dad. I didn't know what was worse—to be on the leash at home or every time you left the house.

"Is this yours?" Alec had found a transcript from my old school—one of the documents I had assembled for when I started filling out college applications. "You're such a nerd! You didn't tell me that!"

"I don't have to tell you *everything*. And I'm not a nerd! I just...study."

"You have even more A's than my brother Matt!" He chuckled. "Now I get why you want to go to med school... Are you aiming for Harvard like him? Have you decided where you wanna go yet?"

"Isn't it obvious? UCLA." I thought he already knew that.

"You're not even trying for Harvard? Or Princeton? Or Yale?" He looked at my transcript again. "I bet you could—"

"I told you, Alec, on the boat! I put on a pretty good show in the spring to convince my parents to let me come to LA. It wouldn't make any sense if I changed my mind now."

"I'm sure they would understand if you were accepted at Harvard, for example."

I couldn't believe he was saying that. Boston was so far away. If I went to Harvard or any of those Ivy League universities, we would never see each other!

Alec studied my reaction, then shortened the distance between us. "I don't want you to do this for *me*, Linda."

"I'm not…"

He brushed a strand of hair away from my face with a crooked smile. "Tell me, if you could choose any college in the world, and I'm serious—I'm talking England, Germany, Japan, Argentina. If you could go anywhere on the *planet*, where would you want to go?"

I considered his question. It was hard to really think about all the possibilities. I'd always thought Australia would be a good place to live. Or maybe Spain. And I'd love to volunteer in Africa someday. But I guess to study, I would have to say… "New York." I sat on the bed, staring at nowhere.

"I went on a trip with Nina's parents once, when we were little. We visited her aunt at the NYU campus, and we felt so *free* in that city, so *inspired*. As if anything was possible, you know?" I grinned up at him, remembering. "After that, we both started dreaming about going to school there."

"Great. You're applying to NYU, then!" Alec beamed, sitting next to me.

"What? No!" I rested my knee on the bed as I turned toward him. "Things changed, Alec. I really want to stay in LA." I reached for his hand. "I found something else that makes me feel inspired. I don't need a city anymore."

Alec rubbed his thumb across the back of my hand, staring deep into my eyes. And that's when we heard the screams.

"This is *my* house! And I swear to God—get the hell out or I'll call the police!"

We ran downstairs, alarmed. Dad was on the street, yelling at a group of paparazzi while Jimmy tried to convince him to go back inside.

"They're not *on* your property, Mr. González. They aren't doing anything against the law."

"You go mind your own business!" He pushed Jimmy away. "I'm warning you all! Get out of this street right now, or I will—"

"Dad!" I shouted, running after him.

And then the flashes became even more blinding.

Inside the house, Jesse started crying, scared. Carol rushed to pick him up, and Claire took advantage of her mother's distraction to sneak out and pose for the pictures.

Dad went *furious*. More angry than I'd ever seen him in my whole life.

I glanced at Jimmy, asking for help—fearing what Dad could do. And Alec was suddenly ahead of us all, speaking directly to the paparazzi.

"Please, Dad. Let's talk inside!" I hugged my father in despair, pushing him toward the house.

Jimmy held his arm too, and Dad didn't resist this time. He knew he needed the intervention to stop him from losing his mind.

"They aren't disrespecting the law, Mr. González. We can't just call the police," Jimmy explained after we closed the door.

My father was so angry he couldn't even formulate an answer to that.

I turned around to go after Alec, but Carol gestured for me to stay inside, before taking the kids upstairs.

"We can't make them leave, sir. I'm sorry," Jimmy repeated.

"You're saying these people can camp outside my house and take pictures of my family and I can't do *anything* about it?"

"It's temporary, Dad!" I blurted. "Soon they'll get used to Alec coming here and won't—"

"That's *always* gonna be a problem, isn't it?" He glared at Alec, who was still outside trying to send the paparazzi away.

Fear overtook me. And at the height of my panic, I had an idea. My plan was audacious and highly risky, but if I pulled this off, I would be solving multiple problems at once.

"Dad, please listen… This is only happening because you forced Alec to come see me here. If you had let me stay at his house, the paparazzi wouldn't—"

His glare turned to me, and I was smart enough to shut my mouth.

"I can take them back to Malibu, sir." Jimmy understood where I was going and jumped in to help. "The cameras will go away the minute we're out of here."

Dad stared at Jimmy, as if considering what to do. And I was filled with hope again.

"Please let me spend the weekend there, Dad? They have security gates—the paparazzi can't get this close. And his parents and his brother are there too; Alec and I won't be alone in the house. I promise I'll come back on time tomorrow. Just tell me when…"

He sighed, looking at me. His eyes were more scared than angry now.

I knew my dad was trying his best. But this whole situation with Alec was too much for him. He didn't know how to handle it.

And I could understand. I mean, he hadn't had time to get to know Alec and slowly transition to his world like I did. He had been sucked into it without any notice. And now this new scary world was literally at his door, forcing its way in.

"Please trust me, Dad. Just with this." I touched his hand. I really didn't want to put him and the kids through all that media attention, but I wouldn't give up on Alec either. Dad would have to accept that we were a duo now, that he couldn't have me without Alec. And if he wanted to keep Alec's world far away from him, he would have to extend my leash.

"Fine. 6 P.M. tomorrow," he murmured.

I bit the inside of my lip to control my excitement. "Thank you! I'm gonna go grab my things." I squeezed his hand in a reassuring clasp, then headed to the stairs.

"But stay in your room until I call you. I want to have a talk with *him* first." He glanced at Alec through the window.

♪♩♡

"You're a genius! I can't believe you turned this in your favor," Alec said as we climbed into the car for the drive back to his house. "I have to admit, I'm impressed."

"What did he say to you?" I had waited in my room for half an hour before Dad finally let us go.

"Well, to make this short… If anything happens to you, I'm *dead.*"

"Sounds like him." I laughed. "I'm sorry about that."

"No, it was very interesting, actually. I got to learn about your family's values, and your future medical career, and his expectations…"

"Oh gosh." I hid my face in my hands.

But Alec pulled them away, searching for my eyes. "He just wanted to hear that I'm serious about you. That I'm not going anywhere." He smiled slowly.

And my heart expanded in my chest. I wanted to kiss him so bad. But I couldn't. Not now…

I glanced back at the cars still parked on my street. "What about the paparazzi?"

"We made a bargain…" Alec leaned forward, resting his elbow on the passenger seat. "Can you please take us somewhere crowded, Jimmy? They agreed not to sell any of the pictures taken here if they can have some good shots of Linda and I some-place else."

"Does your father—"

"He would rather explain a walk in the city than a scene in front of her house, don't you think?"

"Yep." Jimmy put the key in the ignition. "To where, then?"

Alec turned toward me. "Where do you wanna go? Maybe a tourist spot? They know you're new in town, so that would be easy to explain."

"All right," I said with a grin.

"Where have you been so far?"

"Hmm… Santa Monica Pier, Beverly Hills, Chinatown, Hollywood…"

"Have you hiked to the sign yet?" His face lit up.

"Please say yes." Jimmy frowned at us from the rearview mirror.

"No." I chuckled. "But I can go another time."

"Thank you," Jimmy mouthed to me.

"Maybe we can go somewhere you've already been… Do you have a favorite spot in the city?"

I did. And his question immediately brought this fantasy to my mind. A fake memory I would be very happy if I could turn into reality.

"There's this coffee shop in Beverly Hills. I've always pictured us—"

I stopped talking. Alec's mood had suddenly shifted.

"We don't have to go there," I said, worried.

"No, it's fine." He gave me a little smile. Then his dimples sank deeper. "But can we make a detour first? You just gave me an idea…"

♪♩♡

The detour Alec wanted to make was to someone's house. But we didn't even get out of the car—the person was waiting for us outside, holding a black violin case.

"It's a surprise for Ben," Alec explained.

He had asked Benjamin's teacher to keep it with him until it was time, and he thought today was the perfect moment to surprise his brother. Ben was spending the whole afternoon at the music school where he volunteered. And since he thought Alec would be at my house, he would never see this coming.

Alec told me Ben had been feeling a little lost lately—that's why he got drunk with Hailey yesterday. Alec was hoping the new violin would help to cheer him up and bring him back to the right path. The last thing Alec wanted was to see his brother running into Hailey's arms again. And the one thing she couldn't distract Ben from was the violin. As long as he was focused on his music, he wouldn't want to go back to her.

I didn't understand very well when Alec explained the appeal of the new violin though. It made no sense to me that the best ones were the oldest. I mean, he was talking about three-hundred-year-old instruments. It was hard to believe people hadn't invented better violins in the 2000s.

Alec said Ben had always wanted an antique violin like this one, but never had the courage to ask his parents. And Alec had been lucky to meet this guy in Europe who happened to be selling one for a very good price. Apparently, violins like this were not only very expensive, but so rare that they only went on sale when their previous owner died or something. I didn't dare ask how much it'd cost—that was none of my business. But I was guessing that little box with us in the car was worth more than the car itself.

"That's my music school!" Alec pointed at the gray building on the other side of the street. "Where I learned how to play the guitar…"

I recognized the facade. I had passed in front of it before—every time I went to the coffee shop! That's when I understood Alec's reasons for this little detour. He knew we'd be close to Ben, and it was the perfect time to surprise his brother.

"So, here's my plan." He turned to me while Jimmy parked the car. "I'm gonna warn the paparazzi that we're coming in for just ten minutes, then we'll walk to the café so they can take their pictures, okay?"

"Yep." I took a deep breath, getting ready for the flashes.

"We can't hold hands, and we can't be too close…" Alec said apologetically.

"I know. It's okay." I shrugged.

"Thank you for understanding." He half-smiled. "And for helping me surprise my brother!"

"I'm kind of nervous now. What if I forget my lines?"

"Don't worry, you can improvise." He patted my leg. "Just remember, your goal is to convince him that you're there for a trial lesson. And then you casually ask for his opinion on this violin that your father bought you."

"Do you think he'll fall for it?"

"I think he'll freak out the moment he recognizes what you have in your hands." Alec laughed.

"And that's when you come in…"

"Yep." He bit his lip in excitement, doing a drum roll on the violin case.

Alec got out first, to talk to the paparazzi. Then he came back for me, and we went straight to the music school, ignoring all the cameras. But the moment I stepped inside the building, I knew our plan wouldn't work. Everybody rushed to greet Alec in the corridors—there was no way Benjamin wouldn't see him coming. But Alec didn't seem worried, and I only understood why when I finally saw Ben.

He was playing by himself in this soundproof room. We could

see the back of his head through the window, but he was concentrating on the notes. He had no clue of anything happening outside his own world.

"Here." Alec handed me the case. "I'll be waiting by the door. Don't forget to leave it open a bit so I can hear you guys."

"All right." The butterflies raced around in my stomach.

I had warned Alec not to get his hopes up. I'd always been a bad actor and an even worse liar. But for some reason, I couldn't say no to this. I *wanted* to make Alec's plan work. I *wanted* to be part of the surprise.

"What the—" Ben winced the moment I touched his arm.

"Sorry I scared you!" I giggled. "I knocked on the door, but you were so focused…"

"What are you doing here?" He put the violin down, trying to steady his breathing.

"I came for—a trial lesson."

Ben studied my face, suspicious. "Where is Alec? I thought he was spending the day with you."

"He was, but then…" I swallowed hard. Lying to his face was a lot harder than I thought. "Your father called, and Alec dropped me here—because I'd like to take a trial lesson," I tried again, using all my confidence this time.

"*You* want to learn how to play the violin?" Ben raised an eyebrow.

I was absolutely sure he wasn't buying my story. I would have to step up my game, if I didn't want to disappoint Alec.

"Yes." I held his gaze. "My dad got me this violin a while ago, and I thought that, now that I'm living with him, he would be pleased to finally see me playing it."

Ben glanced down at the case. I could see he was starting to believe me.

"Okay… I-I guess I can help you with that," he said, his tone soft.

"Great." I smiled, proud of myself. "But I have to warn you, I'm not sure if this violin is any good. It seems old, and I have no idea where my father…" I babbled as I opened the case on the desk in front of him.

The game was on now, he was definitely buying it. He seemed excited, even. It was funny to watch.

"Don't worry. If this one isn't suitable for you, I can—" He stopped talking the second he caught a glimpse of it.

"What do you think?" I looked away to keep from laughing. Alec was watching everything from the window; I could see him smirking.

"Linda…" Ben's voice broke when he took the violin in his hands. "Where did your father get this?"

I couldn't hold back my laughter anymore.

"It's fake, isn't it?" He rolled his eyes, glancing around the room. "Where is my brother? I know this is a prank."

"It's real, bro." Alec walked in our direction, grinning like a kid on Christmas day.

"No." Ben examined the violin again. Then he turned to me, serious. "How… Where did your father find this?"

Both Alec and I burst out laughing.

"It's not hers. It's for *you*, you idiot!" Alec patted Ben on the shoulder.

"You're kidding…"

"Go ahead, try it! I'm dying to see how it sounds!"

Ben stared at the violin for a moment, analyzing the front, then the back. I could see in his eyes how amazed he was—how special this was for him. Then he positioned the violin on his shoulder, took the bow in his right hand, and started playing the most beautiful song.

Goosebumps rose all over my body. I had heard that piece many times before, but never like this. I couldn't tell if it was coming from the violin, or the violinist, or the combination of them both, but I could *feel* that whatever was happening in that room, it was truly magic.

"Yes! I made him cry!" Alec squealed, raising his fist in the air. "I have to tell Matt—Ben is the hardest one to get emotional!" he explained to me.

Benjamin put the violin in its case, choking back tears. "I can't… This is too much; it must have cost you a fortune. I…"

"You deserve it, bro!" Alec squeezed his shoulder. "I know how hard it's been lately… I hope this helps you to stay strong—stay focused on your dream."

Ben lowered his head, wiping his eyes.

"Oh, come on, this was supposed to make you happy!" Alec chuckled, hugging his brother sideways.

And Ben couldn't hold himself back. He hugged Alec tight, in a long, meaningful hug.

My heart completely melted. And that's when I realized I also had tears in my eyes.

Chapter 9

I couldn't believe I'd never thought of surprising anyone before. I mean, of course I had already appeared somewhere unexpectedly—that's not the kind of surprise I meant. No, I meant something elaborate, like Amanda and the angel costume or Alec and the violin. Something meaningful for my parents or my siblings or my friends—for no special reason. Just to make them happy.

I'd bought Nina this purse once, four months before her birthday, when I was visiting Dad at his old home in San Francisco. But even then, I'd waited until her birthday to give it to her. I'd never thought of surprising someone with a special gift out of the blue like that. But after witnessing Alec's joy holding that violin and Benjamin's total ecstasy when he saw it…

"I want to surprise someone too," I announced.

But I immediately regretted saying it out loud, because now Alec would know I was planning a surprise, and he was one of the top targets on my list.

"It was great, wasn't it? He will never beat me on this…" Alec grinned.

To me, that was the best part of the Brocks' tradition. They actually *competed* to see who would make the other one happier. And that was insane for me to think about—I'd been taught how to *prank* my siblings, not how to give them reasons to like me even more!

Maybe I should start with Claire.

"I'm thinking about my sister... Do you have any suggestions?"

"Actually, I do." Alec smirked.

But suddenly, I couldn't focus on him anymore. We had just stopped on the sidewalk to wait for the green light, and the paparazzi were shooting like crazy.

"Back up, guys." Jimmy tried to keep them far enough away so they wouldn't hear our conversation.

I lowered my head, embarrassed, though Alec didn't seem to mind.

"I was observing Claire today. She's always so in tune when she sings with me—I think she has a knack for music. And here at the Conservatory, they have scholarships for," he hesitated, as if deciding which word to use, "low-income students."

"All right." I tried to keep my face straight. We both knew how far apart our worlds were, but hearing the words coming out of his mouth... Well, it hurt a little. I considered myself *middle class* in LA, but if he'd said that after seeing my father's house, what would he think if he saw my mom's?

"Ben became a volunteer teacher this year—he knows everyone in the program. I'm sure he can get her in!"

"Are you serious?" I raised my brows. I would have loved to have learned how to play an instrument growing up. And that school seemed incredible. "That would be *amazing!*"

"We'll make it happen." Alec smiled tenderly, reaching for my hand. And thank goodness I remembered the cameras!

"Look, it's green!" I pointed at the traffic light, yanking my hand away from his.

Alec chuckled, realizing what had just happened. "You're terrible at this."

"*I'm* bad at this?" *I'm not the one who almost exposed us to the paparazzi,* I said with my eyes as we crossed the road.

"I said you were bad; I didn't say I was better." He laughed.

It was so weird to walk on the street like that, followed by a bunch of people. I only relaxed when we got to the coffee shop.

I thought it was over, but Alec said we still had to pose for the last pictures. Then, when I thought it was over again, he got caught up by a group of fans.

It was exhausting to go out with him, I realized. And it had only been two blocks!

Now I understood why he needed Jimmy. It wasn't even because he was at risk of being kidnapped or mauled. He needed someone to set limits around him. To say "enough" and guarantee that people would eventually go away. Otherwise, they would never let him do what he came here to do.

"Is your cappuccino good?" Alec took a sip of his tea.

"As always, yeah." I closed my eyes and raised the cup to my nose, just to inhale the smell. "I think I'm addicted to this by now."

"You come here a lot, huh? Can I ask you why?"

"*Hello.*" I showed him my cup again. "They have amazing coffee."

"Come on, seriously… I asked you in Vegas, but you never answered me. Why did you come here alone that day? Just to wait for hours…"

I couldn't resist his pleading face this time.

"It calms me down. I was anxious because—" *There's no way I'm telling him I was jealous of Tera.* "You were traveling. So I came here to relax."

"And you just sit here and wait?" His voice came out high-pitched in surprise.

"Kind of, yeah. I enjoy…watching people."

He tilted his head. "What do you mean?"

"I like to pretend I'm invisible and just watch them—imagine what's going on in their minds. Like their personal histories or what they're doing here, their worries, their dreams…" *I don't think I've ever said this out loud before.*

"That's actually nice." Alec had a silly smile on his face. "And then…"

"And then what?"

"You don't do anything with these thoughts?"

"What would I do with them?"

"Maybe write them down?"

"What? These ideas?"

"Yes!" He chuckled, watching me. "Those *ideas* in your head are called *inspiration…* I think you could be a great writer if you wanted to."

I snickered. There he was, bringing that up again.

"Would you write a song with me?"

I widened my eyes. "*Me?*"

"Yeah." His dimples showed.

I couldn't tell if he was being serious or not, so I bluffed. "What would I get in return?"

"We will share the copyrights so…money?"

"What? I was teasing!" I threw my napkin at him. "I don't want your money!"

Alec laughed. "What *do* you want, then?"

I lowered my brows, surprised at his tone. He *was* being serious. He really wanted me to do this. He was willing to give me something in exchange for it.

I definitely hadn't planned this, but all of a sudden, I knew exactly what I wanted.

I leaned forward, looking around to make sure nobody was listening. We were safe. Alec had found us this hidden spot at the back, and Jimmy was occupying the only table within hearing distance of ours.

"I have some questions," I said cautiously. So far today we'd been pretending nothing happened. But that party yesterday was too messed up for me to not say anything. That almost fight with Zach, all the mystery around their old band and around James. I had to ask…

"What do you want to know?" Alec moved on his chair, concerned.

"*I don't know,* Alec, that's the thing. I thought I knew everything about you, but the more we spend time together, the more I realize how little I know… You didn't tell me about your exams this week. I was the only one surprised at the party when—"

"This is because of what Zach said, isn't it? He got into your head yesterday."

I dropped my eyes, feeling my cheeks burn. The one who had actually invaded my thoughts all night was James.

"All right." Alec exhaled. "I don't like to talk about this, so I'm only gonna do it once, okay? I'll tell you everything, but then please leave it alone. There's no…*solution* anyway." His voice faded to a whisper.

And I could see the pain on his face. I had to resist the impulse to comfort him—to reach for his hands and hold them in mine.

"Okay?" Alec insisted.

"Okay," I agreed with a sigh.

"We met in fifth grade, Zach and I… He was already playing with James—they'd been inseparable since forever. I arrived later; I was homeschooled before, during the time I was sick. And I only played classical back then—with Ben."

I nodded, remembering the photos I'd seen at his house.

"They were covering punk rock bands, and one day, I saw them playing at school. I thought it was so much cooler than what

I was doing that I decided I wanted to be a drummer." He snickered.

And I grinned, feeling thankful for that. I loved to watch him drumming—he looked *so hot.*

"So my mom called Zach's mom and found out about the music school we just visited. Both Zach and James were taking lessons there."

"All right." *So they all studied at the same music school.*

"Zach and I became very close then. But I got bored with the drums. I was too used to the piano—I missed the notes. So Mom moved me to James's class, and that's when I found my true passion. Not the guitar itself, but the writing! I had just beat cancer, so there were a lot of emotions ready to come out, and the guitar allowed me to turn them into songs, you know?"

"Yeah." I thought about "Wave." And, once again, it broke my heart not to be allowed to hold his hand right now.

"The lyrics were terrible in the beginning. But then I started writing with James, and we connected right away. To this day, I still can't finish a song without him—he's like my musical soulmate."

I leaned back uneasy, remembering the dark blue of his eyes. The chocolate he had left for me.

"So we had our own songs at this point, but we still needed a bassist to be a real band. That's when we met AJ... You know who he is, right?"

"I think I've seen him a couple of times."

"Oh, and you should definitely talk to him about Claire! He was part of the program I told you about. He had one of those scholarships."

"Cool." I wondered if AJ was—like Claire and me—from a "low-income family."

"Anyway, he played cello with my older brother. But I guess he hadn't found his place in the school yet. He was already trying other instruments when Matt brought him to one of our rehearsals. So one thing led to another, and then we were officially a band." He sounded proud, nostalgic.

"We used to come *here*, actually. The four of us—after practice. We wanted to become one of those big punk rock bands. And grow our hair long. And tour the world together." His expression slowly changed from nostalgia to pain.

I remembered Ben warning me not to ask him about this. *I mean it, Linda. It triggers his anxiety.*

"It's okay if you want to stop," I blurted. I could ask his brother for the end of the story; I didn't want to make Alec upset —especially in a public place.

"You need to know the truth. I don't want Zach messing with your head again." His voice was low but decided.

"Okay." I swallowed hard.

"We tried to get a management deal when we were in eighth grade. We got some auditions—and we killed it *every time*—but they said we were too young. They wanted us to come back when we were eighteen." He snickered.

"I knew I was ready, you know? I refused to give up. Every day after school, I sat down with the guitar until I came up with something good. I didn't go to bed until I had something worthy of a song.

"Then, one Sunday afternoon, I wrote 'Wave' with the words Mom used to say to me." He half-smiled. "I had this feeling it would be *big*, and I couldn't wait to show it to the boys. But they all said it was 'too pop' for a punk rock band. They told me I was obsessed with the whole thing, and we should just do what the managers said: come back in five years.

"I didn't listen to them, of course. I thought that if I got us an audition, they would come around and try again. So I went to Dan's office one day—with my mom." His eyes flickered down to the table. "He said he had a few minutes to spare and asked me to play something right off the bat. Mom hadn't heard 'Wave' yet, so I decided to play it—mostly for her. And that's when things got complicated…"

Alec stopped to take a sip of his tea, and I leaned forward on my chair, worried about the regret on his face.

"I know I made a mistake. I shouldn't have played a new song without their consent—I knew it didn't represent the band. So I don't blame them for feeling betrayed… But I thought they would be happy about the audition!"

"What did they say?"

"Nothing! I thought everything was okay between us! But then on the big day, only James showed up."

My mouth fell open.

"AJ was Matt's best friend, so he forgave me a few days later —and he's been working in the crew since. But Zach… You saw it; he hates me! And he *loves* to remind me of every single one of my mistakes."

"Alec, you didn't do anything wrong."

"I did." He nodded. And I could see his guilt, his sadness. "I shouldn't have played 'Wave.' I shouldn't have gotten an audition behind their backs. I shouldn't have signed as a solo artist when I was still in a band. And I'll never know if Dan really liked me for *me*, or because I'm Amanda Parker's son."

I couldn't believe I was hearing this. "Alec, you're crazy talented! At fourteen, Dan could already see it—this has nothing to do with your mom's fame. You played three instruments and wrote songs like 'Wave' before even finishing middle school! How can you possibly think you don't deserve your own success?"

He took a deep breath, and I noticed he was shaking from stress.

I couldn't help myself this time, I gripped his hands on top of the table.

"Let's go home? This place is…" He glanced around, anguished. "Too many memories, you know?"

I nodded in sympathy, still rubbing his hands. And that's when I finally connected the dots. If this coffee shop meant that much to Alec, it was probably important to the others too!

James. My heart raced. "Who else knows about this story?"

"Only the people who were at the party, I think. Our school friends."

And Impostor Alec, I realized. We'd spent *hours* talking about this café. He made me picture coming here with him countless times on the phone. It couldn't be a coincidence! Either he knew this place was important to Alec, or…somehow, it was important to him too.

Chapter 10

I never forgot that conversation with Alec. Three whole weeks had passed, but I still couldn't get over my suspicions about James.

"Ben, can I ask you something?" I said, watching Alec and James play acoustic guitar at the back of the room. They were rehearsing in Hollywood during the week now, so whenever I was free after school, Alec asked me to come see him.

"Sure. Want some?" Ben grinned, casually handing me my daily afternoon snack.

I took it from him, holding back a smile.

He thought I hadn't noticed, but I knew exactly what he was trying to do, carrying all those high-calorie snacks in his backpack every day. I didn't complain, though. I thought it was actually sweet. Even if I had the feeling *Amanda* was the one behind it.

Since our conversation on Halloween, she seemed to have put not only Alec but also Benjamin on my watch, to make sure I was eating right. And I confess all that encouragement was helping. Like, *a lot.*

It had been a month since I'd had that dream. And I still

thought about the impostor whenever someone stared at me on the street—I couldn't say that I didn't. But now I was choosing to live in faith, to be optimistic. And every day that went by—every day that I didn't have any news from him—was a confirmation this nightmare was finally over.

There was just this *one* suspect at the back of my mind that I still couldn't forget.

"What did you want to ask me?" Ben bumped his knee against mine.

I finished chewing, staring at Alec with James again. "I was wondering…"

"Please don't start." Ben frowned.

"You don't even know what I was going to say!" I laughed.

"I do, Linda. You've been trying to make me answer these sneaky questions about James for weeks now!"

I dropped my eyes, feeling my cheeks burn.

And Ben turned his whole body toward me. "He's the nicest guy, okay? *Believe me!* He's not your impostor. You have no reason to be anxious around him."

"*He's* the one who is always anxious around *me*," I protested.

I was doing fine with my anxiety now, but James… It turned out that his self-conscious behavior on Halloween didn't match the sociable guy he seemed to be in front of everyone else. Apparently, he was only shy around *me*.

"Alec told me he has already talked to you about this," Ben said, his tone serious.

And I sighed, giving up. "He did, yeah…"

I'd tried to bring the subject up a few times, so I could get more information about James, but Alec had always gotten so anxious… That's when I started saving my questions for Ben. And he had answered a few of them, yes, but he always sided with Alec. He would never tell me something that his brother hadn't told me himself or didn't want me to know. And the more they avoided my questions, the more I was convinced *this James* was Impostor Alec James.

"So let it go! Relax." Ben bumped his knee against mine again. "James is… I don't even have a word, Linda—he's one of the best people I know! He would never do anything like that."

He would never do anything like that…

"You're daydreaming, aren't you?" Alec's voice brought me back to the present. "Is everything all right?"

"Yeah." I glanced up at him. He was sitting on my bed, leaning against the wall, and I was lying with my head on his lap.

"You're a terrible liar, you know that?" He chuckled, running his fingers through my hair. "You're even worse than James…"

I felt my blood boil. I hated how Alec was always talking about him. How James was in every single one of his stories. That was the reason why I couldn't stop thinking about him in the first place!

"Are you worried about the tour again?"

I took a deep breath to calm myself down. Besides the adrenaline that hit me every time he mentioned James's name, there was something else messing with my nerves.

Alec was leaving for the Jingle Ball Tour on Saturday. For three weeks! And with a bunch of other artists, including his gorgeous pop star ex-girlfriend, Tera Scott.

"I told you, babe, you have absolutely nothing to worry about."

I held his gaze, biting my lip. "Promise?"

"Of course." He smiled slowly.

I smiled back, covering his hand with mine over my stomach. Then I glanced at the bag he'd brought me with one of his shirts inside. "Is there something of mine that you would like to take with you too?"

"Yes! I was about to ask you that. Can you get me a little bottle with your shampoo?"

"My shampoo?" I giggled.

"Yeah—or whatever this coconutty thing is that you use on your hair." He leaned down and kissed the top of my head. "It's intoxicating."

I laughed, searching for his lips. We still had two days before saying goodbye, but I already missed him.

Alec deepened the kiss. And I felt chills all over my body when his hand slid under my shirt, leaving a trace of his warmth on my stomach.

I shouldn't have let him do it. We were at my house with the door open. Dad was downstairs, helping Carol with the Thanksgiving turkey, but still… If he came in and caught us making out, I didn't even know what would happen! But for some reason, the danger and the risk only made me want Alec's touch even more.

I lifted my body, crawling on the bed, then climbed into his lap.

He glanced at the door, alarmed, but before he could say anything, I caught his face in my hands and brought his lips to mine.

He grasped my waist, under the shirt. And I tried to close the gap between us, pressing my chest against his…

"Not like this, babe." Alec broke the kiss.

"Why not?" I moved a little closer and kissed his neck this time.

He held his breath, gently pushing me away. "Makes it harder to resist."

"So, stop resisting," I said meaningfully.

I knew we couldn't go on right now—we were at my house, after all. But even on the weekends, when we were alone in *his* room, he never let me do everything I wanted to do.

Alec sat upright, reading my frustration. "I thought we were waiting." His voice was surprised.

"No, *you* were making *me* wait." I chuckled.

And he showed me his dimples, flushing a little. "Are you serious? Are you sure you're ready for this?"

I looked into his green eyes reflecting mine.

If he was any other guy in the world, my answer would be different. We'd known each other for only two months—that was way too soon for me to be even considering taking things to the next level. But he was Alec Brock. The *real* Alec Brock. *My boyfriend* Alec Brock. And even if our story was a little messed up, I'd been waiting for this—for *him*—for too long now.

"I'm ready." I nodded. And his smile gave me butterflies.

"Well, in that case… I'd love to have a special night to remember during the tour." He tightened his arms around me. "And my parents won't be sleeping at home tomorrow, so…"

Is this really happening? Are we really doing this? My heart pounded in my chest.

But then the doorbell rang. And suddenly all I could think about was the person waiting outside.

I jumped off the bed, already running downstairs. "I'll get it! I'll get it!" I yelled at Caroline.

She laughed out loud as I beat her to the door, reaching around her to open it.

"I can't believe you're here!" I gave Nina a bear hug.

"Me neither!" She leaned back to look at me. "I'm in LA—with you!" She squealed in delight.

And I squealed with her, squeezing my best friend in my arms again.

"Welcome to California, sweetie," Caroline said, bringing her suitcase in.

"I hope I'm not bothering you guys…"

"Not at all! We're happy to have you for Thanksgiving." She patted Nina on the back. "I'll let Linda help you settle in—we're a little busy with the turkey. But, please, make yourself at home!"

"Thank you." Nina grinned as Caroline left. Then she lowered her voice, looking me up and down. "You're not that much thinner than I remember."

"You should have seen her two months ago," Alec said, making her notice him for the first time.

"You…" She exchanged a long look with him. "You're just how I imagined you would be."

"You too, actually." He chuckled, stepping forward to hug her.

"Thank you for the trip," she said shyly.

And he gave her a little smile. "My pleasure."

"Are you upset that we asked someone else to pick you up at the airport?" I bit my lip apologetically.

"Are you kidding? I felt like a Hollywood star! Let me tell you, to get out of a plane with a *chauffeur* waiting for you like that? *Best thing ever!* It's decided, I wanna be *rich* when I grow up."

Alec and I burst out laughing, and I hugged her once again. "I missed you so much."

"Me too." She rubbed my back.

"I'm gonna let you guys catch up." Alec turned to the door. "Mario is waiting…"

"Call me goodnight, okay?" I reached for his hand and laced our fingers together.

"Always." He leaned down to give me a kiss.

"Oh my gosh, you're *so cute* together!" Nina squealed.

We both laughed again, and Alec gave me another "Happy Thanksgiving" kiss.

"See you guys tomorrow." He waved, walking toward the car waiting for him.

"I can't wait!" Nina shouted.

I beamed at her excitement, barely believing my own eyes. My *boyfriend* Alec had just brought me my best friend for Thanksgiving!

Right then, thinking about all the things I would give thanks for at dinner, that's when I realized. Despite everything bad that had happened this year, I'd never had so many things to be thankful for.

♪ ♩ ♡

Among all the plans we had for that weekend, Friday's dinner was my least favorite. Thanksgiving with Caroline's parents had been great. Sightseeing and shopping with Nina today, absolutely awesome. I was looking forward to "sleeping" at Alec's house tonight. And I couldn't wait to see Nina's face tomorrow, when I announced the surprise I'd planned for her. But a double date that involved James… Let's just say I would have passed on it, if I'd had any choice.

"Are they late or did we arrive early?" Nina said when we got to the restaurant.

She was looking like a celebrity in that turquoise dress—it made her dark-brown skin shine. Her long, black hair was falling down her back, perfectly straightened. It matched the cut of the fabric, highlighting her curves in all the right places. She was overdressed, for sure. But Nina was the kind of girl who didn't really follow fashion rules. And somehow, this stubbornness always worked in her favor anyway.

The thing about Nina, though, was that she was never satisfied dressing up only herself. She had to dress you up too.

"They are late." I pulled the bottom of my dress down, feeling claustrophobic and exposed. I didn't usually wear such tight clothes. I knew I shouldn't have let her—

"Wow!" Alec said behind us, staring me up and down. "What have you done to my girl?" He greeted Nina first.

"See?" She gave me a smug smile. "I told you the dress looks perfect on you."

I rolled my eyes at her, then fought the urge for Alec's lips when he caught me in a hug. I hated this can't-be-seen-dating-in-public rule now. It was getting so hard to keep my distance from him…

"Hi." James stepped out from behind Alec.

My heart skipped a beat, looking at them both at the same time. I knew right then that dinner had been a terrible idea.

"Nina, this is my friend James." Alec put his hand on James's shoulder.

"Nice to meet you." Her face lit up.

"You too." James grinned at her, then bit his lip ring, dodging my gaze.

I hated when he did that. I hated how he always looked at everybody but me. I hated being forced to be so close to him. I hated…

I exhaled. "All right. Let's get—" *this over with* "—inside."

♪ ♩ ♡

"I'm gonna have the salmon, please."

"Music is my life. I can't picture myself doing anything else."

"No, thanks. I don't like olives."

"I don't think I'm shy, I'm just more of a quiet guy…"

"Rom-com, for sure. I'm not a fan of scary things."

"No, I'm an only child."

"My dad passed away when I was in sixth grade, and the twins were the ones who…"

"South America, I guess. Do you remember the show in Rio, Alec? I'll never forget…"

"Well, it's hard to make things work with someone when you're always traveling. All my relationships have become long-distance since I…"

"Excuse me, I'll go find the restroom." I got up from the table as soon as I finished my dessert. I couldn't take it anymore. I just couldn't.

I was unable to name one topic they had discussed that night. But at the same time, I could fill pages and pages with all these little pieces of information I had learned about James. My brain had spent the whole dinner checking if they matched with what I knew about Impostor Alec. And now I was feeling drained—and absolutely insane.

I stared at myself in the mirror. I looked as tired as I felt.

Have they noticed anything?

"You still think it's him, don't you?" Nina came in behind me.

I just sighed. I was too exhausted to actually talk about it.

"Linda, look at me." Nina held my shoulders, making me face her. "It's not him, okay? You've got to relax now. Stop thinking about this."

"Was I that obvious?"

"To me, yeah!" She dropped her arms in disapproval.

"Do you think Alec…"

"No." Her eyes softened. "But you have to let this go now, okay? Please! You're gonna end up ruining what you have with Alec if you don't stop with this paranoia."

"It's not just paranoia, Nina. I told you—"

"Linda, this is Alec's *best friend* we're talking about! He would never do something like this! And *so what* if he left the chocolate for you? Or if he likes to go to the same coffee shop? Don't you think the detective—and Alec's father—would have found out if it was him by now? They *know* it's not James, and you should trust their judgment!"

I looked down, my chest tightening.

"Plus, haven't you seen how sweet he is? And caring and cute… I think I might be in love!"

I laughed without humor. "You can't be serious."

"All right, maybe not *love*. But mama needs some sugar, and

I'm dying to bite that lip ring… So please be cool, okay? You already have your candy for tonight." She smirked, fixing her hair in the mirror. "How are you feeling, by the way? About…"

I let out a breath. "I'm not sure it's a good idea anymore."

"Because of James?" She raised her brows. "Linda, you've been waiting for this—"

"I know, okay?" I snapped, turning away.

"Hey." She caught my arm, making me look back. Her face was concerned at first, but then her expression changed. "I think I know why you're so obsessed with James today… You're finding yourself an excuse! You're just nervous about Alec!"

Could it be? I asked myself. And the sudden burn in my eyes answered for me.

I couldn't say she was right, but she wasn't completely wrong either. Since the moment I'd put on that sexy dress, I was feeling on edge. I knew Alec had big expectations for tonight, but mine were a thousand times bigger—and heavier—and terrifying! And the last thing I wanted was for this night to have anything to do with *James*. The last thing I wanted was to be thinking about those midnight calls I'd had with the impostor, when Alec and I finally…

"Aw, come here." Nina hugged me. "It's a little scary, I know."

I choked back the tears. I didn't want him to ruin this for me. I wouldn't let him!

If Impostor Alec James was *this* James, he'd had all the chances in the world to tell me the truth, to let me know who he was, to fight for us! But he didn't…

I shook James's face out of my head. *It doesn't matter if it's him or not…I'm Alec's now, only Alec's.*

"Everything will be all right." Nina rubbed my back. "The first time doesn't matter that much anyway. Things get better with *practice*, you know?"

I had to smile. Even if I didn't have the courage to tell her what was really on my mind, I was happy she was there with me.

"Thank you… I'm so glad you're here."

"Me too," she said tenderly. "Are you ready to go back now? They must be thinking we're taking a dump in here."

I laughed, composing myself, then followed her to the table. And relief washed over me when I noticed the boys had just paid the bill and seemed ready to leave.

"There they are!" Alec got up from his chair, examining my face.

I gave him a reassuring smile, and his expression relaxed a little.

"I have good news, girls," he announced. "James has just agreed to extend this party to my house."

"Really?" Nina's eyes blazed. It wasn't the "Alec's house" part that she was excited about—we were already sleeping there anyway. It was the "James" part. The part that *I* couldn't take any longer.

"Only if you're okay with it, of course." James glanced at her, then at me.

♪♩♡

In the car, Nina couldn't stop rambling. She was trying so hard to impress James that I couldn't decide if it was boring or entertaining to watch.

She told him about her plans to work in fashion. And James offered to talk to Alec's stylist for her—see if he could get her an internship or something. Nina was ecstatic. And I knew her so well that I could *see* the dreams forming in her head, about moving to LA and dressing up all those celebrities.

"You unleashed a monster," I told Alec. "She will want to take on this city now."

"That's good!" He grinned. "We need more people like her ruling things here."

I snickered, resting my head on his shoulder.

"Are you okay? You seem *distant* tonight." He rubbed my hand with his thumb.

"I'm fine." *Or I will be fine…as soon as I can stop looking at James.*

"Are you excited to meet Matt?" Alec asked.

And my spirit lit up. "Oh my gosh, yes!"

With all that paranoia in my mind, I had forgotten Matt was home for Thanksgiving. He'd been my favorite person from Alec's world before. I couldn't believe I would finally meet him in person!

"He's dying to see you too." Alec beamed. "We've talked about you all day."

<h1 style="text-align:center">Chapter 11</h1>

"Maybe the studio?" I said.

We knew Matt and Ben were at the house, but we'd been calling their names for a while, and no one had answered.

"No, Ben hurt himself—he can't play for two weeks. But, listen…" Alec followed the muffled sound of laughter coming from the patio. "I think they're in the hot tub."

"What happened to Ben? Was it serious?" I asked as we walked outside.

"It's tendonitis. He got way too excited with the new violin."

Ouch! Poor Ben. I'd never had it myself, but I knew tendonitis could be pretty painful.

"There you are! Why…?" Alec stopped, noticing AJ in the hot tub with Matt. "I didn't know you had company tonight."

"Last minute plan. You know how this one loves to play with me." Matt gave AJ a little punch in the arm. And AJ responded by splashing water on Matt's face.

It was so adorable that I laughed with them. I knew Matt was gay and that they were childhood friends. But I didn't know they were *that* close. Like, *boyfriend* close.

"How was the double date?" Matt asked Alec, waving hello to us all.

I guess it's a triple date now, I thought when he grinned at me.

"It was great! I brought James—to keep the party going."

"Awesome! Go change and join us."

What? No! Dinner had been bad enough already. I didn't need to spend the rest of the night seeing James half-naked!

"We don't wanna bother you two, right, guys?" I turned to Alec, then Nina, hoping they would realize how inappropriate that was—to interrupt their date like that.

AJ gave me a shy smile, but Matt stood up, grabbing his glasses and a bathrobe. "Don't be silly, honey. I was dying to meet you! It's a party now, the more the merrier."

Nina linked her arm with mine in excitement.

I could imagine how she felt, being in Alec's world for the first time. She'd been euphoric all day—bought a new bikini and everything. I couldn't take that away from her. I couldn't ruin her night with my insanity.

"I'm not in the mood right now, but go ahead. Have fun!" I said, letting go of her.

"You're not coming in?" Alec frowned.

"No, it's too cold." I rubbed my arms, looking chilly. I knew the water was super warm but there was no way I would take off my clothes in front of James.

Alec studied my face, concerned.

"You guys go; I'll watch it from here." I nodded toward the garden sofa with a reassuring smile.

"Go change, bro. I'll keep her company." Matt patted Alec's shoulder, then opened his arms to hug me. "Look at you—you're gorgeous! Alec was not exaggerating."

"Thank you." I beamed. "I can't believe I'm finally meeting you!"

"Yeah… I read a few of those old messages, and I have to say,

I was delighted! It's an honor to be your favorite, miss." He bowed theatrically, making me laugh.

Matt was exactly how I'd pictured him. He was a little shorter than the twins, he wore black, square glasses, and he was blond—like his mother. But he resembled Alec a little. Because of the green eyes and the shaggy mop that made them look cute and hot at the same time.

We sat down to chat, but before I thought she'd had time to change, Nina was already entering the hot tub with James. My face burned at the sight of him. He had broad shoulders and a V-line—I had to look away.

"There you go." Alec put a blanket over me, then sat fully dressed on the couch.

"You're not…?"

"Not without you." He pulled me closer, cuddling me in his arms. Then he buried his face in my hair. "Tonight, I'm all yours, remember?"

"You two are *so cute* together!" Matt said.

"I know, right?" Nina shouted from the hot tub. "I said the same thing yesterday!"

I smiled at them as Alec kissed my cheek. Maybe our date wasn't totally ruined, after all.

"Have a good night, everybody." Ben appeared behind us. "I'm sleeping at Hails's—just so you know." He glanced at his brothers.

"*What?*" Alec blurted. And I could feel his muscles tense beneath me. "No—tell me this isn't happening again!"

Benjamin blushed and exchanged a quick glance with James before saying, "I just wanted to let you know where I'll be… Goodnight."

Alec sighed heavily, as if deciding what to do. Then he got up, letting go of me. "Wait, Ben! You can't—"

"Let him go, Alec!" Matt shouted.

But his brother didn't look back.

"He never listens." Matt rolled his eyes.

"I know!" I snickered. "But he's right this time. I mean, Hailey is…" I couldn't describe her without cursing. "Alec doesn't think she's…the right person for Ben."

"Maybe not for forever, I agree. But I think she's exactly what he needs right now: fun! I've never seen Ben so stressed before—he only thinks about his auditions. And now with this new violin… He's not okay, you know? He's too obsessed. He even hurt himself from practicing too much!"

"I saw the wrist brace… It's tendonitis, right?"

"Yeah. And since he can't play for a couple of weeks, Hailey could be a good…*distraction*."

I bit my lip to keep from saying anything else. I understood Matt's point of view, but he hadn't seen Ben the other night. Hailey wasn't a good distraction; she was too dangerous.

Maybe I could set him up with one of my friends. I thought of Sam. She was a good girl—and so pretty! And she liked classical music too and played the oboe…

"So you were asking me about med school…?" Matt said.

"Oh, yeah." I grinned. "How did you know you wanted to be a doctor? I'm having some trouble deciding."

Matt smiled to himself. "I remember the exact day, actually. Alec's last day of chemo."

My heart skipped a beat. I was *not* expecting that.

"It was my favorite Halloween… I have a picture, wait!" He walked to the table and searched for his wallet among the scattered clothes. Then he pulled out an old photo and showed it to me.

The taller boy—the one in a doctor's costume—was blond, and he was holding his hands behind his back, way too serious. But the other two seemed pretty happy. The one with the red cape was raising his arm in the air, looking healthy and strong. And the one wearing a green suit was a lot thinner, holding a sign that said: "No more chemo."

"They loved to dress up as superheroes for Halloween." Matt chuckled. "But I remember realizing right then that the *doctors* were my real heroes. And that I wanted to grow up and save people's lives like them—like they'd done for my brother."

I looked up at him with watery eyes. I couldn't even...

"Oh no, don't cry. This is a happy memory now!" He hugged me sideways. "I even carry it around for motivation! For when things get hard at school."

"You're gonna be a great doctor one day," I said genuinely.

"Thank you." He smiled. "I'm sure you will too."

But now I wasn't so sure anymore. If Matt returned the question to me, I wouldn't have anything better to say than "I like to watch medical shows, and I have good grades."

Matt stared at me guiltily. "Sorry, I didn't mean to upset you."

"No. I have to thank you, really. No one likes to talk about this." I pointed at his wallet. "And I've always wanted to know—to see it."

"It was hard on everyone, that's why. But Alec has always been the strongest of us all."

My chest tightened. It hurt so much to think of him going through all that... "Tell me about the happy ending! What happened to Alec after this picture?"

"Life went back to normal, I guess. Dad registered us in school again—they were in fifth grade, and I was in eighth. But Mom went all crazy and changed everybody's lifestyle...because of Ben, you know?"

"No. What?"

"Since they are identical, everyone was sort of expecting him to get sick too. So my parents got *obsessed* with keeping us healthy."

"*That's* why you're all vegans!" I said to myself.

"Kind of, yeah. But Dad and Ben never gave up on dairy: they're actually vegetarians."

"Yeah, I know. Ben is my salvation here on the weekends—the keeper of the good stuff. In fact, he's the one to blame for me gaining all this weight back! He's always walking around with all these chocolate snacks I can't resist."

"Alec told me..." He laughed. "Benjamin is *annoyingly* caring, right?"

"Maybe a little." I giggled. "But what happened after that? When you guys went back to school?" I asked, hoping he would talk about Alec's band.

"Well, I decided to come out and gave my family something else to worry about." He glanced at AJ in the hot tub.

I smiled, watching him smile. "So, you two met in eighth grade, then?"

"Yeah..." The affection in his eyes melted my heart. It was so obvious that he was in love with AJ. I wondered if I looked like that staring at Alec too.

But when I followed Matt's gaze to the hot tub, I couldn't focus on AJ. James's arms were around Nina's shoulders. And I snorted in reflex, looking away.

"What was that?" Matt chuckled. "Are you okay?"

Am I okay? I couldn't understand what I was feeling.

Am I jealous? No, I'm not jealous.

I'm mad! But why am I mad?

Because nobody believes me! I'd had this feeling about James since the first day we met. But everybody kept defending him, and trusting him, and—

"Why does everybody love James?" I snapped.

Matt frowned in surprise. But I couldn't control myself anymore.

"Alec is in love with him! Ben is in love with him! And now Nina is in love with him? Seriously?"

"Wow, *you* clearly are not." He laughed. "What did he do to you?"

"Nothing!" I covered my face with my hands, taking a deep breath.

"He triggers your anxiety…" Matt observed.

"I have this feeling about him—about the impostor," I confessed.

"But you know it can't be him, sweetie. He has an alibi and everything."

"An alibi?"

Matt's face went red.

"What alibi, Matt?" I asked again.

And when he avoided my gaze, I finally understood. "He has an alibi that nobody bothered to tell me?" I hissed.

"I don't… You better talk to Alec about this, Linda."

"I will!" I jumped off the couch. I was suddenly so angry that I couldn't even… *Urgh!*

I marched to the house and followed the voices until I found the twins in the library.

"Alec, a word?" I blurted.

"Can't this wait, baby? I'm in the middle of—" He nodded at Ben on the sofa, who looked like he was either about to kill Alec or burst into tears.

"No." I clenched my tingling hands, forcing myself to breathe. I got anxious every time I had to be around James. I'd been paranoid like this for over a month! If there was something else I should know about him, I couldn't wait another minute.

Alec examined my face and came into the corridor right away. "What happened?"

"What's James's alibi?" I said too loud, too fast.

His face lost its color, but he didn't answer me.

"I asked you a question!"

"Baby, I…"

"What is it, Alec?" My heart pounded faster in my chest. My fear grew bigger every second he made me wait.

"Linda…"

"Just tell me!" I shouted.

"He went after you—the impostor," Ben said from the door.

"What?" I looked at him, my eyes wide.

"James was playing in New York on the same day, that's the alibi. But the impostor went after you in your hometown. And nobody told you," he pronounced every word in a tone of disgust and vengeance.

My head went blank.

"Benjamin!" Alec glared at his brother.

"I'll be at Hails's," he said icily, heading to the front door. "Have a good night."

"Is this true?" I mumbled.

"Baby…" Alec grabbed my hand, but I yanked it away.

"He's been to *my house*?" I raised my voice.

"Yes. But—"

"And you didn't *tell* me?"

Alec rubbed both his eyes, taking a deep breath.

"How could you keep this from me?"

"What's going on?" Nina came running in, wearing a bathrobe.

"The impostor went after me, Nina—he's been to Petersburg! And Alec knew, and he didn't say anything!" I scowled at him as she caught me in a hug.

"Baby, breathe!" Alec took a step forward but didn't touch me again. "You should sit down. Let's talk in the—"

"Since *when* do you know about this?" I narrowed my eyes. "How did you even find out?"

Alec swallowed hard, and to my total despair, exchanged a long look with Nina.

My heart stopped.

"We can explain," she said quickly.

"You've got to be kidding me." I pushed her away. "You *knew* about this?"

"Baby, please calm down." Alec clasped his hands, begging.

"I'm such an idiot! So, *that's* the secret you've been sharing, since…" I opened my mouth, realizing for how long they'd been communicating. "When did this happen? When did he go to Petersburg?"

"It was," Nina dropped her gaze, "right after classes started."

Her words knocked all the air out of my lungs. *He wanted to meet me—to show me who he was! He didn't give up on me; he wanted me back!*

"He called me at home, asking if you were there with me. He said he'd searched for you everywhere—at your house, at school, at the restaurant—but couldn't find you. He kept insisting that I tell him where you were and when you were coming back home. So I told him you'd moved to a different town and if he tried to get near any of us again, I would call the police."

I leaned my back against the wall for support, saying between clenched teeth, "Why didn't you tell me?"

"I didn't think it would do you any good. You were in love with him, L. You would have probably taken him back if—"

"You didn't have the right to—" I raised my voice, but the tears didn't let me finish.

"He could have called you, you know?" she yelled back, also crying. "He could have written to you—but he didn't! Why do you think he decided to show up out of the blue? The guy is a psycho, Linda! God knows what would have happened if you were at home that day—or if you didn't have a bodyguard here!"

"What?" I turned to Alec.

"Baby, you have to keep in mind that I was just trying to spare you from even more anxiety, okay? I wanted you to keep eating healthy and to stay calm—"

"Tell me!"

Alec sighed with deep, sorrowful eyes. "He threatened you, the night the first photos went public. He said he was willing to hurt you if you kept seeing me. But Jack had tapped your old phone, remember? He told my dad about the message in the morning—that's why they made you leave the hotel without being noticed. It was for your own safety! And when they told me all that, and I realized you hadn't seen the text yet…"

"You took my phone away from me." I stared at nowhere, numbness creeping over my limbs. *Manipulating me.*

"I didn't want you to worry! We were keeping you safe, anyway. You didn't need to—"

"You never canceled the investigation, did you?" *Another lie.*

"We couldn't. Not when he'd threatened to hurt you."

"You lied to me. And you manipulated me," I said, my voice dead as I felt my heart break. All the pieces I'd managed to put together, they were all scattered on the ground again.

"I just wanted to keep you from worrying…"

"You let me believe everything was okay when it was all a *lie*!" I couldn't hold back the tears this time. "Was this dating thing part of the act? Were you just distracting me? Are we even real?"

"How can you say this?" Alec frowned in despair. "*Of course* we are real! That's why I had to protect you from him!"

I stared at his green eyes. The same eyes that had hurt me before were now hurting me again. I squeezed my own eyes shut. I couldn't look at him anymore.

"I was just *protecting you*!" Alec repeated, wrapping his arms around me.

"You *lied*!" I pushed him with all my strength. "You are no better than him…" I turned around, running away.

Chapter 12

I ran to the front door and out into the street. I didn't care if I had to run all those miles until I got home. I wouldn't stay there, I wouldn't go back.

But then, just a few houses away, there was a parked car I recognized.

"Ben?" I panted.

He jumped at the knock on the window, then unlocked the door, right before I saw Alec from the corner of my eye.

I got in without hesitation. "Can you give me a ride?" My voice was urgent.

Ben glanced at the rearview mirror and immediately put on his seatbelt. I wasn't sure if he was helping me escape or trying to save himself. But either way, I was thankful when he stepped on the gas and took us both out of sight.

"To where?" he said, his voice husky. And then I noticed his puffy red eyes.

"Anywhere." I stared through the window, feeling my own tears fall.

Ben drove along the coast until we couldn't see the city

anymore. He didn't say anything. He just kept driving and driving.

I only looked at him twice—when he turned on the radio and when he turned off his phone so it wouldn't ring anymore.

I couldn't stop crying the whole time. I didn't know what hurt the most… To know that Alec had been lying to me for weeks. Or that Nina not only knew about it, but had also kept her own secrets from me. Or that the impostor was not James, and I wasn't safe at all!

I can't believe he's out there searching for me—planning to hurt me.

I have to see you, at least once… His voice echoed in my head. And I thought about all the times I'd freaked out because someone was staring at me. All the times I'd had the feeling he was there, watching. What if it was true? What if he'd found me already?

I wouldn't even know I was in danger! He could pass by me on the street, and I wouldn't even know!

Maybe he's done that! Maybe we've already met!

How close have we been? How close has he gotten to me?

Ben reduced the speed and pulled over at a gas station. "I'm gonna go get a drink," he announced, stepping out of the car. Then he glanced at my dress, now wet from the tears. "And a tissue box…"

I pressed my lips together in agreement, showing him a strong face. But the moment he left me alone, I couldn't help myself. I curled into a ball, sobbing.

I couldn't believe what was happening. It just couldn't be!

My boyfriend Alec would never hurt me like this. Manipulating me, lying to me!

My best friend Nina would never *not* tell me something important. She would never team up with someone else behind my back. She would never, *ever* betray me!

And the impostor…

I thought about James again. He knew my favorite candy, he'd been weird around me since day one. Had I imagined all that? Was I that wrong?

I was. Now I knew I was. The impostor couldn't be anyone like James, simply because he was…bad.

He threatened you, I saw Alec's face in my head. *He said he was willing to hurt you if you kept seeing me.*

The impostor had never been a fraction of the person I thought he was. He was a liar, he'd committed a crime, he was dangerous. He was indeed the psycho Nina claimed him to be.

Ben opened the door, and I composed myself quickly, wiping away my tears.

He handed me the tissue box, then took two cups from the paper bag and put them in the cup holders in the dashboard.

"How did you buy that?" I nodded at the vodka in his hand.

"Hails got me a fake ID." He took it from his pocket and showed it to me.

"And they believe you're…Mr. Green?" I asked, puzzled, examining the card. He was the identical twin of a teen pop star— there was no way people wouldn't recognize him. And everybody knew Alec was only eighteen.

"Convenience store cashiers aren't exactly his target audience…" Ben gave me my cup, then raised his in the air. "Cheers!"

I watched him drink. His cup had a lot more liquid than mine. "You're driving, you shouldn't—"

"It's water." He nodded at his knee, and I noticed another bottle on the floor next to him. "The vodka is for you. You kept sobbing your eyes out, so I thought…"

My face burned with shame. And I took the shot in one gulp, leaning my head back like they do in the movies.

"Wow, go easy!"

I almost threw up in his face. "Urgh! This is terrible!"

Ben chuckled as I reached out for his water. I didn't even bother using the cup; I drank it straight from the bottle.

"You'll feel better in a minute."

"I doubt it." I sighed, closing the cap.

"Is there anything I can do?" His voice was low now, honest.

"No." I dropped my eyes. "I'm already thankful that you told me the truth. Who knows when they would have…"

That's when it hit me. Ben only told me the alibi because he was mad at Alec! He knew it all along—everybody did! Everybody was lying to me!

I shook my head, on the verge of tears again. But I choked them back and flung the door open, bolting outside.

"Where are you going?" Ben shouted over the roof of the car.

"Home!" I yelled back, heading to the beach.

He called my name a few times, but I ignored him. He was a liar, just like his brother! Just like Impostor Alec! Just like my best friend…

I couldn't trust anyone anymore.

No, worse—I *literally* couldn't trust anyone anymore!

I froze in my tracks. There was too much adrenaline in my veins. And not the kind that gives you momentum and keeps you going. It was the other kind—the one prey feels right before being attacked. The fear that paralyzes you when you realize there's nowhere to run.

He can be anyone. He can be anywhere. And if he really wants to hurt me... My heart got out of control, and I turned around, walking back to the car.

He could stalk me on the street. He could come to my school and pretend he's a student. He could befriend me in the supermarket, at the church, at the bus stop.

My gosh, the bus stop! I remembered my panic attack leaving Dr. Brown's office, when Alec was in Europe. I felt him there—following me! I thought I'd even heard him calling my name! I wasn't sure I was paranoid anymore. What if my senses were actually right?

"What happened?" Ben widened his eyes at me.

I jumped inside the car, doing my best to breathe. But there was simply no air. My throat was completely closed.

"Take a deep breath!" Ben shouted in panic.

I'm trying! The words didn't come out. There was no opening, no oxygen…no light.

"No! Stay with me, Linda! Stay with me!" He squeezed me in his arms, making the pain real again.

I gasped for air over and over, my whole body numb. And that's when I heard the music. This loud majestic music, taking me out of my own head.

I focused on the angry violin, holding on tightly as if it was my lifeline. And when the melody started to calm down, it took me with it, carrying me away from the storm. By the end of the song, I felt like I was lying back on the beach. Completely exhausted but safe and dry.

"Thank God that worked." Ben loosened his arms around me, then lowered the radio volume. "You really scared me!"

"Sorry." I tried to lift my body, but all I could do was rest my head against the door. I had no strength left. I could barely keep my eyes open.

Ben found a jacket in the back seat and covered me with it. He didn't say anything for a while, but it didn't feel embarrassing or weird. The violin kept playing in the background, filling the silence between us.

"I should have told you the whole truth before. I'm so sorry." His voice cracked.

"It's not your fault. It wasn't your secret to tell." I gave him a forgiving smile.

He sighed, sounding regretful. "Do you want me to take you home?"

Only then did I remember he had plans. I was totally ruining his Friday night.

"I'm sorry, I didn't mean to… You can drop me anywhere on your way to Hailey's; I can call my dad."

"It's okay. I'm not going anymore."

I met his gaze, surprised. "How did Alec convince you?"

"He didn't." Ben pressed his lips together. "*You* did."

"Me?" I raised my brows.

"Yeah. We should stay away from what's toxic," Ben mumbled to himself. "I hate to admit this, but Alec was right, you know? About me, *and* about you. He really wanted to *protect* us."

My chest tightened. It physically hurt to think of Alec right now.

"I've been fighting with him to stop lying to you since the beginning, Linda. To me, you deserved to know that the impostor had gone after you—that he'd tried to contact you. But after seeing you in pain tonight, I think I get it. *He* is the one who doesn't deserve a place in your mind. Just the *memory* of him is toxic for you… The same way Hails was—is—toxic for me."

"It's not the same, Ben. I don't know what happened between you and Hailey, but this is way more—"

"I know…" He stared at me, sadness darkening his face. "That's why I understand Alec now. Everything he did was to defend you from this—what just happened. He never lied to protect *himself*, Linda…like the impostor did. He was genuinely trying to do what was best for *you*."

"But he *lied*, period! He manipulated me!" I fumed. "Why does everyone feel like they can fool me like this? Is it something with my face? Do I look that naive?"

"No." Ben touched my arm, concerned. "I know what we did is not okay, but I see what you're doing here… Please don't let that *one* experience chase you for the rest of your life! The mistakes *he* made with you—you have to move on from that. Not everybody is like him, you know? Alec is not like him."

Our eyes locked for a moment, and I knew Ben was right. Whatever pain I was supposed to be feeling, it was hurting a thousand times more because of Impostor Alec. Because *he'd* hurt me that way first.

"Let's go home," Ben said, finding his cell. "He must be worried sick about you."

"No." I grabbed his hand before he turned the phone on. I couldn't look at Alec yet, I was just too mad.

"Or we can join Zach's hate club if you prefer. I confess I'm very tempted tonight." He laughed wryly.

And suddenly I remembered the Halloween party. *You deserve better than this,* Zach had said. *I'm just trying to warn you, love. Stay away—for your own good!*

I wondered if Zach knew Alec was lying to me. He seemed to be the only person who tried to warn me somehow. The only one on *my* side.

"So, are you coming with me? Or do you want me to drop you at your house?"

I glanced at Ben, hopeless. If I went back home, I would have to explain to my dad why Nina had stayed at Alec's. And if I went with Ben, I would have to face Alec—and Nina. Both of them.

I hid my face in my hands. "Can't I just disappear from the world? Just for tonight?"

"You know what? I think I can help you with that…"

♪♩♡

I fell apart on the couch the second Ben closed the door of the studio. I was so thankful for his idea—for his help. Even more now that it had actually worked.

I'd thought I wouldn't be able to sneak my way to the guest

house without being seen. And I was terrified of answering the door and bumping into a face that wasn't Ben's. But he kept his word; he didn't tell anyone I was here. And he even brought me my bag, and a blanket, and a snack.

Ben was a good friend. I didn't have many people I could trust right now, so I really appreciated him. And he was giving me something I truly needed tonight: *time*. I would have some hours to think straight and get some rest. I wouldn't have to face anyone or explain anything before I understood it myself. And I could cry —I could scream, even—without anyone there to judge me.

So that's what I did. I tried to process what had happened and cried myself to sleep.

At some point during the night, though, I felt someone there with me. I didn't need to turn over to know who it was; I recognized his scent. His arms were warm and tight around my body, cuddling me from behind. But I didn't realize he was awake until I heard him sob.

I grasped his hand in reflex.

"Sorry. I didn't mean to wake you up." Alec's voice was small.

My heart pounded, but I didn't look at him. I didn't say a word.

"I can leave if you want," he said, taking his hand away.

And I let him.

My whole body complained. I really didn't want him to go. But he had hurt me too much; I wasn't ready to deal with him yet.

Alec's breathing changed, and he didn't move any further. "I'm sorry."

I stayed silent.

"Can we talk? Please?" He sobbed.

I took a deep breath, choking back my own tears. And he wrapped his arm around me again.

"Please, Linda. Let me explain…"

"You *hurt* me," was all I could say.

"I know. I'm so terribly sorry." He buried his face in my hair. "I didn't realize I was doing *exactly* what he did. I didn't mean to—"

I climbed over him on the sofa, getting up. I couldn't take it anymore, I was on the verge of a meltdown. If he wouldn't leave, then *I* would.

"Where are you going?" Alec straightened up.

I stopped in shock when I looked at him. His hair was matted down, and his eyes were swollen.

I felt my heart break.

"Please don't leave," he begged.

There were tears streaming down his face. I could barely breathe, staring at them. "Alec, just for tonight, okay? Please let me have this."

"Why?" His voice broke. "It's better if we talk…"

"I need time! To understand all this!" I snapped. "There are too many lies! I don't know who to trust—what to believe! I don't know what's real or not anymore."

He knit his brows, then reached for my hand, pulling me closer to the couch.

"Alec, please don't—"

"I'm real." He looked up at me, pressing my palm against his heart. "You can trust *me*. We are real."

I dodged his gaze, trying not to burst into tears. But then I had a flashback from that day on his boat—the first time he'd let me feel his heartbeat like that. It was steady and quiet. It didn't react to me.

I met his eyes, affected. His heart was loud and fast this time. And, to my surprise, just as anguished as mine.

I felt it racing under my touch as he waited for my answer.

Alec was real. *We* were real.

"Tell me *everything* that is not," I demanded.

He swallowed hard, looking down. I thought he would ask for us to have this conversation another time or give me some kind of excuse. But when he met my gaze again, his eyes were determined. He was ready to talk.

I only understood why he was suddenly so desperate to be honest with me when he said, "I promise you, I won't ever keep anything from you again. I mean it—no more lies! You can trust me again, okay? I promise you, I'm *nothing* like him."

I went quiet, remembering what Ben had said to me in the car: *Please don't let that one experience chase you for the rest of your life! Not everybody is like him, you know? Alec is not like him.*

"No more lies, okay?" I cupped his face with one hand.

"No more lies," Alec affirmed his promise, pulling me closer into his arms.

<h1 style="text-align:center">Chapter 13</h1>

"Sorry I gave you away." Ben stood in the hall in his pajamas, watching me close Alec's door.

"It's okay." I half-smiled. "I'm actually glad you did."

"So you guys talked it out, then?"

"Yeah. We're getting there."

"Good." He held my gaze, pressing his lips together. "What about Nina?"

"I haven't seen her yet. But I'm not gonna do this right now; Alec is leaving in an hour…"

My heart was already aching. I'd been preparing to say goodbye today, but I had no idea I would have to let him leave like this—right after all this mess.

He'd told me the truth last night, and we did work things out. But it was like the fight had made us realize just how much we wanted to be with each other. And now, it was a hundred times harder to let him go.

"You're right." Ben nodded. "You'll have plenty of time to talk to her at the park anyway—waiting in line for the rides."

"No, I don't think that's a good idea anymore."

"Are you serious?" He widened his eyes at me. "You're canceling her surprise?"

"To be honest, I'm not sure she deserves it," I said between my teeth.

"Of course she does… I talked to her yesterday; she seemed pretty bad."

I dropped my gaze, spinning the ring on my finger.

"Come on, don't cancel your plans." He punched my arm playfully. "You said it was your *dream* to go to a theme park together… This will be your first ever roller coaster ride!"

"I really don't want to spend the whole day alone with her, Ben. Not today… At least at my house, we will—"

"What if we come with you?" His face lit up.

"What?" I raised my brows.

But Benjamin didn't even look at me. He went straight to the next door and opened it without knocking. "Matt, you're up? Get ready, we're going to the park with the girls."

"Really? Yay!" Matt said in his morning voice.

"No, Ben, you're not doing this." I shook my head.

"I sure am!" He grinned, excited. "My parents have this super boring event planned for us today. I was desperately in need of an excuse."

"Excuse for what?" Alec asked behind me. His hair was still wet, but he already had his carry-on luggage with him.

My chest tightened. *Three weeks apart—I don't know how I'm gonna survive.* I wrapped my arms around his waist.

Alec hugged me with one arm as Ben explained, "The Formans' party. Matt and I are going with the girls to the park instead."

"Oh, that's great! I wish I could go too." Alec rested his chin on top of my head.

And I couldn't help myself. I searched for his lips.

"I'm—gonna go get ready, then." Ben closed his door. And Alec dropped his bag on the floor, tightening his grip around me.

"I don't wanna leave." His voice was small in my ear.

I squeezed him harder. I didn't want to let him go either.

"We are okay, right?" He leaned back to look at me.

I nodded at his anguished eyes. "Please just come back soon, okay?"

"As fast as I can." He pressed his forehead against mine.

And for the first time, I really thought he would say it. *He loved me.* The words were there, on the tip of his tongue—I could tell. But he stayed quiet, then kissed my mouth instead.

♪♩♡

It felt like Alec had taken my heart away with him—in the bag hanging off his shoulder.

I wanted him to go live his dream; I wanted to support him on tour. I was actually used to it already—the whole long-distance thing. But *today*, I really didn't want him to go. Not like this. Not right now.

After everything I'd discovered yesterday, I kind of needed him with me. I didn't think I could face this wave without him by my side. And it was terrifying to know that I would *have* to, that I was all alone this time.

Alec had ten shows scheduled in the next three weeks, including one in London. Plus all the radio and TV promo he would do for his Christmas song—to raise money for his charity project in Africa. He would barely have time to call me on the road. And when he finally came back, we would only have forty-eight hours to be together before *I* had to catch my plane to go spend the holidays with my mom. I would see him on the night of the Jingle Ball concert in LA, but still… That was less than *three days* with him in the whole month of December.

Three days! It was too sad to think about.

Maybe that's why Alec had supported me with this surprise for Nina. He knew I would feel blue today. He probably hoped this would cheer me up.

It wasn't working, though. It wasn't working at all.

The boys were definitely helping to lighten the mood, but the tension between Nina and I was too thick. And being in the happiest place on earth when you're feeling that bad only makes your misery show even more.

As much as I tried, I couldn't bring myself to look at her—to talk to her. I felt heavy and remorseful. And she didn't seem to be having any better of a time.

When I planned all this, I thought Nina would be ecstatic, like Ben seeing his new violin. We'd always dreamed of going to a park like this together—like, since we were five years old! I was expecting squeals and laughter, not the sorrowful smiles she was giving Matt and Ben. This wasn't my best friend. This wasn't my Nina.

And I knew it was my fault. *I* should be the one to say something. But I didn't know how. I didn't know when. *What should I even say to her?*

"I can't take this anymore." I stopped without warning, right after we entered the princess castle.

Probably not the best way to start a conversation, I know. But I swear I was doing my best.

"Ben, you wanna go ride a roller coaster?" Matt patted his shoulder.

"Sure." He didn't look at his brother. He gave me an encouraging smile instead.

I took a deep breath but still couldn't face her. "Maybe we should…" I nodded at a bench in front of the souvenir shop.

Nina followed me in silence. And despite all the noise in the park, I could hear every racing beat of my heart. I'd never fought with Nina before. Never, in twelve years of friendship.

"Before you say anything," she sat down next to me, "I just wanted to… I… I'm really sorry." She broke down in tears.

And just like that, my own tears were back.

"How could you do this to me?" I sobbed.

"I was afraid!" She raised her head to look at me. "Linda, I was the *only person* in the world who knew about you two. If he found you and did something bad to you, it would be entirely my fault! And I was sure you would forgive him—you would call him the minute I told you! You wouldn't realize how weird it was that he'd just showed up like that. You were too in love, too blind!"

"It was *my* choice to make, Nina! You didn't have the right to keep this from me!"

"I didn't know what I was doing, okay? I really didn't!" She rubbed her eyes. "You were being so…*cold* those days. You stopped calling me back, and every time I tried to talk to you about him, you got angry and came up with an excuse to hang up the phone!

"At one point I even thought you were still dating in secret— and your silent treatment was my punishment for not telling you that he'd called. I only understood what was going on when you met Alec and started to open up to me again!"

I felt a knot in my stomach. I remembered those phone calls. I had ended them because of anxiety, not because I was avoiding her. My breath shortened every time I even *thought* of him—I simply couldn't bear saying the words out loud. This had nothing to do with her. And I had no idea she didn't know that.

"Then Alec called me, and he seemed willing to help… I knew this would be important for the investigation—I had to tell him, you know?" She lowered her head in tears. "I'm sorry if this alliance went too far, but all I wanted was to make sure you were *safe*."

I sighed, putting an arm around her shoulder. I didn't have a choice, I had to forgive her. If I were in her place, I would probably have done the same thing.

"I'm sorry," she said again, hugging me tight.

"It's okay…" I rubbed her back.

"Did Alec tell you about your bodyguard?" She pulled away to look at me. "Because I told him I'm not keeping secrets from you anymore!" Her voice was resolute.

Which made me smile. "He told me, yeah. I'd noticed the car before, but I thought he was a paparazzi."

"And the investigation? Do you know about the other cases?"

"Yeah." My smile vanished. In everything I'd learned yesterday, that particular bomb was the one that hurt me the most.

Alec told me that thanks to the multiple warnings posted on his website, four other cases had been reported by his fans. And since then, Jack had been working closely with the police on the investigation.

Two of the girls lived in California, and both of them had received invitations to go meet "Alec" in person—which didn't happen to the ones who lived in different states. So Jack was convinced this guy lived somewhere near, and that's why they'd gotten me a bodyguard.

The impostor knew I'd been the one who exposed his game to Alec's management. And he'd already gone after me once; they didn't think he would hesitate to do so again. Especially if he connected the dots and realized I was living in LA.

Arthur was the one in charge of studying my routine—not of taking pictures for Alec's stylist, like they let me believe. Though he had indeed been the one who took those pictures.

He had stalked me for a week, actually, in order to draw my security plan. That's why he'd looked so familiar in Vegas. And

Alec had said *that* was his main reason for not telling me about the text: my reaction when I thought Arthur was the impostor.

Arthur had told Oliver about the scene I made at the hotel as soon as Ben took me out of the living room that day. And when Oliver told Alec what had happened, he realized I would probably have an anxiety crisis like that on a daily basis if I knew the impostor lived in California and that he was now threatening me. So he decided to just reinforce security and keep the information to himself. He really *was* trying to protect me in every way possible. He thought he was doing what was best for me.

That's why I forgave him, you know? How could I not?

The thing that crushed me, though, was that now there was no hope anymore. I had *proof* that the guy I fell in love with was *bad*. He'd fooled at least four other girls—he was a professional liar! A sick, disgusting, unscrupulous liar.

"And how do you feel about all this?" Nina frowned in sympathy.

"Hurt," I confessed.

She could have said, "I told you he was a psycho." She'd warned me a hundred times before. But she chose to hold my hand instead.

"I think I'm gonna talk to Jack; Alec said I could. He doesn't know all the details. He said it made him too angry, so he stopped asking for updates."

"I only know what Alec knows, so maybe, yeah—you should get things straight with the detective."

I looked away, sad. "I've always believed he was *good*, you know?"

"I know." Nina squeezed my hand. "But you'll get through this. You're strong—and you have Alec."

"I don't know… I feel like I can't trust *myself* now. I've been living so many lies that I'm not sure what's real and what's fake anymore."

"Like your paranoia with James?"

"To start with, yeah. You could have warned me about that one, by the way!" I frowned at her. "If you knew his alibi, you should have convinced me that it wasn't him somehow—to help me move on. You know I've been anxious about him since the first day we met!"

"Sorry. I guess I didn't realize it was that bad until I saw it with my own eyes."

"Do you get it now? I swear I had this *gut feeling* about him… My intuition is all messed up, Nina. I genuinely think I'm going crazy!"

"You're not going crazy." She laughed. "I understand why you thought he could be hiding something or running away from you. There were some coincidences, and he is indeed very mysterious and introverted…"

"You two really hit it off, huh?" I could tell from the glow on her face.

Nina smiled. "He reminds me of *you* a little—of your soft heart. Seriously, you should give him a chance. He's a very nice guy."

That's what everybody keeps telling me. Maybe I should start trusting their judgments instead of mine.

"Sorry I ruined your date," I said, meaning every word.

"No, it was totally my fault. And Alec's…" She met my gaze, serious. But then her expression changed. "He's head over heels for you, by the way. You should have seen how crazy he went when you left with Ben."

"Really?" I grinned.

"Yeah… I guess my plan worked better than I ever imagined it would."

I raised an eyebrow. "What plan?"

"The chat history! Who do you think told him to read it?"

"No…"

"Yes!" Her face lit up with joy. "On our first conversation— the day you two went sailing! He called, asking what he could do to help you, then told me he'd even written a song about 'the girl that left her CD with him,' and I realized maybe you had a chance! I thought if he knew you the way I did—the way the impostor did—maybe he could love you too."

My heart warmed toward her. "Why didn't you tell me? *This* you could have."

"I know. I just didn't wanna brag." She shrugged, making me laugh.

"I'm gonna miss you," I said, looking into her eyes.

"Me too." She wrapped her arms around me again.

"We should go find the boys." I got up. "*Now* I think we're ready to have fun."

"Yeah." She grinned, following me. "Thank you. For this surprise."

"It was supposed to be just you and me, but…"

"It's all right, I like them. Ben is so sweet, and Matt is—"

"And Matt is what?" he said from behind her.

"Matt is nosy and gossipy!" She chuckled, giving him a side hug.

"I told you she would forgive you." Matt smiled at her.

"Yeah, you did." She smiled back.

My heart melted a little.

"So, Linda." Matt turned to me. "Since I'm your absolute favorite, I have a special surprise for you."

I bit my lip, glancing at Ben. It was not that I liked Matt any less, but now I couldn't say he was my favorite person from Alec's world anymore. Not after everything Ben had done for me.

"*What?*" Matt put his hands on his hips. "You like him better than me now?"

I frowned apologetically, and Ben laughed out loud.

"Well, then, *this*, my lady, is about to change!" Matt

announced in a deep, theatrical voice. "Because I just called my father and asked him to revise your security arrangement."

"What do you mean?"

"He switched your bodyguard!" Matt grinned. "AJ doesn't want to travel with Alec anymore, so I convinced Dad to let him work with you."

"Really?" That was so sweet of him! I didn't know AJ that well, but he was Matt's boyfriend—I would definitely feel more comfortable being escorted by him than by that other guy. "Thank you!"

"It's my way to say sorry for being the one who started all this, you know? I thought it would be easier for you to deal with *everything* if you had a friendly face taking care of you." Matt tilted his head in sympathy.

And his words made things real for me.

I'd been feeling paranoid for months now, wondering if any of those unfamiliar stares could be from *him*. But now I had a body-guard. *The Brocks* had gotten me a bodyguard. This wasn't my anxiety speaking anymore—they were convinced I needed phys-ical protection!

I'd never imagined a simple chat room conversation could end up like this, with someone stalking me, threatening to hurt me if I didn't do what he said. It was surreal to think that the guy I'd once loved was being chased by the police—for fooling not only me, but four other girls. And the worst part was that...this person I had to run away from, I didn't even know what he looked like!

"Are you okay?" Ben touched my arm.

"Yeah," I lied. I didn't want to keep spoiling their fun.

But I was not okay. Nothing was okay.

My life had become a mess. A big dangerous mess.

Chapter 19

On Monday morning, as Matt had promised, there was a friendly face waiting to take me to school.

I grinned the minute I saw my new bodyguard. AJ had this open-mouthed smile graced with perfect white teeth—it made me happy just to look at it. His eyes were thin, his short hair was black and thick, and his skin golden brown. But what caught my attention the most was that he wasn't wearing a suit nor driving one of those fancy sedans. His car was average and ordinary. *He* was average and ordinary. Just like me, just like my world.

I decided I liked him right then. He wasn't a bodyguard to me, he was already a friend.

"You look happy today." He unlocked the passenger door. "I confess I wasn't expecting that."

"I'm happy it's *you*, not the other guy."

"Then I'm happy too." He grinned, watching me find the seatbelt. "I think we'll have a great time together…"

I had no doubt of that. We already had so much in common, so much to talk about.

We were both in the same situation, living between two different worlds so we could be with the Brock we loved.

We were also in long-distance relationships: his boyfriend lived in Boston, and mine…he lived on the road for now. Plus, AJ had known Alec since they were kids. He was part of his former band; I could totally get him to tell me more about it!

"So, tell me about yourself!" I said too fast. It was hard to hide my enthusiasm.

AJ half-smiled, then turned on the engine. "What do you want to know?"

"I don't know… Everything!" I chuckled. "All I know about you is that you're Matt's boyfriend."

AJ's face went serious, and he closed his hands on the steering wheel, focusing on the road.

All right, maybe it's a little too soon to start talking about boys. We're technically not friends yet.

"I also know you used to play bass in Alec's former band!" I tried again. "Oh, and that you asked not to travel as his bodyguard anymore, right? *Why?*"

"Yeah, it's just too messed up—I don't know how he stands it." AJ snickered, his mood back to playful. "I hate not having a routine. Going to sleep at a different time every night…"

"But you also get to travel and see a lot of different places!"

"That's total BS, you know?" He glanced at me. "You barely have time to go from one place to the next, and when you finally have a day off, you're just too exhausted to go out."

"Oh." I thought about Alec on the road. Ten shows in three weeks, plus all that Christmas promo. Would he have time to call me at all?

"You look…*normal* now. I'm happy to see it," AJ said, his voice quiet.

I held his gaze, confused. "What?"

"I remember you—at the mall. And then again at the studio… I mean, I'm glad you look healthy again."

"Oh. Thanks." *That's very considerate of him.* I stared for a minute, trying to remember AJ at any of those places.

I didn't. I had no memory of him. Of course, I'd *seen* him with Alec many times before. And we'd even chatted briefly at a few rehearsals and at the Halloween party. But I guess I'd never really *noticed* him until now.

AJ was about the same age as Matt. I was guessing twenty-one, twenty-two. But he was taller and stronger than his boyfriend, although his childish smile made him look more like a high schooler than a grown-up. Especially when he was wearing regular clothes.

"I think I'm gonna tell my father you're a friend from school, okay? And that you live in the neighborhood…" *Yeah, that's believable. And he'll be happy to see me hanging out with someone "from school" for a change.*

AJ smirked, seeming amused. "You think I look young, then."

"Well." My cheeks burned. "We need an excuse for these daily rides. Do you have a better plan?"

"No—high school it is." He laughed. "But we should set up the details. Backstory is *very important* when you're telling a lie." He met my gaze.

"All right. So, you're a senior like me…" I turned my body toward him. And we talked about all the classes we had together, all the teachers we hated and loved.

He paid attention as if he was being told the most important thing in the world. I guessed AJ was one of those people—when he was talking to you, it was like no one else existed. He made you feel heard, he made the time stop.

The ride passed in the blink of an eye. And it was so good to simply *talk* to him that I didn't get out of the car when he parked in front of my school. I felt like he understood me—like I could talk to him about anything. So we kept babbling until the last minute. Until I really had to go.

"I'll pick you up at 3 P.M., okay? So I can take you to…you know."

"Okay." I closed the door, drawing a deep breath. I was already nervous just knowing I would see Jack that afternoon.

"And, Linda!" AJ called from the car.

"Yeah?" I turned around.

"It was nice to…officially meet you," he said with a smile.

"You too." I smiled back.

♪♩♡

Liar, I thought as I laid eyes on the detective.

The day we met, he had looked me in the eye and said he would do only what I wanted him to do. He told me I could trust him and that we were in this together—as a team.

I guess everybody lies. I remembered my conversation with AJ this morning. All the backstory we had invented to convince my dad he was one of my high school friends.

And then I couldn't help but wonder how many other lies people were telling me. My family, my friends—everyone! How many secrets I didn't know, how many truths only existed in my head.

My abuela always taught me to listen to my heart. But my heart *believed* in people. My heart didn't question anything, didn't get suspicious—it just trusted everyone! And I was starting to realize maybe people shouldn't be trusted at all.

I might not know what he looks like, but I know his soul. I know he has a good heart, I used to tell myself. Was I really that naive? Was I really that stupid?

The impostor had lied to me, yes. But I must also have lied to myself, because it was impossible not to see it now—the guy he really was. The *monster* he really was!

I had to hold on to my chair when Jack started telling me about the other girls. It was absolutely disgusting.

They were all younger than me, from twelve to fifteen. Two lived in California, one in Texas, and one in Florida. But they had all met "Alec" in a chat room, then started a romantic relationship with him shortly after that. The difference between me and these girls was that none of them had agreed to send him any sexual content—I thought about my photos again—they were all smarter than me.

Jack explained that the moment he received the report from the other girls and realized what type of criminal he was dealing with, he was forced to contact the police. As a private investigator, Jack's powers were limited—he could gather information and work on the evidence, but he couldn't make arrests, for example. So he couldn't proceed without their help.

The police had started by following the latest clues and already had not one, but three suspects. Apparently, catfishing was an easy way to win children's trust, so a lot of online predators used this strategy. But Jack told me that, though they couldn't confirm anything yet, this guy from Sacramento was suspected to have traveled to another state to meet with a fourteen-year-old girl in the summer. So they were guessing he could be the one who went to West Virginia too.

And it immediately made sense to me, that conversation the impostor and I had when I was in San Francisco. Sacramento was less than two hours away; that's why he seemed so serious about coming to see me at my dad's!

I told Jack about that extra clue, and he added it to the investigation. Then he kept telling me everything they'd found out so far. And when he finished talking, I wanted to disappear.

Like, literally bury myself in the ground right there and never be seen again. I didn't know how I could face Alec or Nina or anyone else who knew my story—who had warned me about *him* before.

I'd been defending this guy since the day I found out the truth. I'd convinced myself that what we had was somewhat real. That he needed help, not punishment. That he'd had good intentions in his heart.

But, no—I was wrong. And I couldn't believe how wrong I was.

I tried to hold myself back, but I can't. I won't be able to… Not knowing you're there with him right now.

You said you would forget everything about him, Linda. And I can't keep my promise if you don't keep yours.

Please stay away. Please!
I don't want to end up hurting you more than I already have.

I read the message again and again. I didn't recognize the number, but I had no doubt it was him. Because he was throwing our promise in my face! He was using my fear as his weapon. He had given me his word that he would stay away from me and my family with *one* condition. And now he was reminding me that I was breaking that very condition by choosing to be with Alec.

Hypocrite. As if he hadn't broken the promise first, by going to West Virginia after me in August…

I still couldn't understand why he'd done that. My only explanation was that he wanted to silence me before I told anyone about him. That's why he didn't warn me by email or text—he had to catch me by surprise.

And I had not only slipped through his fingers but also become a threat to him. That's why he'd tried to use our promise to keep me away from Alec. He knew I had exposed his game when they put the note on Alec's website, but until the photos went public, he didn't know Alec was on my side. And the closer we got, the greater the chances of Alec putting the police after him. *That's* what he didn't want to happen.

I wondered how he'd reacted when I didn't answer him. When the pictures of Alec and I kept appearing in the magazines. He surely knew he was being hunted by now. And he probably hated my guts for it.

A shiver ran down my spine. Things had taken such a bad turn that I couldn't believe this was my life.

I asked Jack about the backstage clues, and Mr. Bear, Alec's shirt, his autographed CDs... I was so sure the impostor was someone from the crew that day at Alec's house—what had happened with all the evidence I brought him?

But Jack reminded me I had no proof to any of my backstage accusations, and that at this point, they were convinced the impostor had simply manipulated my perception of him. He could have mentioned the clothes Alec was wearing right after he appeared on TV, for example, then made me *think* he had actually mentioned it before the show. They thought *I* was the naive one, that's why he'd managed to fool me.

If the impostor was someone from Alec's circle, he would have told me about his vegan diet, for example—or that it was Ben in that photo with Hailey, not Alec. None of the information he gave me could be considered a real secret from the public eye, and Jack didn't believe this guy had privileged access to Alec anymore.

When I asked him about the objects, Jack told me that predators often go that far to fool their victims. They are very dedicated and smart, that's how they keep people believing in them. Details and backstory usually become an obsession, because they feel like they're playing a game. And the more addicted they get, the more they are willing to spend time, and money, and do whatever it takes to convincingly sustain the lie.

"What about James?" I played my last card. I thought I had good arguments; I thought I had proofs. But I felt as mature as a five-year-old when I heard myself saying the words out loud. "He looks at me strangely… He knows my favorite candy…"

I was pathetic for insisting on this. I knew it was a lost case. But Jack patiently explained why the impostor couldn't be someone from the crew anyway.

He had indeed investigated each one of them. James, for example, had been watched closely after his suspicious behavior at the studio. AJ had been cut from Alec's trip to Europe because of his emotional reaction to my panic attack over James. Jack had even considered Ben, when they realized he didn't have a solid alibi for the day the impostor went to West Virginia. Until Hailey confirmed Ben had secretly spent the weekend with her.

Jack told me he'd gone through every lead, but there was no proof to be found—against anyone. He really had exhausted all reasons for believing the impostor was someone from Alec's immediate circle. All the clues they had were leading to this guy in Sacramento. All the evidence proved that my heart was wrong.

Before I left the office, Jack told me he would personally keep me updated from now on. But I told him it wasn't necessary.

To me, the impostor died right there. I had zero interest in knowing anything about *him* anymore. I just wanted to be notified when he was arrested, so I could take one look at his picture and live my life as far from his face as possible. That was all.

Chapter 15

"So how was it with Jack?" Alec blurted the second Amanda left the dressing room with Carol and Claire.

I hadn't seen him in five days, and he'd been taken up by the press since the moment I arrived—I couldn't even kiss him yet. Then the first thing he asks me is this?

"Babe, I *really* don't want to talk about this now."

"But you already didn't want to tell me anything over the phone…" He frowned, leaning back on the dressing table.

The worry on his face made me think of my conversation with Nina—how she felt in August, when I was avoiding her questions. I didn't want Alec to start imagining distorted reasons for my silence. I didn't want him to think this had something to do with him.

"I'm just…I'm *disgusted*, okay? I don't want to recall it, that's all. Can we please not talk about this anymore?"

"Okay." He looked down, reaching for my hand. "Is there anything I can do to make things better?"

"Yes! Kiss me!" I raised my eyebrows, smiling at him.

Alec chuckled, then pulled me into his chest, kissing me gently.

"I missed you," he whispered.

"Me too." I wrapped my arms around his neck, playing with the little curls at the back.

"I wrote a song this week. I think it might be my best yet."

"Really? Can I hear it?"

"Not now—I want to make it special. It's about you…"

I bit the inside of my lip to control my excitement. "Does it have a title?"

"No More Lies," he said meaningfully.

"Oh." I had the feeling it wouldn't be one of his happiest songs.

"Seriously, fighting with you inspires me even more than being with you!" He let out a laugh.

"I'm gonna fight with you more often, then—to get you a couple more Grammy nominations," I teased. We'd just received the news yesterday that his new album had earned him two this year.

"Don't you dare!" He tickled my stomach. "I'd rather run out of songs."

I writhed, laughing out loud. Then I held his face in my hands and kissed his cheek. "I'm so proud of you."

"Thank you." His dimples sank deeper.

And he looked so cute that I couldn't resist. I had to kiss him again.

Then again. Then again.

He enjoyed my attack, chuckling. "I'm so happy we'll get to celebrate it tonight."

I stopped, serious.

"We're not?" he said in a high-pitched voice.

Alec wasn't going to Malibu after the show. He would be sleeping in a hotel in LA, and he'd invited me to stay with him.

I'd tried everything. Every argument, every bargain. But it

was all in vain. "Dad said I can go for an hour or two, but it's a school night—I have to sleep at home."

"What about Atlanta next week?" he said, hopeful.

And I sighed. "Sorry. It's the weekend before finals; he said I have to study."

Alec stared at me with a frown, then locked his arms around my waist. "Well, I'll take whatever I can get tonight, then." He lowered his lips to mine, urgent and hungry this time.

I grabbed the curls at the back of his head, deepening the kiss. And my heart pounded as I got lost in the warm taste of him, the familiar scent of his cologne. It'd been less than a week, but I missed him so much.

In one quick movement, Alec lifted me off the floor and changed our positions, sitting me on the table. I immediately wrapped my legs around his waist to pull him closer. And Alec pressed himself against me, searching for my mouth again.

"Jeez!" someone shouted.

I pushed him away in reflex, afraid it was one of our parents.

"You could at least... Anyone could have..." James's face went red, and he couldn't finish his sentence.

"Sorry." Alec shoved his hands into his pockets. "I forgot where we were."

I jumped off the table, embarrassed, adjusting my shirt. James was right, that was very reckless of us. There were way too many cameras in the building for Alec and I to be doing something like that.

"We have to go in ten minutes," James announced.

"Got it," Alec said, still trying to steady his breathing.

James didn't hear the answer, though. He had turned around and disappeared down the corridor.

How rude. He could have at least closed the door! I took a step forward so I could close it myself.

But Alec pulled me by the hand, his lips already back to my neck. "I missed you so much. Can we continue this later?"

"Yes." I breathed in his ear, completely helpless in his arms again.

"I can't wait." He tightened his grip on my waist, smashing our lips together, then went to the other side of the room to get ready.

"I think I'm gonna go." I headed to the door. I didn't want to keep distracting him. "I'll be watching with your mom and Ben, okay?"

He glanced at me while attaching his in-ear monitor to his waistband. "Now you're making me nervous."

"Me?"

"Yeah, I… I never had you in the audience before."

"That's not true, you know?" I giggled.

"But I barely knew you back then, so…" He took a deep breath.

"Are you serious? You're really anxious?"

"A little."

"Don't be." I walked to him, then took his heavy hands in mine. "I'm sure you'll be *great*."

"I'll be thinking about you." He tilted his head, dazzled.

And I grinned, searching for his lips one last time.

♪♩♡

"She looks like a mini version of you." Ben nodded at Claire, staring down at the crowd from the edge of the balcony.

"AJ said the same thing." I chuckled. "Thanks again, by the way, for her scholarship. She's loving her guitar lessons."

"You're welcome." He smiled.

"You're there on Mondays and Fridays, right? It's a shame it's not on the day of her lesson. I missed you this week—our snack time talks at Alec's rehearsals."

"I think next week I'll be there on Wednesday as well…"

"That's great! Maybe we can go for a coffee, then! AJ and I went to the café yesterday, while she was in class."

My father was forcing me to take Claire to the school myself. I guess he thought he was punishing me for getting her into music —or into Alec's world. But I loved to take her there. Especially now that I had AJ to wait with me.

"This seems to be going well, huh? You and AJ. You can't stop talking about him."

"Oh." I hadn't realized that. "I like him a lot, yeah. He's very pleasant to be around. And so funny." I giggled, remembering his morning jokes. "Matt is a lucky guy…"

"Wait, what?" Ben raised an eyebrow.

But Claire was suddenly in front of us, pressing her palms to my cheeks, forcing me to look into her eyes. "Why is this taking so long?" she shouted into my face.

She was wearing a pair of those sound-dampening earmuffs; she had no idea she was being that loud. So I took them off, pointing at the stage. "It's almost time, look! Everything is ready, and he's the first to perform."

"You've been saying this for ages! This is so boring!" She huffed, plopping down on my lap.

"I know, sweetie. I'm bored too." I thought about everything I could be doing with Alec right now… We definitely didn't need to have said goodbye so soon.

"So, you were telling me about you and AJ." Ben bumped his knee against mine.

"AJ is the best!" Claire spoke for me.

Ben's mouth fell open in surprise, so I explained, "Everyone in my house is kind of in love with—you know—my new *friend from school*."

"I see…" Ben nodded, serious.

"He's so cool! He gives us rides, and he brings us lollipops!"

I laughed at her enthusiasm.

"He's trying to steal Linda from Alec."

"*What?*" Ben and I said at the same time.

"That's what Daddy said—that he wants to be your new boyfriend."

Well, this explains things! I'd noticed my father seemed a little too accepting of my new friendship with AJ. He'd barely asked any questions before deciding he liked him, and he'd started to come say hello every time AJ picked me up for school. He'd even let AJ drive Claire and me to the music school yesterday, without any hesitation at all. Was that why? He thought AJ was trying to steal me from Alec? And he was actually rooting for him?

"Should I be worried about this?" Ben blurted. "I mean, for Alec…"

"No, of course not!" *He's gay! And he's dating your brother! And I'm dating your other brother, for God's sake!* I told him with my eyes. Or tried to. I hoped he understood.

"All right." Ben raised his palms defensively.

"Does it hurt?" Claire's attention had been caught by his wrist brace.

"A little. But it's getting better now." He smiled at her. And that's when he noticed the autograph on her T-shirt. "So you guys met *Tera*, huh?"

"We did." I rolled my eyes. "Claire insisted."

"And how was it?" Ben said, amused.

How was it to meet my boyfriend's beautiful, talented, and rich ex-girlfriend?

Let's just say, not great.

Until today, I could only imagine she was that perfect. Now, I had not only the confirmation in my head but also a few memories to prove it and keep as souvenirs. And to make things worse, she had been so nice to my sister—even gave her a shirt.

"It was awesome! I got her autograph, and we took pictures! I told her I was learning how to play the guitar so I could..." Claire rambled on.

But Ben kept staring at me. He wanted to hear *my* answer.

I exhaled. I couldn't believe he was making me say it out loud.

"She's cool, isn't she?" He read my face. "I'm glad she showed you there's no reason for you to keep hating her."

"No! I refuse to like her, okay?" I punched him in the arm. *Especially when* she's *the one traveling the country with my boyfriend for the next two weeks!*

Ben laughed so hard that I almost threw Claire's earmuffs at him. He was saved by the bell when the lights went off.

I put my sister's headphones back over her ears as the sudden earthquake of screams took over the room. The intro played on the big screen, announcing all the artists that would perform tonight. And I could only think of Alec, hidden somewhere behind that stage.

Was he nervous? Had he managed to control his anxiety?

I felt a little guilty for coming to the show. I didn't realize my presence here could make him even more anxious. I knew he had some serious pre-show crises sometimes, and I really didn't want this to happen today.

I held Claire in my arms, hoping everything was okay.

But then I realized, *of course* he was okay! They wouldn't be announcing him if he wasn't ready for the show!

The butterflies hurt my stomach. And when the screen started showing pieces of his face and clips of his biggest hits, I couldn't control myself anymore. I got up with Claire and screamed at the top of my lungs, like all the other fans.

Ben laughed mockingly next to me, but I didn't care. Not

about him, nor about who else was watching. I didn't even care about Tera anymore!

So what if she was pretty and nice and rich…and everything a guy could ask for? She wasn't the one Alec would be thinking about on that stage. She wasn't the one making out with him in the dressing room. She wasn't the one he was in love with.

He was mine, he loved *me*.

Reggie started the beat on the drums, and I noticed they were all in their places—Tom, Evan, and James. I searched for Alec through the flashes of light; the anticipation sent chills all over my body. And when he suddenly appeared on the stage, my heart raced. My head went blank. Alec Brock! My Alec! My baby! My *boyfriend* Alec Brock!

"It's him!" Claire looked up at me, ecstatic.

"Yeah, it's him." I hugged her tight, choking back tears.

I watched his voice taking over the arena, his presence filling up the stage. I think I'd never felt so proud in my entire life.

Alec's energy was unrecognizable. He was a completely different guy from the one I was kissing before—or the one I'd watched rehearsing all month at the studio. He grew bigger onstage, his soul expanded. So much that it touched every person in the crowd. We could all feel it. We could all feel *him*.

I glanced around at the venue, taking it all in. It gave me goosebumps; it made me stop breathing.

"LA, let me hear you screeeam!" He raised his microphone in the air, making everybody react to him.

And when I say everybody, I mean *everybody*! I couldn't see one person in the room who wasn't living that moment with him —singing out loud, crying their eyes out, or at the very minimum, paying close attention.

Alec had everyone's eyes on him. Thousands of eyes. Intense, watchful eyes.

But he didn't seem to be nervous at all. He was jumping and smiling and staring back—as present and focused as they were.

It wasn't a monologue, it was a conversation. A heart-to-heart. They understood each other; they were connected. And, to this day, that was one of the most beautiful things I have ever witnessed.

I beamed at him, singing his lyrics out loud. I was part of the crowd. I was one of his fans.

There were these girls in the front absolutely losing it. They had signs professing their love for him and kept their hands in the air, begging for physical contact. I thought I would, but I didn't have a single drop of jealousy in me at that moment. I was happy, actually, when Alec finally bent down and touched their hands.

I *wanted* him to give them his attention. One glance, one smile—it had the power to brighten up their lives. And I wanted to share him, I wanted him to give away as much of his light as he could. I wanted to see him lighting up the entire world.

"Feels like a dream come true?" Ben shouted in my ear.

"Yeah…" *Oh gosh, am I crying?* I chuckled, wiping away my tears.

"Good." He smiled. A very warm, dimpled smile. "I'm happy to see you happy. You really deserve it."

"Thank you, Ben." I gave him a side hug.

Benjamin wasn't one of the easiest people to connect with. He had this natural wall around him—not just anybody was allowed inside. But I was so glad he had let me in. So glad to have someone to live moments like this with me.

It felt like home to watch the concert by his side, because I *knew* he understood me. We had something in common—we shared Alec. So I didn't have to explain to Ben what I was feeling. He just knew. Because he was feeling it too.

For those who knew Alec like we did, watching him perform was like seeing a part of him hidden deep inside. It was rare to catch a glimpse of it. Maybe it took too much of him to show us; that's why he didn't do it so often.

But I recognized now the guy I'd been kissing before. All that energy, all that light—that wasn't an act. He wasn't pretending or putting on a show for anyone else. He was just all in, all there. He was showing us the highest expression of who he was. He was giving us one hundred percent of himself.

I grinned at the stage. His hair was all messy now, the curls sticking to his forehead. I could see the sweat, the pink on his cheeks, the effort he was making to sing. And I was so proud of him. So, so proud.

Chapter 16

There was this one problem, though. Alec's fans…they hated me.

I mean, really, really *hated* me.

I'd tried to ignore the glares I got at the concert yesterday. Which was very hard for me to do, because not only were they pretty obvious, but since I'd found out *someone* could be stalking me, I kind of panicked every time I caught people staring.

AJ had even invented a technique to keep me from going crazy. He poked my cheek every time he noticed I was anxious. He said it was a personal offense to see me stressed in his presence, since his only job was to make sure I was safe. And I didn't know how, but it actually worked. Whenever I was with him, I felt fine. It was like he had a special talent to distract me from my worries.

But the second he dropped me off at school, I felt vulnerable again. Girls' stares weren't as terrifying as men's. But still…it bothered me.

It was also getting harder to pretend it didn't annoy me to find their hate notes in my locker. Every. Single. Day.

And I'm not kidding—I'm talking actual hate notes. Like,

You're ugly, your cheeks are too big, or *Alec deserves so much better than you*, or *Go back to Mexico, you—* Some of them were too offensive for me to repeat.

I didn't even think they were all from my schoolmates anymore. I'd received so many today that I was convinced the news had spread and now his fans were sending notes through their friends. Because, seriously, this was ridiculous!

"Uh-oh, tough Friday?" AJ frowned when I hurried into the car after school. "What happened?"

"Nothing new. Just more of *the same*." I sighed, putting on my seatbelt. Then I glanced at myself in the external rearview mirror. "Do you think my cheeks are too big?"

"No! Your cheeks are perfect! Who told you that?"

"Thanks." I gave him a little smile but preferred not to explain.

He turned on the engine, studying my face. "I thought things were better after the photos with his brothers at the park."

"Yeah, I guess they were starting to believe we were all just friends. But today with the pictures from the concert…"

"But you weren't even *with* Alec! You were just watching the show with Ben!"

"I know… Apparently someone told the media they'd seen us making out backstage."

And to be honest, I had no idea if they had actually seen us or guessed right or if James had blabbed and people overheard it.

"You should tell Alec about these notes. Maybe he can—"

"No, I don't want to bother him with this. He already has too many reasons to worry about me. He doesn't need to go sleep at night thinking that besides having a stalker, I'm also being attacked by his fans…"

AJ snickered.

"What?" I looked at him sideways.

"Ben is right, you guys are making a storm in a teacup." He

laughed. "I mean, I like this job—I'm having fun with you. But do you really believe you're in *danger*?"

"I do! Don't you?" I turned my whole body to him in surprise.

"Well." He met my gaze, tense. "Don't tell anyone I said this, okay? I don't want to get in trouble. But have you ever thought that maybe this threatening message he sent you could be like one of these hate notes? Like, an impulsive act of jealousy or something?"

I narrowed my eyes. What was he talking about?

"I don't think this girl actually believes your cheeks are too big; she probably just wants to be in your place. The same way I don't think this guy is about to show up and physically hurt you— you know what I mean? Maybe he was just jealous that day because you were on a date with Alec."

"You don't know the details, AJ." I recalled all the horrible things Jack had told me. "He even went to my house in August, to catch me by surprise!"

"Maybe he had other intentions, who knows?" He shrugged.

I couldn't believe what I was hearing. Nobody had ever *defended* the impostor to me before. "Are you saying that you don't believe he's *bad*?"

"I don't know, Linda. I'm just saying that people don't always say what they mean. Or mean what they say… Or do! Urgh, forget it." He shook his head, exhaling.

I smiled at his troubled face. I really liked AJ; he had a good heart. With him, things were never black or white—he was willing to go deeper and analyze all the different shades of gray. He believed in good, he believed in people. Just like me, just like my heart.

But this time, my heart was wrong. And so was AJ.

I remembered my conversation with Jack again—the stories I'd heard about the four other girls. Impostor Alec wasn't the guy

I thought he was. As much as I wanted to believe he was good, I couldn't lie to myself anymore. I couldn't have that kind of hope.

"Great. Now *I* got you upset!" AJ rolled his eyes at himself. "Please, just stop thinking of him. Or any of this, okay? You're beautiful, and you're safe." He poked my face. "Let's talk about something else…"

I giggled, listening to him ramble about this burger place I had to try. And by the time I got home, AJ had managed to take the impostor out of my mind.

But the hate notes, I couldn't forget. I kept thinking about them all weekend.

How can I make them stop hating me? What can I do to win over Alec's fans?

On Monday, I decided not to clean my locker—only to find double the volume of letters on Tuesday morning. So I fought back and wrote a message to put on the door, addressing all the haters. But by lunchtime, I had an extra bunch of notes, even more aggressive than usual.

I really didn't know what to do. This was snowballing into a nightmare!

"Seriously, they can't be just from our school." I dropped my backpack filled with two days' worth of notes on our lunch table.

Aisha leaned forward to examine them. "Maybe. People talk —his fans might be asking their friends to bring these to you."

"I have to find a way to make them stop." I sighed.

"Why don't you send everything to Alec? This is *his* problem, not yours," Liz said.

"I don't want him to worry about this. Plus, they're addressed to me, not him. It's *me* that they hate…"

"This one is nice." Sam showed me one of the letters.

I took the paper from her hand.

Dear Linda,

I know you probably won't read this but I just wanted to say that I support you and Alec. He looks happier in the pictures, and that means the world to me. So as long as he is happy, I'm happy.

Sincerely,

Sarah Williams

I grinned at Sam. "Do you know who the girl is?"

She shook her head.

"Who?" Liz glanced at the name on the note. "I think she's the blonde with the braces, from English class."

"No, that's *Cara* Williams," Aisha said, scanning the room. "Sarah is the brunette over there." She pointed at the fourth table behind ours. "The petite one with the glasses."

I was so moved by that one cute note in the middle of all the hate that I didn't think twice. I thanked Aisha and walked straight to Sarah.

She slid down on her chair, her eyes wide behind the big, round glasses.

I stood in front of her, with the note in my hands. And suddenly, everybody fell quiet to pay attention to us. The whole school had been witnessing the bullying for over a month now, and they'd never seen me react—ever! This was the first time I'd personally confronted someone, and they obviously expected something different from what I was about to say.

"Thank you, Sarah. This was very kind of you. I'll make sure Alec reads it." I smiled at her. And her face lit up like a Christmas tree.

"Th-thank you," was all she could say.

I gave her another smile, then walked back to my table—kind of enjoying the shocked stares being thrown at me.

The girls helped me scan the rest of the notes, and I was excited to see there were two other kind ones—both from freshmen. I put their letters in my backpack and personally thanked them too before the last bell rang.

"You seem happier today." AJ half-smiled, watching me get into the car.

"I am." I told him all about the kind notes on our way home.

The next day, I couldn't believe my eyes. There was still a lot of hate, yeah, but over half of the notes in my locker were nice! They were all addressed to Alec, not me—but it didn't matter, at least they were *nice*.

I got curious, of course, so I took them with me to read during class. And that was a big mistake, because they were way too distracting. One of the letters was from a girl who was literally still alive because of him! She had almost committed suicide last year, but Alec had become part of her life on such a deep level that his music gave her strength to stay strong. I had tears in my eyes when I finished it. I couldn't wait to tell him all this on the phone tonight.

At lunchtime, I hesitated over whether I should go talk to her. But it didn't seem enough to just reassure this girl that I would give her letter to Alec. I felt like she deserved more. I wanted to give her a little bit of his light—to get her a little piece of him.

So I texted Ben: **Hey! Do you think you can get me something from Alec? Like a guitar pick or an autograph? Did he leave anything like that in the house?**

Yeah, I can find something. Why? he replied.

It's for a fan, I'll explain later. You're still coming to the music school this afternoon, right?

Yes. I'll meet you there, he sent with a smiley face.

I kept reading the letters during my next classes, so I had to text Ben again and ask him to bring as many autographs as he could. AJ laughed out loud when I told him my plan. But I couldn't leave these girls without an answer, really! If Alec was in LA, I think I would have invited them all to my house and asked him to show up so they could actually meet him.

"You can't do this—you know that, right?" Ben widened his eyes in shock. "If you throw an 'Alec party' at your house, you'll never have peace again. And he has his own mailbox; why are you even receiving these letters?"

"They were initially hate notes—to me," I started to explain. But Ben knit his brows, even more alarmed than before.

"Let her play fairy godmother, bro." AJ exchanged a glance with Ben. "I think it might help with *the stress*."

"All right." Ben met my gaze, concerned, then reluctantly gave me the little box that held autographed postcards and a few guitar picks. "I'm gonna go gather my things, but you'll have to explain what's going on at your school when we get to the café, okay?"

"Sure. Thanks, Ben." I grinned.

He turned around, searching for his violin. And that's when my heart stopped.

"Claire!" She was sitting on the floor, staring at the open case. "Don't touch that! Come here!"

That thing was three hundred years old. It was worth more than a car! How could Benjamin leave it on the floor like that? Especially with a kid in the room?

"Can I play it?" Claire asked Ben, totally ignoring me.

"No!" I rushed in her direction.

"I asked Benjamin, not you," she said icily.

And he chuckled behind me. "Sure."

My stomach froze. "No, Ben! It's too expensive, she's gonna ruin it!"

"I'll be holding it too; it's okay." He knelt next to her, taking the violin in his hands.

"It's so beautiful." Claire's eyes blazed.

"I know, right?" Ben's eyes blazed just as much.

"Please, don't." I squeezed his shoulder. "It's too fragile, Claire. You saw it out of the case, that's good enough. Now let's go!"

Ben glanced up at me as if saying, *I don't mind, you know?*

But I kept my stern face. It was just a stupid and unnecessary risk that I didn't want to take.

"You know what, Claire? This one is too big anyway. Come here, I have something more appropriate for you to play." He put his violin back and led her to a full wall cabinet.

Claire's jaw dropped when he showed her a mini case.

"There you go!"

"Is it a baby violin?" She beamed.

"It's a one-eighth size." Ben positioned it on her shoulder. Then he straightened her arm so she touched the top. "See? This one is your perfect fit."

"I bet she's gonna switch instruments," AJ whispered to me when Ben gave her the bow.

And I knew he was right. I'd never seen Claire so enchanted by anything in my life.

Chapter 17

So far, I had surprised Claire with the music scholarship and Nina with a fun day at the park. And I was kind of proud—it had been good to see the joy in their eyes. Plus, I loved them with all my heart, so to see them happy automatically made *me* happy.

I had no idea, though, that surprising a stranger would feel so much better.

It's just a guitar pick, I said to myself. But Anna—the girl who'd almost committed suicide—hugged me as if I'd given her a diamond or something. It even took me a minute to remember I also had an autographed photo for her. And when she saw it in my hands, she cried! I'm serious—actual tears!

I guess we never know how much things mean to people. And we definitely don't need to do anything big to make someone happy. We just have to find out what's important to them.

All I knew was that I'd never felt so *alive* before. The look on her face was simply…I didn't even have a word for it. Now I understood why the Brocks were so addicted to these surprises. I couldn't stop thinking about my next one.

I spent the whole Thursday reading more letters in class. Alec had helped one girl to get over her parents' divorce and another girl to come out to her family as a lesbian. There was also this kid who'd started playing guitar because of him and these two best friends who met while waiting in line for one of his concerts. The stories were so heartfelt that I decided to answer them—all of them. I would write a little note, telling the fans I would make sure Alec received their letters, and send it back along with an autographed postcard.

AJ didn't think I should do it; he thought it was too much work for nothing. But, honestly, I felt like I was getting more out of it than the fans. Reading those letters made me feel closer to Alec. He'd been on tour for two weeks now—he barely had time to text or talk on the phone. And with all this distance between us, I felt myself slowly plunging into the darkness again. This constant anxiety of not knowing who the impostor was, combined with the fear of maybe being next to him right now and not even knowing it, was leaving me in desperate need of Alec's brightness. And to me, every single one of those letters…they came with a bit of his light.

I guess that was also why I enjoyed AJ's company so much. He was part of Alec's world, and every time we were together, it was like Alec was there with us. So spending time with AJ not only made me feel safe, but also warmed me up inside.

He was right, by the way. All Claire talked about now was her baby violin and how much she wanted to learn how to play it.

Dad and Caroline were so impressed by her sudden change of instrument that they decided to come to the music school with us on Friday afternoon. That's when Ben taught his beginners' lessons to five- and six-year-olds. Dad asked him if my sister wasn't too young. But Ben said he'd started when he was only three and that Claire seemed to learn things fast—he wasn't worried about her at all.

I was surprised, actually, to see how well Dad interacted with Ben. I thought he didn't like Alec's world, but I guess he just didn't like *Alec*. He only had a problem with Claire wanting to become a pop star; her wanting to be a classical violinist was totally okay. He even put an end to my punishment, saying that since her lessons were now on Fridays, Caroline was available to take her—they didn't need me to do it anymore.

But I told Dad I would probably keep taking her anyway. I was happy to have an excuse to see Ben every week. Besides, he said I could watch the lessons if I wanted—and I had to agree with Dad, baby violins were way cuter than baby guitars. When I saw her new classmates all holding those little things, my heart just melted.

The sound, on the other hand, was a lot sharper—and painfully high-pitched. Yeah, it was cute to see her with the instrument, but it was a whole different thing to hear her playing it. Especially when it's on Saturday morning—at your house—in the room right across from yours.

"Ahhh! I can't take this any longer!" I said to AJ, covering my ears with my hands. I could barely listen to my thoughts, let alone concentrate on the pile of papers in front of me.

"Look on the bright side—the more she practices, the better she's going to sound. It might take a year or two, but she's gonna get there." AJ chuckled, giving me another form to sign.

"Oh my gosh, I'm gonna have to move out! I can't—the guitar wasn't so bad, but this? It's like she's killing a cat!"

He laughed out loud. And the amusement on his face made me laugh at him.

I was so glad AJ had offered to come help me with my college applications. I was only applying to UCLA and a few other fall-back options in California, but each school had its own list of requirements—it was a total nightmare! Some submissions were online, others on paper; I had to make sure the essays were perfect, all the documents were there, everything had been filled in and signed and organized. I'd been feeling overwhelmed for weeks, just thinking about it. But with AJ here, helping me focus, things had gone a lot smoother. And what I'd thought would take me all day was done by lunchtime.

"I can't believe I did it." I let out a breath, staring at the two envelopes on my desk. All that was left was to put them in the mail—the other applications had already been sent online.

"Yeah, now you just have to wait." AJ smirked, flipping a USB drive between his fingers.

I tilted my head. "Where did that come from? Is it yours?"

"Yep." He got up, shoving the flash drive into his pocket. "Are you ready to go to the post office?"

My stomach froze as I glanced at the envelopes again. "It's all right, I'll post them on Monday."

"Let me guess… You want to double-check everything."

"You know me." I chuckled.

"You seriously need to stop overthinking things." He rolled his eyes.

"And you need to start being less…*carefree*. How can you even live like this? Never worrying about anything?" I honestly didn't get how he could stay so calm at all times.

"I do worry about things…"

"Oh yeah? Tell me *one thing* you worry about."

He held my gaze for a second, as if preparing to say something serious, but then his mood shifted. "Lunch! I'm very worried about that. Let's go somewhere?" He turned around, heading to the door.

"I can't. This is the weekend before finals, I—"

"Come on, girl—live a little! You've studied every night this week! And you know you won't be able to concentrate with this serenade." He nodded toward Claire's room.

I sighed, rubbing my face with my hands. My head was already aching from the hours of torture. And AJ was right, I did deserve a break.

"All right." I reached for my bag. "But you have to take me to that burger place you've been bragging about!"

"It's like you're reading my mind." He beamed.

♪ ♩ ♡

The tiny diner was located in AJ's neighborhood. He showed me his house on the way there, and I was happy to see it was even a little smaller than mine. We really belonged to the same world. And since our boyfriends both lived across the borders of the other world, AJ and I understood each other like no one else—despite having such different person-alities.

"I'm telling you, this is going to be the best meal you've ever had," he said, after ordering the famous burger he'd been pitching to me all week.

"We'll see." The waitress seemed more worried about the TV behind the counter than about sending our order to the kitchen, so my hopes weren't high.

"I know, the service sucks. But I promise you, the burger is worth it. Even their veggie option is out of this world! Matt is crazy about this place." He grinned.

I held back a smile, studying his face. It had lit up at the mention of his boyfriend's name. "You never talk to me about Matt…"

AJ dropped his eyes. Which I thought was cute, because this seemed to be the only subject he was shy about.

"You don't have to—if you don't want," I continued. "I just… I don't know. I guess I just realized we're always talking about *me*. Never about *you*."

"What do you want to know?" His voice was low.

·I thought my first question would be about Matt, but all of a sudden, something else crossed my mind. "Why didn't you want to keep playing with Alec? I mean, if James is still in the band, why didn't you—"

"I never felt like I was good enough to play professionally," he said with a shrug. "I started playing with them for fun. It was never serious for me—like it was for Alec."

"Oh." I really wasn't expecting that. From what Alec had told me, I was guessing it'd been because of the disagreement between him and the rest of the band. I thought AJ had been offended or something. "Are you still friends with the others, then?"

"James, yeah—love that dude. But Zach..." He rolled his eyes. "He's too stubborn, you know?"

"No, actually. Everybody refuses to tell me anything about him..." I glanced up at AJ from under my lashes.

He laughed out loud. "I assure you there's a good reason for that, miss. So, don't you try to take advantage of me!"

"Come on, is he really that bad?" I made a pleading face.

"Yes! He's been a jerk to Alec for years! Now, drop it, okay? That is all you need to know about him."

"Fine," I muttered. "I'll ask him next time."

"What do you mean *next time*?" AJ narrowed his eyes.

"We talked a little bit at the Halloween party. And to be honest, he seemed pretty nice before Alec arrived—as if he was genuinely worried about me. I think he was trying to—"

AJ shook his head. "It's unbelievable how he does it..."

"Does what?"

"Tricks people into thinking whatever it is that *he* wants you to think." He snorted. "If you see him again, you ignore him, okay? I mean it, don't listen to him—just call me or Alec!"

His reaction surprised me. AJ was the kind of guy who searched for the good in people. If he had given up on Zach, maybe there was really nothing good to be found there.

"Okay?" he repeated, louder.

"Okay," I murmured. But then something didn't make sense in

my head. "Why is James still friends with him, then? If he's *that* bad?"

"They're cousins. You can't break that kind of bond."

"So *that's* why Zach listened to him at the party…" It all made sense to me now. "That's why he prevented the fight!"

"*Fights*, plural. James has been trying to mediate things between those two since Alec got signed. But, as I said, Zach is just too stubborn… And enough with these questions about him! I've already told you more than I should."

"All right." I leaned back against my seat, still thinking about that night. "What about Hailey? What is this toxic thing going on between her and Ben?"

After our little talk that day in his car, I thought Ben would break up with her for good. But Alec was all stressed out this week because he'd found out they'd been secretly seeing each other again.

"Oh, that one, I guarantee, is a total player. They deserve each other, her and Zach."

"Are they a thing too?" I raised my brows.

"I don't know. Hailey is—she has a lot of *friends*, you know what I mean?"

"Yeah." Alec had already told me that she slept around a lot. That was one of the reasons he hated her: she had repeatedly cheated on Ben.

"And Benjamin knows it, but…" AJ shrugged.

"I don't get it. He's such a deep person; how can he date someone shallow like her?"

"Well, they say a man never forgets his first love… But I think there's something wrong with him lately—these college auditions are messing with his nerves. Maybe that's why he started partying with Hailey again."

"I'm thinking of introducing Sam to him. She's going through the same thing with her oboe auditions. It might be good for them both, to have someone to talk… And she's pretty, right? Do you think she's his type?"

"A redhead? I don't know. The twins have always had the same taste in girls—I think you'd better find him a Latina." He chuckled, checking me out.

It made my cheeks burn, so I dodged his gaze, glancing at the waitress. I was hoping to see her bringing our order, but she seemed distracted, her eyes glued to the TV.

"What about you and Alec?" AJ rested his elbows on the table, still watching me.

"What about us?"

"Isn't it—confusing for you? You were in love with this person and now you're dating only his body…"

"I'm not dating only his body!" I laughed.

"You know what I mean." He half-smiled. "Don't you ever get confused and think about the other guy?"

"No," I said sharply. "Especially now that I know he's a monster—a professional *liar*."

"And before that?" AJ insisted. "Did you used to get confused in the beginning? Right after you met the real Alec?"

"Not really… Back then, I wasn't in love with *Alec*, you know? It was actually easy to separate them in my mind because I didn't recognize the guy I loved in Alec.

"I've always been crazy attracted to him, of course, but it wasn't love. What I feel for him today started later…after we became friends." I grinned, remembering our last kiss at his hotel. *Six more days, and I'll have his kisses back.*

"So you really moved on, then," AJ said. "From one to the other."

"Yeah. I guess I did."

"But if you had to move on, it means that it was *real*."

I knit my brows, not sure where he was going with that.

"Do you really think you *loved* the impostor? I mean, do you honestly believe that true love happens on this *soul level?* And that it doesn't matter what he looks like, or his race, or body shape—or even his gender?"

"Yes," I said without hesitation. "I know he never deserved it, but what I felt for him back then was real." So real that it still hurt me, the fact that for him it had all been a joke.

"That's—beautiful." AJ pressed his lips together. "You're very brave for admitting you loved someone like that... Especially after everything he did to you."

His eyes lingered on mine. And I had this bad feeling. A cold shiver.

I didn't realize AJ's phone was buzzing until he put it to his ear.

"Hello?" I watched his face fall, his expression turn darker.

My stomach tightened. AJ never worried about *anything*.

Something was wrong. Something was really, really wrong.

"No, she's with me... Okay... I will." He said goodbye to the person on the line.

But when I asked him what happened, he avoided my gaze and rushed to the counter instead. "Can we have our order to go, please?" he spoke to the waitress.

"What's happening?" I grasped his arm.

"I'll explain in the car, okay? We have to go home." His face was a mix of fear, sympathy, and regret.

My heart pounded, anticipating the wave. I knew it was coming, I knew it was about to hit me.

And that's when I heard the TV.

"...Alec Brock has been arrested..."

I spun around to look at it. There was another face next to Alec's on the screen. The face of a white middle-aged man.

"The forty-six-year-old pedophile..."

Realization knocked all the air out of my lungs.

"Two cases confirmed and hundreds of photos..."

"…in Sacramento…"

"…by the Internet Crime Against Children…"

Each word burned in my chest like consecutive bullets. I couldn't move, I couldn't dodge. I just stood there—taking the hits.

Chapter 18

"**I** love you," Alec said on the other end of the line.

My heart skipped a beat. It had only been a couple of months since we exchanged phone numbers, but I couldn't say I was surprised.

First, the daily conversation in the chat room wasn't enough. Then texting all day wasn't enough. Then calling every night wasn't enough... I knew we would have to say it soon. It was the last barrier—the final way to feel his touch.

I couldn't explain how it was possible to be in someone's arms when we were that far apart. But that's how I felt. That's how his words made me feel.

With Alec, there was no time or space. No physical limitations, nothing to get in our way. Whenever we talked, we were connected from heart to heart. We were two souls in this different dimension, perfectly capable of touching each other.

"It's okay, you don't have to say it back. I just said it because—"

"I do." I smiled, pressing the phone to my ear. "I love you too."

. . .

"AJ, let me talk to her right now!"

"You're on the speaker, Alec! She's listening to you! I'm serious, I don't know what to do—I think she's in shock!"

"Babe? Babe? Linda, talk to me!"

"I'm gonna take her to the hospital…"

"Baby, can you hear me? Linda? LINDA?"

"I'm here," the words fell out of my mouth, though I didn't feel any of them.

"Thank God." Alec exhaled on the phone. "How are you? Is it a panic attack?"

I took a deep breath, regaining my senses. I was in AJ's car, parked outside the diner. *How did I get here?*

"AJ, tell me how she looks!"

"I'm fine. No panic attack," I answered first. I felt calmer than usual, actually. My whole body was…numb.

"You tuned out, Linda!" AJ widened his eyes. "You scared the hell out of me!"

"Sorry," I murmured.

"How is she?" Alec shouted.

"I'm fine, Alec! Relax!"

"Take me off the speaker," he ordered. "I want to talk to you alone."

"I'm gonna…wait outside." AJ opened the door, handing me his phone.

"Babe?" Alec's tone was soft now.

"Yes?"

"I'm *so sorry*. I wish I could come to stay with you tonight."

"I'm okay. Don't worry," I said, my voice dead.

"Is there anything I can do? I'll call you after the show, of course—but do you want me to do something else?"

"No, I'm fine."

"I'm gonna ask Dr. Brown to—"

"No, Alec! I don't want to talk about this."

"Okay." He breathed.

We both fell silent, feeling each other's presence. I couldn't help but notice that his light didn't touch me this time. Maybe the darkness in me had become just too heavy.

"I'm really sorry," he whispered.

"It's okay, I'm okay."

It's okay, I'm okay...

SUNDAY, DECEMBER 14

"They arrested another one?" Caroline widened her eyes at the TV.

"Not one, two!" Dad said, turning up the volume. "The FBI is going after all the catfishes using teen artists' profiles."

"That's ridiculous! How can these kids fall for this?"

"It's the parents' fault." Dad shook his head. "If they spent more time educating their children, they wouldn't be out there—talking to strangers on the internet."

"Did you see the number of photos they found with the first one? He's been doing this for years!"

"It's disgusting… People like him should never be allowed to leave jail."

Happy birthday, Alec texted.

Thank you! I grinned at my phone and searched for a quieter room, ignoring the party happening around me.

Did you get my surprise?

I did. Thank you so much! It's the most beautiful teddy bear I've ever seen, Alec. It was hard to explain why I was receiving gifts in the mail, but it was totally worth it. I love it!

I'm so glad you liked it! It took me half an hour to choose which one was the best. LOL. I wish I was there to see you open it...

Me too...

"There you are!" Dad found me in the kitchen. "What are you doing there? It's your birthday party—people are here to see you!"

"I'm coming," I answered, distracted, sending Alec another text.

"It's like this now, Joel..." Abuela said in Spanish. "When she's not on the computer, she's on her phone. It's like suddenly her family is not as important to her anymore."

"It's a phase, Mother. She's just being a teenager." Dad rolled his eyes. "At least she's safe at home—not out there doing drugs or getting pregnant."

"Did you hear about the guy pretending to be Alec on the internet?"

Sam's comment tied my stomach in a knot.

"I saw it on the news! Everyone is talking about it!" Aisha raised her brows.

"How is Alec doing, Linda?" Sam turned to me. "I saw that he refused to talk to the media—did he say anything to you?"

"No." I dodged her eyes, pretending to be busy with my plate.

"Poor girls." Aisha shook her head.

"More like *stupid girls*… Seriously, I'm struck by how dumb a person can be to believe Alec Brock would be on the internet, talking dirty to you." Liz scoffed, making everybody laugh.

"Yeah." I sighed. *Very dumb.*

"Did you receive the photos?" I asked, already regretting the email I'd just sent.

"Yes." Alec's voice faded to a whisper.

"So…" I bit my lip, my heart racing in my chest.

"You're so beautiful."

I breathed in relief.

"More beautiful than any other girl I've ever seen."

I cracked a smile.

"Thank you for trusting me."

"Don't forget your promise! You can't ever, ever, EVER show these to anyone, okay?"

"Of course, baby, I would never do that. I love you!"

TUESDAY, DECEMBER 16

"I can't stop *remembering* him. What's happening to me?" I broke down in tears.

"These are called flashbacks, honey." Dr. Brown wrote something on her notepad. "It's another symptom of post-traumatic stress disorder. Like the intrusive thoughts we've been working on."

"No, this is different. It's not just a thought—it feels like I'm there, living the scene all over again!" I shook my head in panic, trying to slow down my breathing.

"That's a flashback, yes. Whenever a trigger evokes the memory, your brain activates the same neurochemical cascade as the original event, making you experience the same feelings and emotions as if they were happening right now."

I glanced at her, startled. She kept talking to me about possible treatments, but all I could think about was that he had officially done it. He had literally made me go insane.

"Close your eyes," Alec said.

"Done." My face warmed, anticipating what it would be this time. He was asking me to imagine a lot of things lately.

"Now, feel me lying next to you... Our legs are tangled, your knee over mine. I have one arm around your neck, and my other hand is rubbing yours."

"I'm actually feeling you right now. Can you believe it?"

"I do—I can feel you too. The smell of your hair, the warmth of your skin..."

"The sound of your heartbeat," I added with a grin.

"Let's not say goodbye tonight, okay? I want to sleep with you."

"All right." I hugged him in my head and fell asleep in his arms for the first time.

"Linda, you have to talk to me. Please, don't go down that road again."

"There's nothing to talk about, Nina. They caught all the main suspects; it's over!"

"Did the detective confirm it was him? The guy from Sacramento?"

"They haven't found my pictures yet, if that's what you're asking," I snapped.

"Linda—"

"No, Nina, enough! What part of 'I don't want to talk about this' don't you get?"

She sighed on the line.

"I'm fine, okay? Stop worrying about me!"

"Thank you for trusting me."

"It's nothing, Sam. I'm fine…"

"You're so beautiful."

"It's okay, Liz. I'm fine…"

"Can you feel it? Can you feel me there with you?"

"Thanks, AJ, but I'm fine…"
"I love you."
"Please, Dad—leave. I said I'm fine!"

"No, it's okay. I'm glad you came." I heard my father in the hallway outside my room. "But I think she's already asleep."

I turned to the other side of the bed, pretending I was indeed sleeping. I bet it was Ben again. Alec had sent him to check on me a couple of times since Saturday.

"She hasn't been feeling very well this week," Dad continued. "She says she's stressed because of finals, but I think she—she misses you."

"I miss her too, sir." Alec's voice made my heart jump.

What is he doing here?

No, I must be hallucinating. Alec had a concert this evening— he's not coming back till tomorrow!

"Linda?" Dad opened the door a crack.

I turned on my lamp. And I couldn't believe my own eyes—it was really him!

"You're awake!" Alec grinned, coming toward me.

"I'm gonna let you two…" Dad stepped aside, then closed the door behind him.

Alec frowned in reflex. "Did he actually close the door? With *me* in here?"

I let out a laugh, reaching for his hand, and pulled him down onto the bed with me. "What are you doing in LA? I thought you would—"

"I got on the plane right after the show," he said, snuggling me into his chest.

I raised my head to look at him. "I can't believe you're here."

He brushed his lips against mine, then smiled at me with worried eyes. "I'm so sorry. I came as fast as I could."

I buried my face in his chest again, feeling my darkness take over the room. And by the way Alec tightened his arms around me, I knew he could feel it too.

We stayed like that for a moment, just being with each other. We knew what was coming. We would have to have *that* conversation. But neither of us seemed ready for it yet.

"How are you?" He broke the silence.

"I've been better," I said, honoring our No More Lies policy.

"I know…" He rested his chin on top of my head. "Everybody is worried about you—AJ, Ben, Nina, even your dad!" He chuckled. "He wouldn't have closed the door if you were okay."

"I will be." I thought about the treatments Dr. Brown had suggested to fix me, then grabbed his hand, lacing our fingers together.

But suddenly, it didn't feel so right anymore. It didn't feel like it was *fair* to him.

I sat upright, letting go of his hand. *Alec deserves better than this.*

"What are you doing?" He lowered his brows. But realization was crashing through my mind and the tears didn't let me speak.

I crawled to the foot of the bed so he wouldn't see my face, but it only made me cry even more. I had taped up photos of Alec and I to decorate that wall—the two of us in his house laughing, kissing, making fun of each other. Ben had this Polaroid camera that he let me borrow whenever I was there. And now I had all these memories—real memories—of Real Alec. And not even that had been enough…

My hands started trembling as I remembered the words Alec had said to me on the boat: *If I rewrite your story with me, like this… Doing things you never imagined you would do with him, creating new memories for you to rely on—I'm sure I can make you forget. Before you realize it, you won't remember the fake moments anymore.*

He was wrong. The old memories…they would never go away. They couldn't be replaced! They couldn't be erased!

"Linda, please, talk to me." Alec stroked my arm.

"Don't!" I yanked it away, having another flashback. I felt so dirty, so used, so stupid—I couldn't even let him touch me anymore.

Every single one of those hate notes, they were right. He deserved better. He deserved so much better! He shouldn't be here, he shouldn't be with *me*. He should be with someone like Tera, who was clean and bright like him.

"Baby, what's happening?"

This guy—this man—he'd never touched me, but there were fingerprints of him all over my soul. And I couldn't wash them away. I couldn't rub them off. I couldn't scrub my skin hard enough. As much as I tried, I couldn't get myself clean again! I was marked for life—I would never be the same!

"Hey…" Alec walked around the bed and lowered himself to his knees in front of me. "It's okay if you don't want to talk about it. I just want you to know that—"

"It's just a wave," I finished his sentence. That's what he always said whenever we had a challenge coming our way.

"Well, that too… But that's not what I was going to say." He smiled, taking my hands in his.

And I surrendered to his touch this time. I didn't want to contaminate him with my darkness, but I was too selfish not to enjoy the last moments I would have with him.

"What I wanted to say is that… Baby, to me, you're a heroine! I can't even imagine how you must be feeling right now, but I want you to remember that your pain saved those girls, Linda. Who knows how many others would have fallen into the same trap after you? And now that the media is talking about it, you will probably save a lot more—all over the country!

"You not only stopped what was going on here, but you helped to raise awareness of this happening to people! I'm so proud of you—for being the one who had the courage to start this war!"

I didn't do anything. He did! He—and his father—and Jack. I'm just one of the hundreds of victims—a public humiliation.

"Talk to me, baby…" He kissed my palm. "You know you'll feel better after you say it out loud."

I need to let him go. I can't do this to him anymore. I opened my mouth, and tears streamed down my cheeks—but it hurt too much. I didn't have the guts to say it.

"Talk to me," he whispered again. And our eyes locked.

My God, his eyes—his green eyes! Will I survive this? Will I be able to go through all of this without him?

I will have to! He deserves better. I need to do right by him.

"Alec, I…"

"I'm here. I'm listening." He sat next to me on the bed, rubbing my hand with his thumb.

"I'm…" I took a deep breath. "I'm really thankful for everything you've done for me. For illuminating my life when I needed it the most. For helping me get to the end of this—to the truth. And I have no idea how I'm gonna survive this without you but… you have to go."

"What?" He widened his eyes at me.

"You deserve better." I sobbed. "So much better!"

"Are you breaking up with me?" His voice cracked.

"You're pure *light*, Alec. And I'm all *darkness*. I don't want to hold you back, I want you to shine! And I can't get rid of it—his hands, his fingerprints—I've tried!" I scrubbed my arms hard in despair, wishing for the millionth time that I could wash away the memories of his touch. "He marked me *for life*. You deserve someone clean!"

All of a sudden, Alec wasn't listening anymore; his attention had been caught by my forearm. He held it tight and rolled up the sleeve of my pajamas, uncovering my red, irritated skin.

"I wanna kill him!" He got up, his hands on his face. "If he wasn't already in jail, I think I—" He stopped mid-sentence to take a deep breath.

"You should go." I pulled down my sleeve in shame. "I'm really sorry I involved you in my mess. I should have never told you anything."

Alec took another deep breath, then moved my desk chair to sit across from me. "Listen to me, I'm not gonna let this *monster* make you believe you don't deserve to be happy, okay?" He looked me in the eyes. "I know you don't really want me to leave, and I'm not going anywhere. We're gonna get through this together!"

"No." I shook my head. "I *want* you to go. I want you to have *more*, Alec! Please, you know it's the best for you."

"*You* are the best for me!"

"How can you say this? Haven't you heard what everybody thinks of me? What they're saying about the victims? Haven't you realized how *stupid* I am? How much damage he did to me?" I burst into tears.

"Baby, you're not damaged." He caught my hands again, his eyes in pain. "This is just an opportunity to grow from your mistakes. What he did to you—what happened to you—doesn't define who you are! Your actions do! That's what counts, how you choose to *react*! And you've been fighting back with so much grace, Linda. Look what you did last week with the bullying at your school! You fought hate with kindness until you turned it into love. Literally! You're receiving love letters now!"

"They're for *you*!"

"No—don't you see? It's *you*! Everything you touch, baby, you turn it into love. That's how you always react—that's who you really are!" He gave me a tender smile. "When I met you, your world had been completely wrecked by this guy. And instead of just falling apart, you came after me—you decided to speak up! Then you took your pain and turned it into hope with this investigation, for all these girls you are helping to save now. They've arrested *nine* pedophiles, Linda—in less than a week! Do you realize how many kids you've saved so far?"

Nine already? My chest tightened, thinking about all the girls out there feeling as dirty and used as me.

"You are *amazing*, babe. I saw it the first time we met! I remember—you looked at me as if I was yours, and your eyes touched me so deeply that here we are now." He chuckled. "I'm all yours!"

"You know you deserve better than me, Alec," I said, meaning every word.

And he sighed. "How can you still not see it?"

I lowered my head. I just wanted him to leave. I was too ashamed to look at him.

"Do you know the first thing I told my mom about you? After our breakfast at the hotel?" He cupped my face in his hands and wiped my tears with his thumbs. "That I'd never met anyone brave enough to follow her heart like this. To move across the country chasing love, with no guarantees at all. Right then I knew you were a real believer—like me.

"I deeply admired you for that. Because you'd turned fear and uncertainty into courage, into faith. And you were so driven, baby, that despite everything, you ended up getting *exactly* what you came here for." He showed me his dimples, pointing at himself.

I had to smile. "How did this happen?" Now, looking back like this, I couldn't explain how we'd ended up here.

"*You* did it! By being courageous and selfless and kind. You turned your tragedy into love. You turn everything you touch into love…" He tilted his head, watching me.

My eyes burned with tears again. My thoughts were running too fast—my head and my heart were having a fight. I was feeling so confused, so lost, so anguished…

"It's going to pass, baby. It's just a wave. We're gonna get through this together!"

No. I love you too much—I can't drag you into the darkness with me, I wanted to say, but the tears didn't let me.

"I've never met a girl as beautiful as you, Linda." Alec reached out to wipe my cheeks again. "And it's not just because you're gorgeous…" He tucked a lock of hair back behind my ear. "It's because you are genuinely *good.*

"I'll always remember what you told me in Vegas. That you didn't believe anybody was *bad*, remember? People are just hurt, lost…that's why they make bad decisions." He stared at me for a second, then grasped both my hands in his. "Don't let this liar stop you from being a believer. Because that's your light, baby— you're pure *love*! And you're much brighter than you realize."

I glanced down at our hands, feeling the warmth of his touch —of his words.

"Nobody is only darkness or only brightness, you know?" Alec continued. "Even stars have scars, if you look at them closely enough. And that doesn't keep them from shining—that's what shapes their light! That's what makes them beautiful." He grinned at me with his I'm-writing-a-song-in-my-head face.

I cracked a smile.

"See what you do to me? I look at you, and it feels so warm that…you make me want to write!" He laughed. Then he squeezed my hands. "I wouldn't rather be with anyone else, baby. I mean it!"

I let out a breath. I didn't know what to do…

Alec kept waiting still, with this cute glow in his eyes, so I nodded at the desk. "You can use my notebook. I know you have lyrics in your head right now."

He gave me one of those delicious, dimpled smiles. "I'll do it another time."

"No, please! I love to see you write." *And this might be my last opportunity, so…* I rubbed his palm, encouraging him to go.

Alec nodded, then turned around, finding himself a pen. And I watched as this beautiful boy scratched out a song in front of me.

He kept looking down, concentrating, his hair falling in front of his face, making me want to brush this little curl away from his eye. His dimples were showing—he was happy with what he was writing. And I was happy to see him write…

That's when I realized. The blackness in me wasn't so dark anymore.

I couldn't tell when it happened or how it happened. But I was feeling stronger; I could see the light. And it wasn't Alec's this time, it was actually mine.

Only then I understood. It wasn't Alec's brightness that illuminated me all those months in LA—it was my own! This shy and blurred little light burning in my chest right now—that's what kept me alive!

Alec was right, I was a believer. I believed in good, I believed in people, I believed in love! And that's why I was feeling so dark lately. Somehow, admitting my heart was wrong about the impostor made me question everything I knew—everything I was. But like Ben had said in the car, I couldn't let this *one experience* chase me for the rest of my life. Not everybody was like the impostor. I'd made a mistake trusting this liar, but I couldn't lose hope in the rest of the world! I had to keep believing. I *needed* to keep believing. Because that was my light—Alec made me realize.

I glanced at him again. He didn't think I was dumb and naive like everybody was saying. He thought I was brave. And kind. And beautiful. He *believed in me*; that's why I felt so much brighter next to him. Not his light, but his faith in me had illuminated me all this time. And now it was there, healing each one of my wounds—covering my marked skin with a new layer, a new armor.

I really didn't deserve him. I was still convinced he should go find someone better than me. But now I knew I would be okay. I could survive anything. Alec had taught me how to swim in the ocean, how to be brave. And even without him by my side, I wasn't afraid. I knew how to live in faith now. I knew how to face the waves.

"I remembered another one. Maybe the thing I admire most about you." Alec read the words on the notebook, "'You turn resentment into peace, by choosing to forgive and move on.' You really don't keep scores, Linda—with anyone. You forgave me, you forgave Nina. I still didn't forgive *myself* for hurting you like that, but you did." He held my gaze, making my cheeks burn.

"You even forgave *him*!" Alec scoffed. "Well, maybe not anymore… Do you remember what you told me on the rooftop? That you had forgiven him so you could move on? Do you still feel like that, now that you know the truth? Did you really forgive him?"

I looked away, searching for the answer in my heart. I confess that back then, I thought the impostor was someone my own age —and that I was the only one he had lied to. Things were very different now. Was I able to forgive someone that immoral? That cruel? Anger coursed through my veins again.

Alec quickly read my face. "Stupid question, I know. I'm sorry I asked."

And suddenly my answer was there, written in his eyes. His beautiful green eyes.

"I did. I forgave him." I felt the tears fall, overwhelmed with my own realization. "Because I wouldn't have met you if it wasn't for this. There's no *resentment* in me right now because it was all worth it. *You* were worth it."

Alec stared at me, dazzled, then sat by my side on the bed. "How did *I* get so lucky?"

My heart warmed toward him.

But then I panicked. I felt like he was about to kiss me, and I couldn't let him do it. I wouldn't be able to do what I needed to do if he—

"I love you." He looked deep into my eyes, saying the words for the first time.

IMPOSTOR ALEC

When I realized what I'd done, it was already too late. I was too blinded by love before, I wasn't thinking. I'm so sorry. From the bottom of my heart, I'm sorry.

I knew I had made some big mistakes by lying to you, then by not telling you the truth when I introduced myself to you as me. But it was only through the course of the investigation that you opened my eyes to how bad of a person I was.

I'd never felt so ashamed in my life. I was so terribly guilty, I couldn't even face myself in the mirror. I couldn't believe I'd had the guts to do all of that, to be that cruel. You looked so fragile, so bruised… I was heartbroken. I hated myself for being the one who did that to you. So much so that I decided to stay away. I didn't think I deserved your forgiveness anymore.

You might not believe this, but deep down I was happy watching Alec fall in love with you. I knew he would take care of you for me. He would make things okay again and give you everything I couldn't.

I wanted you to be happy with him, Linda. That's why I chose to remain silent.

Chapter 19

The bright side of hitting rock bottom is that there's nowhere left to go but up. It took me two more days with Alec—and this very insightful self-help book I read on the plane—to show me that. But it was true. The worst thing that could have happened had *already* happened. And I'd survived it. Now it was time to assess the damage, rebuild, and move on. And what better way to restart than by coming home, right?

It felt so good to be back in Petersburg. My old town, my old room, my old friends.

I missed Mom! I hadn't really realized how much until I saw her waiting for me at the airport. I burst out crying the moment I hugged her. After everything that had happened this semester, I felt like all I'd needed all along was that hug.

It would be just us two for Christmas this year. Her parents had decided to spend the holidays with my uncle in the south.

I didn't mind, to be honest. I didn't hate my grandparents, but I couldn't say I really loved them either. And that was probably not my fault, since they were the ones who decided they didn't like me first—before I was even born. If it wasn't for my dad's family, Mom would have given birth to me in a shelter. They'd come around once she finished high school and they realized a non-white grandchild was also cute and everything. But I never felt one hundred percent welcome in their home. I never really felt like we were a family.

Or maybe my other grandparents, my dad's family, had raised the bar too high, that's all. They were both Mexicans and *a lot* more family oriented. But I liked that. I liked the warmth, the connection, the love. I'd missed that too, all those months in LA.

Mom and I went to their party on Christmas Eve. But on Christmas Day, it was only us two. No Grandma's house, no fancy dishes, no shiny clothes. We spent the whole day in our pajamas, just talking and eating the cookies we'd baked together.

Norah Davis was that kind of mom. I told her all the news about my friends in LA and about school and about Alec. She already knew what he'd gotten me for Christmas…

It started with the song he'd written after Thanksgiving. It was called "No More Lies," and he played it to me on the piano. I cried my eyes out, of course. It was the most beautiful song I'd ever heard. Because it was about me—it was about *us*. Then he told me the best part: he was taking me on a six-day vacation with his family to a Caribbean resort! He'd already asked my parents' permission and everything. We were leaving on December 30.

"You guys got serious very fast, huh?" Mom looked at me sideways on the couch.

"Yeah. I guess it was just…meant to be." I smiled at nowhere, holding my hot chocolate mug with both hands.

"I'm so happy for you, honey." She stroked my leg.

"And what about you?" I turned toward her. "Did anything change while I was gone? Any new boyfriend?"

"Oh, baby, things did change." She chuckled. "But not in that sense."

When Dad married Caroline, Mom got a little bit lost. It's not like she didn't see it coming—he'd left when I was two, so I didn't think she still expected he would come back one day. But it hit her hard, the fact that he'd managed to move on with his life and she hadn't. Dad had left the small town and built himself a career and gotten a new family. And Mom… She'd been busy waiting tables so we could survive. She'd been busy taking care of *me*.

So that Christmas, I got the best gift she could have ever given me: she was moving on too! I was absolutely thrilled when she told me that, after I went to California, she felt so empty inside that she decided to occupy her mind by going back to school. She was taking a few courses at a community college nearby, and she was thinking of applying to their nursing program next fall. She said she was very grateful for all those years working at my abuelo's restaurant, but she couldn't wait to do something else with her life. She'd always felt like the restaurant wasn't her place.

"I'm so proud of you!" I hugged her with watery eyes.

"I still have a long way to go, baby. But one day I'll get there." She smiled. "Sorry I didn't tell you sooner, by the way. I wasn't sure I'd be able to keep up with the classes, so I didn't want to get your hopes up."

"And how was it? Did you pass everything?"

Her smile grew bigger. "I'm one of the top students, can you believe it?"

I let out a laugh. I couldn't even put into words how happy I was for her.

"Maybe we can work together—when you finish med school! I could…"

She kept talking about the future with the enthusiasm of a five-year-old. I listened to all the procedures nurses can perform and all the people she was going to help. And through her passionate eyes, I could see myself.

Suddenly it became so clear to me why I'd always wanted to

be a doctor. My interest in hospitals, my pleasure in assisting people, the medical shows I liked to watch—it had never come from *me*. It was *her* passion, *her* vocation. It had always been *her* dream.

"And once I get my degree, I can join you in California! Or move someplace else… Just leave this town, you know?" Her face lit up.

"You've always wanted to leave, haven't you?"

"Yes. And you inspired me, baby. You're showing me how to chase my dreams. They will never come to me unless I get up from where I am and go after them. I know that now." She hugged me again.

And that's when it hit me: I'd never had a dream. I'd never felt compelled to leave this town like she did. I'd never felt strongly drawn to a specific career. Not even any subject at school —I kind of liked them all equally. I'd gone to LA to chase love, not a dream.

What am I chasing now? I should be chasing something, right? Besides love?

That question didn't leave my mind for days.

I certainly wasn't as excited as Mom about a career in healthcare. And I didn't have any reason to want to be a doctor either, not like Matt. When I started talking to Nina about all this, she'd seemed so sure she wanted a career in fashion that I didn't even have the guts to continue. I knew she wouldn't understand anyway. That's why I couldn't talk to Alec either—or Ben! They both lived for their music. They would just feel sorry for me—the girl who didn't have any passion.

So I called AJ. I knew he hated being a bodyguard, and he'd given up on music before that… Maybe he was lost like me.

"Oh my gosh, yes! I totally understand you!" He laughed on the line. "But I had no idea you felt like that. You've always seemed so sure you wanted to study medicine."

"I was. Until now…"

"You're taking this 'moving on' thing pretty seriously, huh?"

"I think it's that self-help book Ben gave me for Christmas—I can't stop thinking about it! I know I have a lot of things to rebuild in my life, and I want to do everything right this time, you know?"

"You should, yeah," he encouraged.

"But after what my mom told me…I don't know. I think medicine has always been *her* dream, not mine."

"And what's yours?"

"That's the thing. I don't know!"

"Are you sure you're not just afraid of admitting it to yourself?"

"I'm sure. I don't have a clue, AJ." I shook my head. "Do *you* have any idea of what you really want?"

His mood changed. And he hesitated a few seconds before saying, "I do."

"Then why aren't you doing it? It's not working for Alec, is it?"

"No." His voice was small.

"So, what is it? Why don't you go after it?"

"It's…complicated."

"Come on, tell me!"

"No, Linda. It's nothing…"

"I bet you're worried about other people's opinions, am I right? Is that why you don't want to tell me?"

"Maybe." He chuckled.

"Then don't! I'm not gonna judge you. We should be what we were meant to be, AJ—like Alec and Matt! They aren't living in vain; they are chasing something! I feel like I'm just doing what people expect from me, without even knowing where I'm going. You know what I mean?"

"I do…more than you can imagine. Sometimes it's like I'm

trying to be the guy I was supposed to be, instead of the guy I really am."

"Exactly! I envy Alec for this. He's so sure of who he is…and what he wants…and where he's going!"

"Yeah, me too," AJ murmured.

"Well, at least it's good to know I'm not alone."

"You certainly are not."

"What should we do, AJ? I don't think I can just ignore this anymore… Can you?"

"I got this advice once. That I should start doing the little things that make me happy, and then the bigger picture would unfold itself."

"Does it work?"

"I don't know. I still couldn't do any of the little things."

I laughed out loud. "We are both pathetic. We have to make some changes next year."

"I guess." He chuckled.

"I mean it!"

I told AJ he was way too special not to live his dreams—not to become the guy he wanted to be. Maybe we hadn't found that calling in ourselves yet, like our friends, but I believed we would get there one day. We just needed to start being true to ourselves and stop doing things just because they were what the world expected from us.

"You're right," he said, and I could hear the smile in his voice. "You're always right."

I smiled back. I felt so much lighter after talking to him about this.

"We should probably hang up." I looked at the screen. "It's been an hour already!"

"Thank you for calling. It was good to see you're being your-self again."

"I feel better, yeah… Those three days with Alec brought me back to the light."

"I'm happy for you two. You really deserve each other."

"Thanks." My heart warmed. "So talk to you soon then?"

"Sure… And Linda?"

"Yeah?"

"You're good at this—giving people hope. You called me for advice and ended up inspiring me to be myself. Maybe *that's* your thing."

I cracked another smile. *Giving people hope. What college should I go to for that?*

♪♩♡

I never thought I would say it, but after a week in West Virginia, I missed home. I mean my LA home.

I couldn't explain how, but I didn't feel myself here. I didn't fit in like I used to. It's funny how you don't realize you've changed until you're expected to be the person you've always been. I couldn't do it—I didn't know how to be that girl anymore.

Yet, I did my best to pretend. And apart from Mom and Nina, I guess everybody still recognized me as the old Linda. That was, until December 30, when I tried to say goodbye to my grandparents.

"Are you crazy? Absolutely not!" Abuela said in Spanish, putting the box of grapes she'd bought for the New Year's party into the fridge. "Your father just arrived here; the family is finally complete! How can you say you're leaving?"

"But Abuela, everything is already set up. I have to leave for the airport in two hours! My boyfriend and his family are waiting for me."

"So you think your boyfriend and *his* family are more important than your own family?" She closed the fridge, meeting my gaze. "You're already spending the whole year on the other side of the country, Linda—we miss you like crazy! Claire and Jesse are finally here; please tell me I'm gonna have all my grandchildren with me on New Year's Eve!"

I huffed. I hated when she did that! When she made me feel guilty for not wanting to do whatever she wanted me to do.

Do what's important to you, not what the world expects from you. I remembered my talk with AJ the second I picked up the phone to call Alec. I couldn't believe my New Year's resolution was already getting off to a bad start.

"This isn't you trying to break up with me again, right?" Alec said in a high-pitched voice. "Because I told you—"

"No, baby. Calm down!" I clutched the phone in my hand. I hated to do this to him. "I love you, we're *not* breaking up. But my grandparents take these family reunions too seriously, and my dad has just arrived… They said I can go on Thursday; they just don't want me to miss the party on New Year's Eve."

"Oh," Alec said reflectively.

"I know this is going to mess up your plans. I can't go meet you in New York today, so this means—"

"Don't worry about that, I'll reschedule everything. Just *promise* I'll see you on January first."

"I promise." I smiled.

I couldn't wait to see him. Alec was always so busy that he had changed my perception of time. With him, every single day counted. And we were losing almost forty-eight hours with this little delay—that was such a waste! I wanted to enjoy every hour, every minute, every second I got to be with him.

Urgh! I was so angry at my abuela!

So angry at myself for not having the courage to go against her!

This was important to me. I should have stood up for myself! I spent the whole night regretting it.

"Are you sure you don't want me to stay, honey?" Mom said, putting the pot in the coffee maker. We were both in our pajamas, having a lazy last morning of the year.

"Yeah." I sighed from my chair. She had other plans for tonight, of course, since I wasn't supposed to be here. But just because *my* plans had been crashed didn't mean I had to spoil hers too. "I'll leave tomorrow morning anyway. Go have fun with your friends in the mountains… And be careful with those skis! You remember what happened the last time."

"All right, *Mom*!" She chuckled, hugging my head. Then she gave me a kiss. "I already miss you, baby. I can't believe I'm only gonna see you again in the summer!"

A lump rose in my throat as I stared back at her. I already missed her too.

That was so weird—and so unfair! When I was in Petersburg, I missed LA; and when I was in LA, I missed Petersburg! I wondered if I'd ever feel complete again.

"Finish the coffee," Mom ordered, walking to the living room. The bell was ringing.

I didn't even have time to get up from the chair.

"Oh my God!" She gasped at the door.

I ran to her, alarmed, anticipating the worst. But then my heart stopped.

Standing on my sidewalk—in my hometown in West Virginia —was Alec Brock. The real Alec Brock. My boyfriend Alec Brock.

"Nice to meet you, Ms. Davis. I'm Alec." He held out his hand to take hers.

But Mom caught him in a bear hug instead. "I can't believe you're here, sweetie! Come in! It's so nice to finally meet you!"

I clasped my hands over my mouth, still not believing what was happening in front of me.

"This is my friend Jimmy. Can we—"

"Of course! Of course! Make yourselves at home!" Mom gestured for them to come inside.

And that's when he saw me. Our eyes locked, but he didn't move. He just stood there, smiling at me.

"What are you doing here?" I finger-combed my hair, then straightened my shirt. Thank God I was wearing a bra—and had brushed my teeth!

"I couldn't start the year without you," he said, flushing.

"Aw!" Mom held her hands over her chest. "Wait a minute, I'm gonna go grab my camera!"

"No, Mom! No photos!" I shouted. The last thing I wanted was to be registered for eternity greeting Alec in those old pajamas.

But he didn't seem bothered at all. He chuckled in fact, walking in my direction.

"I can't believe this!" I shook my head, my hands on my cheeks.

His dimples sank deeper, and he leaned down to give me a kiss. "Can you believe it now?"

"This is so cute!" Mom shot a flash in our direction. "And it's *you*! I mean... I'm a big fan of your mom, Alec—I remember when she had her twins. But who would have thought one of her babies would end up with *my* baby!" She giggled in delight, making Alec laugh.

"Mom, please!" *Stop embarrassing me!* I glared at her on my way to greet Jimmy. "Seriously, what are you doing here? You two were supposed to be in the Caribbean right now!"

"Believe me, miss. I tried to stop him."

"I had to see you!" Alec grasped my hands. "I couldn't wait any longer. This year is going to be tough enough already; I didn't want to waste a day that I could be spending with you."

My chest tightened, and I leaned in for another kiss. I felt exactly the same way about him. With the World Tour coming soon, I didn't want to waste a second!

Click.

"Mom!" I hissed.

"I have to record this, baby—sorry. This is like…the proof that fairy tales are real!" She chuckled. "You have no idea, Alec, how crazy this one was about you. She watched all your TV shows and has this collection of magazines. Your music is practically the only thing she listens to since—"

"Mother!" I yelled.

And Alec laughed out loud. "Really? What else, Ms. Davis? I'd love to hear more."

No, no, no! My face burned, anticipating what Mom would say.

"Oh, please call me Norah, sweetie! Come, let me get you some coffee. I'll tell you everything…" She touched his arm, leading him to the kitchen.

Chapter 20

And that was the start of the most embarrassing hours of my entire existence.

Mom told Alec every single one of my stories.

You know those fangirl things we do, believing no one is watching? Guess what? She was watching.

She told him about the calendar I'd made to keep track of his TV appearances—and how happy I was whenever I heard his song playing unexpectedly on the radio. She told him I used to spend all my free time on the internet, looking at his pictures and voting for him to win his music awards. She even told him about the cake I made on his eighteenth birthday! Although for her, Nina and I were just being hardcore fans—she didn't know about my celebration with Impostor Alec later that day.

I was shocked by how much she knew. She hadn't connected the dots, obviously. But I never imagined she'd been this close to guessing it! She was fully aware I was obsessed with him, but she thought the texting and the phone calls were just me fangirling with Nina.

I was so worried Alec would take it the wrong way and be uncomfortable listening to "my ex-boyfriend's stories." But he loved them. I'd never seen him so amused before, as a matter of fact. He liked to know I was his fangirl—it inflated his ego. Which made things a little less embarrassing, I guess. But still…

In the afternoon, Mom went skiing with her friends, so I decided to take Alec on a little tour. Jimmy didn't come—the town was tiny and safe, and half of the inhabitants weren't home anyway. Including Nina.

Alec was sad that he didn't get to see her, so I showed him her house. And it was there, parked on Nina's driveaway, that he had the craziest idea.

"A trip down memory lane?" I raised an eyebrow at him.

"Yeah, I think it can help you confront your past and get rid of these flashbacks. It would be like that day on the boat, remember? You punching your fears in the face?"

My whole body stiffened. But I cracked a smile, already feeling the butterflies. It was incredible how he did that—made me *want* to do the scariest things I'd ever done in my life.

"I know I can help you get through this, babe…" He reached for my hand, hopeful. "Please, let me help you?"

I nodded at his green eyes.

I never thought I'd have the courage to recall any of those shameful memories. To allow myself to remember—to actually talk about them! But Alec made me feel so safe, so loved, that somehow they didn't seem so scary anymore.

So we took a trip back to my old life, and I showed him everything—my favorite spot on the river, my abuelo's restaurant, the church, the supermarket. It felt good to finally be with him in all of those places. I had planned this in my head for so long that I knew exactly what to do, exactly where I wanted to take him.

We even stopped to take a picture in front of the old courthouse, like I'd always imagined we would. Alec was thrilled, helping me recreate my memories—showing me that I had nothing to be afraid or ashamed of. But we both agreed that our favorite part of the trip was the moment we decided to go off the script.

It started when we got to my old school. The doors were closed, so I couldn't kiss him in all the spots I'd dreamed. But we had enough fun covering the outdoor locations. And when it got too cold for us to stay outside in the snow, we went back to the car and turned on the heater.

It's strange, the logic of being totally exposed in a public place and still feeling more privacy than when we were alone in his room. But that's how I felt. That's how *we* felt.

"I wanna try something new, okay?" Alec whispered, breaking apart from my lips.

My heart raced before he could even finish his sentence. We'd started trying "new things" the day of his last concert in LA, and every time he said the words, my whole body reacted in anticipation.

"If you don't like it, we can stop." He held my gaze, serious.

"I'm pretty sure I'm gonna like it." I smiled at him.

And he smiled back, then glanced out the windows to make sure there was no one else in the parking lot.

♪♩♡

I couldn't think of anything else after that. I wanted him *so bad*.

And not just his hands, not just his mouth. I wanted *him*—all of him.

"You're being too obvious, chica." Joaquín laughed. "Cool off, your dad is watching you."

My face burned as I met Dad's eyes in the crowded room. "Thanks, Uncle Quin." I composed myself, trying not to look back at Alec.

He was *gorgeous* in that navy turtleneck sweater; it was even hotter than the red one he'd worn during the day. I could see his muscles beneath it. I could picture his tattoos. I wanted to touch them—redraw every single line with the tip of my fingers.

"What kind of man doesn't eat meat?" Abuelo said, making Alec explain himself for the tenth time tonight.

He was trying hard, I could tell. He wanted to prove to everybody that he fit in—even if he didn't eat the same things and looked extraordinarily white and tall among us.

I'd never noticed before—how tall he was. Of course I knew the exact height difference between him and me, but we fit so perfectly together that I never cared about the measurements. I was taller than most of my relatives, though—maybe that's why I'd never realized it. I'd gotten so used to feeling small among his family, that I'd forgotten how tall I felt among mine. And since here *I* was considered tall, poor Alec looked like a giant.

A *very* hot giant…

"Did you see me play?" Claire asked, proudly holding her violin under the right arm like Ben taught her.

Apparently, she had not only gotten a brand-new violin for Christmas—so she didn't need to borrow the one from the music school anymore—but it had also been delivered by Santa himself, like he'd promised in October. And I was guessing Dad had really surrendered to the whole Santa Claus thing, because I'd asked Alec and he told me he had nothing to do with that.

"Of course! It was beautiful!" I lied. She only knew how to play one song, and though it wasn't as bad as before, she still sounded like a dying cat.

"Alec saw it too! He said he's going to tell Ben!" Her eyes blazed.

"You really like him, don't you?" I smirked.

"Yeah," she said with a bashful giggle. "I wanna marry him when I grow up."

I laughed out loud. *These Brock boys and their charm—we have no defense against them.*

"I'm so glad you live with us in LA!" She hugged my waist. "Now you're really my sister—because I don't see you only when we come here."

My heart melted. But I didn't know if I was happy or worried to be hearing that.

"No matter where I live, I'm always gonna be your sister, okay?" I squatted down to look into her eyes. And she gave me a shy nod, then turned around, rushing off.

"Don't run with the violin! You're gonna—" I stopped. Dad was suddenly standing next to me.

"I'm happy you stayed, honey." His voice was soft.

I got up, glancing at Alec with Abuelo. "Me too."

"I'm sorry, I…"

I widened my eyes at him. I'd never heard Dad start a sentence with the words "I'm sorry" before.

"I misjudged him. I can see now that he truly cares about you."

I couldn't hold back a smile. "Thank you."

He nodded, pressing his lips together. "You guys are leaving tomorrow morning, right?"

"Yes, 9 A.M."

"Have fun." He stroked my arm, then kissed the top of my head. "I'm gonna go put the kids to bed…" He looked at Caroline, who was holding sleeping Jesse in her arms.

"Yeah, I think I'm gonna go too." If Dad was allowed to leave, then so was I.

"Is Alec staying at your mom's with you?"

"*What?*" Abuela shouted. "No, Joel, you can't leave them alone there!"

"Alec is actually staying at a motel, Abuela."

"That's the same!" She kept talking to my dad, completely ignoring my presence. "How can you leave these two kids unsupervised like this, Joel? Look what happens when parents make this mistake." She pointed at me.

"Ouch!" I felt myself blush. She was speaking so loudly the whole family was now staring at us.

Alec walked over to me, concerned, and Abuela pointed between him and me. "You two are too young to be so free. One of you stays under my watch tonight!"

Dad laughed but didn't defend me.

And I got angry—at both of them! "Are you serious? You know I'm going to travel with him tomorrow anyway, right?"

"His parents will be there, then it's going to be *their* responsibility to keep an eye on you. But in this town, you're under *my* watch!"

Alec looked down to keep from laughing, his dimples sinking into his cheeks.

"But I need to finish packing!" I tried to argue in Spanish. It would be better if he didn't understand this anyway. "And Alec has Jimmy to watch him. They are both staying at the motel, not at my mother's house!"

"Do you think I trust *him* to watch you two?" She pointed at Jimmy. "Look at him, no authority at all—as soft as a teddy bear."

"Abuela!"

"No, Linda! You're too young," she said in Spanish, then switched to English, turning to Alec. "One of you two stays in this house tonight! I'll let you choose who it will be."

I glanced at my dad, but I knew he wouldn't dare go against Abuela. No one in that house would. No one except…

"Alec stays, then," I said firmly, surprising everyone. "There's a place for him with Uncle Quin, right?"

"Yes, there's plenty of room for him with Joaquín." Abuela smiled, rubbing Alec's arm.

I had to bite the inside of my cheeks to keep my face straight.

And from the corner of my eyes, I noticed Uncle Quin smirking. He knew exactly what I was planning in my mind.

"Linda?" Alec said, confused.

"Sorry, babe—I need to finish packing. You understand, right?" I exchanged a look with him, hoping he would trust me and go along with it.

"Sure…" He knit his brows. He knew I was lying about packing, he just didn't get *why*.

"Great. Let's get you all settled, love." Abuela pulled him by the arm.

Alec glanced back at me, but I let him go alone. I still had to work on the second half of my plan.

"Is it okay if he stays here, Jimmy?" I asked, trying not to sound too eager. "I can assure you he will be safe."

"I have no doubts, miss. He should hire *her* to be his bodyguard." Jimmy snickered, watching Abuela drag Alec up the stairs. "She would scare a lot more fans than me."

"I know, she's a little—"

"Badass! All the women in the family, as a matter of fact… I like it!" He smiled, shooting a glance at Aunt Julia again.

They'd been flirting all night. Maybe now that Jimmy didn't have to guard Alec, he would have the courage to try something with her. I hoped he would.

"I'm gonna run to the motel and put together an overnight bag, then." Jimmy turned toward the door.

"That would be great. Thanks!" I fought to hide my excitement. Then I said goodbye and headed upstairs to check on Alec.

He was helping Uncle Quin with the air mattress while Abuela searched for clean sheets in the other room.

"So…" He met my gaze, uneasy. "Not that I'm against staying here at your grandparents' house, but why *me*? Why didn't *you* stay?"

"She's a *bad girl* after all." Uncle Quin smirked at us again.

"Trust me, okay? Quin will tell you what to do." I grabbed his hand, already feeling the butterflies. "We're gonna be alone tonight, baby. Like, *really alone*. No parents around, no body-guards. Just us two."

Alec cracked a shy smile.

Chapter 21

One hour and forty minutes later, I got a message from Quin.

Clear!

I put on my boots, grabbed my coat, and walked out Mom's door. I didn't even worry about a scarf or gloves. It was just a ten-minute walk to my grandparents' house, and I knew a shortcut anyway.

My hands kept shaking, though. And it wasn't from the cold. I had watched Uncle Quin doing things like this my whole life, but I'd never imagined one day *I* would be the one sneaking around behind the adults' backs.

Not that I was officially becoming a *bad girl*, like he'd said. I was very proud of myself for always following the rules. Being a *good girl* kept me out of trouble—unlike Uncle Quin. He was four years older than me, but so much more immature. I'd covered for him more times than I could remember. I knew what his punishment would be if they caught him, and I didn't want that for him. I didn't want that for anyone.

That's why I'd always thought it was stupid to be reckless. I never understood his motivations; none of them seemed to be worthy enough for me to risk it.

Not until that night. Not until Alec.

"Ready?" Quin mouthed to me from his bedroom.

I gave him a thumbs-up, ignoring the knot in my stomach.

Quin helped Alec pass through the window with his back-pack and everything. I was so nervous when he started sliding down the roof over the porch that I could see the headlines in my head already: *Alec Brock dies from a roof fall in West Virginia!*

I took a deep breath, trying to relax. He was almost at the tree, everything would be all right.

But when he finally reached it, I got even more worried. Alec seemed to have no idea what he was doing. I was sure he'd never climbed a tree before!

"Your feet first, baby." I guided him to the nearest branch.

"Shhh," Quin whispered, making my heart race even faster.

I kept staring at the dark windows of the house, hoping none of the lights would flip on. Adrenaline had already overtaken me. But Alec was only halfway down—and moving slowly.

Like, *too slowly*. I had to hold my laughter at the end.

"You can let go. You're not far." I held his waist, to show him how close he was to the ground.

But Alec thought he was actually at the bottom and completely let go, making us both fall down into the snow.

I gasped, thinking about the noise we'd made. They would find out tomorrow anyway—after we were already far gone. But if they caught us tonight…

Alec laughed his delicious loud laugh. And I rolled over him, covering his mouth with my hand.

"Shhh!" He clearly didn't know the risk he was taking. He looked so happy—childish even. "What happened to you?"

"I've always wanted to do this!" He grinned from ear to ear.

And my heart melted at how genuinely happy he was. How much he liked to be in *my world*.

"I love you." I leaned in and gave him a kiss.

"I love you too." He smiled my favorite dimpled smile.

That's when my phone buzzed: **Run, you idiots! You've never done this before? You're going to get caught, jeez!**

"Let's go! Now!" I got up from the snow as Uncle Quin scowled at us from his window.

We couldn't stop laughing after that. It was like the adrenaline had done something to us. I tried to shush Alec as we crossed other people's backyards, but watching him try not to laugh made me want to laugh even more.

"Stop it, I mean it!" I giggled when we got to my sidewalk. "You're making my cheeks hurt!"

"Come here, then." He grabbed my hand, pulling me back to the street, then planted a kiss on each cheek. "Better?"

I shook my head, giggling again. "Let's go. It's cold!" I folded my arms. My hands were freezing; I definitely regretted not having brought my gloves.

"Can you give me just a minute?" Alec opened his coat, inviting me in, then wrapped it around us both, warming me against his chest. "I want to feel this for a little longer."

"Feel what?"

"*Freedom.*" He glanced at the snow on the empty road. "Do you realize that there's no one else in the entire world who knows where I am right now? I think this hasn't happened since…ever!"

I grinned at the joy on his face.

"Thank you for today," he said tenderly.

"*I'm* the one who should be thanking you for the surprise! For helping me face my memories! I did nothing for you—just drove you around town."

"You make me feel *human*." His voice was low.

"The word is *ordinary*, remember?" I chuckled.

"No, baby, it's not just about doing ordinary things. You really make me *feel*... Freedom, happiness, boldness, butterflies... You make me feel all sorts of things that I only feel when I'm with you."

I bit my lip to keep from smiling.

"What about you? How do I make *you* feel?" He held my gaze, tightening his grip around my waist.

My body reacted to his stare, responded to his touch. Exactly like it'd been doing since the day we first met.

"I wanna show it to you. Do I still have that 'all-access pass' you gave me?"

"Sure," he said, amused.

I unfolded my arms, looking into his eyes. Then I slowly slid my freezing hands under his shirt.

Alec gasped, contracting his muscles.

"That's how you make me feel... Since the very first time you touched me." I smirked. "It's like this little electric shock—cold and shivery. But all I can think about is that I don't want it to go away. I don't want it to stop," I whispered, sliding my hand up his chest.

He breathed through his mouth with his eyes closed.

And he looked so hot, I couldn't resist. I kissed his bottom lip.

Alec ran his fingers through my hair and pressed my head against him, deepening the kiss. So I moved my hands to his back, bringing him closer.

He gasped again, but didn't break apart from me.

I felt his heart race, his breathing change. And before I realized it, we were stumbling our way to the house.

"If I'm going too fast, or if you want to stop, just let me know, okay?" He leaned back to look at me. "I don't want to do anything that *you* don't want to do."

"I really want to." My heart pounded in my chest. "I couldn't stop thinking about it all night."

"Good." He chuckled, then kissed me again, walking us both to my room.

My back hit the bed, and Alec moved his lips to my neck. I was so happy that I had to open my eyes. I had to make sure I wasn't dreaming!

"I think I've always wanted it to be here," I said, staring at the neon stars shining on the ceiling.

Alec followed my gaze, and smiled slowly. "I'm glad we waited then."

I cupped his cheeks, pulling him back to me. And I got lost in my memories, remembering how many times I'd imagined this. How many times I'd lived this night in my head.

"Are you okay?" Alec said with a frown.

"Yeah." I grinned. He looked absolutely gorgeous, shirtless in those black jeans.

I brushed my fingers against his skin, touching the hull of the ship on his stomach. I'd lived this exact scene before, in my dreams. But I could never have guessed it would be so much more meaningful. The scar hidden in that ship, the fact that he was the *Real Alec*. All the "waves" I'd had to face to get to this day. Even the escaping-from-my-abuela's-house adventure! Everything was a thousand times more special…and deep…and real! And they made this moment a thousand times better than I could have ever dreamed.

"Baby?" Alec's voice brought me back to the present.

"Yes?"

"You don't seem okay." He tilted his head, serious.

"No, I am! I'm happy! It's just that…it feels like a déjà vu, you know?" I half-smiled.

But Alec kept his face straight. "Maybe we shouldn't do this here."

"What?" I raised my brows.

"I don't want this night to be part of your 'trip down memory lane,' Linda." He let out a breath. "I need you to be present in this with me, and there are too many memories here—in this room. I feel like they are haunting you."

I glanced around, thinking about what he said. Maybe he was right.

"I'm sorry if I'm being selfish, but I really want to make this about *us*—just the two of us."

"I know. I agree…" I gave him a reassuring smile.

Alec planted a kiss on my lips, then lay by my side on the bed.

I sighed deeply, staring at him. I had imagined this scene too. And he looked exactly how I'd pictured. His curls, his eyes, his mouth, the black ink on his arm, completing the masterpiece. The Alec of my dreams was so beautiful. But the boy in front of me was so much more than that. So much more than I ever imagined he could be.

"I just realized something…" I held his gaze. "Why the new memories will never *replace* the old ones."

"Why?" He stared, puzzled.

"Because even if they *look* the same, they *feel* different… I pictured this night in my head a million times before, baby. But when I look at you right now, it feels so much better. And it's not just because it's real…it's because it's *you*!" I grinned, reaching for his hand.

"I feel *grateful* tonight—so grateful that the memories from my past can't even hurt me anymore. I think deep down I've always wished things had worked out the first time around. That I'd really met you in that chat room and you had recognized me in LA. I thought my life would be *better* if the Alec of my dreams was real. But now I know I was wrong…*this* is better." I laced our fingers together. "And I would go through all of it again, baby— the pain, the tears, everything—just to be here, with *you*, right now."

Alec smiled at me. "I love you so much."

"I love you more." I smiled back.

"Please never leave me…" His voice was quiet, worried.

"Of course! Why would I leave you?" I giggled.

But Alec didn't reply. He just kissed me. A long, warm, passionate kiss.

"I have something for you." He sat up on the bed, then ran to the living room.

When he came back, there was a little gift box in his hands. "I wanted you to open it at midnight, but instead of kissing you, I had to eat all those grapes…"

I laughed out loud. "You did great, by the way—with their Mexican traditions."

"It was…*different*, for sure." He chuckled. "But go ahead, it's for you."

I held my breath, undoing the ribbon. I wasn't expecting a ring, of course. But I felt a little on edge, receiving jewelry out of the blue.

To my total surprise, when I opened the box, I saw a necklace. More than that, a guitar pick necklace! It was matte silver, and a lot smaller than the picks he normally used. But there was his signature *AB* on it, and a single white pearl hanging alongside.

"This is so beautiful, Alec! Thank you." I beamed, touching the *A*, then the *B*. It was a mini version of his autograph—together they resembled a star beside a heart.

"Turn it over." He smirked.

I knit my brows, intrigued, taking the necklace out of the box. *As fast as I can* was written on the other side.

"Can I?" Alec took the pick from my hands to put it on me.

"What does it mean?" I pulled my hair up, a little embarrassed for having to ask.

"That, for the first time, I don't want to go on tour…" His sorrowful eyes lingered on mine. And right then I understood what he'd meant before. *Why* he'd asked me not to leave him.

"This year I won't be able to be around as much as I wish," he continued. "But this is to remind you that every time I leave, I'll be thinking of you. And I promise to always come back to you…*as fast as I can*."

My heart ached in my chest. Love and pain, they were all one thing. At least when you're in love with Alec Brock. The *distance* was the only constant between now and then. It had always been like that. It would always be like that.

The thought of him leaving made me bury my fingers in his curls and pull his head closer, locking our lips together. Alec felt the urge too. The clock ticking, the lonely nights ahead of us. He took me into his arms, rolling his body over mine. And neither of us wanted to stop this time.

Chapter 22

"Oh, come on! Get a room!" Matt groaned from his lounger, throwing his hat at Alec.

I laughed out loud, watching Alec throw it back at his brother and then kiss me again as if nothing had happened. It was like, since New Year's Eve, we couldn't take our hands off each other.

"Seriously, you guys. Just because here you can kiss in public doesn't mean you should be doing *this* in public! Poor Ben had to cover his eyes already." Matt pointed to where Benjamin lay under his improvised sun shelter.

Ben yanked away the towel from over his face but kept his gaze on his parents, who were swimming in the ocean. And the pink on his cheeks made me break apart from Alec. Maybe we *should* take it easy—at least when there were other people around.

"Thank you, honey." Matt smiled as I sat cross-legged on the lounger.

"Oh, come on. We're just cuddling!" Alec sat upright too, then snuggled me from behind. "I bet you would be doing way worse if you hadn't broken up with your boyfriend."

"What?" I gasped, bringing my hand to my chest. "You two broke up?"

"Right before Christmas, yeah." Matt pressed his lips together.

"I'm so sorry!" I'd always thought Matt and AJ were a perfect match for each other.

"It's okay," Matt said with a shrug.

"It's a relief, that's what it is!" Alec snickered. "Sorry, brother, but Sebastian is a douche. The only reason you don't get the trophy for Worst Taste in the family is because Ben is still messing around with Hailey."

"Hey, leave Hails out of this!" Ben glared at Alec, grabbing his book. "But, yeah… I have to agree, Sebastian *is* a douche."

"Wait, who is Sebastian?" I narrowed my eyes.

"Matt's ex-boyfriend." Alec seemed surprised that I didn't know.

"I thought he was dating AJ!"

"He wishes." Ben chuckled.

"No, babe. AJ is straight, they're just friends."

"AJ is straight?" I raised my voice in shock.

That made no sense to me. Matt had looked so in love with him that night at his house. They were having a hot tub date, for God's sake—I could *see* the sparks flying between them when they had that water fight! And AJ had always shown so much affection when we talked about Matt, so much love. I was one hundred percent sure they were a couple.

"Yes. You assumed he was gay?" Alec laughed.

"Well, yeah. I've been referring to Matt as his boyfriend this whole time. I can't believe he never corrected me!"

"Maybe he didn't notice it," Alec said. "He was dating this girl—are they still together, Matt?"

"No, they broke up too."

"I never had the chance to meet her." Alec tilted his head.

"Me neither," Ben added.

"Really?" Matt turned toward us in surprise. "He talked so much about her. I thought he was showing her off everywhere."

"Not at work." Alec shrugged.

"That's odd…" Matt leaned back on his chair. "Well, it's over anyway."

"Maybe now it's your chance, bro." Ben smirked from behind his book.

And Matt threw his hat at him this time.

"He has a lifelong crush on AJ," Alec explained to me.

"I don't!" Matt shouted. "Not anymore… You should have seen him talking about this girl—I finally understood he's straight, okay?"

My heart broke for Matt. I could tell that whatever he felt for AJ was strong—and *painful*. He seemed a lot more upset about him being straight than about his recent breakup with Sebastian.

"I hope you find someone else soon." I gave him a sympathetic smile.

"Thanks, honey." He smiled back. "Now, *please*, can we talk about something else?" he said to his brothers, then glanced at me. "Are you joining me in Boston this year or what?"

"No, sorry." I grasped Alec's hand. "I'm staying at UCLA."

"You haven't even applied anywhere else?" Ben raised his brows.

"Not out-of-state, no. I think it will be hard enough already—with the tour and everything. I don't want to make this even more complicated."

"Wow. You guys are really serious, huh?" Matt nodded at us.

"Yep." Alec grinned, planting a kiss on my cheek. "But I've gotta tell you, babe—I'm probably getting an apartment in Manhattan in the fall."

"What?" I widened my eyes at him.

"It's always been our dream—" he exchanged a look with his

twin "—to go to school in New York and get a condo for the two of us. Now that Ben is going to Juilliard, we can finally do it."

My jaw dropped. *I could have applied to NYU!*

"Poor girl. She hadn't realized it yet…" Matt chuckled. "You got yourself a combo, honey. These two don't break apart—you take one, you get both."

"No, it's not that." I stared at nowhere, suddenly sad.

"What is it, then?" Alec smirked, tightening his grip around me.

"Nothing…" *Now it's too late anyway.*

"Don't worry, okay?" He stroked my arm. "Wherever you choose to study, we will make it work."

As if I had the choice to go anywhere else… I sighed. I couldn't believe I had just missed the NYU deadline.

Alec watched me for a moment, his dimples peeking out. Then all of a sudden, he stood up, excited. "I think I'm gonna go for a swim. Do you guys wanna come?"

"I'll go with you." Matt got up, taking off his glasses.

"Go ahead, I want to finish my book." I reached for it on the table. "I'll join you later."

"I'll be waiting." Alec gave me another kiss, then walked to the sea with Matt.

I tried to focus on what I was reading, I swear. But I just couldn't take my eyes off him. I couldn't stop longing for him, his kisses, his touch…

My face burned as I noticed Ben watching me drool over his brother.

"Don't!" I hid myself behind my book. "I already know what you're gonna say."

"I wasn't going to say anything." He laughed.

"Sorry we're being a little too obvious."

"That you two had sex? No, not at all!"

"Oh gosh, don't say it like that!" I lowered my head, making a curtain between us with my hair.

"It's okay." His voice softened. "I'm happy that you…seem to be feeling better."

"Thanks, Ben." I met his eyes. I knew he meant what he said —he'd seen me at my worst a couple of weeks ago. He'd even gotten me a self-help book, trying to make things better. "Your Christmas gift worked, by the way. I read it on the plane, and it really touched me. I couldn't stop thinking about it for a week."

"I'm glad to hear it." He smiled shyly.

"Do you know another one like that? I enjoyed reading about feelings and emotions—mental health, you know?"

"Yeah! We have a bunch of those in the house. If you want, I could pick out a few that I think you might like…"

"That would be great! Thanks." I grinned at him.

"My pleasure." He pressed his lips together.

♪♩♡

The next three weeks flew by before my eyes, though it felt like forever since our little break at the beach. I didn't know if it was Alec's intense rehearsal schedule or the fast-paced classes I had taken at school. Or the fact that I didn't have AJ by my side anymore.

He'd really brightened up my days, I realized. I missed his open-mouthed smile and his terrible jokes. My commute to school was definitely not the same without him.

But that was also a good thing. It was liberating to go out of the house alone and walk on the street without fear, looking people in the eye. The police had arrested all the impostor suspects now. And though there was still no proof that this guy from Sacramento had been the one who'd gone to my house, he had indeed traveled to other states to meet with minors. So that, associated with the timing and the similarity of the messages he sent to his victims, had convinced Oliver and Jack that they'd caught the right guy. They were actually anticipating the impostor would have destroyed any evidence about me at this point, since he knew I'd been the one who exposed his game to Alec's management in September. That's why the investigation had been focused on the other cases—Jack never really expected to find anything about *me* on this guy's computer.

But I confess I felt even more relieved listening to all that. Not only was the impostor in jail, but no one would ever see the pictures I'd sent him. I couldn't have asked for a better closure. It was truly over—all the nightmare, the anxiety, the pain. After six months underwater, I could breathe again. I had finally broken through the wave.

And you know what? I'd never felt so *strong* before. So aware of who I was—of who I wanted to be. Alec was encouraging me to be *more myself* and to *take care of myself*. And that's what I was doing.

I was eating healthy. I was exercising. I'd read three other self-help books Ben had picked out for me. And I guess all of that was making me more confident. I felt *good* around people again —I didn't need to be invisible to feel safe anymore.

Sam, Liz, and Aisha noticed it. Dad and Caroline noticed it. Even Dr. Brown was proud of me for facing everything so bravely. And I couldn't deny that I was proud of myself too. I wasn't scared or anxious or ashamed. I didn't feel like I was less than anybody else because of what he'd done to me. I hadn't let this one jerk make me give up on loving myself.

But among all these things I was doing, the one I was most proud of was my project with the fan letters. I'd spent the last few days selecting the best ones for Alec. I was making him a scrapbook to take on tour. There were so many great stories—I was sure he would love my surprise!

I was answering every single letter too. I was addicted to

reading how much Alec inspired his fans. And I loved to have the opportunity to write them a few encouraging words back. It empowered me somehow, it strengthened my light.

I was even reconsidering studying medicine now. But not the physical practice—I still thought that was my mom's thing. I wanted to work with the mind. Psychiatry, psychology…I didn't know. I just knew that I wanted to work with that—fighting the darkness, giving people *hope*.

"That's so cool, Linda." Ben beamed at me. "I think you're gonna be an awesome mental health advocate one day."

I glanced down, my cheeks burning. "I'm still thinking about it—it's not decided yet. And I haven't told anyone, so…"

"Don't worry. You know I'm good at keeping secrets." He smirked.

"You better be! If Alec finds out I made him drink regular milk with his coffee that day at the beach, I'll kill you!"

"That was so funny." He laughed. "But it was an accident; he wouldn't be mad if—"

"You promised, Ben!"

"All right!" He raised his palms, amused.

"So do you have more books for me or not?" I put my hands on my hips.

"Sure." His dimples showed. "I'll bring them to the music school on Friday."

"Thanks." I smiled at him, then glanced at Alec's rehearsal stage. "Isn't it time already?"

Ben checked his watch. "He must be a little late. We should go." He nodded toward our seats in the front row.

It was Alec's last days of preparation for the tour. Production Rehearsals, they call it. When they put together the big screens, the lightning, the effects—everything. We were in this huge studio, where they'd built an actual stage for him to practice on. Alec said there would be even more cool effects in the US shows but that his performance today would give me an idea of what his concert would look like. At least on this first leg of the tour.

He was kicking off in Australia. Then he would go to New Zealand, Indonesia, Singapore, Malaysia, Thailand, Philippines, South Korea, and Japan. Six weeks on the road... I would only see him for a couple of days in February when he came back to LA to perform at the Grammys.

"I'm tired of waiting!" Claire sighed, standing in front of me.

"He'll start in a minute. Go play another round!" I stroked her arm. "Or are you gonna let Anna win?" I nodded at the girl two chairs away from me, starting another word-guessing game on her notebook.

"Hey, it's *my* turn!" Claire scowled at her. Then she leaned in and whispered to me, "Tell me a difficult word."

"Hmm, let me think..." I bit my lip theatrically. Then I pulled her closer, saying in her ear, "Impostor."

"Cool." Her face lit up, and she ran back to Anna.

I glanced around the room, anxious. Alec was late, and Claire wasn't the only one bored.

There was a little audience waiting for him. Besides his crew, his friends, and his relatives, I recognized some very important people from his record label. And Alec had let me bring Claire, of course, who absolutely loved to see him playing. And Anna, the girl who hadn't committed suicide thanks to him. He'd asked me if he could meet her, so I thought this would be the best possible opportunity. It was something she would never forget, a memory that would give her strength whenever she had to fight depression again.

"I'm very proud of you, by the way." Ben bumped his knee against mine. "For what you're doing for his fans."

"Thanks." I grinned. "I love it—I think it's benefiting me more than them. It's literally helping me find my way out of the darkness."

"Good." His lips turned up at the corners.

"What about *you*, Ben?" I bumped my knee against his this time. Alec was worried about his twin's mental health too. He told me Ben had been spending way too much time practicing and that he seemed anxious, even depressed, when he wasn't playing. "How are you feeling?"

"I'm okay." He avoided my gaze.

"Come on… I thought you'd learned your lesson with that Bluff game at the beach. You know you can't fool me anymore."

He cracked a smile. "I *will be* okay. Once I get into college and move to New York."

I nodded in sympathy. "I'm sure you will kill it at those auditions. Claire and I were watching your rehearsal the other day at the music school, and…wow!" I really had no better word to express how talented he was.

"Thank you." He grinned down at his hands.

"She's absolutely loving your lessons, you know? You even made her forget about AJ! She only talks about you in the house now."

"Smart kid." Ben chuckled, watching her play with Anna.

"What happened to AJ, by the way?" I knit my brows. "He disappeared! We texted a few times, but he seems to be always busy with something else."

"He's probably finishing some stuff for my dad, since—you know—his two weeks notice."

"What?" I widened my eyes. "He quit?"

"Yeah, right after New Year's. You didn't know?"

"No. He didn't tell me…"

I thought about our conversation on the phone, our New Year's resolution. And suddenly I felt this warm blast of pride in my chest.

He was doing it. He was going after his dream.

IMPOSTOR ALEC

I knew you would never think I was as cool or charming or worthy of your time as he was. He's always been better than me at everything—there was no way you could be interested in me after meeting him first.

And I was right. My first attempt to fix this mess was talking to you as me. I don't know if you remember this, but I tried! We chatted for an hour, but you friend-zoned me. And I'll never know if it was because you didn't like me for me or because I was too late and you were already in love with Alec.

Chapter 23

"We're ready, everybody," Alec's tour manager announced from the stage. "Sorry for the little delay; we'll start in a minute."

Finally! Excitement overtook me as the lights went off.

I had watched Alec rehearse for weeks; I knew the setlist by heart at this point. But I couldn't help but feel like a fan—like Anna! I was over the moon just to be here, watching another one of his concerts.

The introduction played on the screen at the same time the musicians walked to their positions. And my stomach froze in anticipation. It was so different from a normal rehearsal already. The effects and the lights gave a whole new context to everything.

Claire squeezed my hand, euphoric, and I hugged her sideways, smiling at Anna. I was happy to have at least two people to scream with me—because there was no way I wouldn't behave like a fangirl.

This show meant a lot to me. I would recall it in my head again and again every night Alec spent on the road. And I wanted him to remember me there, watching him, every time he played a different show.

From the moment he stepped onto the stage, though, I knew something was wrong. He kept staring at the back of the room, so concentrated that his moves seemed automatic.

I paid close attention to his hands. They were tense but not shaking. I guessed he was nervous about having to perform in front of those people from the record label. He would be relaxed by the third song, like he always did.

But this time, he didn't. When he finished the fourth song, I could tell he was emotionally exhausted. There was a battle happening inside his head. He was fighting anxiety.

The next one was "No More Lies," the song he wrote for me. He'd decided to add it to the setlist to surprise his fans with something they hadn't heard yet. So I screamed the lyrics even louder to make him look at me, to help him relax.

But Alec ignored me. He heard me—I knew he had heard me—but he didn't want to look my way. He kept staring at the piano instead, pretending I wasn't even there.

Did something happen? I asked Ben with my eyes.

Not that I know of, he answered silently.

I watched the rest of the show, just waiting for it to be over. I knew Alec would break the moment he left that stage. He was clearly not okay.

"Do you go or I go?" Ben said at the end of the last song, right before Alec stormed out to the dressing room.

"I'll go." I got up, telling Claire to stay with Ben.

I'd never seen Alec behave like that. And I had no idea what could be wrong—he'd seemed fine when I arrived. When I gave him my scrapbook. When he met Anna.

"Alec, it's me. Open the door." James got there first.

"Can I come in?" He tried again with no success.

"Let me talk to him," I interrupted. And before James could even step aside, the door cracked open.

Alec was breathing fast, his eyes full of pain.

"I'm here, baby." I hugged him, closing the door behind us.

He held me tightly but didn't say anything.

"I saw you weren't okay the moment you walked on the stage. What happened?"

He kept hyperventilating without saying a word.

I pulled Alec to the couch with me, cuddling him. And he wrapped his arms around my waist, resting his head on my chest.

"It's okay. Just breathe with me. In… And out… In… And out…"

For several minutes he just gasped, but I didn't give up. I kept taking deep breaths while rubbing his back until his muscles started to relax around me.

"Do you want to talk about it?" I said softly, playing with his curls.

"No," he muttered.

"Come on…" I caught his chin. "You know you'll feel better after you talk to me," I teased, repeating the words he always said when *I* felt bad.

Alec cracked a little smile.

"What's wrong? Are you mad at me? Is that why you were ignoring me onstage?"

"No. I just… I don't wanna mess this up. But I have to go…" He choked back the tears. "You have no idea how lonely it is, the road. I couldn't even look at you tonight because I knew I was going to break. I'm gonna miss you *so much*."

"Me too." I kissed the top of his head, my chest tightening.

"When I read your chat history for the first time—you two talking about my last tour—you made me wish I had a relationship like that. I thought it would make me feel less lonely on the road. But now that I actually have to say goodbye to you, it feels like I'm ripping my heart out and leaving it here in LA."

I smiled. "You're taking mine with you, so I guess you'll be all right."

He laughed without humor. "I love you."

"I love you too…" I stroked his hair.

"You're coming to Europe with me, right? Over spring break?"

"Yes." I hadn't asked my parents yet, but I knew they would agree.

"Okay." Alec breathed deeply, calming himself down.

"The tour is not gonna change anything between us, baby. I promise you. I'm good at this long-distance thing, remember?"

"Yeah." His dimples showed. Then he leaned in and gave me a kiss.

"Are you ready to go back? There are a lot of people waiting for you out there…" I nodded at the door.

And Alec's mood shifted.

"This wasn't only because of me, was it?" I sat upright, forcing him to do the same. "What happened, Alec?"

He dodged my gaze.

"No More Lies, remember?" I caught his chin again.

"I saw Zach today," he murmured. "He found out that AJ isn't working with us anymore, and he had some *comments* to make about it…"

"I can't believe you're letting Zach get into your head again!"

"He's right, Linda. That's the thing!" Alec exhaled. "Zach is smart—he *sees* things. And he's so right: I made a mistake with AJ. The same mistake I made with Ben. And that's why I want you to go to NYU—I don't want to make that mistake with you too!"

"What?" I said in blank confusion.

"AJ was happy, you know? When he quit. He said he wants to find himself—do what he really wants to do. And I support that; I want him to do it too! I wanted Ben to have gotten into Juilliard last year, but I was selfish enough not to let him practice at home! I shouldn't have dragged him on tour with me—

the same way I shouldn't have kept AJ in the crew all these years."

"I'm really not following you, baby. What—"

"I thought I was getting the band together again! I've always hoped someday I would, but I never will… I can't undo what I did when I went alone to that first audition. And because I was alone that day, I'll be alone for the rest of my life."

"What are you talking about, Alec? You're not alone, you still have a band! Reggie, Evan, Tom—they all love you so much. And you have James! He's not going anywhere. He's always gonna be there for you!"

I thought I was making things better by saying that, but I guess I wasn't. All of a sudden, Alec was in full panic mode again.

"Breathe, baby. Breathe." I held his shaking hands in mine. "What's happening? Did you guys have a fight?"

"It's not fair, you know?" he said in tears. "Zach is right, it's not fair! He's been with me since day one and nobody sees that! He has to play in the shadows while I get all the attention… I never *wanted* all the attention!" he shouted. "We dreamed about this *together*—the four of us. It was never supposed to be just me!"

That's when I finally understood. Alec's anxiety didn't come from *fear*, like mine did. It came from *guilt*. He still hadn't made peace with his past. He kept trying to take his friends with him and recreate what they'd once had—but it was gone. And he felt so guilty about it that he didn't even think he was worthy of what he'd built without them.

"Alec, listen to me." I squeezed his hand. "You did nothing wrong. You just followed your dream! *They* were the ones who didn't want to keep up with you. You went alone to that audition because *they* let you!"

"And since then, the bigger I get, the lonelier it gets—this dream." He sighed. "Sometimes I wonder if it's really worth leaving all these people behind…" His eyes lingered on mine. I knew he was talking about me this time.

"Of course it's worth it!" I said, serious. "First, because those who truly love you will always be by your side, no matter where you are! And second, because you get to do what you love every single day of your life! Do you know how rare this is? Not to mention that you were lucky enough to have *found* your passion. God knows how much I'm struggling with that." I snickered.

"What? You don't wanna be a doctor anymore?"

"No. Not like that, at least. And it's because of you!"

He knit his brows, puzzled.

"Baby, when you're up there on the stage, it's so magical that you light up everyone around you. Anna is out there *alive* to prove that! You do what you love with so much heart and so much passion that it touches us."

He smiled shyly.

"I want that too! To do something meaningful. To change people's lives for the better! That's why they come see you, Alec. And buy your CDs and love you for real. Because you make their lives better!

"I'm sorry you have to deal with all the pressure alone, but don't blame yourself for getting all the recognition. Because you worked harder than anyone else for this—you deserve it! If James is still with you, it's because he believes in what you're doing. He doesn't care about the spotlight—he knew it would be like this from the beginning, and he chose to stay with you anyway.

"And as for AJ, he told me last year that he never felt good enough to play bass professionally! That's why he didn't want to stay in the band, not because he felt like you'd betrayed him."

"He said that?"

"Yes!" I touched his knee in reassurance. "You have to make peace with your past, Alec. You can't live people's lives for them

—you have to accept the choices they make. And the three of them made a choice that day! They could all be here with you, but they didn't believe in your dream like you did. That's why you have it all for yourself now. Not because you stole it from them, but because it has always been only yours!"

"And James's," he added.

"All right… And James's." I chuckled, rolling my eyes. "He really is a loyal friend, isn't he?"

"Yeah." Alec smiled.

"I see it now."

IMPOSTOR ALEC

It wasn't easy for me, you know? To see you with him, to watch you give your love to someone else. And that's why I kept making these stupid mistakes…

I shouldn't have sent you that message when you were in Vegas. I went insane, thinking about what you were doing on that date and all the times I would be forced to watch you with him if you two got together. It was a poor choice of words. I was just drunk and jealous.

Then again at Halloween, when James almost gave us away. It was entirely my fault… You were so gorgeous dressed like an angel that I couldn't stop rambling about you to him—and how cute you looked, searching for the Reese's Cups in every bucket in front of you. That's why I had to leave the party, you know? It hurt too much to look at how beautiful you are. I wasn't used to having you so close. I felt like I would lose my mind if I saw Alec touch you one more time.

Chapter 24

I didn't cry this time—watching him go. Alec was upset enough already; I had to be strong for us both. But the moment that plane took off—the moment I realized he was gone —I broke down in tears.

Nine months away. He would only come back home in October! There would be a few breaks between each leg of the tour, but still… That was a long time to not see your boyfriend. A long time to be alone.

One week went by… Then two… And I was keeping the promise I made to Alec: that I would stay strong and take care of myself and do all the right things. But today, all my strength had been drained…by flower arrangements and heart-shaped cards.

I hated Valentine's Day. It never worked for me anyway. This was the second time I had a boyfriend that I couldn't celebrate with.

I knew last year didn't really count, but that only made me miss Alec even more today. He was real, and he was mine—but he was in Singapore tonight.

And the worst part was that I felt guilty for even *complaining,* since I'd just seen him last weekend, when he came back to LA for the Grammys…

I sighed at myself in the mirror, remembering how gorgeous he'd looked in that suit. What was he doing right now? Was he thinking about me too?

"Linda? Your friend is here!" Dad shouted downstairs.

Good, she's on time.

"I'm coming!" I quickly finished my makeup before grabbing my purse.

I was so not in the mood for a party. I wanted to stay in my room and snuggle in bed with Mr. Bear, eating all the chocolates Alec had sent me that morning.

I'd only agreed to go because I couldn't say no to Ben. He'd just auditioned for UCLA, and tonight was some sort of celebration with his friends.

He was so cute yesterday when I brought Claire to her lesson, telling me that he'd killed it in front of the jury—as if he actually believed things could have gone any other way. And it felt like a flashback, because I'd had that exact conversation with Sam the day before, after *her* UCLA audition. I knew right then I had to introduce those two. And what better opportunity to play Cupid than Valentine's Day, right?

Plus, the setting was perfect. A beach bonfire at sunset! I couldn't think of a better way to set them up. Of course, that required my presence at the party as well, but I had a plan. When I saw they were getting along, I would sadly receive an emergency call from home with a last-minute babysitting request. By then, I was hoping Sam wouldn't mind staying without me, and Ben would be satisfied that I had at least showed up. So everybody would be happy, and I'd be eating chocolates in bed before the clock struck eight.

"Bye, Dad," I said from the stairs.

"Remember your curfew!"

"Don't worry, I won't be long." I double-checked to see if I had my keys. Then my mouth fell open as I opened the front door. It wasn't Sam waiting for me on the street, it was AJ!

"What are you doing here?" I ran to hug him.

"Ben asked me to give you a ride." He squeezed me in his arms. "I thought he'd told you."

"No! I mean, he did say he would send someone, but I was expecting Mario or another one of their drivers. You don't work for them anymore, right?"

"Right," he said, and I could see the pride on his face. "I'm sorry I haven't had time to stop by and catch up—I've been *very* busy."

"I saw that; you disappeared! Why did you stop answering my texts?"

"Oh, sorry." He knit his brows. "I got a new number…"

I laughed in relief. "I thought you were ignoring me!"

"I'm so sorry!"

"It's okay." I shrugged. "I'm glad to see you today! How are you? What have you been doing?"

"I'm doing the *little things*." He beamed. "Do you remember our talk after Christmas?"

"Yeah!" *I knew he had quit because of our New Year's resolution!* "So you're finally becoming the guy you want to be, then?"

He nodded. "I'm getting there…"

"Am I late?" Sam came rushing in our direction. "Sorry, guys."

"No worries," I said. "AJ just arrived."

"Let's go, then?" He pulled the keys out of his pocket. "Or are we waiting for someone else?"

"No, let's go." I grinned at him, walking to the passenger door. I had the feeling I wouldn't want to go home early tonight after all.

♪♩♡

"How are you and Alec?" AJ asked in the car. "I was so sad he didn't win anything at the Grammys! How are you guys handling the tour?"

"Yeah, everybody was a little disappointed… And we're doing okay, I guess. He calls as often as he can; I can't complain." I sighed. "He misses *you*, actually! He's been a little anxious without you and Ben."

Alec had started well in Australia and New Zealand. He was enjoying playing the new songs and excited to meet his fans every night. But when he arrived in Indonesia, anxiety got the best of him. He said he was jet-lagged and tired, but I had a feeling it was because of Ben. The two of them weren't used to being apart for that long; so far Ben had always gone with Alec on his headline tours. His father still traveled with him—and James was also there, of course. But they were both too quiet, too serious. Without his twin to keep him company and AJ to make things more fun and entertaining, tour was definitely not the same. And Alec was feeling that.

"I'm sure he'll get used to it." AJ smiled to himself.

"I hope so…" I worried about the upcoming legs of the tour. Alec still had *eight months* to go.

AJ kept filling the silence with small talk and Valentine's jokes, but we couldn't really talk—not with Sam there. And I wanted so much to talk to him. I had so many questions!

"I'm gonna go say hi to Ben and introduce him to Sam. But then I wanna talk to you, okay?" I said to AJ when we got out of the car.

"Sure!" He pulled a brown case from the trunk. "I wanna talk to you too."

"Hey, I didn't know you also played the guitar. Cool!"

"It's part of my list of little things: to go back to playing." He grinned at me.

"That's so romantic—a guitar and a bonfire," Sam said. "There'll be guys throwing themselves at you by the end of the night, AJ!"

My face burned with shame. "No, Sam—he's not gay! I misunderstood things! I'm *so sorry*." I touched AJ's arm nervously. "I knew Matt was gay, so when I saw you together in the hot tub, I thought… I had no idea you were just friends, until they mentioned Sebastian's name—"

The embarrassment in his eyes shut me up.

"I better get going." AJ locked the car, rushing to the beach. "Talk to you guys later, okay?"

"Oh, no." Sam frowned at me. "Do you think I offended him?"

"I think *I* did…" I watched him go, regretting all the times I'd said something inappropriate about his friendship with Matt.

"I'm sorry."

"No—it's *my* fault. I'll apologize to him later… But first, let's go find Ben!" I linked my arm with Sam's, remembering my purpose for the night.

"Wait!" She pulled me back. "Just give me a minute."

Her shyness made me smile. "It's gonna be fine, relax! You guys have so much in common—and he's even more shy than you."

"No pressure, okay? It's already Valentine's Day. And not all guys like curvy girls…"

"You're *beautiful*, Sam. I bet he won't be able to take his eyes off you."

Her face immediately matched her red hair.

"Let's go! I can't wait to introduce you two." I tightened my grip on her arm, searching for Ben in the crowd.

And twenty minutes later, I was free. Mission complete. My job here was done.

Ben was thrilled when he realized I had come. I'd never seen him so happy before actually, so proud of himself. We all knew his dream school wasn't UCLA, but he'd taken that first victory as a sign that he was ready for Juilliard. It had filled him with confidence for his audition next month.

Sam wouldn't even try Juilliard; she said it was too hard for her. But that particular comment quickly caught Ben's attention, and within seconds, the two of them were lost in this very serious conversation about prescreening auditions, the songs they'd played, and their love for classical music.

My favorite part of those twenty minutes, though, was Hailey's stare when she saw me walk off to talk to AJ. He was playing by the fire, surrounded by people, so I didn't have the guts to interrupt. But at least I'd managed to leave Ben and Sam sitting there by themselves. Alec would be so proud. I couldn't wait to tell him about this tomorrow.

Tomorrow for me, I mean—for him it would be the next day already. Which meant today wasn't Valentine's Day for him anymore.

I sat on the sand to watch the sunset, picturing him waking up alone on the other side of that ocean. I would have given anything to be in his hotel bed with him.

"I see what you did there." Long tanned legs blocked my view.

"Hi, Hailey. Enjoying the party?" I smirked at her.

"You think you're clever, huh? Brought your little friend to steal him from me." She snickered, shaking her head. "You really *are* as dumb as they say."

"Excuse me?" I raised my voice. If she dared say one more thing, I—

"*You* jealous, Hay Hay? I thought you enjoyed a little competition… That's what makes things fun, after all." Someone sat down next to me on the sand.

My heart skipped a beat. *Zach*.

He half-smiled, holding my gaze, then offered me a marshmallow on a stick. *"This* is how we treat our visitors." He exchanged a long look with Hailey.

I had no reaction. I just glanced from Zach to Hailey and back to Zach. It was like they were having a silent fight—a territory fight. And Hailey was the one who lost.

I watched as she rolled her eyes and marched to the other side of the bonfire. I couldn't help but notice this brunette practically throwing herself at AJ. Sam was right, after all. The guitar did work as a love magnet.

"It's nice to see you again, Linda." Zach was still holding the stick in front of me.

I glared at him, remembering how much he'd messed with Alec's head that day at rehearsals. "What do you want?" I refused his marshmallow.

"Are you sure? It's *delicious*." He took a bite, staring at me. And his eyes were so deep, so intense, that they made me shiver.

That's when I noticed it—his hair had changed! He still had the long emo fringe, but it wasn't all black anymore, the ends were blond. And not dark blond like his cousin James; it was that platinum tone that looks almost white. It highlighted the brown of his eyebrows. And the gray of his eyes. And the red of his lips.

"What do you want, Zach?" I said again, focusing on the ocean. All those colors were distracting me from hating him.

"Nothing. Why do you think I want something?"

"Because last time, you only talked to me to provoke my boyfriend!"

"Oh, so now you're allowed to say he's your *boyfriend*?" he said sarcastically, making me see red.

"He's not here tonight, so you're wasting your time—"

"Hey, chill out, love!" Zach raised his palms. "I know he's not here. I was just hoping I could talk to *you*…"

"You already did. Now leave!" I searched for my phone inside my purse. I thought it was time for me to receive that emergency call from home. It didn't look like AJ would have time for me tonight anyway.

"Your hair is longer than before." Zach reached over and grabbed a lock.

"What are you doing?" I yanked his hand away. He'd almost touched my chest!

"I like it, the tone. Dark brown. Is it natural or…"

I narrowed my eyes at him in disbelief.

"What? I like *colors*, that's all!" He pointed at his own head.

I had to laugh this time. "It's natural, yeah."

"Even the highlights?" His voice came out high-pitched in surprise.

"Yes." I giggled. "I think this is actual sun damage."

"It's beautiful," he said with a smile.

"Thank you." I scoffed, smiling back.

Zach turned to the view and just stayed there, quiet. His serenity was so unexpected that I didn't have the guts to ask him to leave—he wasn't doing anything wrong, after all.

Part of me was actually enjoying his company, if I was being honest. It was comforting to know that I wasn't alone at the party. And, at the same time, there was no need to fill the silence between us. No need to pretend I was having fun.

The sun finally set before our eyes, the sky a mix of pink and blue. Zach kept watching the ocean by my side in silence. And I couldn't explain why I was still at this party. Why I hadn't left half an hour ago. Why I kept waiting for something to happen…

I turned my gaze to AJ.

He put the guitar down to go get himself a drink, and the brunette quickly followed him. That's when I decided it was time to go home. It was Valentine's Day—everybody was either with a date or searching for one. There was no place for me here.

"I should go." I got up, glancing at Zach.

"It's boring, isn't it? I think I'm gonna go too."

"Bye." I gave him an awkward smile, then walked back to the parking lot with the phone in my hands.

I had decided it would be better to text Sam and Ben, instead of saying goodbye in person. I knew it seemed cruel to leave Sam at the party like that, but I could tell from the way they were standing that one of them was about to make the first move. If I went over now and said I was leaving, Sam would feel like she should go too, and then my whole point in coming here would be in vain!

It was better to just leave and let them enjoy the rest of the night together. This way, at least *some of us* would get some romance on Valentine's Day.

I had just finished my text to Ben when I heard someone coming up behind me. "What now, Zach? Why are you following me?"

"I'm not following you. I'm going to my car." He pointed to this fancy convertible, parked on the right.

"Oh, sorry." I shook my head and continued writing my message to Sam.

"How are you getting home?" Zach said, serious.

"I'm gonna find a cab."

"Come, I'll take you!" He smiled crookedly, twirling the keys in his hand.

"No, thanks." I kept walking.

"Hey." He grabbed my hand, pulling me back. And for a second, our faces were just inches away.

"Sorry." He let go of me after meeting my cold gaze. "I just think there's no reason for you to try to get a cab when I'm offering you a ride."

"I said: *no, thank you.*" I turned around.

"You're gonna have to walk for miles—they don't stop anywhere near here. Let me at least drop you off at a taxi stand." His voice was soft this time, concerned.

I looked at him again. "How far is it?"

"At least a twenty-minute walk." He frowned.

"All right." I gave up with a sigh.

And Zach grinned as I walked to the passenger seat.

Chapter 25

They tried to call me, Ben and Sam. And even AJ. But I didn't want to have to explain where I was right now, so I turned off my phone. I would call them back once I got home.

"You can drop me off anywhere here," I said to Zach, recognizing the road he'd just turned down. I didn't know the city that well yet, so I'd been lost for the past five minutes. But now I knew how to find my way back to Dad's house.

"Wait, no—I'll take you home! I'm about to get onto the right highway."

I raised my brows in shock. "How do you know where I live?"

"Not important." He smirked, turning onto a different street.

My stomach froze. I hadn't realized it before—what I was doing, who I was talking to.

If you see him again, you ignore him, okay? I mean it, don't listen to him—just call me or Alec! AJ's words popped up in my head.

"Please, drop me off now." I took off my seatbelt and grabbed my purse.

"Seriously? I said I would take you!" Zach glanced at me, annoyed. "Why are you suddenly all cranky again?"

"*Why?* Because it's super creepy that you know where I live!"

"All right, fine!" He sighed. "I don't know exactly where you live. I just… My cousin James told me a few things about you—including your neighborhood. Happy? Can I take you now?"

I stared at him, suspicious. I confess I was more worried about James than Zach now, but still… "No. I'm Alec's girlfriend, I shouldn't be in a car with *you*."

"I'm not as bad as you've heard, you know?" His voice was low.

"I actually didn't hear anything about you…"

"Oh, no?" He looked at me again.

"No. Nobody wanted to tell me," I said sharply.

"So you asked, then?" He half-smiled.

"Well, yeah. I got…curious."

"And what were you curious about? Maybe I can help you with that."

I studied his face. "Are you seriously volunteering to answer my questions?"

"Yeah. Why not? Nobody ever has the courtesy to ask me—they just make assumptions."

"Okay." I turned toward him. "Question number one: why are you being so nice to me?"

Zach laughed out loud. "Because I *am* nice."

"No, you're not. You like to torture my boyfriend!"

"I don't…*like* it." He shrugged. "It just comes easy for me."

"But why do you do it?"

"Because he deserves it," he said seriously, his eyes on the road.

"You're wrong." I folded my arms.

"You don't know the whole thing, Linda. It's easy to judge when you've only heard one side of the story."

"Tell me yours, then!" I challenged.

"Sure." Zach stopped at the traffic light, half-smiling at me. "But not in the car—it's a long story. I wanna do this over a milk-shake. You in?"

Curiosity suddenly overtook me. I thought of Alec. I knew he would freak out when he heard about this. But it could be good for him—for his anxiety! Maybe I could help him resolve his stupid fight with Zach…

I opened my mouth to answer him, but then I heard AJ's warning in my head again.

Then Ben's.

Then Alec's.

A part of me was *afraid* of Zach. Afraid of his bad-boy record people had warned me about. But that fear didn't really come from *me*. Zach had never done anything to me in particular. On the contrary, both times we met, he had been nothing but…nice.

"So…" Zach parked the car right behind a taxi stand. "What do you want to do?" He stared at me with hopeful eyes.

And I decided to trust my heart this time. "Let's go talk."

♪♩♡

Zach McLaren was a *bad boy*. Everybody knew that—he'd never pretended to be anything different. And that's why he *wasn't* really a bad boy. I could confirm it that night.

He told me his side of the story, as promised. And it was pretty much what Alec had told me—besides the betrayal part. I tried to listen without judgment, but I honestly didn't understand how two eighteen-year-olds could still be fighting over something that happened in eighth grade.

Especially when they were both so successful! Zach told me he was in college and already had a nice position in his family's business. Something to do with a hotel, he said. And he still played the drums…with this other punk rock band on the week-ends. He wasn't frustrated at all for never joining Alec and James—he thought their songs were way too pop for him. He confessed that ever since they were kids, their music styles had never really matched.

I couldn't understand, seriously. But somehow, this fight still made sense to them. Zach thought Alec was fussy and arrogant, and Alec thought Zach was stubborn and deceitful.

I personally agreed with them both in this situation, so my only advice for Zach was to talk to Alec about all of it. I assured him Alec would be thrilled to have the opportunity to say "I'm sorry" and be his friend again. And I hoped Zach would listen to me and send him a message, because that would really make Alec the happiest guy on earth. He needed Zach's forgiveness so he could forgive himself and finally move on. And that's what I wanted for him. That's why I'd agreed to have that milkshake with Zach.

I had no idea what I'd actually done until I got home.

"Are you all right?" Ben opened my door as soon as Zach stopped the car. "I was worried sick, Linda! Where were you? Did he touch you? Did he do anything to you?"

"Jeez, Benji, relax!" Zach rolled his eyes at him. "We just went for a snack!"

"Shut up, you son of a—" Ben leaned into the car.

"Hey!" I put myself between the two, shocked at Benjamin's reaction. "He didn't do anything wrong! Stop it!"

"Is everything okay, Linda?" Dad appeared at the door.

Great, now I'm gonna have to explain why there were two boys *bringing me home tonight.* "Yeah, Dad, I'm coming in a minute!"

"You leave right now, McLaren, before I lose my damn mind!" Ben slammed the passenger door shut.

"What the hell do you think you're doing?" I shouted at Ben.

"This is *my* house, and he is *my* guest! You have no right to ask him to leave!"

Zach laughed in delight, rolling down the window. "Thank you, love, but I think I better go. This was fun, though—we should do it again!"

"You're gonna regret this!" Ben threatened.

"Oh, please try…" Zach narrowed his eyes at him. "Your name has been on my list for a long time, Benji. I *can't wait* for a reason to cross it off!"

A shiver ran down my spine. His tone was so menacing that it scared me for a second.

"Goodbye, love." Zach turned on the engine, staring deeply at me. "You can't imagine how good it was to see you tonight."

I watched his car disappear down the street, speechless. This weird feeling flowed over me, and I couldn't understand what it was—or where it was coming from.

"Do you have any idea what you've done?" Ben said between his teeth, trying to stay calm.

"I did nothing, okay?" I rolled my eyes. "We just talked and had a milkshake. And what are you even doing here? You should be at the party! Where is Sam?"

"I took her home," he hissed. "We've been searching for you everywhere, Linda! AJ is still out there driving around! I was so worried! Why did you turn off your phone?"

"Are you kidding me?" I huffed. "Why all this? You guys *really* need to chill out about Zach and this whole thing."

"You have no idea who that pig is!"

"Don't call him that—he's been nothing but nice to me!" I glared at Benjamin again.

"Nice?" He snickered. "Why do you think he did this, Linda? Did you ask *him* why?"

"Because he *is* nice, Ben! He's not the bad boy—"

"Are you sure? I want to see you explaining this to Alec when he sees the pictures."

"What pictures?" I froze.

"You were completely oblivious, weren't you? I saw his friend sneaking pictures of you two in the parking lot. I bet Alec has seen them already, yes, all the way in Singapore!"

My heart raced in my chest.

"How are you going to explain it, Linda? You going home with *Zach*—on Valentine's Day?"

"He wouldn't do that." I shook his head. "I'm sure that's not why—"

"He would do *anything* to hurt Alec. Haven't you realized it yet? It's his game! His addiction!"

"No, Ben… He's not the monster you guys think he is."

"He *lies*, Linda!" Ben rubbed his eyes with both hands. "He would have told you anything you wanted to hear tonight! That's his thing. He's manipulative and persuasive! He's been taking advantage of James for years—just to get to Alec! When I saw you leaving with him, I…" He frowned, clenching his fists.

I took a step backward. His reaction had scared me too. I had no idea what he would do next.

Ben let out a long breath, then murmured, "I knew you would believe anything he said to you, that's why…"

"Look, I understand your worries." I touched his arm in reassurance. "I know Zach has done some pretty bad stuff in the past. But we talked for over an hour today and I really think—"

"You have *got* to learn who you can trust and who you can't!" Ben snapped.

And his eyes—the anger, the anguish in them—terrified me.

He looked away quickly, taking another deep breath. "I know you believe in people, Linda. You're just like James—you keep digging, you never lose hope. But you've got to stop trusting everyone! Some people are just too bad—they don't have a good side! Do you hear me?"

I did. All too well.

Suddenly thousands of conversations and old memories were running through my head. It was like he'd poked a wound with a knife, and now I was torn open, bleeding again.

"I'm sorry. I didn't mean to—"

"Go home." I held my tingling hands over my heart, feeling it break all over again.

"Linda…" He opened his arms to hug me.

"I said *go away*!" I pushed him hard, unable to control my tears.

"What's happening here?" Dad came out of the house, glaring at Ben.

"I'm so sorry." He hung his head and walked back to his car.

IMPOSTOR ALEC

I could have stayed like that forever, just being your friend. I liked having you back in my life somehow, and I knew Alec made you happy. You finally had everything you deserved—I couldn't have asked for anything better. And even if my mistakes had given you some wounds, he'd help you heal. You'd grown brighter by his side, and I loved seeing that.

But while you two rose stronger together, the lies, the shame, and the guilt made me weaker and weaker. Every day I felt a little less myself. I was forced to live in the shadows, to hide every-thing I was feeling from the world and suffer in secret. I knew it was my own fault—*I* was the one who had started all this, there was no one else to blame. But it was a very heavy burden to carry, and I was all alone.

Chapter 26

"I'm here to see Mr. McLaren, please," I said firmly, glancing around at the lobby of the hotel.

"Do you have an appointment?" the receptionist asked.

"No, but I'm—his girlfriend." I swallowed hard, opening the magazine in front of her.

We were front page, Zach and I. *Alec Brock Got Cheated On? Valentine's Day Affair,* the headline read, with five close-up pictures to illustrate it. Me and Zach watching the sunset at the beach, laughing over a milkshake, going home together. They even got one of him touching my hair, and another of the moment he held my hand in front of his car. I still felt nauseated looking at them.

"If you'll just take a seat, Miss González, I'll let him know you're here." The girl smiled at me.

I didn't smile back. I marched to the lounge instead, my heart pounding. I was asking God to help me stay calm, because I swear I wanted to actually kill him!

"Honey!" Zach's face lit up. "I didn't know you were coming, what a nice surprise!"

I felt my blood boil.

"Tiffany, could you please get me the key to the presidential suite?" He shot her a charming grin. "And also…" He lowered his voice, looking me over. "Tell everyone I'll be busy for the next hour. We're still celebrating Valentine's, you know?"

The receptionist giggled, handing him the key.

I almost threw up watching that. How dare he? Was he enjoying all this? Didn't he realize what—

"Don't even *think* about it!" I hissed when he tried to put his hand on my shoulder.

"All right!" Zach chuckled, gesturing for me to enter the elevator first.

I followed him to the room in silence. He'd told me on Saturday that he worked at this hotel, and that it was some kind of family business. But he didn't tell me there were other hotels like this all over the country, and that his family owned all of them. I had to find out for myself, reading the article about us in the magazine.

"So, to what do I owe this pleasant surprise?" Zach locked the door of the presidential suite behind us.

I'd never seen so much luxury in my life. We were in a double-height living room—inside a hotel room! How much more extravagant could it get?

"Make yourself at home." He sat down on the sofa, spreading his arms along the back.

"This won't take long." I threw the magazine onto his lap. "You tell them this is a lie. Or I'll tell them something even worse about you!"

Zach laughed out loud. "You have nothing on me."

"You're right, I got nothing *real*. But two can play this game… I can invent a lie that will hurt you even more than you hurt me!"

He held my gaze, making my face burn. "Sweetie, it's not a threat when you're bluffing, you know?"

"I mean it, Zach! Tell them it's a lie—today!" I clenched my fists. "I know you're the one who sent them these pictures. So you call them right now, or I will—"

"You're not gonna do anything, Linda." He got up, shortening the distance between us. "Because you're a *good girl.*"

"You don't know me." I held my breath. He had gotten too close, but I didn't want to back down. He would know he was scaring me, and I didn't want to give him that pleasure. "I can be bad if I want to!"

"No, you can't." He snickered, raising his hand to my collarbone. Then he brushed his finger against my skin, touching Alec's words on my necklace. "I do know you, love…"

Our eyes locked. And for a second, my heart stopped. My head went blank. If I didn't know for sure that Impostor Alec had been arrested, I…

"You would never have the guts to be like me," Zach continued. "You're just too good—like your *boyfriend.*" He let go of my necklace, walking away.

It took me a minute to regain my senses. I could still see his gray eyes in my mind.

Zach was staring at the window now, dead quiet. And I turned around, searching for the door. Suddenly, I didn't know what I was doing here anymore.

"That's right. Stay away from now on…" He watched me go. "You're too pretty—and too naive—for me not to take advantage of it."

I glanced back at him, not believing what I was seeing. What happened to the lighthearted boy I met on Saturday? This suited guy in front of me looked nothing like him.

"I'm not afraid of you, Zach. I know you're not bad. You're just terrified of showing people who you really are." I thought of our conversation again. "This act you're putting on right now, it's just self-protection. I know you would never hurt me."

"I'm pretty sure I already have." He walked toward me slowly, threatening me with his stare. "Plus, you're my *girlfriend*, remember? *You* came to *my* hotel—by your own will. Tiffany is my witness. I wouldn't be doing anything wrong if we…"

I widened my eyes, taking a step backward.

And Zach burst out laughing. "Gosh, you're so easy to fool. I can't get enough of it!"

"You jerk!" I tried to calm my heart down.

"I've heard worse." He shrugged in complete indifference.

"Who *are* you?" I frowned at him. There was no remorse on his face, no guilt, no empathy.

"I'm *bad*, Linda—I thought you'd learned that already. Now do us both a favor and stay away, okay? Go…"

"I don't believe that." I remembered the hurt in his eyes when he told me how Alec had betrayed him. I knew there was a heart —a broken one—behind his bad-boy façade. "Nobody *is* bad, you know? They just *do* bad things."

"You remind me of James." Zach snickered, sinking onto the couch again. "You two like to fix things—you think you can fix me."

"I'd never try to help someone who doesn't want to be helped."

"Then what are you still doing here?" he said, casually flipping through the magazine.

And I stood there, angry, without anything reasonable to say.

"How did Alec take the news, by the way?" He looked up at me.

"Your plan didn't work. He didn't even get mad!"

"Oh really?" Zach said, amused.

"Yes!" I held his gaze with pride. "He knows I would never cheat on him—especially with you! And he doesn't care about what the media says… You probably did us a *favor*, if you wanna know the truth. You made it sound more convincing, the story that we're just friends."

"Congratulations, then." Zach raised his brows, nodding. "You're publicly someone else's girlfriend, and your boyfriend doesn't even care…"

Urgh! I squeezed my eyes shut.

"You know what? I don't care what people think either!" I yelled, storming to the door.

"Send my hello to Alec!"

"Oh, go to hell!"

"You're so adorable." Zach chuckled. "You can't even *curse*."

I glanced back at him, feeling it all at once: anger, frustration, hate, disgust.

Some people are just too bad—they don't have a good side! I remembered Ben's words on Valentine's Day. And then *his face* popped up in my head: Impostor Alec. Almost as if *he* was the one there in front of me.

Everything in me stopped. And suddenly I knew exactly what I wanted to say to Zach.

"I refuse to let this haunt me… I forgive you."

He almost choked from laughing. "You *what*?"

"I'm not even mad anymore, Zach. I feel *sorry* for you," I said, meaning every word. "It's not right what you did to me. To manipulate people like that, to mislead, to cause pain. You might think this is cool, but it's not.

"But you know what? It only makes me *stronger*—more resilient. It's not *me* who's getting hurt, Zach. It's *you…*"

He shook his head, snickering.

"You're never gonna win this little battle against Alec, and you know why? Because he *cares* about you. He really does! He was sad for *you* yesterday, not for himself. What hurts him the most is not what you do to attack him. It's knowing that after all these years, you're still lost—you've never found your peace, your passion! Because you wouldn't be doing these things if you had. You wouldn't have time for it.

"He's sorry that you still need to live in hate, because you don't have enough love in your life... And the more you lie, Zach—the more you choose to be a jerk to people—the less you're gonna have it: *love.*

"So, if you don't want to take this back," I pointed at the magazine, "fine! Let everybody believe this lie—we don't care. But never forget that every time you do something like this, you're hurting nobody but yourself."

I gave him one last glance, then stormed out the door, grabbing my phone.

You were right about Zach. I'm sorry, I texted Ben. **Can you meet me somewhere in the city? I really need a friend today.**

Tell me where you are. I'm coming right away.

Chapter 27

"Alec!" I bolted from the car.

He caught me in his arms and lifted me off the ground. "I missed you *so much*."

"Me too!" I held his face in my hands, taking him in. His eyes, his dimples, his mouth… I couldn't believe he was finally here!

It was March 9, the day before his birthday. He'd come back last night, and I hadn't been able to focus on any of my classes today, dreaming about this moment—about being in his arms again, safe and loved. After six *long* weeks, I was finally *home*.

Alec must have felt the same way, because he didn't put me down. He pressed me against the wall instead, right there in the living room, kissing me hard.

"What about your parents?" I said, out of breath.

"Mom is working, and Dad went out."

"And Ben?" I dropped my legs to stand in front of him.

"Spending the afternoon with Hailey." He rolled his eyes.

I confess I was disappointed too. I was so sure Ben would love Sam! But apparently she'd given him her number, and he even said he would call, but he never did.

Alec stayed quiet, concern darkening his face.

"So, you were telling me that…" I slipped my hand down his chest to take his mind off his brother. "We're completely alone?"

"Yep." His dimples showed. And he locked our hands together, pulling me upstairs.

I felt like my heart was finally back to its rightful place. Every single piece of it, every broken part. There, snuggled into his chest, I was complete again. I was healed.

The past few weeks had been full of anxiety, full of tears, full of "I wish you were here." But there, in his arms, I felt like it was all worth it. *Alec* was worth it. Even if we didn't have as much time together as we wished, the moments we had were so special they compensated for the wait.

"How is everything?" He broke the silence, running his fingers through my hair.

"Better." I raised my head to look at him. "Especially now, here with you…"

Alec gave me a long, tender smile. "Zach didn't try to contact you again, right?"

I sighed, wishing the past hour could have lasted forever. I wasn't ready to get out of our bubble and start talking about problems yet.

"Did he?"

"No," I said reassuringly.

"He sent me a message this morning—saying he's sorry and wants to talk."

"Really?" I propped myself up on one elbow, so I could look at him more easily. "What did you say?"

"I invited him to the party on Saturday. I thought it could be a start…"

I nodded at Alec. But deep down I wasn't sure if that was a good or a bad thing. Zach was very difficult to read. One moment he behaved like a demon, taking pleasure in lying to your face, and the next, he did something unexpected and heartwarmingly human.

He had publicly turned down the rumors about us, a few days after we met at his hotel. And then he sent the magazine with the interview to my house, with a flower bouquet and this little note.

I never got you a Valentine's gift.
Thanks for the talk.
Z

I almost couldn't believe it, seriously.

But then, a week later, he gave another interview explaining that the only reason we weren't dating was because I was indeed Alec's girlfriend—reestablishing the chaos with the media and finally giving them the confirmation they needed. Zach showed them a zoomed in picture of my necklace and everything, so it was kind of hard for Alec to deny it.

Especially because he didn't *want* to deny it anymore. He ended up talking to his management instead, and they all agreed it was time. So now I was officially Alec's girlfriend. And the person I had to thank for that was *Zach*.

"I hope he's being honest," I said. "You two really need a fresh start."

"Yeah." Alec sighed, hopeful. "What about AJ, have you heard from him?"

"No, actually—I think this time he really is ignoring me! We exchanged a few texts after Valentine's, and I suggested we go out for a coffee, but he never has time to meet me!"

"It's not just you, everybody is saying that he disappeared. The last news I had is that he's planning on moving to the East Coast."

"What?" My breath caught in my throat.

"Yeah, Matt said he's been talking about maybe going to Boston."

"I thought he was working on a project here in LA! He told me *that's* why he's always busy…"

"Well, he's following his own path—and I'm happy for him. He must have been wanting to do this for a long time."

"Yeah." I rolled onto my back. I was happy that AJ was finally going after what he wanted in life, but…I missed him. We'd barely talked since the year started. And now he was moving away?

I hope he comes to the party; I really need to talk to him.

"You're so beautiful, you know that?" Alec lay on his side, staring at me. "Thank you for the way you supported me on the road." He kissed my shoulder. "Now I know we can make this work—I don't have to choose between love and music anymore."

I knit my brows, surprised. "I would *never* make you choose."

"I know." He smiled slowly. "I can't wait to take you on the road with me…"

"I'm so excited!" I glanced at the ceiling, already daydreaming about the Eiffel Tower.

Alec was home for the next ten days. But the following week was my spring break, so he was bringing me along to the first shows of the European leg of his tour: Berlin, Paris, and Amsterdam.

I focused on Alec again, then cracked a smile—he was still watching me. He looked so silly, so in love. I wondered if I looked like that too. Because I did love him—just as much.

"Happy Birthday!" I said quietly.

"It's not until tomorrow." His cheeks went pink.

"Yeah, but you're still jet-lagged. I bet it's already March 10 in your head."

He let out a laugh. "You're so right."

"So, let's celebrate!" I stroked his hair, grinning. "I'm making you a cake today!"

"Oh yeah? Like the one your mom said you baked for me last year but forgot to add the sugar?" He snickered.

"*Better*, okay?" I gave him a little punch.

And he chuckled, locking me in his arms again.

♪♩♡

I had big expectations for that Saturday night. First, because it was the twins' birthday party; I really couldn't be more excited. There was also the fact that Zach was coming. And though I had no idea of what to expect from that, I was *curious*, to say the least. But I confess the person I was most excited to see at that party—besides my birthday boy, of course—was AJ. I had so many questions for him, so many things to talk about.

But the moment I saw him coming my way, I was so shocked that I forgot everything I was going to say.

"What did you do with your hair?" I blurted. He had gotten a blond streak in the front.

AJ half-smiled, bending down to hug me. "I wanted to try something different. Do you like it?"

"Yeah!" I wouldn't have thought it would, but it did suit him well.

"We need to talk… I have something to tell you."

"So, tell me!" I grinned. I was excited just seeing the joy on his face.

He looked around to see if we were being watched. "I'll tell you later, okay? Or maybe tomorrow, I really need some priv—"

"Have you seen Ben?" Alec wrapped his arms around me from behind, then kissed my neck as if we were in his room, not at a party full of people.

I didn't know if it was because he was only home for a week

or because now we could actually behave like this in public, but Alec was extra affectionate these days. And I was absolutely loving it!

"No." I turned around, searching for his lips.

"I don't think Benjamin is in *there*, Alec." Matt's voice made my face burn.

"Sorry, bro. I got distracted." Alec pulled away.

And Matt gave me an apologetic look. "Hailey disappeared too, so we're a little worried."

"Say no more. How can I help?" I stepped forward.

"Well, he's not in his room; he isn't picking up his phone. Maybe he's hiding in his car again..." Matt said to himself, heading toward the garage.

"Wait, I'll come with you!" AJ rushed behind him.

"Should I take a look upstairs?" I glanced at Alec.

"Can you please, baby? Try the TV room; I'll go check the studio. I don't think they left the house—not today. But he is... you know."

"Yeah. I'll help you cheer him up." I gave Alec another kiss before going back to the house.

The party was happening on the outdoor patio, around the pool. Most of the Brocks' friends and relatives were there—I'd even met their British grandparents this time. Everything was decorated in black with these cool details in neon colors. It was their nineteenth birthday, and Alec had purposely chosen this week to take a break from the tour so he could spend it with his brother. And although he couldn't have known, I was happy he did it.

Ben had hurt himself again. And he didn't tell anyone until after his audition for Juilliard last week. Apparently, his tendonitis was back, and he'd been in severe pain for days. But he refused to give up; he refused not to try.

From what he told us, his effort wasn't enough though, and he kind of blew his audition. But worse—since that was his second trial, he really couldn't go to school there anymore. Not as an undergraduate, at least. He could apply again for grad school, but only after he'd earned a bachelor's degree somewhere else.

Ben was devastated, of course. We'd all seen how much he'd practiced for this thing, how much he wanted it. That's why I was glad that he at least had Alec here to help him work through everything.

"Ben?" I knocked on the guest bedroom door. I had already tried all the bathrooms, the TV room, the gym, the library.

"Benjamin?" I was just about to give up when the door opened.

Hailey. I felt myself blush. "Sorry, I didn't mean to interrupt."

She didn't bother talking to me, but her eyes were…sad. Like, really brokenhearted. I wondered if they'd had a fight. *Maybe they broke up for real this time…*

"Come in," Ben said.

I entered the room as Hailey walked away, her head down. "Is everything all right?"

"Yeah, I'm coming down in a minute." He got up from the bed, rubbing his red eyes. "I was just…resting. These pills make me sleepy."

Ben was a terrible liar. It was so obvious that he'd been crying—he looked even more miserable than Hailey. Not to mention they were literally hiding in here. *Whatever happened between these two must have been pretty serious.*

"Sorry about that." I nodded at the door. "About every-thing…" I added, glancing at his wrist brace.

He bowed his head. And I knew he wasn't overreacting—Alec had told me what his doctor said. It must be the worst thing in the world for a musician to be told you may never play profes-sionally again. Especially knowing it'd been your own fault.

"You have to stay optimistic, Ben—please don't lose your

faith. It's gonna be just a few months of rest, you'll see… You're gonna be an even better violinist once you let your wrist heal and recover. Don't listen to what they say; I *know* you're gonna play again—I feel it in my heart!"

He took a deep breath, putting on a brave face for me. But then his chin trembled, and he covered his eyes with his good hand.

"It's gonna be okay…" I wrapped my arms around him. And the second I did so, he burst into tears.

I let him sob on my shoulder, stroking his short hair, until he calmed down.

"Look on the bright side—now you're coming to UCLA with me!" I grinned at him. "You have a *great* future ahead of you, Ben. This is just a wave, it will pass. I can already see myself in one of those fancy auditoriums watching you shine as the great star you were born to be."

He gave me a tearful smile, falling back onto the bed. "I just wish I didn't have to deal with all of this tonight, you know? All these people, all these questions. If I could just disappear…"

"I know how you feel." I sat next to him. "I said the same thing that night you hid me in the studio, remember?"

He nodded, staring at nowhere.

"Well, maybe I can help *you* today! Return the favor."

"It's my *birthday*." He shook his head.

"Yeah, it's definitely gonna be a little tricky. But nobody should be forced to look happy for pictures if they don't feel like it, right?"

He glanced at me, hopeless.

"Okay, let me see…" I stroked my chin. "How can I hide you from a hundred people?"

Ben let out a chuckle.

And his reaction gave me another idea. "Hey, maybe I have two options here! Instead of hiding you from them, I can hide in here *with* you until you're happy enough to want to join them!" My sudden enthusiasm made him laugh.

"See? I think the second option might be even easier!" I grinned, poking his cheek, then sent Alec a text explaining my plan.

♪♩♡

After a pep talk, a heart-to-heart, and a few more tears, Benjamin was ready to leave the room. And I confess I was proud of myself. Not for making him come down to the party, but for helping him to be optimistic—to hold on to his faith. Alec was right, I really was a believer. I didn't know how it would happen, but I believed with all my heart that despite what his doctor had said, Ben would be playing again soon. And the more I helped him believe it, the stronger he became inside.

"There you are!" Alec came running the moment he saw me on the stairs.

His eyes were a little red, but he had a big smile on his face. Like the one he gave me in the snow after sneaking out from my grandparents' house.

"What happened to you?" I raised an eyebrow.

But his attention was on his brother now, grinning shyly behind me. And a look of relief washed over Alec's face at seeing Ben looking happier.

"You really are an angel, you know that?" He caught my hands in his and kissed one, then the other. "*Everything* you touch, you turn into love."

"All right, now you're scaring me," I said, suspicious. "What happened?"

"I talked to Zach! We're all good!" Alec beamed. "AJ and James are helping him set up the drums right now—we're gonna play tonight!"

My mouth fell open.

"Come! I was going upstairs to call you two. You can't miss this!" He pulled me by the hand, euphoric like a little kid.

"How did you do this, Linda? These four haven't played together in five years!" Matt caught me in a hug the second I walked out onto the patio.

"This is literally the best gift you could have given him, sweetie. Thank you!" Amanda hugged me next. And even Oliver came over to say that he appreciated my intervention. They all knew how much losing Zach's friendship had affected Alec, and they were thrilled to finally see the two talking things out.

I felt like they were thanking the wrong person, though. I hadn't done anything, had I?

"Let her move, guys. Zach was asking for her." Alec guided me to the improvised stage they'd set up beside the pool.

I glanced back to make sure Ben was still following me. "Don't go hide again!"

"Don't worry, I'm right behind you," he said with a smile.

"Only you, Linda." AJ opened his arms for a hug. "You never stop inspiring me."

I hugged him back, glancing around at the party. That's when I realized how *happy* they all looked. Not only Alec's family, but the other guests too. Everybody was joyful, grinning at each other.

Everybody but one person.

Everybody but James.

He seemed stunned, frozen in place with the guitar in his hands. I had a flashback from that day at the mall—it was the first time since then that he didn't run away from me. He stared back intensely, meaningfully. As if he was trying to tell me something. Something I couldn't quite understand.

"There she is!" Zach exclaimed, catching my attention.

He had one arm around Alec's shoulder and a self-satisfied smile on his face.

"Look what you made me do." He met my eyes.

And my heart stopped. I had no idea if I was staring at the *good* Zach or the *bad* one.

IMPOSTOR ALEC

When you found out I'd lied, I knew it was over. You asked me to stay away, and I thought that was the most decent thing to do, after everything I'd put you through. But I couldn't forget you. I missed you every minute of the day. And I started having this hope that if a part of you really loved me for me, maybe we could work things out somehow.

I knew you wouldn't just listen to me, though. You would never believe I was telling you the truth about who I was through the phone or the computer. And I was terrified you would end up calling the police on me if I tried—if you hadn't done that already. My only hope to fix my mess and get you to listen was showing you my face.

I thought if I came to your door, begging for a second chance, proving how hopelessly in love I was with you, maybe you would forgive me. And you can't imagine how wrecked I was when I couldn't find you there.

I didn't go only to Petersburg, Linda. I went to your dad's place in San Francisco too. I tried to find you everywhere. I needed to *see* you! It was the only way I could win you back.

<h1 style="text-align:center">Chapter 28</h1>

I spent the rest of the night anxious. I was glad to see Alec happy. But I just couldn't forget how I felt after Valentine's, when I saw the photos in that magazine. When I realized Zach had betrayed me.

He would do anything to hurt Alec. I kept thinking of what Ben had told me the day we met in town, after I confronted Zach at the hotel. He had finally opened up about all the things Zach had done to Alec, and let me tell you, it wasn't pretty. To Zach, this fight, this rivalry between the two, it was like a game. He took pleasure in playing it. And he'd been doing it for too long— it was hard to believe he had changed like that in one night.

"You should have seen his face, Nina. He was too…*happy*."

"And is that a bad thing?" She chuckled over the line.

"Well, yeah. I mean—I don't know. I just think it all happened too fast. I'm not sure if it's real or not."

"You said the other guests were happy, not worried, right?"

Everyone but James. I remembered his deep stare.

"Maybe you're being a little paranoid… And if he is indeed lying, Alec will find out soon anyway."

"But it will break his heart, Nina. That's what I don't want to happen! You should have seen how relieved and at peace he was when we went to bed."

"Wait, so you slept there? I thought you'd come back with your parents. What are you doing at home, then? Is Alec there with you?"

"No, he wanted to go sailing with Matt. We're meeting again for dinner."

"Still afraid of the boat?" She teased.

"No. It has grown on me, actually. But Matt had something important to talk to Alec about, and I didn't want to spoil their brother bonding time."

"You did right… But go on! Keep telling me about the party!"

We spent another half hour on the phone. I told her all about my conversation with Ben, how happy Alec was after playing with his old band, and that once again AJ and I hadn't had the opportunity to sit by ourselves and talk.

I had just hung up the phone when my cell buzzed. I thought it was Nina again, but when I glanced at the screen, I didn't recognize the number.

Can I still trust you? If I say I want to meet you as me, would you go alone? Would you promise not to tell anyone?"

Everything in me stopped. No heartbeat, no breath, no senses.
It can't be him.
He's in jail! Jack caught him.
Could he be out already?
I called Nina again with a racing heart and tingling hands.

"Calm down!" she said, alarmed. "Can you read me the text? I wanna know exactly what he said."

I grabbed my cell, staring at the screen. But before I could read the message out loud, two more came in from the same number.

I really need to tell you the truth—just the two of us in private.

Can you meet me at the café today at 3 P.M.?

"Linda? Linda?" Nina shouted on the line.

I couldn't listen anymore.

We need to talk... I have something to tell you. I thought about AJ at the party, what he'd said to me. *I'll tell you later, okay? Or maybe tomorrow, I really need some priv—*

"Linda? What's happening? Talk to me!"

"They never arrested him—they never caught the right guy. I think it's AJ, Nina."

"What?"

I curled into a ball on my bed, remembering every single one of our conversations. I'd been oblivious before because I thought he was dating Matt, but now...

Don't you ever get confused and think about the other guy?

Do you really think you loved *the impostor? Do you honestly believe that true love happens on this* soul level?

I don't think this guy is about to show up and physically hurt you... Maybe he was just jealous that day because you were on a date with Alec.

He'd *defended* him. He wanted me to think of the impostor as someone insecure and jealous and flawed—not the monster Jack had painted for me. He knew I wasn't in danger; he knew I had nothing to worry about. *That's why he always made me feel so safe around him.*

Now I understood the message he'd sent when I was in Vegas! He really couldn't keep his promise if I didn't keep mine because he *literally* couldn't stay away from me—not as long as he worked for the Brocks.

That's why he quit! That's why he's going to Boston! He's moving on—far away from me.

I couldn't believe I hadn't seen this before.

AJ had been traveling with Alec's crew since the beginning. There was nothing about Alec, his family, his agenda that AJ didn't know. Everybody trusted him. They'd even told him about Impostor Alec!

Jack said he had investigated everyone from the crew, but AJ had always had access to privileged information. Matt was his best friend—and he was not only bad at keeping secrets but also had a major crush on AJ. I bet AJ could get any information he wanted from Matt!

Plus, I loved Matt too. And the reason I loved Matt—the reason he was initially my favorite person from Alec's world— was because he was the one *Impostor Alec* seemed to like the most.

"Linda, talk to me!" Nina shouted.

I took a deep breath. My heart was beating too fast—the adrenaline had completely taken over.

"Please, say something! You're scaring me!"

I forced myself to say the words out loud. Everything I'd just realized. All the evidence no one else had noticed.

Things were so clear to me now.

I loved AJ! Since our first real conversation, I'd felt connected to him! He understood me somehow—we got along almost too well.

I hadn't connected the dots so far because I was trusting the detective, not my own instincts. But I'd always believed Impostor Alec was good! I knew he'd made a mistake, but he wasn't a cold-hearted liar—not like those Jack sent to jail. I was sure there were no other victims; that what we had was real. I knew it all along. I knew it! My heart was never wrong.

"You need to talk to him about this, Linda. Like, *right now*— go ahead and call him! You guys became such good friends, I'm sure—"

That's when it hit me.

"He was there *all along…*" I said, my voice barely a whisper. "He knew about my struggle with anxiety, with depression. When I saw the news on TV, he was the one who took me home! If he's really the impostor and let me go through all that, Nina—just so he could keep his stupid secret. I…" The lump in my throat didn't let me finish.

"I don't even know what to say, L…"

Tears blurred my eyes. *I can't believe he would do this to me.*

"Why don't you go talk to Alec and the detective first? I think it's the best way—"

"They're gonna laugh in my face!" I scoffed. "They would never believe me if I told them it's AJ. I have no idea how he managed to fool everybody, but Oliver wouldn't have hired him to be my bodyguard if they believed there was even one tiny little chance of him being the impostor! I have to confront AJ by myself; they will only scare him away."

"If they were so convinced it wasn't him, there must be a reason for that. The impostor must be someone else!"

"Who else, Nina? He told me yesterday that he wanted to talk to me in private, to tell me something. Now I understand every-thing—*I'm* the girlfriend he told Matt about! The girlfriend no one has ever met. It's AJ, Nina. I know!"

"But Alec was so sure that they'd arrested the guy…"

"They did catch an Impostor Alec—several impostors, actu-ally! They just didn't catch *mine*. I always knew it was someone from the crew, Nina! Someone with access to privileged informa-tion. They tried to convince me I was the one who was naive— that the impostor had simply manipulated my perception of him. But I always had this feeling—"

My cell buzzed again. **I'll be waiting at 3 P.M., and I'll understand if you don't come. But please don't tell anyone, okay? I will know if you do, and you'll be the one to blame for the consequences.**

"What did he say this time?"

I read the message out loud.

"That's pretty much a threat, Linda. I think you should call Alec."

"Come on, it's not a threat. The same way that other text never was! We even talked about this once in his car—I'm telling you, Nina, it's AJ! He's probably just afraid. He fooled too many people with this; he must be terrified that I'll tell someone and they'll send him to jail or something. He's even moving from LA, I told you! He wants to run away from here."

Nina exhaled. "I just don't think you should go alone."

"It's AJ we're talking about… He's not gonna hurt me."

"What if it isn't? You said the messages aren't coming from his number."

"Maybe he's testing the waters, trying to figure out how much I know. Or maybe he just changed his number again. He's changing everything! He quit his job, he's moving to Boston. Even his hair was different yesterday! He got this blond streak in the front."

"You're joking!" She snickered. "I *really* don't see this working for him."

"Yeah, I didn't think it would either, but it kind of suits him well." I half-smiled, remembering him at the party.

I couldn't believe it was AJ. It had always been AJ…

I rolled onto my back, wiping my eyes. I was flooded with all sorts of emotions—anger, relief, sadness, empathy.

I thought about how many times AJ had seen me with Alec.

How many times he'd had the opportunity to tell me the truth.

How many times I'd been in his arms.

"Please tell me you're not doing this alone," Nina said, her voice low.

"We're meeting at a coffee shop; there'll be plenty of people there. And he just wants to talk."

"Then call him right now! You have his number!"

"I can't let him know I figured it out. He's finally decided to open up—I don't want to risk scaring him away."

♪ ♩ ♡

Things might have ended differently if I'd found out about AJ earlier.

I was relieved knowing it was him. After everything I'd been through, thinking it was that pedophile, I was grateful to be *his* victim. To know he wasn't a professional liar, and what we had was somewhat real. But even if I'd already forgiven him long ago, what I felt for him at one time had changed, and now my heart belonged to someone else.

That's what I was going to tell him. That was the right thing to do. He didn't even have to tell Alec if he didn't want to—I was willing to keep his secret. But regardless of what he would say, there was no decision to be made. My heart really belonged to someone else now.

"Are you ready to order, miss?" the waitress said. "Or you're still waiting…"

I looked at my watch. *3:15 P.M.*

"A chamomile tea, please." I gave her a polite smile. If AJ was going to be late, then I needed something to calm the butter-flies in my stomach.

I had gotten to the café ten minutes earlier. I wanted to sit at our table. Not the one where we'd sat a few times before, during Claire's lessons. The one he had described to me during our conversations. The one he always said he was texting me from.

I guess a part of me always expected this. I'd always known this was the place he would choose for us to meet. He used to make me picture coming here with him so often that when I entered this café for the first time, it felt like a déjà vu, not a first sight.

That's why I got so addicted to this place after that July 15. It was my only "familiar setting" in LA; it felt a little like home. Before I met Alec, I used to sit at this table for hours, watching faces go by, wondering if he was one of those guys. And every time someone stared back, I thought it was him. I secretly *hoped* it was him.

I thought about AJ again. When Alec brought me to this café in November, I was too suspicious of James to think of anyone else. But of course this place was special to AJ too! The four of them used to come here together! I bet it meant as much to AJ as it did to Alec—or James, or Zach.

My heart raced. I still couldn't believe it was him. It was so messed up and awkward and awesome at the same time. I couldn't believe—my friend AJ!

I checked my phone in expectation. My *very late* friend AJ.

It was already 3:30 P.M., and I'd had no news from him.

Breathe, Linda. Breathe, I kept telling myself. *He must be a hundred times more nervous than you. That's why he's late...*

Ten minutes later, my patience was gone, so I texted him: **Where the heck are you?**

And it took him five more minutes to finally text back. **Thank you for the ambush!**

What is he talking about? I got up, glancing around. *I'm waiting here alone for an hour, like a complete idiot, and he...*

That's when I noticed a man at the table next to me. He'd been reading a book since the moment I arrived, and all of a sudden, he stood up alert, with one hand on his ear and another one on his waistband.

"Linda!" AJ came running in my direction.

Oh, thank God. I let out a breath, my hand going to my chest. "What took you so long?"

"I'm so sorry." He kissed the top of my head, hugging me tight.

"It's okay, you're here now."

"No, Linda." He leaned back to look at me. "I'm really sorry, honey, but…it's not me."

My heart sank.

"I'm so, so sorry." He sat down on a chair next to mine, pulling my hand so I could do the same. "I didn't realize you were still thinking about the impostor; I had no idea you thought it could be me! I would have told you sooner if I knew—I'm gay, Linda! I'm in love with Matt!"

"What?" My voice cracked.

"That's why I loved to hear you talking about us as a couple— and invented that girlfriend when he started bragging about Sebastian! I've known it for years now, but I didn't have the courage to admit it to myself until I met *you*.

"I'm sorry I ignored you after Valentine's; I wasn't ready to tell people the truth yet. I didn't even know if Matt wanted to be with me or not. But then we started talking about Boston, and this weekend we finally…" He tilted his head, grinning at me.

"You're such a special girl, Linda." AJ squeezed my hand. "So brave and so pure. You really believe in *love*. Like, the real kind of love that transcends physical boundaries, age, gender… When you love the essence of someone, you know? Regardless of the package.

"I love Matt like that! Pretty much since the day we first met —there's never been anyone else for me. But I was in denial! I had convinced myself that being his best friend was enough because I couldn't bear the thought of not being what my family expected me to be. But you reminded me of what really matters— of what real love is. Then you encouraged me to be myself and go after what *I* wanted in life. It's because of you, honey, that I had the courage to surrender to love and start being the guy I really am.”

I stared at him in silence, unable to control my tears. I knew he understood me, he always had—that’s why we got along so well. But I thought… I wished… I couldn’t believe it wasn’t him!

AJ wrapped his arms around me, pulling our chairs closer.

“I’ve always thought you two were perfect together, you know?” I wiped my eyes with a dry laugh.

“I know! That’s why I couldn’t correct you when you started talking about us as a couple! You really believed Matt loved me back, and it gave me hope while he was still with Sebastian.” He smiled tenderly. But then his face fell. “I’m so sorry I didn’t tell you the truth before. It’s *my fault* that you put yourself in danger today—you thought you were meeting *me*.”

“Gosh, this is so embarrassing!” I hid my face with my hands.

“No, don’t be.” AJ rubbed my back. “You were right after all; your impostor really isn’t the guy they arrested.”

Only then I realized… “What are you doing here? I mean, if it isn’t you— I’m gonna kill you, Nina!” I fumed.

“Don’t be mad at her; she did the right thing!” he hissed. “How could you agree to meet this guy like this? Without taking any security measures at all?”

“Calm down! This is a public place, he wouldn’t be able to do anything…”

“So you think you’re *safe* here?” AJ snickered. “The police told me most teen victims do exactly what you did—they leave their homes *willingly* to meet up with their predators! Somehow, they are convinced that what they’re doing is ‘safe.’ But you know what happens? They end up being sexually abused—or kidnapped—or even killed!”

“I thought I was meeting *you*!” I frowned in despair, fear washing over me.

“Yeah, but you weren’t! Do you realize now the risk you took coming here? Alec is *furious*, Linda! He can hear you, by the way."

My eyes immediately searched for him.

But AJ showed me a hidden microphone in his shirt. "He's in a van with the detective and the police. There are officers in here too—they were expecting to catch him in the act." He nodded at the guy with the book next to me.

"You set up a trap for him?" I raised my voice in shock.

"Shhh! He might still be around, we never know."

"Oh my God." I lost my breath. "I'm back to square one, aren't I?"

I had no idea who he was again! Worse, now I knew he hadn't been arrested—he was out here in LA, stalking me!

You'll be the one to blame for the consequences. I remembered his text this morning.

"He must be beyond mad, AJ. He warned me not to tell anyone, otherwise he would know. And he did find out! He sent me a text right before you arrived, saying—"

"I know. I was in the van too. They tapped your phone—they're following everything."

"But how…I don't understand. How did this happen?" I stared at the officer at the next table, my breath getting shorter and shorter.

"Nina called Alec explaining about the meeting, so they contacted the police. And when Matt told me it was all my fault, I… I'm so sorry, Linda." He sighed. "Alec wanted to be the one to come burst your bubble when they realized the impostor wouldn't show up, but I needed to talk to you. You were expecting to see *me*, after all…"

"I'm *so* stupid." I let my head fall onto the table. I felt dizzy and nauseated. I couldn't believe I was back to that nightmare.

"I'm gonna get you some water." AJ stood up, stroking my

back. But before I could say thanks, he fell into his chair again. "*What?*"

I raised my head, alarmed, and my stomach froze. He was pressing his hand to his ear, with wide, panicked eyes.

"What is it?" My pulse skyrocketed. AJ never panicked. He didn't even get worried—he was the calmest person I knew!

"What happened?" I shook his arm, making him look at me.

"He took Benjamin… Instead of you."

Chapter 29

"Alec, I wanna go with you. Please, let me come! I can help—"

"You've done enough, Linda!"

I held my breath, frightened. He'd never looked at me like that before.

"I'll keep you updated, okay?" His voice softened. "Just stay in the house and let us take care of this. I can't handle worrying about both of you right now—I need to find my brother!"

I swallowed hard, nodding at him.

I only dared speak again when his phone buzzed. "Do they have any news?"

"No. They're searching for clues in the car, but they still can't tell if the guy went to the coffee shop and realized he was being watched, or if he knew about the trap and didn't even show up."

I glanced down, thinking about Ben. My chest was so tight I could barely breathe.

We were in the car with Jimmy, a few minutes away from my house. Alec's plan was to drop me off and go join his dad, AJ, Jack, and everyone else who was out there looking for Ben.

He'd been abducted on his way to Hailey's house between

3:00 and 3:30 P.M., and the police had just found his car abandoned on the road with everything inside—his phone, his wallet, his violin.

"Don't leave the house, do you hear me?" Alec said when Jimmy parked on my street. "Stay with your dad! I need to know you're safe so I can focus on Ben."

I couldn't hold back the tears this time. "I'm so sorry. I shouldn't… If I hadn't…"

Alec caught my face in his hands and kissed my forehead. "We're gonna find this guy and make him pay for *everything* he's done to us." His tone was deep, his eyes ice cold. "Now go. I have to go find my brother."

I wiped away my tears and got out of the car.

"I'll send someone to escort you to school in the morning," Alec said through the window. "But call us immediately if anything happens during the night!"

"All right." I walked inside, watching him go.

♪♩♡

I spent the next six hours in my bed, staring at the ceiling. I couldn't stop thinking about what else I could do—how I could help them. I was the one who knew the impostor best, after all. I felt like I could be helping…if only they'd let me.

Alec was keeping me updated, but there was not much to be updated about. They didn't know where Ben was or who'd taken him—it was always the same news.

You'll be the one to blame… I recalled the impostor's text over and over. It alternated with the one he'd sent me in Vegas: ***Please stay away. Please! I don't want to end up hurting you…***

He'd warned me. Multiple times.

He wanted me to keep my distance from Alec, to stay quiet.

He'd told me there would be consequences if I didn't do what he said.

I wondered if that was why he went to West Virginia in August—to kidnap me. This was actually the second time he'd tried to catch me alone. But when he got to the coffee shop and realized it was a trap, he decided to improvise. He decided to take revenge.

Where is he right now? What is he doing to Ben? I wished he had taken *me* instead. Ben didn't deserve this—Alec didn't deserve this. They were both so happy last night. Alec was so euphoric about playing with his old band and reconciling with Zach that he'd transformed the Happy Birthday song into a cake fight with his twin. They both had to go wash their faces before actually tasting the cake. And Ben was all smiles after that. Even if for just one night, we really made him forget about his wrist and what his doctor said.

I thought of his antique violin abandoned in the car, and my heart broke all over again. That was the proof Impostor Alec didn't do it for money. The Brocks were still hoping for a call asking for ransom, but if this guy wanted money, he would have taken the violin!

My eyes filled with tears. And I started praying again—asking God for an intervention.

Tic... I heard a noise coming from my window.

Tic... My heart jumped. The shot of adrenaline was so strong my whole body tingled.

Tic... I grabbed my phone, ready to call the police, but forced myself to take a quick glance outside, before officially launching into panic mode.

James. I let out a breath.

"What are you doing here?" I mouthed to him from the window. It was almost midnight, and everybody was sleeping.

"Come down," he whispered, gesturing to the door.

But I searched for his number on my phone instead. I'd added it right before the tour started, in case I needed to reach Alec. And I confess I never thought I would use it until—

"No!" James shouted in the front yard, his arms in the air. "Don't call me—they will know! Just come downstairs," he whispered again.

And that's when it hit me. *All this time, all these months. I knew I wasn't paranoid. I knew it was him! I could feel it!*

I exhaled, furious, then changed into some jeans and a hoodie. When I marched downstairs, I didn't have one drop of fear in me anymore—it was all toughness and anger and boldness. I was ready for a fight! Whatever unfinished business he had to resolve, it was with me, not with Ben!

"You bastard. You never fooled me!" I hissed at the door, from the inside of the house.

"I know…" James sighed.

"Since that day at the studio… No! Since that first sight at the mall!"

"I know, all right? *I'm sorry!* Can you please open the door?"

I laughed without humor. "You must be crazy if you think I will—"

"We don't have time for this, Linda. Please open the door! You have to come with me right now!"

"You really *are* crazy." I scoffed. "I'm calling Alec, he will—"

"No, please!" James put both hands on the door. "I know you never trusted me, but you gotta trust me on this one, okay? It's for Benjamin!"

My stomach froze. "Where is he?"

"That's where I need to take you! So please, open the door and come with me!"

I felt the air escaping my lungs. He was here to kidnap me

too! This was his plan all along: he was using Ben as bait to get *me.*

"Come on!" James groaned, trying to force the knob.

And a shiver ran down my spine. "Wh-what did you do to Ben?"

"I didn't do anything but send you that stupid text this morning! But *he will,* Linda! Please, you've gotta trust me!" James pressed his forehead against the door. "What do I have to do? Tell me what I have to do, and I'll do it—anything! Just come with me, *please!*" He was crying now.

I mean, actual sobs.

It was then that I understood. "You're not the impostor, are you?"

"No. I just…*helped.*" His voice was small.

Helped who?

I squeezed my eyes shut, realization washing over me.

How had I not seen it before? How had I not noticed?

There was only one person in Alec's life cruel enough to arrange all this—to lie for leisure for a year and a half. Someone who'd always wanted to be in his place. Someone who happened to be James's cousin—and *coincidently* liked to provoke Alec by spending time with *me.*

He's manipulative and persuasive! He's been taking advantage of James for years… Ben had told me.

"What did you do? How did you do it?" I said firmly. "I'm not going anywhere with you until you tell me the truth!"

"*I* set up the meeting today, okay? I pretended to be him!" He blurted, his voice desperate. "He'd been acting so weird this week; I was afraid he would do something reckless! But then I saw how much you affected him yesterday—his mood, his attitude. It's like he's a different person when he is around you! And you're so forgiving and good at these things… I've been trying to get Zach to talk to Alec for *five years*, and you convinced him in *one day*!"

James slid his hands down the door, sobbing. "I just wanted to help! I thought if I could make you two talk, you would forgive him and things would be fine again. He really needed this right now… But then you broke your promise and ruined everything!

"He's mad now, Linda—he's mad at everybody! Because they called the police again, and he thinks they will figure it out this time. But he listens to you—you're the only person he listens to! And you can also talk to Alec! You can shut down this investigation in no time!

"You're my only hope, Linda. Please, come talk to him! Please! He's so mad! You have no idea what he's capable of…"

Your name has been on my list for a long time, Benji. I can't wait for a reason to cross it off! The memory popped up in my head. The two of them had almost gotten into a fight that night. If I hadn't been there to stop them…

I opened the door, putting on my sneakers. "Let's go!"

"Thank you." James breathed in relief, already rushing to his car.

I'd never felt so scared in my entire life. My heart was pounding so fast I couldn't even breathe. But I had to do it; I had to go. This wasn't about me or Zach or James anymore. I had to do this for Ben. I couldn't let anything bad happen to him because of *me*.

♪♩♡

James looked terrible, I noticed in the car. His blond quiff was a total mess, and he had dark circles and puffy eyes. They were so red it made the blue of his eyes look brighter.

"Is it because of you that he told me his name was James?" I murmured.

"Yeah. He was texting me at the same time. It was a wrong message."

I looked down at my hands, spinning my ring.

"*You* recognized me in the line that day at the signing, didn't you? You're the one who told him I was there at the mall."

"Yes." He sighed. "But I thought you were just the secret girlfriend he'd told me about! Until that day, I had no idea he was pretending to be Alec. That's why he got the texts wrong, you know? He was having to explain himself to both of us at the same time."

"And why didn't you tell Alec after that? You kept helping him for *months*, even knowing he'd made a fool of everyone."

"He was feeling bad enough already for losing you to Alec. I couldn't betray him like that."

"So you chose to betray Alec instead," I accused.

"He had other people to support him. He wasn't *alone*."

"You saw Alec defending you, thinking you were his most loyal friend…" I scowled. "How could you do this to him?"

"It *killed* me, okay?" James snapped in tears. "It's hard to pick sides! There's no right answer—you always end up hurting someone anyway!"

I stared at the window, listening to him cry. Alec would be devastated when he found out about this. He trusted James as much as he did his brothers.

I'm about to get onto the right highway. Zach's gray eyes popped up in my head again.

How do you know where I live?

My cousin James told me a few things about you…

"Since when does he know where I live? When did you give him my address?"

James wiped his eyes. "I didn't give him anything. He found out for himself."

"And how did *you* know, then? You even got my window right!"

"I came here with him once. When he was trying to tell you the truth."

I swallowed hard. "When was that?"

"September, I think. Right after you talked to Alec at the hotel. But he kept trying in October too—when Alec and I were in Europe."

"*Trying.*" I snorted. "As if it was the hardest thing in the world to just *talk* to someone."

"He told me he almost reached you once on the street, but you got scared when he called your name and ran away on a bus."

My mouth fell open. *My panic attack at the bus stop!*

I'd felt him watching me—I *knew* he was there. I couldn't believe I was actually right.

"What else? Did he really go to West Virginia after me?"

"Yeah." James bit his lip ring, glancing at me sideways. "He cares a lot about you. More than you can imagine."

I thought about the flowers he'd sent me after Valentine's Day, and my heart tightened. I had no idea what I was doing—what I was going to say. This was totally the opposite of waiting for AJ at the café.

Focus, Linda! I took a deep breath, shaking those thoughts out of my head. *Before you talk to Zach about all this, you have to find Ben.*

"Are we close?"

"Yes," James said, taking the exit on the left. But then his phone rang.

Not his actual phone, I realized. A cheap plastic one buzzing in the cup holder.

James took one glance at the screen and immediately put it to his ear. "Yeah, I got her. You're sure that's the address, right? Did you find out what he bought? Please tell me he didn't get a gun—

Oh my God," he gasped. And his distraction made the car swerve.

"Careful!" I grabbed the steering wheel.

But James seemed oblivious. His face had gone pale; his eyes were unfocused.

"James! Pay attention!" I punched him hard in the arm. And his phone fell into his lap.

"No. No!" He stepped on the gas, suddenly crying again.

I picked up his phone in panic. "What did you tell him?"

"Linda?"

"*Hailey.*" My heart skipped a beat.

"You have to go as fast as you can, do you hear me?" Her tone was sharp, urgent. "I'm sending an ambulance after you, but he has to see *you* first! If he sees anyone else, he's gonna lose his mind! I'm serious! I've never seen him so out of himself before."

I couldn't focus on a single word she was saying. All I could think about was the way Zach had stared at her that day at the beach, making her go away so he could be alone with me.

Then I remembered Mr. Bear... *Which one do you like better, the first or the second one?* she'd asked me at the Halloween party.

She knew all along. She'd been helping him since then! That's why she'd enjoyed messing things up for Alec and kept playing with Ben's heart, just to take advantage of him! He was going to *her* house when he disappeared—she'd probably been the one who gave his location to Zach!

"You son of a—"

"Did you hear what I said?" She brushed me off.

"I'm gonna kill you! I can't believe you—"

"Bitch, I hate you too, okay? It's mutual! But you've gotta concentrate here!"

I held my breath, feeling my head spin. The anger, the fear, the hate...

"You have to run! Do you hear me?"

"How could you do this to Ben?" I snapped. "He trusted you! This is all *your* fault!"

"I know…" Hailey burst into tears. "If I could go back in time, I… I can't believe *I'm* the one who started all this."

You what? My breath caught in my throat.

"If the worst happens, I'll never forgive myself… Please go as fast as you can! I'm too far away, but you and James— please!" She sobbed. "I can't live without Ben. You have to save him!"

She hung up the phone at the same time James ran a red light. And that's when I understood: she really cared about Ben. Hailey and James, they both did.

Whatever game Zach was playing, he was playing alone. Maybe they'd been involved at the beginning, but things had gotten out of control—Zach had gone too far. And apparently, *I* was the only one who might still be able to stop him.

I'm bad, *Linda,* he'd said to me at the hotel. No remorse in his eyes, no guilt—like a real sociopath.

I don't believe that, I'd told him then. And deep in my heart, I still meant it. Even more now that I knew the guy I once loved— the guy who had talked to me for over a year—was hidden some- where inside him.

I didn't know where it'd come from, but suddenly I was ready. There was this strength, this energy, this bravery in me I didn't recognize. But at that moment, it was all mine—I owned it. And I was ready to use it. I was ready to do whatever it took to save Ben from Zach…and to save Zach from himself.

"Room fourteen!" James yelled from the car.

I was already running to the cheap motel up ahead. Ben was at risk—I didn't have a second to waste.

Nineteen, eighteen, seventeen… I searched the numbers. *Please, let me be on time. Please, tell me I'm not too late.*

Fourteen! I hurried to the door and knocked. But nobody answered.

"Zach!" I forced the knob.

And to my surprise, it was unlocked. The room was dark and quiet—he wasn't here anymore.

That's when I turned on the lights.

"Ben!" He was lying on the bed, unconscious.

I'm gonna kill you, Zach! I checked for a heartbeat, trying to wake Ben up. But it didn't take me ten seconds to realize he wouldn't. His pulse was weak, and his breathing was so shallow I couldn't even see the rise and fall of his chest.

I opened his mouth immediately, blowing air into his lungs.

"Oh my God!" James fell to his knees by the door.

"Call help!" I shouted.

CPR, Linda. You've studied this—thirty pumps, two breaths. You can do it!

One, two, three, four... "James, go get someone!"

Breathe, Ben. Breathe.

One, two, three, four... "JAMES!" I glanced back at him. But he was in shock, talking to himself—not listening to me at all.

"It's my fault. It's always gonna be my fault..."

No! Wake up, Ben! Breathe! I cried, giving him my breath.

I was on my fourth CPR cycle when I heard the siren.

"Here!" James got up, waving the paramedics over. "They're gonna save him, right? Please, tell me it's not too late!"

I held his cold face in my hands, choking back tears. "Come on, Ben, please! Wake up!"

"He really wasn't kidding," James mumbled. "He'd rather die than tell you guys the truth."

"What?" I turned toward him.

"He said it last week... He'd rather *die* than hurt you and Alec like that."

And that's when *my* heart stopped beating.

IMPOSTOR ALEC

College was my only hope for a new beginning. I thought if I moved to New York and rebuilt my life far away from you guys, I would find peace again. So I became obsessed with playing. The violin was my painkiller, my only relief. But I over practiced, and my body collapsed.

Music had been my passion for as long as I could remember. I couldn't even *imagine* a life where I wasn't able to play. So when I realized I'd lost the violin too—like I'd lost you—I broke down.

James saw it; he realized how low I'd sunk.

He thought if I told you the truth and you forgave me, my depression would go away. He was just trying to help; he'd been inspired by the way you fixed things between Alec and Zach. But I'd literally rather die than hurt you and my brother the way I knew I would if you guys knew the truth. So when I realized what he'd done and that the police were involved again, I just couldn't take it anymore. I felt like I had nowhere to run this time. How could I face my own family if they found out it'd been me all along?

Chapter 30

"Ben!" I raised my head, searching for him.

The lights, the siren. I couldn't breathe! I couldn't wake him up!

"You gotta lie still." A woman touched my face.

A nurse, I realized. I was in a hospital.

"Where is Ben? Is he okay?" The words came out of my mouth too fast. Faster than I could breathe. Faster than my heart was beating now.

"You gotta relax, honey. You're gonna have another panic attack." She forced me back down while another nurse stuck a needle into my arm.

I could feel this lump in my throat—blocking the air, making my eyes go blurry. But I forced them to stay open. I had to keep looking for Ben. "Please, tell me he's here! Tell me he'll be okay!"

"He's breathing on his own!" a girl shouted from the corner of the room. "They told me he'll be all right."

Oh, thank God! I let my head fall back on the—

Was that…Hailey?

That's when I started to remember…

♪♩♡

I didn't want to open my eyes this time. I didn't want to wake up. If this was the life I had to live from now on, I didn't want to do it anymore. I wanted to die—like Ben.

Everything was quiet now, apart from the steady beep of a monitor in the background. But I knew I wasn't alone. There was this large hand rubbing mine.

His touch was familiar and warm and soft—I thought I was dreaming. If Alec was still here, holding my hand, then it had to be a dream.

I squeezed his hand tight, praying I wouldn't wake up.

For the first time in my life, I *wanted* to have been a victim of the guy they'd arrested. I wanted my impostor to be someone cruel and cold-hearted. I wanted him to be anyone else—any other situation would have been better than this. *Anyone* would have been better than Benjamin.

"I think she's waking up." Alec leaned in, stroking my hair.

I couldn't resist. I had to see his eyes. His green eyes.

Ben's eyes.

I hid my face with my hands, suddenly nauseated. *Please tell me this is a nightmare. Please tell me it's a lie!*

"It's over now, baby." Alec kissed my head. "You're safe. Ben is safe. And the police won't let this guy get away with it—they will catch him soon. Everything will be all right."

Oh my God, he doesn't know.

Oh my God! Oh my God! This is going to destroy him.

"Thank you so much, Linda!" Amanda smiled, her eyes red and watery. "You saved my son."

My stomach dropped. *I didn't save him at all. I'm the very reason he wanted to die!*

"They're still caring for him, but he wouldn't be alive if it wasn't for you." She hugged me. "Thank you!"

Oh God, they need to know the truth.

But I can't—I refuse! I can't be the one to tell them.

I swallowed the lump in my throat. "Where's James?"

"He's with your father. And Oliver, Matt—everybody is here. I'm gonna let them know you're awake." Amanda smiled at me again before leaving the room.

"How are you feeling, baby? My heroine—"

"Don't!" I winced. My chest was so tight, so painful. It was like someone had really ripped my heart out of it.

"Are you okay?" Alec knit his brows.

And I couldn't take it anymore. I rolled to the side of the bed, breaking down in tears.

"Baby…" He tried to hug me, but I pulled away, crying even harder.

Dad came running in my direction. "What happened?"

"I don't know!" Alec said, alarmed.

My father's arms slid around me, and I collapsed right there in front of everybody. The guilt, the pain, the love, the anger…it was all too much.

"Take me home, Dad. Please." I sobbed, burying my face in his chest.

"Linda." Alec reached for my hand again, but I yanked it away.

I couldn't bear to feel his touch, to talk to him, to look at his face. At *their* face.

"Take me home, Dad. Take me home!" I held on to him in agony.

"What did you do to her?" Dad shouted.

"Nothing! I don't understand…"

"We need to talk, Alec." James's voice suddenly silenced the room.

♪♩♡

It was July 15 all over again. For the second time, my world had fallen apart. For the second time, Benjamin had wrecked my heart, had killed a part of me.

I couldn't even react for the next few days. I was in shock, grieving. There was only silence in me—and I welcomed it, like an old friend. Silence was good. It was cold, but peaceful. I didn't think I could handle feeling anything stronger than that right now.

Dad didn't ask for more information. He knew I had lied to him, kept things from him, but he didn't force me to explain. Not even when I cried my eyes out in the car. Not even when I said I wanted to go back to West Virginia.

"I'm here to listen whenever you're ready, okay?" he said after we got home from the hospital. "No matter what happened, just let me know what to do—how I can help. I know I'm not the best father in the world, but I want to get better at this. For you and for Claire and for Jesse. I don't know what I would do if I lost one of you the way Benjamin almost—" He kissed the top of my head, choked up. "I've been watching you, Linda. I know something's been going on since you moved to LA. Please tell me what to do. Please let me help…"

And at that moment, I was so done with secrets and misunderstandings and lies that I told him. Everything.

He didn't get mad. He didn't yell or even scold. He just held me in his arms and cried with me.

The next day, we heard on the news that Benjamin had been admitted to a mental health facility after being hospitalized in critical condition Sunday night. I guessed Oliver couldn't keep his family safe from the media this time. Although they were saying it was because of a drug overdose, not a suicide attempt.

I was glad he was getting help. I'd always thought that's what Impostor Alec needed all along: *help*.

Oliver showed up at my house the day after that. He came to apologize—for everything. From Benjamin's lies to his suspicions about me when Alec and I got together. He also talked to my father and offered to write him a check, paying for any mental health expenses I might need in the future. But Dad told him we didn't need his money and asked him to stay away. None of us wanted anything from the Brocks anymore.

And I guess Alec had gotten Dad's message, because it was Thursday evening and he still hadn't called. *I can't believe he's leaving for the European Tour tomorrow without talking to me at all...*

"Eat a bit more, honey." Caroline touched my arm. "At least finish your soup."

I sighed, grabbing my spoon again. I couldn't wait to leave that house—to leave LA. I'd already bought my ticket and everything. I was going right after my final exams; I wouldn't even wait for graduation.

The girls would help me deal with school until then, they'd said. I ended up telling them my story—Sam, Liz, and Aisha. I was too miserable to pretend I was okay this time; I needed their support.

"If you don't like the soup, you can have two desserts." Claire slid her half-eaten chocolate pudding in my direction.

"I like the soup. Don't worry, okay?" I smiled, setting it back in front of her.

I was almost done with my plate when Dad excused himself to answer the door. I thought it was AJ again—he'd stopped by on Monday to see how I was doing. Claire's reaction told me I was wrong.

"What are *you* doing here?" She glared up behind me at the person who had come into the room.

My whole body froze. I didn't have the courage to look. I wasn't sure I wanted to.

"Can we talk?" Alec said shyly. And I breathed in relief.

"No! She doesn't want to see any of you anymore! That's why she's moving back to—"

"Come, Claire. Let's go watch TV." Caroline carried her out to the living room, giving Alec an apologetic look.

"What are you doing here?" I got up from my chair. "I mean, you didn't even call…"

"I know, I'm sorry." He dropped his eyes. "Can we go to your room?"

"Sure." I led him to the stairs.

I'd never felt so ashamed around Alec before. It was worse than that day in his dressing room. Worse than our brunch, when I told him the truth.

He watched as I closed the door, then sat awkwardly on the bed. "I'm sorry I didn't call before. I needed some time to think."

"It's okay." I shook my head, sitting next to him.

Alec went quiet for a moment, as if deciding where to start. And I could feel it—his grief, his silence. It was as painful as mine. We knew our relationship was dead, and we felt exactly the same about it.

He kept staring at my face without saying a word. And I had no idea of what to say either. I wasn't even sure there was anything to say.

"How is he?" I regretted my question as soon as I let it out.

"Better," Alec muttered. "This is for you, by the way." He reached into his back pocket and handed me a piece of folded paper—a letter.

I threw it onto my desk. I would burn it as soon as Alec left.

"James quit the band," he said, his head down.

My heart broke for him. I knew this whole thing had wrecked him even more than it had wrecked me.

"Dad isn't coming on tour either. He—" he paused as if choking back tears "—he wants to stay with Ben."

I couldn't help myself this time. I closed the gap between us, wrapping my arms around him.

"I don't think I can do this anymore." He rested his chin on my head, hugging me tight. "Not without *you*, Linda… Please, say you're still coming with me tomorrow. Please—choose *me*."

"Alec…" I leaned back to meet his eyes. "I can't—choose. I can't do this."

I explained to him there was no choice to be made: I loved him with all my heart. But how could I be with Alec, knowing his impostor was Ben? Especially now, after everything he'd just done?

"I—understand." He stared at his hands.

"But you have to be strong, okay? You have to stay strong!" I rubbed his back.

"I really don't think I can…"

"You *have to*, Alec—for your fans! There are a lot of people waiting for you, waiting to give you *love*. You're not gonna run out of that, I promise you."

"But I love *you*." He turned to me in tears. "I can't even picture my life without you anymore! How can I—"

I buried my face in his chest, falling apart all over again. I didn't think I could live without him either. I didn't *want* to!

Alec held me in his arms, cuddling me on my bed. And we stayed like that—just crying—until there were no tears left.

I could feel his breath on me, the sound of his heartbeat, his warm hand locked with mine over his stomach. I wanted the time to stop so I could live that scene for the rest of my life. I didn't want to live anything that came after that. How could I wake up tomorrow knowing I would never be with him like this again?

"Please tell me it's just a wave." I glanced up at him. "This pain…"

He nodded with a tearful smile. "I don't think I'll ever stop loving you, though."

"I know I won't stop loving *you*." I sobbed, hugging him again.

Then a thought crossed my mind. "Promise me you're gonna forgive him one day?"

Alec shook his head.

I climbed over him on the bed and took his face in my hands. "*Promise me…*"

Silent tears streamed down his cheeks.

"Promise me!" I shouted in sobs. "For *me*, okay? I can't live this life knowing I'm the reason you two—"

"Okay! Okay!" Alec pressed his forehead against mine. Then he kissed my lips for the last time.

IMPOSTOR ALEC

Dear Linda,

I'm sorry. I know saying the words a million times will still not be enough. I just want you to know that...I never thought my cowardliness would allow things to go this far, and you have no idea how much I regret every single one of my mistakes.

Since the first day, I knew you were special, Linda. I was enchanted by you, then addicted to you. Falling in love was my punishment for enjoying too much "playing Alec" on the internet. I didn't realize what I was doing could end up hurting people... until I started wishing I had introduced myself to you as me.

I was the first one to get hurt. I knew you would never think I was as cool or charming or worthy of your time as he was. He's always been better than me at everything—there was no way you could be interested in me after meeting him first.

And I was right. My first attempt to fix this mess was talking to you as me. I don't know if you remember this, but I tried! We chatted for an hour, but you friend-zoned me. And I'll never know if it was because you didn't like me for me or because I was too late and you were already in love with Alec.

I tried to tell you the truth again—many and many times. I forced myself to say the words, but I got choked up. I wrote you dozens of letters that I never sent. I ran away for a while and stopped talking to you. I even tried to make you so mad that *you* would end up breaking up with me. But nothing worked. I just couldn't do it. Even if I knew you were in love with Alec, not me, I loved you too much. I couldn't bear the thought of losing you.

When you found out I'd lied, I knew it was over. You asked me to stay away, and I thought that was the most decent thing to do, after everything I'd put you through. But I couldn't forget you. I missed you every minute of the day. And I started having this hope that if a part of you really loved me for me, maybe we could work things out somehow.

I knew you wouldn't just listen to me, though. You would never believe I was telling you the truth about who I was through the phone or the computer. And I was terrified you would end up calling the police on me if I tried—if you hadn't done that already. My only hope to fix my mess and get you to listen was showing you my face.

I thought if I came to your door, begging for a second chance, proving how hopelessly in love I was with you, maybe you would forgive me. And you can't imagine how wrecked I was when I couldn't find you there.

I didn't go only to Petersburg, Linda. I went to your dad's place in San Francisco too. I tried to find you everywhere. I needed to *see* you! It was the only way I could win you back.

But you disappeared. And when I found you again, you had found Alec. You had told him the truth.

When I realized what I'd done, it was already too late. I was too blinded by love before, I wasn't thinking. I'm so sorry. From the bottom of my heart, I'm sorry.

I knew I had made some big mistakes by lying to you, then by not telling you the truth when I introduced myself to you as me.

But it was only through the course of the investigation that you opened my eyes to how bad of a person I was.

I'd never felt so ashamed in my life. I was so terribly guilty, I couldn't even face myself in the mirror. I couldn't believe I'd had the guts to do all of that, to be that cruel. You looked so fragile, so bruised... I was heartbroken. I hated myself for being the one who did that to you. So much so that I decided to stay away. I didn't think I deserved your forgiveness anymore.

You might not believe this, but deep down I was happy watching Alec fall in love with you. I knew he would take care of you for me. He would make things okay again and give you everything I couldn't.

I wanted you to be happy with him, Linda. That's why I chose to remain silent.

But it wasn't easy for me, you know? To see you with him, to watch you give your love to someone else. And that's why I kept making these stupid mistakes...

I shouldn't have sent you that message when you were in Vegas. I went insane, thinking about what you were doing on that date and all the times I would be forced to watch you with him if you two got together. It was a poor choice of words. I was just drunk and jealous.

Then again at Halloween, when James almost gave us away. It was entirely my fault... You were so gorgeous dressed like an angel that I couldn't stop rambling about you to him—and how cute you looked, searching for the Reese's Cups in every bucket in front of you. That's why I had to leave the party, you know? It hurt too much to look at how beautiful you are. I wasn't used to having you so close. I felt like I would lose my mind if I saw Alec touch you one more time.

But all that selfishness went away the moment I saw myself through your eyes after Thanksgiving. When they convinced you that I was a threat to you. When I realized how you felt about "the impostor" now.

Seeing you in panic, completely broken by me, opened my eyes once again. So I toughened up and started giving you what you really needed: a friend.

I knew I could just tell you the truth instead of letting you believe you were in danger or that you'd been a victim of one of those pedophiles. But if I did that, I would end up hurting your relationship with Alec. I didn't think you two would be able to move on, knowing it was me and that I'd been there watching you all along. And I knew you depended on Alec to stay strong. The last thing I wanted was to break you two apart when you needed him the most.

So I didn't have a choice anymore, you see? It was too late for the truth. The only thing I could do was help you get through it. And that's what I tried to do…

I could have stayed like that forever, just being your friend. I liked having you back in my life somehow, and I knew Alec made you happy. You finally had everything you deserved—I couldn't have asked for anything better. And even if my mistakes had given you some wounds, he'd help you heal. You'd grown brighter by his side, and I loved seeing that.

But while you two rose stronger together, the lies, the shame, and the guilt made me weaker and weaker. Every day I felt a little less myself. I was forced to live in the shadows, to hide everything I was feeling from the world and suffer in secret. I knew it was my own fault—*I* was the one who had started all this, there was no one else to blame. But it was a very heavy burden to carry, and I was all alone.

College was my only hope for a new beginning. I thought if I moved to New York and rebuilt my life far away from you guys, I would find peace again. So I became obsessed with playing. The violin was my painkiller, my only relief. But I over practiced, and my body collapsed.

Music had been my passion for as long as I could remember. I couldn't even *imagine* a life where I wasn't able to play. So when I realized I'd lost the violin too—like I'd lost you—I broke down.

James saw it; he realized how low I'd sunk. I never actually *planned* on hurting myself before Sunday, like he'd thought. But I confess that since I lost you in July, most days I wished I didn't have to wake up. That I could float in dark oblivion forever.

That's why I opened up to Hails on Halloween. (She kind of knew about you already, because I'd stopped seeing her when I fell in love with you.) And she's the one who helped me cope with everything while James was on tour. I honestly don't know what I'd have done without her.

We're *friends*, by the way—there's nothing romantic going on. We just thought it would be easier to explain us spending so much time together if people believed we were dating. That's how good of a friend she is…

James too… I know he only did what he did because he was worried about me. He thought if I told you the truth and you forgave me, my depression would go away. He was just trying to help; he'd been inspired by the way you fixed things between Alec and Zach. But I'd literally rather die than hurt you and my brother the way I knew I would if you guys knew the truth. So when I realized what he'd done and that the police were involved again, I just couldn't take it anymore. I felt like I had nowhere to run this time. How could I face my own family if they found out it'd been me all along?

That was one of my top three fears: to disappoint my family. The other two were to lose my brother and to hurt you again. And all my efforts were in vain because I did all three things anyway. But at least now you know why I did what I did. I know you've always wanted to learn my truth.

I don't expect you to forgive me. I know I don't deserve it. I just thought that after you saved my life, the truth was the least I could give you.

Please know that I never meant to hurt you and my greatest regret in life will always be having done that.

Sincerely yours,
Benjamin Brock

Chapter 31

I'd been trying very hard to *understand* what happened.

Why people did what they did. Why so many lies.

There had to be an explanation for all of it. For *why* things had to be like this…

It'd been seven weeks since I read Benjamin's letter, and these were my last days in LA. But there were so many things I still didn't understand. So many pieces of the puzzle I hadn't figured out.

Everybody thought I was going crazy when I started my little research on "why." But I refused to just be sad this time. I knew that if I didn't do anything, if I allowed myself to lose my faith, I would fall into the darkness again. I needed to keep believing in *good*, believing in *people*, believing in *better days*. Because that was the source of my light, Alec had made me realize.

That's why I began searching for *answers*. I felt like if I could understand the mess and learn something from my past, I could help others not to make the same mistakes, and then my pain wouldn't have been in vain. And there had been so many mistakes. So much pain…

I confess I was expecting a complex web of conflicting answers—if I was able to find any answer at all. But the more psychology books I read, the more I came to the conclusion that all mistakes had the same reason: *shame.*

Why is it so hard for us to admit we made a mistake? To look someone in the eye and say, "I'm sorry I did this, it wasn't my intention to hurt you?"

Why are we so afraid of being honest? Of what people will think? Of letting them down?

Why would we rather break down in secret than show them that we aren't perfect? That we feel hurt, weak, tired? That we might not be able to live up to their expectations?

We like to say we're "only human," but only when our mistakes aren't really that bad. Because the truth is there's rarely a safe space to express our humanity without shame. To be imperfect, to show our fears, to need help, to do something wrong. That's why we're so afraid. That's why we keep things clean and in order, and whenever it gets messy, we don't let anyone see.

We suck it up and keep it to ourselves, like James.

We hide behind hate and resentment, like Zach.

We pretend to be someone we're not, like AJ.

And we lie, trying not to worry those around us, like me.

The thing about shame, though, is that it's lethal. If we don't speak it out, if we don't do something about it, it grows inside us. And when things eventually get out of control and the pain becomes just unbearable, we…lose hope. Like Ben.

Things would have been so different if he had let himself be *seen.* If he'd showed us what he was feeling inside. If he'd had chosen to be vulnerable instead of "strong" and taken the risk of telling the truth.

I had no idea where my life was going to take me, but this one thing I knew: I'd just started a lifelong war against *shame.* I wanted to live every day being bold enough to show the world who I was—even when I screwed up, even when I was imperfect. That was the biggest lesson I'd learned from Benjamin: there should be no shame in being our true, flawed selves.

And I guess, somehow, Alec had learned it too.

As soon as the European leg of the tour started, rumors exploded all over the world about our breakup. He had a meltdown singing "No More Lies" in Paris, then cut it from the setlist —which made the media speculate we weren't together anymore. And since it happened at the same time as the whole overdose drama—where Ben and I had been taken to the hospital together —nobody believed it was just a coincidence. They started babbling about me cheating on him with his brother and how dysfunctional their picture-perfect family had become.

So Alec decided to put an end to the circus by giving them something even more scandalous to gossip about: the truth about himself.

He didn't reveal any of his personal problems, but he opened up to the media about his mental health struggles. And about being a cancer survivor. And the real inspiration behind some of his songs… Spending time away from his dad had been good for him, after all. He was being honest about everything; the only questions he didn't answer were the ones about me and Ben.

But my favorite news from him was when he confirmed Zach's punk rock band would be his opening act for the North American leg. AJ told me they'd really restored their friendship after the party. Zach had not only been helping Alec stay strong during the European Tour, but also trying to mediate things between Alec and James. And apparently, Zach's intervention had worked out because James was officially back in the band. AJ even decided to rejoin the crew during the summer, so the four of them could share a tour bus like they'd always dreamed. I had tears in my eyes when I heard all that. I was so happy for them—so happy for Alec!

He was going to be okay. He was already moving on. And I knew that at some point in the near future, I would have to do the same.

It's just a wave, I kept telling myself. And I was being brave—I swear I was fighting with everything I had to find my way back to the surface. But it was so hard…

I still missed him. Every single day.

Nina was policing me over the phone. No TV, no radio, no internet—no news about him allowed. She was trying to make me focus on the future instead, and all the things I had to look forward to in life.

College wasn't one of them. At least not for next year.

I had gotten a full scholarship to UCLA, but I turned it down the day I received the letter. I didn't care if I would waste a semester or two before I could apply to any other school; there was no way I would stay in LA any longer than I had to.

But at least now I knew what I wanted: to keep doing my research on human behavior and mental health. It really fulfilled me somehow. I wanted to understand the mind—understand people. I still didn't know which major I would choose, but that's what I wanted to learn in college one day.

Until then, I would work at my grandparents' restaurant and keep studying on my own. That was my plan. Before that afternoon.

"Hey, beautiful!" AJ said when I picked up the phone. "How are you doing?"

My heart warmed. I could picture his open-mouthed smile in my mind as if we'd seen each other yesterday, not a month ago.

"I'm okay! What about you? How are things in Boston?"

"Great. We've just finished decorating the apartment! You

should come visit us, by the way—when you're back on the East Coast. It would be such a pleasure to have you!"

"Thanks," I said with a grin. "I can't promise anything right now, but…I'm sure we're gonna bump into each other again one day."

"I really hope so." He went quiet.

"But how is life?" I sat cross-legged on the bed. "Did you finish your novel?"

It turned out *that* was the secret project keeping him busy since January. He told me he'd had this idea in his head for years but never found time to write it down.

"I'm almost there—I'm still working on Matt's notes. But I've been meaning to ask you—do you think I can send you the manuscript too? I'd love to have more feedback before trying to publish it."

"Oh my goodness, of course! What an honor." I beamed. "Congratulations, AJ. Seriously. I'm so proud of you for chasing your dreams, for taking a chance on love. You're an inspiration to me, you know that?"

"Thanks, honey. It means a lot, coming from you. You're my inspiration too."

I swallowed hard, trying not to think of Ben.

"But tell me about you!" He changed his tone to distract me. "What have you been doing? Is everything packed for West Virginia?"

"Yeah. I just have my final exams next week, and I'm leaving on Friday."

"Good… What else? Are you still obsessed with those self-help books?" he teased.

"Kind of, yeah." I chuckled. "If there's one thing I'll miss about LA, it's the library."

He laughed out loud. "Well, it's great that you enjoy studying, because I have some news for you."

"Oh yeah? Tell me!"

"I need you to go check your mailbox."

"What?" I raised an eyebrow.

"Go ahead! And take me with you—I wanna hear your reaction!"

"Are you here at my door? Is that it?"

"Nope. But you got mail, girl. Go check it out!"

I got up from my bed and walked downstairs with the phone in my hands.

"Are you there yet?" he asked.

"Almost… What are you doing to me, AJ? Did you send me a postcard or something?"

"No, it's not from me. It was all Alec's idea."

My heart raced at the mention of his name, so I sped up my pace.

There was a red rose in the mailbox. I was so overwhelmed, staring at it, that it took me a moment to realize it was attached to something. A big envelope with two smaller ones inside and indications of the order in which Alec wanted me to open them.

I choked back tears, recognizing his handwriting. We hadn't seen or spoken to each other since that goodbye at my house— since he went to Europe. I knew he was coming back to LA this week, and it was taking all the strength I had in me not to go knock at his door. I missed him so much. So, so much.

I took a deep breath and opened the first envelope only to find another one inside.

"NYU?" My heart skipped a beat.

"Did you open it?" AJ squealed.

"What's this?" *Some kind of cruel joke?*

"You got into NYU, Linda! Congratulations!"

"Shut up!" I ripped the envelope open.

"It's for real! Alec sent them your application last year! I saved him a copy of your other submissions with my flash drive

—remember that day at your house? Your parents helped too, but it was all Alec's idea. He wanted to make it a surprise."

I sat on the sidewalk, big warm tears streaming down my cheeks. The papers were all there—they had already accepted the offer in my name. All the fees were paid, everything was set up. I was going to New York. I was going to live my childhood dream.

I moved on to the second envelope, sobbing. It had a journal inside—a red vintage journal with the Eiffel Tower on the cover. And when I opened the first page, an origami heart fell into my lap.

I saw this in Paris, and it reminded me of that night in Vegas. So I had to give this back to you. I had to set you free.

Although I wish I could keep it safe with me for the rest of my life, I need to say that it's okay if you want to give it back to its previous owner. Or to anyone else who makes you happy in New York or wherever you go.

Because all I want now is to know you'll be happy. Of all the people I know, Linda, you're the one who deserves it the most.

All my love,
Alec

That was the end of an era for me.

I'd been in love with Alec Brock for over two years now; I didn't even think I could live any other way. But here he was, showing me how, pointing me in the right direction. Making me love him even more than I already did.

I didn't have the guts to say thank you. One day I would—I promised myself I would. But I wasn't ready yet. If I saw him or talked to him, I knew I would break down again.

I needed to pick up the pieces first and think about the future. Think about my new life. Now that I finally understood *why* Impostor Alec had done what he did, there were no excuses anymore. It was time to let go, rebuild, and move on.

Some days were worse than others, but I confess it got a lot easier once I went back home. Things were *simpler* in Petersburg. And my family was being so supportive, so understanding. Nobody cared about the fact that I'd lied, they only cared about how I was doing right now. And *that* alone was enough to make me feel better. Much, much better.

I think honesty is some kind of antidote to shame. Because from the moment you speak the truth, the pain is gone. There might be some consequences in the external world, but it can't hurt you inside anymore. It loses its power over you.

I felt so relieved not to have to lie or to pretend. It was like lifting a burden off my shoulders. And I wanted to keep living my life that way, being honest. Not only with the people I loved, but also with myself.

"Are you ready?" Nina walked into my room in her strapless purple gown.

"Yeah." I frowned apologetically.

She went to my bed and touched the fabric of the dress she had sewed for me. "You're not wearing it?"

I sighed. The dress was tight and shiny, and it had this weird mermaid skirt. I hated the fact that I hated it.

"No, I'm sorry. It's *beautiful*, you know? You're very talented! But it's just…not for me."

"It's okay." She smiled slowly, then looked me up and down. "I like this one too. Red is definitely your color."

"It's the dress Alec gave me in Veg—" I stopped myself. I

was fighting the habit of talking about him at every opportunity I got.

"I know." She smirked, offering me her right arm. "Let's go?"

I was already convinced the best thing I could do for myself was to stop looking back at the past. But there was this one thing I still wanted to do before officially turning the page and saying goodbye to the previous chapter of my life: *prom.*

It wasn't my prom, of course—I had already missed it. But the calendar in her school was different, and Nina had invited me to go as her date. I normally would pass on this kind of thing, but after spending our senior year apart, I was happy to have this one last memory of high school with her.

Especially because, once again, we would be living on opposite sides of the country soon. As James had promised at Thanksgiving, he'd sent Nina's portfolio to Alec's stylist. And Leah Watson had called her in person a few weeks ago, offering a twelve-month internship at her agency, starting in the summer.

Nina was absolutely ecstatic, but she came to talk to me first before saying yes. She was worried about how keeping this connection with Alec would affect me. As if I would ever stand between her and her dream of dressing up Hollywood stars! Her parents, on the other hand, were a little less supportive. But Nina was stubborn and didn't hesitate in postponing her college plans to go after what she really wanted.

I was so happy for her—so proud of her. Tonight was our official celebration. We knew everything was about to change, and this was our last goodbye to our old lives.

"Look at the decorations, Linda. Purple and white! It's like they know about NYU."

I smiled, stepping out of the car. I couldn't wait to go to New York. College was the only thing in my life right now that was exciting enough to distract me from missing Alec.

"All right." She took a deep breath, leading me to the entrance. "Now, remember that I love you, okay?"

I chuckled. "I love you too, but why—"

Ben.

I froze where I stood, my heart pounding. All of a sudden, I was angry. And embarrassed. And sad.

"Hi." He smiled at me. He was standing next to James, with a white corsage in his hands, matching the boutonniere on the lapel of his tuxedo.

I was so overwhelmed, I couldn't even… "What are you doing here?"

"I made you a promise, remember? That when the time came, I would come to Petersburg to take you to prom?"

"And among all the promises you broke, *this* is the one you decided to keep?" I snapped.

Benjamin widened his eyes but didn't say anything. And a storm of emotions washed over me. Suddenly, it was too painful to look at his face.

"Wait! I just want to talk to you."

"You had your chance. It's expired now!" I rushed back to the parking lot.

"He has a plan, Linda." Nina caught me by the arm.

And I glared at her. "I'm gonna *kill* you for this!"

"This is not what you're thinking." Benjamin blocked my path. "I'm not here to—"

"Go. Away!" I said between my teeth, fighting to stay strong. We were right at the entrance of the school, and there were way too many people staring.

"Just listen, okay? I didn't come to talk about me or to win you over. I'm here for Alec! I want to bring you back to LA—for him!"

The simple mention of his name filled my eyes with tears.

"He is in bad shape, Linda. He's trying to look strong, but I know him—you need to come back. This probably makes no sense to you, but I'm fine seeing you two together, you know? I had almost a year to accept that I lost you. But I can't take this… The guilt of knowing what I did to him—to you both. I wanna fix it. Please, help me fix it!"

"It's too late." I shook my head, walking away. "You really ruined *everything*."

"No! We can still fix it!" Ben followed me. "We've been able to function as friends this year, right? We *can* live around each other—we've already proven that! I know things got a little more complicated and awkward, but I don't think it will last forever. It's just—"

"You don't even *realize* how much you hurt me, do you?" I stopped in my tracks.

"I do… You have no idea how sorry I am. And I'm willing to talk about it or to drop it—you choose. I'll do whatever you want me to do. Just please don't make my brother pay for *my* mistakes." He knit his brows in pain, and my heart ached. "It doesn't have to be like this, Linda. You can still be together! I *want* you to be together! I'd rather know you guys are happy with each other than miserable apart!"

I rolled my eyes, hopeless. "We can't just pretend nothing happened."

"Let's make this a test, that's all I'm asking! That's why I chose to come here *today*! If you can survive this one public event with me—without wanting to kill me or whatever—you'll know things will be okay if you come back. I want to prove to you that you can be his girlfriend again, that I won't be in your way!"

I buried my face in my hands. I wanted to kill him already—there was no way his plan would work.

"*One night*, Linda." He clasped his hands. "I just spent six weeks locked in a clinic, regretting everything I did wrong—and this is the only mistake I might still be able to fix. Please, give me *one night*. I'm begging you!" He frowned. "If you can't do this for me, then do it for my brother…"

I stared into his eyes. And I could see it for the first time—the guilt, the regret, the shame.

"Please say yes?"

Chapter 32

"Oh my gosh, look who's here!"

"Is that…?"

"It's the twin; it's not him."

"The rumors must be right, then! She really cheated on Alec with his brother!"

"His drug addict brother…"

I regretted having agreed to this before even entering the gym.

"Stay cool," Nina whispered, smiling at the camera. "You don't care about what people think anymore, remember?"

"This was a mistake," I hissed between pictures.

"Everything will be fine! It'll be like ripping off a bandage, you'll see." She locked our arms together, then pulled me along to where the boys stood waiting. "Let's go find a quiet table, shall we?"

Nina went ahead with James, leading us all to the back of the room.

"Thank you for agreeing to this." Benjamin smiled shyly.

"I'm not doing it for you."

"I know, but still…" He pulled up a chair for me. "I really appreciate it."

I ignored his gesture and sat in another chair.

I knew I was being childish. I'd said yes to this, after all—no one had forced me. But even if a part of me wanted to be there, the other part needed to at least make it clear that I was still mad at him.

James sat down on the chair Ben had pulled out for me, patting his friend on the shoulder. "Congratulations on getting into NYU, Linda!" He tried to start a conversation.

"Thanks," I said icily. I was still mad at him too.

"*Okay.* Let me get you guys a drink…" Nina got up.

"I'll help you!" James followed her.

Seriously? I rolled my eyes. *Could you be any more—*

"So this is your school, huh?" Benjamin glanced around.

"Yeah. The gym."

"I was imagining something a lot bigger."

"It's a small town," I said, offended.

"I know. But from the way you described your school—the whole town, actually—I thought… You're not very good at descriptions, you know?" He chuckled.

How dare you! I frowned. "At least I know how to spell! You have no idea how many mistakes I stopped myself from correcting."

"I'm a musician, not a writer." He laughed again.

"I'm not a writer! I don't know why you two keep saying that!"

"Because you are! I hadn't realized that until Alec pointed it out, but you totally are." He tilted his head, smiling at me.

And there it was again—awkward.

Benjamin dropped his eyes, self-conscious.

"This is too weird." I shook my head.

"You're gonna get used to it. It was hard for me too—being around you in the beginning. But I promise, it gets better."

I stared at nowhere, remembering all the times he'd been

there, watching me—watching me with his brother! I was sick just thinking about it.

"So Alec is home this week. But he leaves for the North American Tour on Wednesday… How is your schedule? Do you think you can come back tomorrow with us, or would you prefer to go meet him on the road?"

I turned to him, speechless. I couldn't believe that after everything he'd done—including trying to kill himself—he was there in front of me, acting as if nothing happened.

"What are you doing, Benjamin?" I held his gaze. I swear I didn't understand him. Not even a little bit.

"I want to take you to Alec! This is going to be the surprise of his life. He's never gonna beat me on—"

"What the heck are you even…" I let out a breath, calming myself down. "Do you think I believe you? Do you think I'm buying any of this?"

He went quiet for a second. "I want to fix it, okay? I feel too guilty; I need to get you two back together!"

"Well, guess what? You *are* guilty! And what you're saying doesn't even make sense! Not after everything you did."

"I've changed, Linda. I'm trying to be someone better. And I need your help! I can't undo everything that I did, but I can still fix this—at least this!"

"No, you can't." I lowered my head. Even if I went back, things would never be the same between me and Alec. It was ruined. *He'd* ruined it.

"I promise to be one hundred percent honest with you from now on. I'll never lie to you again."

"I don't believe you, Benjamin, that's the problem! It doesn't matter what you say or promise, I don't believe you anymore. I don't think I ever will."

"I'm telling you nothing but the truth from this moment on."

He crossed his heart with his finger. "Go ahead, try it out! Ask me anything you want."

"All right." I stared into his eyes, thinking about the first of a million questions I had for him. "How did it start?"

"I…" He swallowed hard. "Back in those days, Alec was constantly talking to people online—to see if his music was being played around the country. And sometimes, when he left the computer to take a break, I would answer in his place. It started like that… I wasn't trying anything or planning anything—I was just doing it to help him out. I didn't realize I was enjoying 'being him' a little too much until I fell in love with you."

"Why didn't you tell me before?" I folded my arms over my chest. "In the beginning?"

"The short answer is: when I realized what I was doing, I had already fallen in love. And I couldn't risk losing you."

"You have the same damn face! How could you be insecure about—"

"That's the thing, Linda! All I've ever been is a lesser version of him! You would never have been interested in me after meeting him first!"

I rubbed my eyes to control my anger. "You had so many opportunities to tell me—to end this sooner!"

"I tried! You can't imagine how many times! I tried to talk to you, to write to you, to fight with you. I tried to make you break up with me practically every time Alec was seen with a girl! But no matter how bad we fought, you always called me back *begging me* not to give up on us!"

"You're delirious…" I scoffed.

"You don't remember?" he said, startled. "The photos with Hails, for example! We weren't dating anymore back then—she knew I was in love with someone else. But since she and Alec never really got along and she wanted to boost her career, I asked her to help me out!

"*I* set that all up so the paparazzi would think I was Alec and publish the photos. I thought that would make you want to break up with me for good, but you never did!"

I clenched my fists, reliving every one of those arguments about Hailey—and Tera and all the other dating rumors. Now I knew why I hated them so much. Benjamin had literally manipulated me into it!

"What is the matter with you?" I snapped. "Do you have any idea of how stressed I was? Of what you put me through back then?"

"I thought you would forget me a lot easier if I gave you a reason to hate me!"

"Jeez, Benjamin!" I got up, pulling my hair in despair. "Why can't you be normal and act like everybody else? It's like you purposely choose the worst and most inconvenient ways possible to do things!"

He hung his head, quiet.

"This, for example. Prom!" I glanced at all the people staring at us. "Did you really think it was the best moment to come see me?"

"All right, I think we need to move a little bit…" Nina pulled me to the dance floor while James sat down next to Benjamin.

"I can't do this, Nina." I hid my face in my hands. I was so angry, so disgusted—I wanted to go back there and slap him!

"Breathe. Just breathe." She rubbed my arm. "Think about Alec! You can be with him again. He loves you; he wants to be with you! You just have to talk things out with his brother first."

"I'm *trying*, but I don't think I can…" I looked at her, tears blurring my vision. "He ripped my heart out. Twice!"

Nina bit her lip, watching me. "Maybe prom was really not a good idea. Do you wanna go home?"

I nodded, collapsing in her arms. But then someone pulled me away from her, locking me in *his* arms instead.

"I'm so sorry!" Benjamin squeezed me. Too tight. Too strong. "If I could go back in time—if I could do *anything*—I would! You have no idea…" His voice broke. "I made a lot of mistakes in my life, Linda. But the one I regret the most is this—hurting you. I'm so sorry!"

I kicked him in the shin, pushing him hard, then sprinted for the nearest exit.

There were so many tears I couldn't see where I was going. And my heart was too loud for me to think, too fast for me to breathe.

I fell to the floor, sobbing and gasping at the same time. All these memories of him were crashing back into my head. And the pain was so unbearable I prayed to just run out of air and stop breathing already.

"Come, I'm taking you home." He was suddenly there again —picking me up from the floor.

I stood on my own two feet, but couldn't control my anger anymore. The words poured out of my mouth without asking for my consent.

"I *loved* you! With all of my heart! I gave up *everything* to be with you! And you saw it! I went to your home! You looked at my face! And you didn't have the courage to tell me it was *you*!"

"I never believed you loved *me*!"

"Well, *I did*! What I feel for Alec today didn't even exist back then! And you…" I sobbed. "You didn't even love me enough to tell me who you were!"

"You're wrong." He frowned in anguish. "I loved you *so much* I even got you a ring!"

My heart skipped a beat.

"You told me to stay away in July, but I couldn't stop thinking about you. I was going *insane*!" he cried, staring at me. "I knew you wouldn't believe me if I told you it was me. I had to *show you*, to tell you in person! Otherwise, you would think I was lying again and would call the police on me. So I booked a plane and came after you. If you were here—if you'd said yes—I was ready to spend the rest of my life with you! That's how much I loved you!"

His words completely disarmed me. All I could do was to stand there, watching the tears stream down his face.

When I found out it was all a lie that July 15, my heart didn't give a damn if he wasn't Alec—I didn't care at all what he looked like. The only thing I needed to know that day was if he loved me for real. If what I'd lived that past year of my life was even partially true.

And now he was here, looking me in the eye and telling me that it was. But I still couldn't believe him. I still couldn't trust his words.

"If you loved me like that, why didn't you fight for me?" I murmured.

But Benjamin didn't react.

"Why didn't you *fight* for me?" I shouted, making him wince this time.

His eyes were wide and full of pain, but he wouldn't let me in. And I couldn't trust him. I couldn't know for sure if he was really telling me the truth.

So I kissed him.

I grabbed Benjamin by the lapel, bringing his lips to mine.

They were tense at first, but then his hands found my waist and my neck. It didn't seem like a first kiss. It felt like we'd done this before—hundreds of times. Our souls knew exactly what to do. They'd been practicing for too long now...

My anger started to fade. My heart finally calmed down.

I knew the truth now. The whole truth. This had been the only way to find out. The only way Benjamin couldn't lie to me.

You did love me. I watched as he opened his eyes. *You still do.*

Ben gasped, as if awakening from a daydream, then stared at

me, afraid—regretful. He knew his biggest secret had just been exposed.

I'd always thought the impostor didn't tell me the truth because he didn't love me enough. I had believed this whole time that he never loved me back—not the way that I loved him. But that kiss proved me wrong. Benjamin did love me. With all his heart.

But just loving *me* wasn't enough. In order for him to tell me the truth—to fight for us—he needed something else. He had to love *himself*.

I remembered the night I'd tried to break up with Alec. I was so sure he deserved better than me that I didn't let him get closer. Not until the moment I realized I had my own light too.

Now I understood why Ben never believed I truly loved him. Why *my* love for him hadn't been enough. You can give a person all the love there is in this world, but if he doesn't love himself first—if he doesn't feel like he deserves it—it still won't be enough.

"Linda, I…"

I turned around and climbed onto the bleachers. We were outside, on the football field. I hadn't realized it until now.

Everything was quiet, apart from the muffled music coming from the gym. Ben slowly climbed the bleachers, then sat down next to me.

"We can still make it work—you, Alec, and me."

I dropped my eyes, hopeless. I guess part of me had believed we could still fix this—I could still go back to Alec. But not now. Not anymore.

"I know I already lost you," Ben said quietly. "And it's okay. I did too many things only thinking about myself; I deserve this. Right now, I honestly just want to see you happy again…"

I kept my head down, fighting the tears.

"He's the right guy for you, Linda—I knew it from the beginning. To be honest, this was one of the main reasons I was so afraid to tell you the truth. Even if you forgave me for lying online, I would still have to introduce you to Alec one day. And I knew you guys had a lot more in common than you and me. I thought it would only be a matter of time until you hit it off and realized you two were a better match.

"And I was right! You guys are good for each other! I love seeing the way you grow stronger next to him. It's like he lights up something in you—this never happened when you were with me."

My chest tightened right there; that was so hard for me to hear. Because at the same time that it reminded me of how much I loved Alec, the fact that Ben was here telling me all this made it impossible for me to hate him.

"I've never seen Alec so hopeless before. You make him stronger too, you know? He's absolutely lost without you. He just keeps writing and writing. You should have seen him in the studio yesterday, obsessed about this 'song you never wrote together' or something…"

I remembered the promise I'd made him at the café. He'd asked me so many times to sit down and write with him. But I never did.

"Come back to LA, Linda. At least until you start at NYU."

I met his gaze.

I couldn't unsee it now: his love. But, once again, he was choosing not to fight. He loved me—with his whole heart. But he was choosing to step aside.

"Then you're going to New York, and I'm staying in LA. We're not even gonna see each other that much. Nobody will know—"

"*I* will know, Ben," I murmured.

"I'm gonna move on, you know? I'm not gonna love you forever." He chuckled, but it had a faint, hollow ring to it.

I kept my straight face. "You just tried to take your own life. How in the world do you think I can go back and consciously hurt you—"

"It was not your fault, okay? I need you to know that!"

Tears immediately flowed from my eyes. Of all the wounds Benjamin had inflicted on me, this was the one that hurt the most. I still thought about it every day—it was the only reason why I'd been able to keep my distance from Alec. I knew I would never recover if Ben decided to finish what he'd started because of *me*.

"It was never because of you and Alec, I swear!" He read my face. "It was because of the lies and the shame. I thought I was stuck in that guilt loop forever; I didn't have any way out—"

"There's *always* a way out!" I sobbed. "You should have talked to me! Or to your family! Or anyone!"

"I know. Now I know it." He touched my shoulder to calm me down.

And I couldn't help myself. I hugged him tight, surrendering to the tears.

"I'm sorry I put you through that," he said in my ear. "I promise you I'll never do anything like that again. I feel so much better now that everybody knows the truth. I had no idea my family would be so supportive…"

"I'm still mad!" I scowled, pulling away from the hug. I hated the thought of losing my friend Ben to suicide, but I hated knowing that he and the jerk who manipulated me were the same person.

"It's okay, I deserve it. I just want you to know that… I'm so grateful I'm still here, Linda. I don't want to ever live like that again. I want to start over and build a new life. A life I'm not ashamed of, but actually proud of, you know?"

"Yeah… I'd like that for you too."

"Thanks." He smiled. "I know you'll probably never forgive me, but just this—just talking—makes me feel so much better."

I stared at him, feeling the same peace he was feeling. It was like for the first time since that July 15, there was no rain, no waves. The storm was over, the ocean was finally at rest.

"I never thanked you for saving my life. I have a future only because of you, Hails, and James. Thank you," he said meaningfully.

I wiped my eyes, then looked across the field. My heart was at peace, but that didn't mean it wasn't hurting.

We both went quiet for a moment. And the silence between us was soft and warm. *Familiar.* I couldn't believe I'd never noticed it before—how comfortable it felt to be around him. How used to it I already was.

Ben seemed to be at home with it as well. His breathing was calm and steady as he unconsciously massaged his hand.

"How is your tendonitis?" I couldn't help but ask.

"Better." He showed me his bad wrist. "I can't touch the violin for another month or two, but it's healing well. My new doctor said it was caused by stress—I was tensing up too much while playing. But now that the stress is over, I might have a chance to fully recover."

"That's really good news," I said genuinely. "Did you hear from Juilliard?"

"Yeah, I didn't get in."

I frowned, my lips pressed together.

"It's okay, UCLA is starting to grow on me."

"Good." I cracked a smile.

"See? We can still be friends… It's not that hard to be around each other, right?" He bumped his knee against mine. "Please come back with me tomorrow?"

I looked into his green eyes. And my heart expanded with a warm blast of hope. Was that possible? To be with Alec, having Impostor Alec as a friend?

No, it wasn't. Not when they lived in the same house. Not

when they were so close.

"I can't, Ben. I don't wanna be the girl who stands between two brothers."

"That's exactly what you'll be doing if you don't come! Alec will never get over it—deep down, he'll always hate me for this."

"He'll forgive you. We've already talked about it."

"He might forgive me, but he'll never forget. Don't you see? Right now, you're hurting all three of us. But if you come back, everybody wins!

"I need you in my life too, you know? It's not just him. Since I got depressed, Linda, you're one of the people who've helped me the most. And I kind of need you right now—as my friend."

I thought about my *friend* Ben. The guy who fed me chocolate all those months in LA so I could put on some weight. The guy who came to visit me in my room with a self-help book when I was too depressed to get out of bed. The guy who rescued me and comforted me when I fought with Alec, when I didn't know how to talk to Nina, when I got fooled by Zach.

While he did his best to help me, he knew he was the one twisting the knife—secretly making me bleed. And if I went back to LA, if I went back to Alec, I would be doing the exact same thing to him.

I saw Alec's face in my mind. Then I sighed, staring at Ben.

I loved his brother with all my heart; there was no doubt about who I wanted to be with. But I couldn't do this to Benjamin. Not when I knew he was still in love with me.

"It was really nice to talk to you, Ben. Thank you for coming here and ruining prom." I got up with my arms spread, making him laugh. "But I can't come to LA with you…"

His face fell. And in my heart, I felt even more sure of what I was about to say.

"I can't choose Alec…because I love you too." I met his eyes one last time, then with a silent goodbye, I walked away.

Chapter 33

"No, you don't." Ben caught me by the arm on the football field. "Not anymore. Not the same way you love *him* now."

I didn't recognize that look on his face—so decided, so fearless.

"I fell in love with this girl, two years ago." He slid his hand down my arm, slowly letting it go. "She was the *best* thing that ever happened to me… And I was so dumb I didn't realize she loved me for real until after I lost her."

My heart tightened, remembering everything we'd lived together before that July 15. Every conversation, every memory, every imaginary kiss.

"But this girl…" He choked back his tears. "She deserves the *world*. So I mean it when I say she can come home and be with my brother, because I honestly can't think of a better person to give her that. And I'd rather see them happy together than know neither of them are happy because of me."

His green eyes were hopeful now, reminding me of his twin's—and my heart broke all over again.

I couldn't do this to them. I just couldn't.

Things would never be the same between me and Alec, and Benjamin needed help, not a constant source of stress. As long as I stayed out of their lives—as long as I wasn't there to keep making them bleed—I knew they would be okay. All they needed right now was some time to heal.

All *I* needed right now was some time to heal.

"I have to go, Ben… I'm sorry." I turned around before the tears started to fall.

"I've always thought he was better than me at everything, you know?" He shouted after me. "Every time I failed, my first thought would be 'this wouldn't have happened to Alec.' This, for example! Right now! I'm here thinking that if it was the other way around, he'd have managed to convince you to come."

I stopped where I stood and glanced back at him.

"I only recently realized that *I* was the one who kept trying to be better than him *at being him.* And that if I wanted to stand out somehow, I had to stop comparing and just start being myself.

"So, this is *me*, Linda—tonight. I know it took a while, but I'm here—telling you the truth—showing myself to you—trying to be the best possible version of *me*.

"If I've failed, if this is still not enough, I will go back home, and I'll have no regrets. Not about this, at least. Because I *did* do everything I could to fix you two. But I hope, from the bottom of my heart, that you realize you're making the *biggest* mistake of your life. And I *know* you are! Because you're doing exactly what I did.

"If you walk away right now, you're giving up without even *trying*. And believe me, you won't want to look Alec in the eye one day and have to explain *why you didn't fight for him*."

♪♩♡

"You can still choose *me*, you know? Forget about Alec! Let's walk out that door and never look back—"

"Leave her alone, Zach," Ben said from behind us.

"Get in line, I know." Zach rolled his eyes, making me laugh.

"Are you ready?" Ben smiled at me.

And suddenly there were thousands of butterflies in my stomach.

"Wait a second, I'm just gonna…" I reached for my makeup bag again, but AJ grabbed it before I could.

"You look gorgeous, relax!"

"He's right, Linda." Nina slid out from under James's arm to adjust my skirt. "I think this time around, you might really give him that heart attack."

I grinned at them all.

Everybody knew I was here in the musicians' green room— his parents, his band, his crew. Everyone but Alec. He had started the North American leg of his tour in Florida, then gone to Georgia, and tonight was his first of two shows in New York.

I didn't go back to LA with Ben after prom. I needed some time to put my life in order. But I knew he was right, I had to at least *try*—I couldn't give up without a fight. And I had to start right then; I couldn't waste another day.

These were the biggest and most nerve-racking concerts of the tour. Alec had been anxious about them since the tickets sold out in November! And although I knew everybody would come to support him, all I could think about was how much I wanted to be here too. How much I still wanted to be with him.

That's when we came up with the idea for this little surprise. Ben was paying back for the violin, and I was paying back for NYU. The plan was to approach Alec as a fan during the Meet and Greet, and then announce I was joining him on the road.

I'd never been more excited in my entire life. I couldn't *wait* to watch him play every night. And to be by his side. And to give him all my heart. I'd come ready to get on that bus with him and go everywhere he wanted to take me...

Until my classes started, anyway. I needed to be back in New York by the end of August. But I was sure he would support me in that, like he always did.

I had no idea *how*, and I definitely wasn't expecting it to be easy, but I knew we were going to make this work. The distance, the turbulent history, the awkwardness, the shame—everything. My heart was telling me that. And my heart, it was never wrong.

"This is going to be the biggest surprise of his life! He's never gonna beat us on this," Ben said, guiding me to the Meet and Greet area.

I watched as he opened the door enthusiastically. And I wondered if we ever stop loving someone we once loved.

I didn't think so. That's why we have to be so careful—hearts don't have exit doors. If you let someone in, and what you lived together was real, they will stay there forever.

Of course the feeling changes, in size and intensity, depending on the paths life may take you. But you never stop *caring*. You never stop wishing them well. If one day you both said "I love you" and meant it, that person will always be there—somewhere in your heart.

"Are you okay?" Ben asked.

"Yeah." I grinned. "Are *you* okay?" I looked into his eyes, searching for the truth.

And he smiled slowly, staring back at me. "Yeah."

"Are you Linda González?"

"Yes, it's really her! Ben said she came to surprise Alec!"

"Are you serious? So you're back together?"

"Oh my gosh, he's gonna be so happy!"

"This will be *the best* show of the tour."

"Can you make him put 'No More Lies' back on the setlist?"

"Oh, please! It's my favorite song!"

"You two are my couple goals…"

"Yeah! We never believed the rumors—about Ben and that other guy on Valentine's."

"Is *that* the famous necklace he gave you?"

"Can I take a picture?"

"Is it true that you brought a fan to his rehearsal with you?"

"And that you made him a scrapbook with fan letters?"

The girls in the line were beyond excited to have me there among them. They asked question after question, and I did my best to answer them all, but I confess I was just half present. The other half of me was somewhere backstage—it was there with Alec.

"You don't have a ticket? Sorry, but I can't let you—"

"It's his girlfriend, you idiot!" one of the fans yelled. "Just let her in already!"

"I can't let *anyone* pass without a ticket."

"It's okay, she's with me." Ben showed his badge to the security guard, then accompanied us to the next room. "Don't let him see you before you get to the head of the line, okay?"

"Don't worry, we're gonna hide her," a girl answered for me.

"Great. Thank you!" Ben gave us a dimpled smile, then returned to the staff area.

"Did you see that? Benjamin Brock just smiled at me!" the girl squealed at her friend. And I laughed, watching them fangirl over him.

Ben would be all right. He was trying very hard; he really wanted to become someone better. And now that I knew everything he was going through, I could keep an eye on him—I could help him find his own light. We would make sure, Alec and I, that he learned to fight for his happy ending this time.

"He's here!" The girls started screaming.

And that's when my heart burst open.

He was wearing his favorite The Hope shirt and black skinny jeans. The shoes were one of the pairs *I'd* picked out the day his stylist showed him the selection he should take on tour. And his hair—my gosh, his hair! I couldn't wait to bury my fingers in his curls and smell his mild herbal shampoo.

It was pure agony to see him so close and have to stay still in that line. I didn't have to wait as long as that last time at the mall, but it was so much harder! The girls were doing all the work of hiding me, because I just couldn't take my eyes off him.

"Don't forget about NML!" said the fan in front of me.

"NML?"

"Yes, 'No More Lies.' Make him play it tonight!"

"Oh." I chuckled. "Okay, I'll try…"

"Next!" the security guard said, and the butterflies hurt my stomach.

I watched the girl walk to Alec. Then the next one. Then the next one.

When I got to the front, my heart was beating so fast I thought I would faint. So I glanced around, searching for Ben, and *James* met my eyes instead. With a big encouraging smile.

I smiled back at him, overwhelmed with joy and gratitude.

I *heard* when the security guard called "Next." I *saw* when the girls got out of my way, excited. But all of a sudden, I couldn't move; my heart had stopped.

I was having a flashback of that July 15—I was just seconds away from everything I'd ever wanted. But this time, not only was it *real*, but I was getting so much more than I'd asked for. So much more than I could have imagined existed.

Suddenly, I didn't mind any of the tears that brought me to this moment. All the wounds, all the pain, all the wait—it was all worth it. *His love* was worth it.

Alec turned around to search for his next fan. And the instant he recognized me, he clasped his hands in front of his mouth, tearing up.

My chest tightened, making the blood circulate in my veins again. And I ran to him—I flew into his arms.

"What are you doing here?" He squeezed me against him. "How...?"

"Ben went to Petersburg, and we talked—"

He put me down, stunned.

"So I brought you this." I reached for my pocket and showed him my origami heart. "In case you still want it..."

Alec took the little heart from my hand, trying hard to contain the tears. Then he scanned the room and half-laughed, sobbing when he saw Ben.

He didn't know his brother was there either. The two of them hadn't spoken since the day Alec learned the truth.

"It was just a wave, baby." I touched his chest reassuringly. "Things will be all right... I'll make sure of it."

He held my face in his hands, tears streaming down his cheeks. "I can't believe you came back to *me*...after everything."

"I must really love you," I teased, making him chuckle.

"Please, never leave me again." He pressed his forehead against mine.

"I promise you." I smiled into his green eyes.

THIRTEEN YEARS LATER

Epilogue

Ben

"Is that your book? Can I finally read it?" Alec trailed behind Linda, bouncing up and down like a happy puppy.

I rolled my eyes. It was pathetic how excited he was for this.

Linda crossed the living room, setting us apart from the rest of the family. Then she stopped in front of the couch and gestured for us to take a seat. "Now, before I give this to you, I wanted to say how special this year was for me, and how…"

I confess I didn't hear a single word she said. All I could think about was the two books she was carrying in her hands. But not because I was excited, like Alec—because I was *scared*. I knew she was writing a memoir for her psychology research, but never in a million years would I have imagined she'd let someone read it. That she'd let *me* read it.

"Go ahead, open it." Linda half-smiled, finally handing us her Christmas gift.

I had to wipe my sweaty hands on my jeans. I hadn't been this nervous in *years*. And anxiety was a constant in my life now—since I'd started traveling the world with the orchestra. But none of those performances even came close to how stressed I was in this moment, anticipating all the horrible things Linda must have written about me in this—

"A journal?" Alec frowned, touching his name printed on the cover.

I breathed out in relief. She wasn't sharing her book with us— my gift was exactly like his!

Except for the colors, I noticed with a grin. She loved to do that: mine was always blue, his was always yellow.

"Yeah…" Linda sat down on the coffee table, facing us both on the couch. "I'm gonna let you guys read it, I've already decided." She took two USB flash drives from her pocket, launching me right back into panic mode.

Alec immediately reached for her hand, but Linda yanked it away. "Not so fast! I have a condition first."

"What condition?" he asked.

"I want you to write your side of the story too." She glanced at me. "Both of you."

My heart skipped a beat. How could she ask me that? After all the years of therapy I'd done to move on and forget, she wanted me to go back and relive everything?

"But I've already written hundreds of songs about you!" Alec protested. "Doesn't that count?"

"Not really." She shook her head. "You've only written about *me*—never about what happened or how you felt about Ben."

"That's not true," I interrupted, remembering "No More Secrets"—a song Alec wrote for me when we were nineteen.

"All right, I'll count NMS as *one page*. But this is my condition, guys." She leaned in closer and showed us the flash drives again. "What do you say?"

A twinge of excitement began to creep in with my fear. I was honestly *terrified* of what might be in there, but at the same time, I'd never been more curious in my life. She had written an entire memoir about me. About how she *felt* about me.

Well, about *us*. But still... This was my chance to find out everything she'd felt for me before! After fifteen years of guessing, I'd actually get to learn *her* truth.

"I don't know, baby." Alec leaned back on the couch, anxiety stamped all over his face.

I could tell he was even more curious about her book than I was, but not exactly excited to write down his own memories. And from the way he was looking at me, I knew that it wasn't even Linda's part of the story he was worried about. It was *mine*. Everything that had happened after that show in New York, that's what he didn't want to remember.

"You watched me write it, Alec. You know how good this was for me—for our relationship!" She reached for his hand. "I've grown so much from this experience. I really think you two should try it."

I opened the journal, considering her request.

And Linda quickly added, "You don't have to show it to me or to each other. I just want you to let it all out onto the pages, so this story can finally stay in the past."

"Things are already in the past, right, bro?" Alec dropped his arm around my shoulder.

"*Yes.*" I gave her a reassuring smile.

"I know, but—" Linda sighed, staring at me, then at my brother. "I think this could make things even better. Especially now that we're hoping to start a new chapter in our lives..." She exchanged a long look with Alec.

He swallowed hard, glancing down at her stomach, and right then I knew what his answer would be. His thoughts were so loud, I could practically hear the shift in his mind—his big motivation for agreeing with her.

"I'm in," he said firmly, then sat beside her on the coffee table.

"Ben?" Linda turned to me, hopeful.

And that's when I caught myself smiling. Not because I was happy, no—I was mirroring *her* excitement.

"This is not a good idea." I composed myself, serious. As much as I wanted to read her side of the story, I knew I couldn't let myself go back to the past.

"Oh, come on, Ben…" Her face fell into a frown.

But the disappointment in her eyes made me all the more sure of my decision.

"I made too many mistakes, Linda. If I start recalling them all, I…" The memories were haunting me already—every last one of my regrets. "I'm just too ashamed of my story to write it down. I'm sorry."

"Think of it like this… *Your mistakes are the reason you are who you are today.* You wouldn't want to change the ending, would you?" She raised an eyebrow, nodding at my girl.

I watched her play with AJ and baby Luca beside the Christmas tree. She tried to put the toy we'd bought for him in his hands, but he kept throwing it aside, clearly more interested in playing with the wrapping paper. I caught myself smiling again.

"See?" Linda chuckled. "Stop running from the memories, Ben. It's time to embrace your story, and instead of being ashamed of the mistakes you made, be *proud* of how much you've grown from them."

I looked into her eyes, staring back into mine. And she reached for my hand, her touch soft and warm against my skin.

I'd longed so much for this touch. I'd waited for so long, I'd wanted it so badly…

Why didn't you fight for me? I heard her voice in my head.

And just like that, I was eighteen all over again.

ACKNOWLEDGMENTS

My dear Brockies,

In the last few months, I've been experiencing a kind of love that I didn't know existed. Everything is so new to me that I have no words to describe it. All I can say is that I *feel* it—in every DM, every reaction, every comment, every review.

Thank you *so much* for all the drawings, all the Alec Brock edits, all the fan arts! Thank you for reading my story, for telling your friends about it, for sharing my posts on social media. Thank you for watching my vlogs, for encouraging me with your messages, for being my true friends…

Alec Brock really does have the best fans in the entire world. And I love every single one of you with all my heart!

I also would like to thank all the lovely people who helped me turn my dream into reality…

My super-agent, Stephanie Hansen. My awesome editors, Arielle Bailey and Cheryl Wanner. And my beta readers and dear friends: Mônica Martins, Milena Martins, and Marina Tampieri. I don't know what I would do without you guys. Thank you all so much!

Thank you to the artists who changed my life in 2017/2018: Harry Styles, Shawn Mendes, The Vamps, and 5SOS…and also my girls, Selena Gomez and Camila Cabello. Your songs are the reason I didn't give up on my dream. Thank you for giving me the motivation to keep going, for helping me stay strong when things get hard, and for inspiring me in so many ways.

Thank you, Mom, Dad, Brother, and a dozen of dear friends scattered around the world (you know who you are) for the unconditional love and support, especially in the past four years. No matter how far we live from each other, you're *always* in my heart—always inspiring me.

And finally, thank you, God, for giving me the words and for connecting all the dots in the end! When I started writing Linda's story I had no idea where it would take me, but you guided me through it. And I don't even feel like I deserve credit now, because I know it all came from you. So all I can say is this: thank you for choosing *me* to write this story.

ABOUT THE AUTHOR

Born in Brazil and naturalized French, **LARISSA LOPES** is a real citizen of the world, trying to write her own story the best way she can.

She writes diverse, emotionally charged romances. And when she isn't in her cave, living her characters' lives, she likes to inspire people to follow their dreams and become the best version of themselves with #THEBESTVERSIONOFMYSELFMOVEMENT.

You can find her online at
WWW.LARISSALOPES.NET.

Alec Brock Trilogy
Linda & Alec

Until We Get It Right
Nina & James

Until I Found You
Zach & Emma

Until My Last Breath
AJ & Matt

Until You Love Yourself
Hailey & Charlie

WWW.ALECBROCKSERIES.COM